STORM DANCER

TERRI VALENTINE

ZEBRA BOOKS
KENSINGTON PUBLISHING CORP.

ZEBRA BOOKS are published by

Kensington Publishing Corp.
850 Third Avenue
New York, NY 10022

First Printing: March, 1995

Printed in the United States of America

To Heather and Miranda, my smart, talented, and supportive daughters. I love you both very much.

One

St. Petersburg, Russia
June 1872

More breathtaking than any picture Hunter Kincaid could conjure in his head, the graceful enchantress whirled across the boards of the Maryinsky Theater. Utterly smitten, he watched, unable—no unwilling—to tear his eyes away from the woman's entrancing stage presence.

If he ever admitted to having a weakness—not that he was admitting to it now, not at all, but if he did—it would undoubtedly be his attraction for women who knew how to command an audience. Songstresses, dance hall girls, once even a pretty circus performer, those types of women had turned his head more times than he cared to count. But then, what chance had he had to know any other kind growing up in the shadow of a saloon in the wilds of Wyoming?

Hunter frowned beneath the brim of his gray felt Stetson, glad of the concealment if not of his past. Earlier, he'd refused the offer of the ever-present servant to "see to his hat." Not likely he'd remove it now, in spite of the darting looks and sometimes outright stares of curiosity he received from the audience, not only in the seats far below, but in the private boxes eye level to where he sat.

Well, let the gol-darned Russes look, if they have a foreign mind to, 'cause I'm looking, too.

What he was looking at wasn't a bunch of gussied up Russian aristocrats, or the gilded architecture of the theater that would put the Mother Lode to shame. What continued to capture his fascination and stirred up the until-now suppressible fantasies with the force of a Wyoming dust devil was the long-legged ballerina who floated across the stage like a winged fairy in the arms of her equally handsome male partner.

Fantasies. Hell, it had been so long since he'd indulged in them that he wasn't sure he even knew how anymore. However, the more he watched the gypsy-like she-dervish, the more certain he became that fantasizing wasn't something a man was likely to forget altogether. At least, not for long.

"Lovely, isn't she?"

Startled from his private revelry by the heavily accented English, Hunter collected himself before he lifted his eyes from the stage now filled with a hodgepodge of lithe, whirling dancers. Putting on his best poker face, he turned, acknowledging the man occupying the plush velvet seat beside him, his host while in Russia.

In spite of his undeterminable age and crippled body, Prince Dmitri Nicolaiev was not a man to reckon with lightly. Beneath his lined face, closely cropped gray hair, and twisted legs dwelled a master of manipulation.

"Well now, Your Grace," Hunter drawled in his best Wyoming accent, stretching out his long legs encased in black nankeen to reveal tooled leather boots. "I'm not quite sure which little filly you're referring to." He pushed back his Stetson and scratched his head as if he honestly didn't know.

They stared at each other, unblinking for a long moment. Hunter didn't doubt for a moment that the wily, old prince saw right through his hayseed facade. But it was all part of the game they played—rustic American versus aristocratic Russian.

The truth of the matter: They needed each other. As the representative of the Wyoming Cattlemen's Association, Hunter had an endless supply of beef on the hoof he wanted to sell for a good profit. As the representative of the Russian government, Dmitri Nicolaiev had the need to feed his starving people and, as Hunter saw it, an endless supply of money to spend to accomplish the task.

By the time the unwavering confrontation ended, the curtain had closed on the first act of the performance, the standing ovation thundering like a herd of stampeding cattle through the theater.

The prince smiled, but the expression never reached his eyes. Then he turned his attention back to the stage, adding his own applause to the others' with uncharacteristic enthusiasm.

Without a doubt, the sly old fox was up to something. But what? Hunter wondered, clapping his hands as well. Whatever it was, he suspected it undoubtedly had everything to do with the outcome of the all-important international negotiations.

"Three minutes to curtain, Your Highness."

Unmindful of the many members of the *corps de ballet*, both male and female, milling all about her, Princess Marina Nicolaiev quickly set about her business. Slipping behind a traveler for what little privacy it afforded, she changed her costume right there, backstage. There wasn't time for modesty or to return to her dressing room. She must be dressed and back to center stage before the curtain rose on the second act of *La Source*.

With a drumroll the orchestra began the overture.

Odd, what images the mind conjured at the most inappropriate times! The pain of her long-ago loss had a way of worming its way in unwanted. Many things evoked the frightening memory of the night her mother died. The rumble of distant thunder . . . a drumroll.

"Marina, are you ready? Two minutes to curtain." Sergei Bozzacchi, her dance partner, flitted by her as lithe as a willow branch, as handsome as Adonis.

"Almost," she murmured, peeved at herself for being distracted by a mere drumroll, at Sergei for his impatience. Bending down, she adjusted first the fleshing of her left leg, then the satin ribbon of her wooden box-toed shoe, flexing her foot to test it once to ensure a comfortable fit. She barely had time to glance up before Sergei took her by the arm and whisked her toward the stage, ignoring her protests.

"The second *fouetté en tournant.*" Clasping her about the waist, Sergei pulled her toward him with a relaxed calmness she never felt before the curtain rose, no matter how many times she went through it. "Do not forget to watch the position of your right foot." He spoke softly into her ear.

"I won't," she whispered back, leaning against his strong arm and self-assuredness. "And you must watch yours during the *tour jeté.*"

Sergei laughed low in his throat even as the squeal of the curtain pulleys filled the air.

"By the way, Marinuska. I thought you might like to know. The prince is rumored to be in the audience tonight."

"Dmitri?" she cried softly in concern, knowing how difficult it would be for him physically to come to a theater which offered no accommodations for a man in a wheelchair. Forgetting for the moment who and where she was, she twisted her head to stare out over the footlights to the private box on the left that the prince kept but rarely used. "Are you certain?" In spite of her breach of professionalism she could see nothing beyond the gas jets.

"Nothing is certain in this world we live in, my dear," the tall, blond *danseur* replied, leading her into the first step of their duet even as the thunder of applause rose from the darkness once more to greet them. "Except that I will always be here to catch you."

Yes, many loud noises evoked the haunting memories, but never the thunderous applause of her admiring audience. The wonder of such approval always kept them at bay, set her free to do what she did best.

She danced, forgetting all else but the steps she took and the hands of the partner she trusted without reservation.

"She is quite lovely. Do you not agree, my friend?"

There was no denying of whom the crippled aristocrat spoke in his rolling Russian accent. The fleet-footed sprite who commanded the stage as if it were hers alone was a beauty indeed.

Utterly captivated, Hunter jealously watched every intimate gesture of the accompanying male dancer, not the least feminized by his clinging tights and short tunic. And when his hand slid down the length of the ballerina's leg, coming to rest in the warm spot behind her knee, his other hand grasping her about the waist and lifting her as if she weighed no more than a feather, Hunter downright despised the man who touched her so intimately. His own hands tingled with curiosity, wondering how silky such a beautiful leg must feel, how supple such a small waist.

"Mr. Kincaid?" The prince fished for an answer.

"Yes, of course. What man in his right mind wouldn't find such a woman attractive?"

Ballet. All of his life he'd thought such culture merely the pastime of the namby-pamby, not something a man like himself would find the least bit stimulating. Had he been wrong? He glanced about the vast audience. No one spoke; hardly a head turned away during what was nearly an hour performance. A gasp of approval rose as the ballerina ran across the length of the stage and took a flying leap. Hunter straightened in his seat, fearing she would jump right off the stage and be injured. To his surprise and the delight of the rest of the audience, the male dancer caught her in mid-air and held her high above his head for what seemed an eternity before he slowly lowered her, every glorious inch of their perfect physiques touching on the way down. Could it be that every man, and woman as well, felt the same desire that racked Hunter's oxygen-deprived body?

Taking a ragged breath, Hunter cleared his raw throat and his raging mind, relieved, yet strangely disappointed, when the performance came to a conclusion. He tore his gaze away as the couple clasped hands and moved toward the footlights, accepting their applause with bows and blown kisses. Then when an armload of long-stemmed roses was presented to the woman, she turned and looked straight at him—or so Hunter perceived—and blew a personalized kiss his way. His hand moved up to cover the spot where the imaginary caress would have landed. To be so singled out was a fantasy come true.

"Perhaps you would care to meet her."

"What?" He glanced over to see the old Russian watching him with barely disguised amusement. "Whom?" He tried to sound nonchalant, but didn't think himself successful. God, he was acting like a lovesick stripling. One would think he would have learned his lesson by now.

"Why the lovely prima ballerina, of course." The old prince sidled in close, like a mountain cat moving in for the kill. "It can be arranged, you know."

So that was his game. Offer the uncouth American a taste of Russian finery, then lead him around by a ring in his nose like a sated bull.

"Tell me, Your Grace. Just what do you expect in return

for your gallant efforts?" he asked bluntly, dropping all pretenses.

"Expect?" The old man retreated, his eyes reflecting his surprise, yet they glimmered with cautious respect as they made a reassessment of Hunter. "Why, *I* expect nothing at all. *I* merely thought you might like to converse with someone quite fluent in English. I want only to make your stay in Russia as enjoyable as possible. Just what are you expecting, sir?" he demanded in the same unfettered tone.

What had he expected? A wild night of passion with a woman as intoxicating as Russian vodka?

"I simply want it understood that neither your generosity nor hers will have any bearing on our negotiations. None whatsoever. Business will remain business."

"But, of course. Only on rare occasions have I ever found bribery to be an effective means of negotiation." When Hunter's look didn't waver, the prince laughed aloud. "Not to worry, Mr. Kincaid. I can assure you that the Princess Marina Nicolaiev would never allow herself to be used as a political pawn." He moved in close again. "Nor as a point of any man's or country's negotiation."

Princess Marina Nicolaiev? Did that mean the focus of his most indecent fantasies was none other than this man's daughter? Hunter took another look at the lovely ballerina, searching for a resemblance between her and the crippled aristocrat.

Instantly he thought of Rainee, his own beloved child, whose life and virtue he would defend no matter what the personal cost. He knew exactly how he would react if he suspected some cad even briefly thought of her in ways he had fantasized about this man's daughter. He flashed the prince an uncertain look, one filled with skepticism and momentary self-doubt. Had he read something into the man's words that hadn't been there at all? No, he knew what he had heard. He wasn't wet behind the ears. A bribe was a bribe . . . was a bribe.

Just what kind of barbarians were these Russians? The kind he'd be wise to watch his every step around or he'd find himself at a definite disadvantage. At all cost, loss of control must be avoided. Too many people, friends, and neighbors— to be exact—depended on him to keep his mind strictly on business.

Still he'd have to be some kind of saint not to wonder, even briefly, what it would be like to make love to a beautiful woman like Princess Marina Nicolaiev.

Hugging the roses to her heart as if they were a most precious child, Marina made her way to her private dressing room. Once there, the door closed to the inevitable tide of well-wishers soon to intrude, she laid them on the small table beside her most prized possession, an ornately carved rosewood music box that had once belonged to her mother.

Without a doubt the flowers were from dear Dmitri. Nonetheless, she wanted to read the note, knowing it would say just the right thing to make her smile and feel good about herself before the demanding crowd found her.

Dmitri. He always knew what was best for her and saw that she got it. She owed him everything and gave him back so little in return.

Only too well she remembered the first time Dmitri had come to visit her. She had been seven, and he had been in a wheelchair even then. What an oddity he had seemed to her, a man with wheels instead of feet. How wretched she had been then, a bewildered little girl who had lost her mother to death and her father to his career. Raised by servants paid to do a job, more often than not she was left to her own devices and misconceptions. Not that she could blame anyone.

The nightmares, the terrible fits brought on by the recurring dreams . . . well, those in charge were ill-equipped to deal with them or with her.

Dmitri had been different. At first he had kept his distance from the wild little creature hiding behind the bushes gone wild as well. With the greatest of patience he had merely talked aloud for the longest time as if he hadn't known she was there.

Mention of her mother had made her peek through the shrubbery, eyeing the stranger with longing. Mama had had many friends, most of whom she'd never met since she was rarely allowed in the grand salon. Oh, how she had needed to speak of Mama and all that had happened that terrible day. To learn that Dmitri had been Mama's friend, her confidant, somehow had made him instantly trustworthy in her little-girl mind.

From that day forward, Dmitri had been there for her. He had comforted her when news that her father had been killed in battle reached her. He had seen to it that she entered the Imperial Academy of Dance, giving her the opportunity to fulfill her dreams to become the prima ballerina of the Russian Royal Ballet. He had been mother, father, friend to her. She smiled. And now . . .

"Oh, Dmitri, you scoundrel." Reading what he wrote on the card made her laugh aloud, made her see herself as lucky indeed. Dmitri. Yes, he always saw that she got everything she needed. If only he were not a cripple . . .

Pushing aside such frivolous longing, she concentrated instead of how she would thank him for his never-ending generosity and kindness once she got home.

Kindness, generosity, and devotion. What woman, except an ungrateful one, could in all conscience wish for more in a man?

* * *

The carriage ride through St. Petersburg gave Hunter time to think, to clear his mind, to reestablish his goals—most of all to remember just why he had traveled halfway around the world from his home in Sweetwater, Wyoming.

Beef. He wanted to sell it. The Russians needed to buy it. By damn, no little heifer, royal or not, and no matter how pretty or distracting, was going to run roughshod over his hard-earned advantage.

He glanced across the darkness of the carriage, its ostentatiousness making him feel uncomfortable at best, putting him at a decided disadvantage. He wasn't used to such an overt display of wealth. In Wyoming, a man's material worth was measured on the hoof—his real worth in his loyalty to friends and family and, most of all, in his code of honor.

Nobody wanted or needed to own a vehicle like the one he rode in now. It looked like a rolling palace. The fact that the opposing seat had been removed to accommodate Nicolaiev's wheelchair made the carriage seem even more pretentious, yet the man himself more vulnerable.

Hunter wasn't about to be fooled. He refused to allow the Russian to use a physical shortcoming or a show of wealth to outmaneuver him.

"It's mighty kind of you, Your Grace," he said slipping once more into his "cowboy" persona, "to invite me to your home, but it really wasn't necessary."

"Oh, quite the contrary, Mr. Kincaid. My wife would never forgive me if I did anything less."

His wife. The prince had mentioned her once before. Hunter still found it odd that the woman hadn't accompanied them to the theater, but he had been too polite to question her absence aloud.

"I'm sure you exaggerate. I'm just a dusty, ol' cowboy from Sweetwater, Wyoming."

"Precisely. It's not every day we have one of your kind invade our rather exclusive culture."

Invade? The sly, old Russian made it sound as if an American was some kind of unwelcome plague.

"I know what you mean. One of *your* kind arriving in Sweetwater would stir up a hornet's nest."

"Stir up a hornet's nest?" the prince asked with polite curiosity. "That doesn't sound good."

"Hard to say. Sometimes we Westerners have cockeyed notions about foreigners." Hunter smiled crookedly.

"Ah, I understand." The prince smiled in return, like any man who had just been insulted. "Then it seems Russians and Americans aren't all that much different, after all. We, too—as you so quaintly put it—have 'cockeyed' notions about foreigners."

The carriage slowed, took a corner, then pulled up before a building as big as a Wyoming sky and twice as lit up—a palace by any man's standards. The drive and the street both ways were jammed with an array of fancy carriages. As Hunter descended, patiently waiting for the discreet servant who followed the prince's every move to assist his master out of the vehicle, he had a most disquieting thought.

Russian hornets. Were they as big and mean as the ones back home in Sweetwater?

"Hurry, Olga. I cannot afford to be a moment later than I already am." Marina wiggled in the partially fastened gown of shimmering silver, trying to see behind her back and assess the servant's tedious progress.

The *soirée* had long been in progress when she had arrived home late from the theater, but there had been no way short of rudeness to escape the deluge of fans and admirers that always crowded backstage after a performance. That Dmitri hadn't been among them hadn't really surprised her. His note had tantalized her enough. His promise of a surprise awaiting her arrival had nearly sent her racing home still dressed in her costume. But that would never do. She must make her grand entrance sheathed in the exquisite gown he had had made just for her and this occasion.

She ran her hands down her sides. Yes, sheathed best described the way the flowing material clung to her every curve.

"Patience, Your Highness. These things take time. There must be at least a hundred of these little buttons, and my old fingers do not move like they used to." Hunched from the waist, the maid's broad posterior filled the width of the cheval glass, blocking Marina's view.

Marina's frown relaxed, her annoyance dissipating along with it, leaving indulgence in its wake.

Olga had been a mere scullion when Marina was a little girl. During the "dark years," as they often referred to them, the old peasant had been the only servant among the many in her father's household to make certain she had something to eat—often only a shared crust of bread—something to wear—even if only rags. Now she worried a row of diamond-studded buttons with the same gruffness she had displayed knotting a babushka beneath Marina's chin to hide the hopelessly knotted hair that no one had taken the time to brush.

How well she remembered the day Olga had sheared her head, holding her down like a bawling, squirming sheep. She had hated the practical old woman, had tried to bite and claw her. But the loyal servant's actions had no doubt been for Marina's own good, keeping her free from lice infestation.

Although she could never confirm it, she suspected Olga had been the one to contact Dmitri, risking her position and perhaps even her life, to tell him of the dire condition of the abandoned little girl.

Yes, Marina owed her most unconventional lady's maid

much, and she was not one to forget her debt to those who had been kind and generous to her.

"There, Your Highness. All done." Olga patted the row of diamonds that ran all the way down her back. "Now, let me check your hair one last time and you'll be ready to go downstairs." The servant fiddled only a moment with the two soft rosettes of hair intricately wound above Marina's ears. Then, sorting through the jumbled jewelry box on the dressing table in front of them, she selected a matched pair of diamond-studded combs, inserting them in the center of each black coil.

"There," she said in a voice of approval, stepping back to view her handiwork. "Now, go make your grand entrance. I can assure you everyone is waiting for you, especially Prince Dmitri."

"Bless you, Olga." Marina turned and hugged the old woman. "Whatever would I do without you?"

As giddy as a young girl, she hurried past the beaming old woman, only too aware of the reason for her own impatience. Dmitri had some kind of wonderful surprise planned for her. His gifts were always unique. She had given up trying to guess them ahead of time years ago. Whatever the gift, she was certain he would give it to her in his usual grandiose style.

Face facts, Kincaid. You're disappointed she's not here. Hunter decided to actively seek the first opportunity to offer his excuses and leave.

He suspected it wouldn't take all that much longer. Introductions were brief at best.

"Mr. Hunter Kincaid of *Am'er'ik'i,* Count Tolskivich of Blah Blah Blah."

Why was it that all Russian names ended with "vich" or "sky"?

Hunter smiled and nodded his head for what seemed the thousandth time as the prince rattled on in Russian saying only God knew what about him. Then when roles were reversed, the Russian count did the same as it was explained in English who he was. Nothing more to say as neither of them spoke the other's language. On to the next introduction.

Hunter took hope in the fact they eventually had to run out of guests.

But then, to his chagrin, he was introduced to a woman who thought she spoke English.

"You are cow-boy, *da?*" she asked in her perfectly deplorable accent, pointing at his Stetson.

"Why, yes, ma'am, I am." He fingered the brim of his hat in a halfhearted attempt to doff it politely.

"Bang! Bang! Shoot dem up?" Her eyes glistened with childlike delight. "You have many . . . vat you call dem? . . . on your gun?" The finger of her right hand hopped down the length of the matching digit on her left like a pecking bird indicating notches. Reaching out, she brushed aside his black formal jacket as if she thought to find a gun belt strapped to his hip.

"Well, actually, ma'am . . ." Hunter stepped backward, unsure just where the brazen woman might reach next.

"No gun?" She sounded downright disappointed.

"Left it back in Sweetwater with twenty-three notches so far," he elaborated, mimicking her hopping-bird gesture.

"Tventy-tree? How many is dat?" She glanced at the prince for an explanation.

Before the Russian could answer, Hunter lifted his hands and flashed two tens and a three with his fingers.

Gasping, the wide-eyed woman stepped back as if terrified. Hunter couldn't help the chuckle that escaped as the woman elbowed her way across the room like a bossy pursued by an annoying horsefly.

"Don't mind Minna. She has always been a bit of a . . . how do you say it? . . . a busybody." The prince laughed, too.

"We have 'em just like her back in Sweetwater," Hunter admitted. "There's only one way to handle 'em."

"I am quite willing to wager you can handle just about any kind of woman, Mr. Kincaid."

Unsure just what the Russian meant by that remark, Hunter opted to simply maintain his silence.

That's when he saw her, Marina, the one woman he'd be most willing to handle if given the opportunity, but really wasn't sure what would be the best way.

The grand staircase that led down into the ballroom that took up a good portion of the second floor of the mansion had to have been put there to accommodate a woman like her. She shimmered and flowed like an elusive bead of quicksilver, commanding those stairs like a stage and everyone in the room as if they were her audience. Her hair, as dark as lampblack, was still coiled on the sides of her head. He imagined himself removing the pins that held the silky strands in place, running his fingers through the jet tresses, wondering just how long her hair was. Long enough to wind about his wrist several times and still have plenty to contemplate?

"Damn!" he murmured, totally entranced by a vision he hadn't the strength to tear his eyes away from even if his life depended upon it.

"I beg your pardon, Mr. Kincaid?" The prince angled his wheelchair to see what it was that had captured Hunter's attention. "Ah, yes. I see Marina has finally decided to join us."

And so the struggle began anew for Hunter, even though he should have known better than to fall victim to it. He must remember who he was, where he was, and especially what he had come there to do. He had to remember what a woman exactly like this one had done to him. And if that didn't work, and it didn't seem to be working, he had to remember she was the daughter of the man who even now sat in a wheelchair right next to him and held the future of Wyoming cattlemen in his gnarled hands.

"Please, Mr. Kincaid, do both me and dear Marina a favor." The prince sighed mightily. "Kindly rescue her from her adoring fans and escort her over to me."

She sorely needed rescuing. Looking beautifully vulnerable, already she was surrounded by an impenetrable circle of admirers who didn't seem to think twice about the fact they might well suffocate her in the crush.

"What am I to say to her?" Meaning what could he say to gain her attention over the crowd.

"Why simply tell her I sent you."

"Yes, of course." He needed no more urging. Working his way through the crowd, he decided he'd felt safer in the middle of a cattle stampede. Those four-legged critters had shown him more consideration.

But the worst moment was when Marina's eyes, as dark as midnight and just as unfathomable, skipped over him. Hell, she didn't even know he was alive. Or if she did, she didn't find him worth her time.

Spurred on by rejection, Hunter managed to elbow his way to the front of the crowd. Out of breath, his hat knocked askew, he realized the very moment she finally took notice of him. Actually it was more of a sweeping appraisal. Her eyes skimmed over him thoroughly, yet her expression never offered a single clue as to what she thought of him. Then once again their inky depths moved on to more fertile soil.

Hunter was not a man to be ignored twice.

"Excuse me," he said, touching her bare arm just above

the elbow. Too late, he tried to pull back his hand. Like any fool stupid enough to stand on the open plain in the middle of a thunderstorm, he'd been struck by lightning.

Elevated several steps above the crowd, she looked down at him with an imperial air he did not take to kindly.

"Your father sent me for you." The words came bounding out of his open mouth like a rattled jackrabbit out of its hole.

"My father?" She stared at him, off guard for only a moment. Then her dark eyes slowly filled with amusement and she laughed.

At *him*, Hunter decided. A bitter resentment began to burn in the pit of his belly. She dared to laugh at his bumbling ineptness—as if she knew something he didn't.

"You must be mistaken," she replied, her whimsical expression freezing into an icy glare, as if whatever she'd found so humorous a moment ago was not so anymore. "Now, if you don't mind . . ." Flippantly, she brushed him off as if he were no more than a pesky mosquito.

But he did mind. If the truth be known, he minded quite a bit. Why were women like her all the same? The more beautiful they were, the more arrogant.

"Excuse me, Your High and Mightiness, but you are to come with me." This time he took her firmly by the elbow. She looked down at him, meeting his determination with that of her own, but he gave her no choice. Descend the stairs or make a scene before her adoring followers. Women like her never made a scene—at least not in public.

He'd pegged her well. She trailed behind him without a protest. In fact, she followed so quietly and with such self-assuredness he again wondered what it was that she knew that he didn't.

Well, he'd had just about enough of it and her. Coming to a decision, he made a beeline across the ballroom, skirting the dancers as if they were a herd of restless doggies. As soon as he delivered Marina to her father, he intended to stick to his original plan to make his excuses and leave.

Reaching the spot where he had left Prince Dmitri only moments before, he glanced around. Now where could that scheming old Russian have gone?

"Lose something?"

"Not yet, but I'm about to." Hunter pinned the woman in shimmering silver with an intimidating look that usually instilled silence in whoever was unfortunate enough to receive it. However, he suspected there was nothing usual about her.

"You're the American cattleman, aren't you?" she asked, undaunted by his glare.

Hunter nodded. Against his will he found himself studying her from the corner of his eye.

"My mother was an American." Her upturned face was open and serene, yet her great, dark eyes probed. Was she looking for a crack in his tough exterior? Well, she wouldn't find one if he could help it.

"Oh, really? Your father never told me that." Still, he refused to give her the direct look she sought from him.

"What did he tell you about me?" There was something in her voice—something lightly hesitant, almost musical. Unable to stop himself, he turned his head and glanced down at her.

"Enough. What else should I know?" To his surprise he discovered he still held her by the wrist, so delicate beneath the crush of his calloused fingers. He could feel the pulse beneath his thumb pad, as steady and calm as the uncommonly dark eyes that continued to solicit he wasn't sure what from him.

She was so damn cool, standing there fearlessly, almost as if she could read his thoughts and found them amusing, but he sensed an underlying vulnerability to those very same thoughts. Fearless yet vulnerable. She was too good to be true and deserved a total reassessment.

Who was she? What was she? Witch? Gypsy? Perhaps. Still he couldn't shake off an image of her as a little girl standing in the rain terrified. Hunter Kincaid, the visionary? About as practical as Hunter Kincaid, the romantic. He had no desire to be either.

"Do you dance, Mr. Kincaid?" Nervously, she glanced over his shoulder, then back up at him.

For the life of him he couldn't remember having told her his name.

"I've been known to take a turn or two around a dance floor," he offered cautiously.

"Good. Then dance with me now."

Suddenly his restraining hand upon her wrist became his own self-made trap. She moved into the circle his arm created and stood waiting, her eyes pleading with him to do as she asked without questions.

When he saw the apparent reason for her impetuous desire to dance with him, a tall rather intense Russian glaring at them from only a few feet away, he struggled to brush aside his disappointment. Still, the moment was no less than his dream come true. The siren of the Russian stage waited for him to gather her in his arms and sweep her away. Only a fool would hesitate, might even back off and refuse. Only a fool or an idiot. After all, it was only one dance.

Hunter considered himself many things, but no fool. The hand that still claimed her wrist slid upward and settled over her receptive fingers; his free arm slipped about her long and supple waist. He lunged into the first step, cursing himself for his own clumsiness. However she followed with such style and grace he convinced himself he'd never made the slip-up. Or if he had, she'd not noticed.

"You dance quite well for such a large man, Mr. Kincaid,"

she commented even as she again compensated for his lack of fleetness of foot. Head flung back, she smiled up at him, enjoying herself no doubt at the cost of his discomfort.

"Thank you, Your Highness." He bared his teeth back at her, taking charge of her for a succession of turns that called for some fancy footwork that he was frankly quite proud of. "However I can't say the same about your lying. Or your motives." With a list to his head he indicated the glaring Russian who continued to watch them.

"Or I regarding your manners, Mr. Kincaid." She never even blinked at his personal affront.

In spite of himself, he liked her spunk. In fact, he found it downright refreshing. *Watch it, Kincaid,* he warned himself, *get hurt once, shame on the deceiver. Get hurt twice, shame on yourself.*

"So tell me, Princess, who is he?" With another bob to his head he indicated the glowering Russian. "Some frog prince your father wishes to marry you off to?" He grinned at her. Arranged marriages. That was how it was done in the civilized world or so he'd been told.

"Count Ivan Petrovsky?" Once again she subjected him to a long and studious assessment. Then she laughed ever so condescendingly. "Quite the contrary. He is one in a long succession of men who have asked me to be their mistress."

He'd barely had time to digest her unexpected confession when the music came to a halt.

"Does your father know what you're up to?" he demanded, clasping her tightly so she could not escape.

"Dmitri Nicolaiev is not my father," she replied with a decisive tilt to her well-formed lips. "Now, if you don't mind, Mr. Kincaid." Extracting herself from his arms, she whisked off without a backward glance.

Or further explanation. Not that he was entitled to one.

Still, he wanted to know. At least, he thought he did. Something inside warned him he wouldn't like what he heard.

He watched Marina until the milling crowd swallowed her up. Intrigued beyond the point of retreat, Hunter needed to confirm just who she was if she weren't Nicolaiev's daughter.

"Prastee'te, I beg your pardon, Mr. Kincaid."

Reluctantly Hunter tore his gaze from the spot where Marina had disappeared. His limited Russian kept him from understanding much the servant said to him. However, when an immaculate white glove extended a folded piece of paper toward him, he accepted it.

"Spasee'ba," he said, thanking the man. After reading the message from Prince Dmitri asking that he join him in his private study, he looked up and glanced about the room once more. He halfway expected to find Marina watching him with that mysterious look of hers which even now drove him to distraction. She was nowhere to be seen.

With purposeful strides he followed the servant, unsure just what it was he'd gotten himself into.

Two

The nerve of the man.

Hunter Kincaid. Dmitri had hinted the American would be nothing like what she might expect. Still, it was hard to believe that a reprobate like that and her mother could have come from the same country.

Determined not to look back, Marina continued to thread her way across the crowded room. She paused only when required to sustain her role as the gracious hostess, then she quickly moved along.

She needed to think. Needed a moment to calm her shattered composure, shredded on the inside even if she appeared calm and collected to those around her. Most of all, she needed time to remember who she was and what she was and what she was determined never to become. Now more than ever, she must remember.

Never before had she felt the way she had when Hunter Kincaid had touched her. Did Dmitri suspect her weakness? Her gaze darted around the room, but did not find him. Had he watched them dance? If so, she hadn't noticed him. Regardless of what he had seen, she must find him. She must reassure him that Hunter Kincaid was like all the rest of the men who pursued her. He meant nothing, nothing at all to her. In fact, he meant less than nothing. He reminded her of her father, all bluff and bluster and self-importance.

It was Dmitri she loved. Dmitri, who had been her guardian

and then, in order to continue protecting her, had offered her marriage. What did it matter that he was an invalid? He gave her everything she needed or could ever want. He always had.

She glanced around the ballroom, suddenly growing quite weary of it all, wanting only the safety, the calm, and the solitude of the life she had chosen for herself. Yes, she had chosen it—no one had forced her.

Dmitri. Call it intuition, but she sensed he was thinking of her just as she thought of him. He needed her, that inner voice insisted, just as much as she needed him. An overwhelming urge to locate him sent her striding purposefully to his private study on the floor below.

"Mr. Kincaid. Please do come in."

Sitting behind the concealment of his desk and a pair of reading glasses, the Russian prince no longer looked the invalid, but a formidable opponent who demanded careful consideration. He reminded Hunter of an old range wolf he had spent two summers hunting down. Battle scarred, missing a forepaw sacrificed to a trap, that wolf had managed to steal more calves than a rustler. The day Hunter had finally cornered him in a canyon was one he'd never forget. He'd almost lost his own life, learning a lot about his own weaknesses and vulnerabilities in the process of taking the animal down.

Hunter moved forward, ignoring the soft click as the door closed behind him. From the floor above he could hear the sounds of the ongoing party. Marina was up there somewhere. Who was she dancing with at this moment? Count Ivan Petrovsky, perhaps?

Now was the wrong time to be thinking about a woman and her deceptive ways. He had more important matters to deal with. Namely Prince Dmitri Nicolaiev.

There was no point in asking the eccentric aristocrat what

his intentions were. Hunter figured he would find out soon enough.

The moment came quicker than he'd expected.

"I have been looking over the contracts." Nicolaiev glanced up at him over the top edge of his spectacles, apparently ready to conduct business. His gray eyes sparkled with a subtle shrewdness only a fool or a greenhorn dared to ignore.

Hunter narrowed his blue eyes. Why this sudden interest at this ungodly hour when they had spent the last few days never once mentioning the cattle deal?

"I think you will find the papers all in order," Hunter replied, quickly gathering his wits about him. "The Wyoming Cattlemen's Association has made your government an innovative offer."

"I do not doubt that they think that they have. Please, Mr. Kincaid, have a seat." The Russian indicated one of the plush velvet armchairs across from him.

Hunter decided that to sit put him at a definite disadvantage, so he declined the invitation, preferring to remain on his feet and ready.

"As you wish, Mr. Kincaid. However, could you please explain how this program will work?" Riffling through the proposal, the prince held up one of the documents.

Actually the "program" was more of a working theory. One Hunter himself had stumbled across quite by accident, although he would never admit it aloud. Later he had learned that other ranchers in the association had made similar observations. Together they had worked to perfect a plan. To sell it to the Russians was the final application.

Beef kept idle on the hoof and fed a balanced ration of grain and roughage lost its toughness while gaining poundage, the cattlemen had noted. This in turn added to the profits. Kind of like a retired cowboy who goes soft and flabby once he turns to drink and women, Hunter theorized privately.

The plan was quite simple. Rather than the ranchers bearing the expense of drylotting and then allowing the slaughterhouses in Chicago to take another big bite out of their potential profits, they would sell their commodity directly to the consumer, who would absorb much of the cost of fattening the cattle during shipping. Whether the animals were confined on land or aboard ship really made no difference as long as they were properly fed and tended. It would cost the Russians no more than refrigerating the carcasses during the long voyage would. Once the shipment reached Russian shores, the cattle could be butchered at the docks.

Of course Hunter explained this to the prince in terms that focused on the potential savings to the Russian government rather than the profits of the ranchers.

"I see," Nicolaiev said noncommittally after Hunter finished his well-rehearsed speech. "It sounds rather risky to me."

"Not at all, Your Grace." Damn! He'd hoped for more enthusiasm on the Russian's part. "At least no more so for your side as for mine."

"What if the cattle should die in transit?"

"On page three the contract states that the Cattlemen's Association is willing to guarantee the health of the stock and live-delivery barring shipwreck or any other acts of God—provided our men remain in charge of the cattle's welfare during the voyage."

"Yes, I see that. However, once they reach Russian soil we will be solely responsible for their disposition."

"That is how the contract reads." The wily, old Russian was sharp indeed, but Hunter was more than ready for him.

"I must be honest with you, Mr. Kincaid." The prince sat back in his chair and folded his hands across his chest. "We are ill-equipped to handle such wholesale slaughter."

"With a little luck, a man with vision could turn just such

a situation into a golden opportunity." Hunter moved into the shadows toward the large window of the study that overlooked much of St. Petersburg and the lights of the harbor only a few blocks away. He shoved his hands into the pockets of his sack coat.

"A man like myself, perhaps, Mr. Kincaid?"

"Very much like yourself, Your Grace." He turned to face his opponent aware he was merely a voice coming from the darkness. "As luck would have it, my associates and I can be of tremendous help to you—for certain considerations."

"I have no doubt that you can. Just what did you have in mind?"

"A partnership. We supply the know-how, you the facilities and the manpower." When the prince did not give him an immediate response, he offered his ace in the hole. "Am I to understand that you raise cattle yourself, Your Grace?"

"You might say that I dabble."

Dabble? Not likely. He had heard Nicolaiev owned one of the largest herds of Russian cattle, inferior though they were, in the country.

"Well, then perhaps you would be interested in improving your stock."

"Perhaps," the prince said guardedly, yet he looked at Hunter with real interest.

"As a bonus, I personally will throw in a prize proven bull for breeding purposes. In no time, an enterprising man like you could have a herd of superior cattle from which could springboard a nationwide effort."

"A most interesting proposition, Mr. Kincaid. I do not deny I could use a good bull. I think we can come . . ."

The sound of the study door opening cut off the rest of the prince's hard-earned agreement. Frustrated by the untimely interruption, Hunter frowned at the intruder.

And nearly jumped out of his skin.

Who should come waltzing into the room as pretty as she pleased? Why none other than the Princess Marina herself. If she noticed him, she gave no indication.

"Dmitri!" Marina chided with an exasperation that sprang from affection. Just as she'd expected, she spied her target sitting alone in the darkness of his private study. "I knew I would find you hiding here." She glided across the room to hover over him, placing her hand protectively on the slope of the aged shoulder that carried the weight of the concerns and problems of so many. "How like you to invite a house full of people then simply ignore them."

"I did it for you, my dear." Dmitri spoke in English. "You have been working far too hard of late."

"No more than you," she chided gently, replying in English as well.

Speaking in her mother's native tongue was not unusual for them. Since she had been a little girl sitting on the floor beside his wheelchair, it had been a game they had often played. To keep her in practice, he'd insisted. She smiled at him with genuine appreciation, but she had practiced quite enough for one day, thank you, dealing with that overbearing American.

"What you seem to forget is that I am much younger and possess far greater fortitude than you," she teased. Then to temper her words she lowered her face and placed the gentlest of kisses on his aged brow. "Now, I insist you go on up to bed."

"In a little while, my dear."

"Do you promise?"

"As soon as I am finished here."

"Good. Sitting in the dark alone is not healthy."

"I agree, my dear. Neither is chasing after a crippled old man."

"Nonsense, Dmitri. Now go to bed. As soon as I can be rid of our guests, I promise I will join you upstairs." Straightening, she reached out and squeezed his hand across the desk, noting the lines and age spots. Nonetheless, in her eyes it was the manliest hand in the world.

"Marina, you met the American cattleman tonight. What did you think of him?" Dmitri asked.

Odd that he would ask her that question right then when she was feeling anything but pleased with herself and her runaway emotions regarding that very same man.

"I think he is obnoxious."

"Your mother would have liked him. A handsome man, dashing and adventuresome just like your father."

"Well, I am not my mother, Dmitri. And you know how I feel about my father. I prefer consideration and stability in a man."

"Old and crippled, you mean." His gray eyes danced as he said it. "Someone who has no choice but to do what you tell him to do."

"Poppycock! What I prefer is that Hunter Kincaid leave soon and allow us to get back to our normal lives."

"There's nothing normal about us, Marina."

"Stop that, Dmitri. Stop it now." She thumped him on the shoulder to dramatize her determination. "I'll have no more of your nonsense." Whirling away in a cloud of shimmering silver, she waltzed toward the doorway. But she was smiling, although she was careful not to let him see. As an afterthought, just before she left the room, she confronted him once more, putting on a stern face. "And would you kindly tell your friend Ivan Petrovsky I'm simply not interested?"

"As you wish, my dear." Dmitri smiled.

His soft, loving chuckle followed her out the door and down the hallway. It drove her to distraction.

However, once alone, Marina caught herself smiling once more in the brightly lit hallway. Dmitri meant well, she knew that even when he dangled those so-called gallants in front of her as if she were some foolish, lighthearted girl. To be sure she had her fair share of faults and failings, but one of them wasn't unfaithfulness. It never would be.

And so the mystery solves itself. The princess is already married to the frog prince. By God, he had never coveted another man's wife. After Della . . .

Thinking of his own past experience with betrayal, Hunter swallowed so hard that the terrible truth caught sideways in his throat. He had vowed never to do to another man what had happened to him. Until now, he had had no problem keeping that solemn promise.

"I apologize for my wife's rudeness, Mr. Kincaid." The prince spoke softly—deceptively so.

Quite frankly, Hunter figured the old Russian found the situation downright amusing. Based on his own enlightenment regarding the whims and fancies of women, he couldn't comprehend such a reaction.

"No man is responsible for any woman's actions," he said dryly. God knew his marriage to Della had taught him that much. "We can only hope to sidestep them."

"Still, we do what we can to keep them happy."

"I suppose." Again, he had learned one of life's most bitter lessons attempting to do just that—keep a woman happy. Della hadn't seen it that way.

"Are you married, Mr. Kincaid?" The question could be one of mere rhetoric, or it could have a point. Hunter wasn't quite certain of the prince's intention.

"I'm a widower, Your Grace."

"Dmitri. If we are possibly to be partners in business, call me Dmitri. My condolences."

"Thank you, but it was a very long time ago." So long ago, painfully so, and he tried not to think about it much. "And so, Dmitri, *are* we to be partners?" Hunter pressed.

"I have high hopes of it. However . . ." He trailed off, picking up the multi-paged contract and slowly shuffling through the pieces of paper.

"However, what?" Hunter leaned forward in anticipation. He was so close, so very close to pulling off the deal of the century. It would make him not only rich and powerful, it would make him a hero in the eyes of his fellow Wyomingites. No one would ever again laugh at him for what Della had done.

"There is one small condition."

"Yes?" If it were monetary, Hunter had come prepared to concede it within reason. If it were a matter of responsibility, he was even willing to give in on that—to a point.

"My wife."

"Your wife?" Holy Jesus. Surely the man didn't intend to involve his wife in their business dealings. The thought of answering to a woman . . . well, that just wasn't something he intended to do. He straightened. Or would he, to get what he wanted?

"You must understand. Marina is a unique woman. I married her when she was only sixteen."

Cradle robber, Hunter thought, but kept his face as passive as a cardsharp's.

"I have sheltered her, loved her, given her everything within my power, but there are certain things I am incapable of providing for a woman like Marina."

Hunter knew the question he was supposed to ask; he just

wasn't sure he wanted to ask it, not until he had figured out what the cagey old wolfhound was leading up to.

"What are those things? you may ask." How neatly the prince sidestepped his reluctance. "Physical love, Mr. Kincaid. The one and only thing I am unable to give my beautiful, passionate wife."

"What?" Surely he'd misunderstood what the Russian had said.

Dmitri wheeled his crippled body out from behind his desk. "Physical love," he repeated. "Mr. Kincaid, I will guarantee the acceptance of the purchase contract if you will simply agree to give my wife what I am unable to give her."

Stunned, Hunter stared at the Russian. By God, the man was asking him to bed his wife. Inconceivable. And yet, his mouth went dry with the tantalizing thought of making love to the sultry ballerina who had already danced her way into his dreams of desire.

"No." Hunter edged backward, needing to put distance between himself and temptation. "What kind of a man do you take me for?"

"An honest man," the prince replied, his gaze never wavering. "I know you find Marina attractive."

"I thought she was your daughter."

"And if she were my daughter, would you then consider complying with my request?"

"I'm sorry, but this is no way to conduct business," he said self-righteously. He meant it, by damn. He'd pass up this golden opportunity before he would sink so low to attain it. Picking up the contract, he turned and aimed for the exit.

"Wait, Mr. Kincaid."

Gut instincts, the same ones that had gotten him through many a harrowing scrape, told him not to listen. They urged, no they all-out insisted, that he keep on going and never look back—and never regret his decision.

"Please. The welfare of so many depends upon what happens between us."

Confronted with thoughts of his friends and associates back in Sweetwater who depended on him to make this deal happen, Hunter paused in the doorway. He refused to turn around.

"If I have grievously misjudged you, Mr. Kincaid, then I apologize. Sometimes I forget there are still men of honor and integrity in this world."

A man of honor and integrity. Yes. That was exactly how Hunter saw himself. As long as the Russian saw him in the same light, then perhaps he deserved another chance. Satisfied, to be honest, relieved yet still wary, he turned to face his opponent.

Hunter prided himself on his ability to read other people, but Prince Dmitri Nicolaiev was a master of concealment. The Russian's gaze, still unwavering, met his own head on. No hostility, no regrets, no sign of defeat to be found there.

"Perhaps your wife is right. We should call it an evening."

"Yes, of course, Mr. Kincaid. Tomorrow we can begin our discussions anew."

"Very well." But could they in all honesty? Hunter wondered, never once relaxing his stiff, unyielding demeanor.

"I have a *dacha,* a country villa, not too far from the city. Quite lovely this time of year, Mr. Kincaid. There you could get a feel for the countryside and we could continue our negotiations without further disruption." The prince smiled, a gesture meant no doubt to put Hunter at ease. "In fact I would welcome any suggestion you might make regarding my rather meager cattle operation. Nothing on the grand scale of yours, I'm sure. But I am proud of it, nonetheless."

Back home to refuse such hospitality would be unthinkable. To be certain, he didn't trust the Russian aristocrat or the obvious cat-and-mouse game he played. Still, to find his feet planted firmly on more familiar ground, the country instead of the city, Hunter felt would be to his advantage.

"Until tomorrow morning then."

"Very good." The Russian's smile broadened. "I will send a carriage to your hotel at nine."

"I'll be ready."

With that Hunter departed, confident they had placed the unsettling incident firmly behind them. Then he smiled. He had the bull by the horns. Tomorrow morning he would wrangle the beast to the ground and claim his victory, won fair and square.

Only an emergency could disrupt Marina's early morning ritual.

First, winding up the music box, she drank a cup of hot chocolate. It was the one and only indulgence she allowed herself when it came to food, a habit she'd developed long ago as a child when her mother had invited her into her boudoir each morning to share a cup and a moment to chat. Always they played the ornate music box that her mother unfailingly took with her wherever she went, a habit Marina now had. Her heart lurched at the memory of the last time they had listened to it together. No, she mustn't think of that tragedy, not now. She set aside her empty cup.

Excited barking and the clatter of tiny canine feet scampering on the marble floor returned the smile to her lips, reminding her of her duty. Olga always seemed to know the moment she had finished and needed a prod. At the exuberant encouragement of her pair of tufted-eared terriers, wet tongues and all, she rose from her bed.

"Yes, yes, Sissonne, I am going," she scolded one of her precious pets. Dressing quickly, she headed toward the small, mirrored antechamber just off her bedroom where she always attended to her morning exercises. For reasons she didn't question, she paused on the way and rewound the music box.

It was there at the *barre* in the middle of a series of warm-up *pliés* that she received the practically unheard of intrusion. The sight of Feodor, her husband's personal servant, broke her concentration and sent her scurrying across the room.

"Dmitri? Is he all right?" she asked over the yapping of the excited dogs and the tinkling of the music. Her heart pounded with trepidation.

"But of course, Your Highness." The servant bowed in his usual stilted way, then conveyed the message he'd been sent to deliver, an invitation to join the prince in his private sitting room to break the fast.

Breakfast with her husband? A rare request, indeed, even for a Saturday morning. Something had to be amiss or dear Dmitri would never have sent for her.

Disregarding the fact she wore a half-skirt, fleshings, and a pair of well-worn ballet slippers, she raced across the vast palace to the small designated room, a part of the master suite in the west wing. Her little dogs followed at her heels, barking with delight with the unscheduled chase.

The west wing. How different it was from the east where her rooms were located. The prince loved an opened window and the sunshine; she preferred the security of the curtained dark. The footlights of the stage were all the illumination she desired.

"Dmitri, what is it?" she cried in a voice breathless with the exertion of running so far when she spied him leisurely sitting before a glass of *chai,* hot tea, into which he stirred a spoonful of fruit jelly and a *pónchiki,* a hot, sugared dough-nut. He was dressed as if he planned to go to work. But it was Saturday.

"Ah, Marina, my dear, there you are." Her husband frowned upon seeing that she was still dressed for her morning exercises. "I warned Feodor not to disturb you. I merely wished to speak with you when you were finished."

"I was finished," she lied. "Now tell me what this is all about." She sat down in the chair opposite him, took one of the dogs—Arabesque—into her lap, stroking his silken ear as she waited patiently for her husband to finish stirring his tea and put down his spoon.

"Must it be about something for a man to wish to spend a few moments with his lovely wife?"

"No, of course not." But for Dmitri, yes. "So what is it, Dmitri?" She smiled, confident she knew him well.

He toyed with his *pónchiki* for only a moment; then, giving it to the neglected pup sitting at his feet, he settled back in his wheelchair, eyeing Marina with a steady, yet gentle gaze. "It's the American."

"The American?" she echoed, her hand pausing mid-stroke on Arabesque's head. Why did her heart insist on racing out of control at the mere mention of Hunter Kincaid?

"I invited him to stay at the *dacha* for a few days. We are scheduled to depart this morning. However," he sighed, picking up his glass of tea and taking a sip, "it seems Tsar Alexander has requested my immediate presence at the Winter Palace."

So that was why he was dressed in a crisp white shirt and frock coat.

"I'm sure Mr. Kincaid will understand if you must cancel," Marina offered in all sincerity. She didn't like it when Dmitri was so unsettled and resented anyone who caused the gentle man undue stress, even the tsar.

"No, Marina, you don't understand. The negotiations are very delicate between us. If I should cancel, the entire project stands at risk." He set down his cup once more, piercing her with one of his famous unwavering stares. "Think, my dear, how many might starve this winter if we should lose this opportunity to purchase a much-needed supply of fresh beef."

"Perhaps it is the tsar, not I, who should be hearing this," Marina suggested.

"But of course. And I plan to tell him exactly that the moment I see him this morning. I'm sure he will listen, once I do. Until then . . ." His voice trailed off on a note of uncertainty.

"Until then?" she leaned forward, concerned for both her husband's dilemma and the welfare of the Russian people.

"Until then, I must make sure Mr. Kincaid is kept . . . entertained."

"Perhaps you could arrange for him to tour the city."

"I'm afraid not." Dmitri shook his head. "Mr. Kincaid is not the kind of man to be held captive by our history or our architecture."

No, she supposed not.

"Then what would hold his attention?" she asked.

"The company of a beautiful woman."

"Dmitri," she chided ever so gently, pushing the dog out of her lap and herself out of the chair, "why do you persist in trying to throw me together with these other men?" He did it for her, she knew that, thinking to fill a void he could not satisfy himself. His was truly an unselfish act, but she didn't need it—nor did she want it. Moving to his side, she knelt down next to the arm of his wheelchair and covered his frail arm with her hand. "Dmitri, can't you accept that I am truly happy the way I am?"

"I swear to you. This is not what you might think, Marinuska," he said with undisguised affection, using the Russian endearment of her name. "I honestly need your help."

"Then you are like the boy who cried wolf."

He looked at her, his eyes sparkling with an intellectual challenge. Then he hung his head so endearingly she couldn't help but believe him—and love him—and wish to make him happy, too.

"Very well, Dmitri. I have the day free. I will take your all-important Mr. Kincaid on a tour of St. Petersburg." Convinced, she rose, resigned in her action. A short ride through the city with the man, especially if she brought along her dogs—how threatening could that be?

"No, Marina." Dmitri's age-spotted hand grasped her sleeve. "Instead you must take him on to the country villa for me."

"But . . ."

He cut off her protest with a beseeching look. "Please. I promise to follow only a few hours behind you. Think of all the hungry little children you will save with your generosity."

As a child herself saved by just such generosity how could she possibly say no?

"You promise to follow?" she insisted, feeling guilty for doubting his motivation, but she did.

"By this afternoon at the very latest."

"Very well. But I will only escort him there, nothing more."

"Of course, my dear, nothing more expected. Thank you. And Marina, leave the dogs at home. I do not believe they are the American's glass of *chai*." Lifting his own glass, the contents now cooled, he saluted her before draining it like a thirsty child.

Without agreeing to his request, Marina made her way back to her rooms to pack for what would be no more than an overnight stay at the *dacha*. As for the dogs—what did she care if Hunter Kincaid liked them or not? If Dmitri truly understood the circumstances, he would agree with her decision to take them along for protection.

* * *

The prince's carriage arrived at precisely nine that morning. Hunter saw it pull up in front of the Europa Hotel. He didn't bother to wait for the accompanying footman to come into the hotel to fetch him. Instead, he carried his single bag out the door and tossed it into the boot. He noted that the prince had packed one small suitcase himself. The only other item of luggage was an ornate wooden box. What it held, he couldn't imagine.

And so when the servant swung open the door of the carriage he was ill-prepared to be greeted by the yapping of two small dogs. Why was it the smaller the mutt the more it barked? And God those were the ugliest, no doubt the most useless, mongrels he had ever seen. The fur on their backs hung clear to their feet, their ears crooked and tufted with equally long hair that practically concealed their beady little eyes.

"Arabesque, Sissonne, mind your manners." The none-too-harsh command was issued in a soft feminine voice.

Marina? Bending down to glance into the dark interior of the carriage, Hunter took in what Wyomingites called the East Coast-cut of her stylish dress and the gloved hands that stroked the heads of those worthless lap curs. He'd love to wring their scrawny little necks or, better yet, let ol' Rowdy, his cattle dog, have a go at them.

"Mornin', ma'am." He touched the brim of his gray felt hat in greeting, wondering just what was going on but determined not to show his confusion. Where was the prince? Why had he sent his beautiful wife in his stead? God help him, she was beautiful, even more so than he'd remembered from last night.

"Mr. Kincaid." She nodded in turn, looking as cool and settled as an early morning frost as she gave him a quick once-over. Her dark eyes never revealed what she thought of him.

In silence he sat down on the seat opposite her. To his

dismay he had to remove his Stetson or contend with the possibility of having it knocked off by the low ceiling of the carriage. Sweeping off his hat, he dropped it on the seat beside him, self-consciously running his fingers through his hair. Then, when one of the little pests attempted to snatch the hat, no doubt with the intention of gnawing on it like a piece of old rawhide, he grabbed for it.

"I'm sorry, Mr. Kincaid; he won't do it again." Without a blink of an eye, Marina scooped up the dog and dropped it in her lap.

But the little beast had other ideas, or so Hunter interpreted the way his beady little eyes never lifted from his target and his tongue repeatedly darted out to lick his chops. To be on the safe side, Hunter crossed his ankle over his opposing knee and placed the hat, his favorite one, across his nankeen-covered thighs.

"Really, Mr. Kincaid, I have said Arabesque will behave himself."

"I don't doubt it at all, ma'am." He had every intention of seeing to that personally. In the meantime, he studied the woman sitting across from him, so very close he caught a whiff of her tantalizing perfume. That smell, what did it remind him of?

After a few intense moments of staring back, Marina slowly lowered her dark lashes over her equally dark, unfathomable eyes. Just what did she think of him? But more important, why was she here?

"You must wonder why Dmitri has sent me in his stead."

How had she so neatly read his mind?

"He was called away on business, but has promised to join us . . ." She darted a wary look at him. ". . . join *you* at the *dacha* this afternoon."

He watched her slender, well-formed hand fiddle nervously with a little blue ribbon tied in the hair on the head of one of the dogs. Could there be more to her seemingly innocent slip of the tongue than met the eye?

Hunter reached out and snapped open the shutter of one of the carriage windows. Like a startled deer, Marina jumped at the sudden, unexpected noise. She looked out the window only fleetingly with what he concluded might be fear before her attention settled on her pet. He'd learned a long time ago that people spoke more about the truth with their actions than with their mouths.

So what frightened Marina Nicolaiev—something outside of the carriage or something within? He frowned. Or maybe something left behind, like a husband?

"You don't much like the idea of this trip to the country, do you, ma'am?"

"No." She laughed uneasily, her gaze lifting to stare out the window for only a moment, then returning to that mangy mutt. "I don't particularly care for wide open spaces. They remind me of . . ."

When she didn't finish her statement, he didn't press it, although it left him more intrigued than ever.

"You don't like me very much either, do you?"

His frankness caught her full attention. Her gaze swept upward, dark and intense. If looks could fire bullets, he would have been dead.

"To be honest, I haven't given you that much thought, Mr. Kincaid."

Now that was a barefaced lie if he'd ever heard one. She'd thought about him plenty, just as he'd thought about her. Damn, if that discovery didn't make him feel even more uncomfortable and leave him wondering just where this day would lead him.

Was this some kind of plot cooked up by the prince to throw them together in hopes that he would comply with last night's indecent proposal? Could it be Marina was in on the deception, too? Once they reached that isolated villa would she attempt to seduce him? He wouldn't be the least bit surprised if this simply turned out to be some kind of aristocratic game of rope 'em and brand 'em the two of them played using him as the maverick.

If so, he didn't like it, and he wouldn't be party to such shenanigans. He continued to size her up until that annoying ball of fur sitting at her feet started to growl. Only Hunter's eyes moved, glancing down at this newest threat.

"Sissonne, stop that!" Marina warned, scooping up the ridiculous-looking fur ball and stuffing it next to her as if it were a pillow.

Hunkering down, Hunter returned to his silent examination. He had to admit she didn't act like a woman bent on seduction. In fact, anything but. Her dress, although stylish and attractive, was modest and concealing. Her eyes, sometimes bold, never once assessed him in "that" way. And if she'd wanted the opportunity to be forward with him, why would she have ever brought along those damn little dogs?

She wouldn't have, he decided, wishing for all the world he had his Stetson securely on his head so he could pull it down over his eyes and pretend to fall asleep. Better yet, he wished he'd never agreed to this unnecessary trip to the country in the first place.

With a squirming terrier tucked under each arm, Marina frantically sought the best way to handle her dilemma. It served no point to anger the American any more than he apparently already was. She had to figure out some way to smooth out the situation. Not for herself, but for Dmitri and the Russian people he so desperately felt responsible to feed.

After an indeterminate period of time that could have only

been minutes but seemed like hours, Marina forced herself
to speak.

"Your villa in America. It must have lots of wide open
spaces." Just where that had come from, she didn't know, but
it was all she could think to say at the moment.

"It's a ranch, not a villa, Princess, and there's nothing but
wide open spaces as far as a man can see. I like it that way."
His gaze, as blue as a cloudless sky, continued to assess her.
"Not so different from Russia really."

"Really?" She didn't try to suppress her relief that he had
answered or her interest in what he had to say. For in truth,
the one subject she found most fascinating was America. All
her life she had tried to imagine what that great country
looked like. Clinging to every word her mother had told her
about the land of her birth, she had read any book she could
get her hands on. To her confusion they all described America
so differently, and nothing at all like what Mama had said.
She couldn't be certain which source to believe.

"Didn't you tell me your mother was an American?"

"Yes. Yes, I did."

"How did she ever end up in Russia?"

Was it only her imagination or did he make it sound like
a form of punishment?

"She came to Moscow to perform," she replied, not bothering to disguise her indignation. "My father saw her and
proposed that very night to her backstage. They say theirs
was a whirlwind courtship."

"And how long did that last?" His jaws tensed as if he
had bitten into something distasteful.

"Pardon me?" She straightened, hugging her little dogs
closer. "I'm not sure what you are asking?"

"Nothing," he muttered in that slow, irritating drawl of his.
"Then your mother was a dancer, too."

She stared at him for the longest moment, wondering at his odd attitude and her even stranger reaction.

"No, a singer," she finally replied.

His eyes pierced right through her with an intensity that made her catch her breath. And there it went again, her inconceivably foolish heart, racing out of control, and all he did was look at her in a way that spoke of loss and longing—and incredible passion.

Marina knew then and there she was not made of as ascetic a fabric as she had always prided herself in possessing. She was vulnerable to basic human needs like everyone else. Frantically, she glanced out the window, hoping beyond hope to find they were still in the city—that she could escape not only the man, but the truth about herself.

Wide open spaces, they were all around the carriage, a barrier more confining than the strongest fences, at least to her.

Filled with trembling anxiety, she glanced once more at Hunter Kincaid. Was the cannonade she heard created by her out-of-control heart or something worse? She glanced out the carriage window with dread. Could it be thunder that rattled the carriage window? A terrible fear she was powerless to fend off clutched the shredded remains of her composure.

God, no, please don't let it be thunder.

Three

The rain swept across the Russian countryside like a marauding pack of coyotes that slunk in from the west without warning. Although Hunter had ridden through much worse storms with less cover, he couldn't explain why this one made him feel so uneasy.

Perhaps it had something to do with Marina. She practically turned green around the gills hugging those two dogs to her as if they might protect her. From what, he couldn't imagine. Perhaps from him. No other explanation made sense. No one could be that terrified of a little thunder and lightning, could they?

However, he suspected his unrest had equally as much to do with the unpredictable nature of the weather as with the woman. Wyoming thunderstorms were bold and direct, riding in on gusts of wind and throwing bolts of lightning like arrows with the accuracy of a marksman's aim. Russian storms were not as dramatic. Without honor, they sneaked upon the land, the thunder more like the rumble of an angry bear or a distant battle; then, without so much as a clue, lightning would strike a hapless tree in the forest, not necessarily the tallest one.

In only minutes the deluge transformed the already rutted dirt road into a rushing rivulet. Hunter's first thought was to insist that the driver return them immediately to the city.

"We should turn around," he said. His mind made up, he lowered the window.

"Mr. Kincaid, no."

Disregarding both Marina's protest and the heavy rain that lashed at his face like needles, he stuck out his head to call up to the coachman. He heard the thunder crack, saw the sparks fly—then the tree coming toward him, and barely had time to withdraw into the safety of the vehicle before the hulking giant hit the road right behind the carriage. Its ancient limbs reached out as if determined to snag them. Like the sound of fingernails dragged across slate, the scrapes on the roof over their head grated on his nerves. Marina clapped her hands over her ears. Miraculously the carriage continued on, apparently unscathed, at least for the moment.

"How much farther do we have to go?" he demanded, slamming closed the window against the din of the storm. He resigned himself to the fact there would be no turning back, not now with the road blocked by the fallen tree.

"Four maybe five *versts* at the most," she replied in a shaky voice.

Even as she said it and he calculated the Russian measurement into approximately three miles, he could feel the carriage slowing down, the mud sucking at the wheels. By now the road would be a quagmire and would only get worse, even if the rain should stop. He heard the driver raise his whip to the team of horses, ordering them to keep moving. How long, Hunter wondered, before the road became completely impassable?

The thought of making his way on foot across the unfamiliar countryside didn't disturb him all that much. He could do it alone, but he hesitated to leave Marina behind. He glanced at the woman sitting in wide-eyed silence across from him, assessing her fortitude and stamina. Dressed in her stylish clothing and impractical shoes, she wouldn't get far, if he could convince her to leave the carriage at all. And those dogs of hers. He shuddered at the prospect of having to carry one of the spoiled little monsters under each arm.

And so, inevitably, just as he'd foreseen, the carriage came to a lurching halt. The driver's whip cracked as loudly as the thunder, again, and then again. The horses whinnied their protest, the harnessing jingling as they tried to comply with their handler's order, and the vehicle shuddered, all to no avail.

Hunter stripped off his long-haired sack coat and began rolling up the sleeves of his white cotton shirt.

"Mr. Kincaid, what do you think you are doing?" Marina's eyes grew even wider, if that were possible.

"I'm going to see to it we get out of this mess."

"Heaven forbid, sir, you must leave such menial labor to the servants." She placed a restraining hand upon his bare forearm, then immediately snatched it back.

"If I do that, ma'am," he said, staring down at the spot where she had touched him, feeling the surge of electricity as surely as she had, "we could be here a long time." Grabbing up his hat, he jammed it on his head. "So unless you plan on staying stuck in this carriage all night, Princess, or else walking the rest of the way . . ."

"Walk? In this storm?" The trepidation radiating from her dark gaze was without a doubt genuine even if he didn't quite understand it.

Once out of the carriage and knee-deep in muck, Hunter turned to assess the situation. Much worse than he'd imagined, the mud, black and gummy and like none he had ever seen, rose clear up to the cogs of the wheels.

"How does it look, Mr. Kincaid?"

Hunter glanced up to find Marina's face framed in the open window, the yapping of those little dogs accompanying her query. One of her tightly coiled rosettes of hair was starting to come down. Escaped wisps of hair curled about her fore-head and cheek, destroying the illusion of aristocratic aloofness and revealing in its stead an air of fragile vulnerability.

There it was again. That haunting vision of a little girl, lost and alone. He had to physically shake himself to be rid of the disturbing image.

"Stay put and don't worry, Princess."

It was more than enough that he must worry about their sticky predicament.

In a miff, Marina closed the window and then the shutter. Swiping at the wet frizz clinging to her face, she sat back and crossed her arms over her chest. The dogs began to climb upon her, their little wet tongues seeking to comfort.

"Sissonne, Arabesque, stop that," she muttered, brushing them away. Dmitri had been right. She should have never brought the two of them along. Better yet, she should have never agreed to Dmitri's request to nursemaid the American. Instead, she should have stayed in St. Petersburg where she belonged. Then none of this would be happening to her.

The thought was no more formulated than the carriage began to rock back and forth so hard Marina had to brace herself to keep from being tossed about like baggage.

The baggage. Her concern switched from her personal safety to the state of her mother's music box stashed in the boot of the carriage. If any harm should come to her most precious possession . . .

Any breakage would be the fault of that ridiculous American. Whatever was he doing out there wallowing in the mud with the servants? Whatever it was, she had to admit, it appeared to be working, for suddenly the carriage lurched ahead a few paces. Then, to her disappointment, it halted once more for what seemed an eternity.

Curious, she parted the shutters enough to peek out of the window, a peek that turned into a full-fledged, neck-craning search when she saw nothing but the residue of the rain dripping from the roof of the carriage and not a single soul. Even if Hunter Kincaid might desert her, and she wouldn't put it past him to think only of himself, surely the servants would not be so disloyal. Or would they?

Frightened beyond words, Marina threw open the carriage door to get a better look. With a resounding burst of barking, one of the dogs squeezed by her.

"Arabesque, no!"

He hit the mud with a loud splat, looking more like a lady's wig tossed out the door than a live animal. Without thinking, Marina followed her beloved pet. Of course, Sissonne dogged her steps. Like an umbrella stuck in the sand, Marina found herself planted in knee-deep mud, her silk skirts spread around her.

To make matters worse, the two muddy dogs struck out for parts unknown. When she tried to shepherd them back to the carriage, she toppled forward, her hands instinctively reaching out to break her fall.

Mud. It was everywhere, coating the expensive Belgian lace on her sleeves. It was even in the strands of hair that straggled in her eyes and down her back. She reached up to brush the dark curly tresses out of the way. Now look what she had done. The mud was on her face as well. The more she tried, the worse it got. Finally, she gave up, shaking her arms in frustration.

"I say, Princess, I wonder what ol' Ivan would think if he could see you now."

Marina twisted in place to discover none other than Hunter Kincaid leaning against the back of the carriage. He, too, stood knee-deep in the mud. His shirt was wet and plastered to his lean, athletic body; the brim of his hat was dripping.

But he didn't look the least bit foolish. In fact—she swallowed so hard it sounded like a gulp to her own ears—he looked incredibly handsome.

On the other hand, she knew *she* must look utterly ridiculous.

"Sissonne, Arabesque." She pointed in the direction in which the disobedient dogs had dashed.

"Not to worry, ma'am." His amused perusal of her ended, his gaze following where her finger indicated. "I suspect they'll be back. None the worse for wear, I predict." Then he glanced back down at her, his blue eyes, sparkling with humor, once more taking in her state of total disarray. "Reckon I can't say the same for you, though." Using his shoulder, he pushed away from the side of the bogged vehicle. "Help is on the way. Didn't I tell you to stay put inside the carriage?"

"Who do you think you are to tell me what to do?" Arms akimbo, she asserted her aristocratic station. Too late she realized her dreadful mistake. She glanced down. Two perfect black hand prints graced the once white flare of her redingote. "Oh-h-h. Blast it all!" she muttered.

Hunter started to laugh, but she didn't find him or her situation the least bit funny.

"What are you laughing at?" she demanded. Scooping up a handful of mud, she threw it at that most irritating of men. When it caught him full on one cheek, she couldn't believe her luck. Her eyes widened. Or was it her misfortune?

He came at her like an outraged bear, outstretched paws swinging and grasping. Mud sucked at his every step, but it didn't stop him. Had she been a trapped hare she would have had a better chance of escaping. She managed one retreating step, then two, but that was as far as the sodden canopy of her skirts would allow her to move.

Plunk.

The feel of the cool ooze seeping into her silk underwear

was shocking to say the least. But it was the startling touch of his fingers upon her flesh that made her gasp.

"Let go of me, you . . . you uncouth brute." When he scooped her up, she swung at him, unmindful of the mud they both slung about. "Right this minute," she demanded. "That's a command. Did you hear me?"

She might as well have shouted at the deaf and dumb for all the good it did her. Too late she realized his intent.

"A royal command, Your Highness? Very well." He dropped her, mud and all, on one of the plush velvet seats in the carriage. If that weren't bad enough, the two exuberant dogs chose that same moment to come bounding back. Muddy feet first, they landed in her lap, the only spot on her gown that had remained—until then—miraculously clean.

Feeling utterly degraded, she spied what the dogs had chased after. Through the woods came the hapless servants followed by a *kolkhoznik,* a local farmer, and a team of heftily built dray horses no doubt meant to pull them out of the mud. She shot a wary glance at Hunter, wondering if this were his idea.

"I told you help was on the way." Giving her a crooked, most irritating smile, he tipped his hat at her, then backed out of the door.

"Your Highness? Is that you?" the driver inquired in wide-eyed wonder at her totally disheveled appearance when she leaned out of the carriage to assure the peasant he would be paid for his trouble and kindness.

"Yes, of course, who else did you expect?" she snapped with much more severity than she had ever before used with a servant. But then it wasn't every day she had to deal with the likes of Hunter Kincaid. Slamming the door, she snapped closed the shutter on the window.

Sitting in the darkness, indignation her only companion besides the muddy dogs who simply refused to stay off the seat, she cared not a fig what became of so rude a man. He could walk to the *dacha* for all that it mattered to her.

"Get down, Sissonne," she ordered briskly, slapping at the terrier who persisted in jumping into her lap. Not that it mattered. She was already filthy from head to toe. What difference did a little more mud make now?

The worst part of her dilemma was that she knew Dmitri would simply chuckle when she told him the story, if she ever told him, and accuse her of egging on the American, even of actually liking him.

Like him? Why she couldn't stand him and would do everything in her power to get even with him for the embarrassment he had caused her!

As that thought, motivated by pure frustration, crossed her mind, she spied Hunter's carefully removed jacket draped across the opposite seat. Smiling with victory, she leaned forward and spread the sack coat out.

"Here, my sweetlings," she cooed with encouragement, patting the soft lining.

Arabesque was more than willing to comply. In no time he was happily curled in the middle of the last-remaining clean garment.

The carriage began to move forward, slowly at first, to the tune of the "gees" and "haws" of the *kolkhoznik*. Marina sat back most satisfied, until she remembered just why she was there in the first place.

In her ill-conceived haste, had she just single-handedly ruined what Dmitri had worked so hard to accomplish over the last year?

She brushed Arabesque off his makeshift bed, knowing even if she had, Dmitri would forgive her. However, she would never forgive herself for being so foolish and thoughtless.

* * *

By late afternoon they reached their destination, the Nicolaiev country estate that had been in the family since the days
of Catherine the Great. Marina stepped down from the carriage to discover the sky leaden with the promise of yet more
rain.

Immediately, her thoughts turned to Hunter Kincaid. Upon
finding him none the worse for travel and mud stains and
apparently quite at home in the company of the driver and
footman, she left him to his own devices, at least for the
moment. She would figure out later how best to deal with
him and hopefully make amends.

Her next concerns were purely selfish. A distant rumble
sent dread coursing through her veins. Oh, how she hated
these summer storms, but mostly the accompanying thunder
and lightning.

"My music box. See that it gets inside immediately," she
ordered the steward, the first of the servants to greet the unexpected arrival of their mistress. If he thought anything about
her strange appearance, he said nothing. For that, she felt
relief and, with the assistance of that same discreet servant,
picked her way across the rain-drenched walk to the front
steps of the villa.

Glancing down the road they had just traveled, she noted
the deep ruts left by the carriage wheels. Only by a miracle
had they managed to reach the *dacha* at all. If it hadn't been
for the peasant and his team of dray horses . . .

Remembering her promise to compensate the man who had
accompanied them on the rest of the journey atop the back
of one of his horses, she turned once more to the steward.

"The man with the horses." She waved her hand vaguely
in the direction of the carriage. "Pay him for his efforts and
offer him shelter for both himself and his animals for the
night if he so wishes it. The prince will hopefully be arriving

soon. Prepare a room in the south wing for our guest, Mr. Kincaid."

"As you wish, Your Highness."

Without further explanation, for none was necessary, Marina turned the muddy dogs over to him and made her way inside the villa and to her own rooms in the north wing, confident her orders would be followed.

"Izvinítye. Excuse me."

What frustrated Hunter most was his lack of communication skills. He sized up the servant, apparently some kind of high-falutin' butler, who continued speaking to him in lightning-fast Russian.

When his limited Russian failed him, the one phrase he had learned and used now—*Ya nye panima'yu*—I don't understand—usually got him through.

So why was this uppity servant shoving money in his hand, and not much of it at that? And why did he keep pointing at the outbuildings? More important, why was the Russian walking away and leaving him standing in the drive when he could have sworn he'd just heard Marina indicate that he was her guest?

"Ya nye panima'yu! Ya nye panima'yu!"

The Russian paused at the front door and stared down his nose at Hunter as if thoroughly annoyed by his persistence. Then Hunter thought about how he must look covered from head to tail with mud. Could it be the man mistook him for a peasant?

"Mr. Kincaid." Hunter stated, thumping himself on the chest. "I am Mr. Kincaid."

It took quite a few moments and the assistance of the driver to convince the hoity-toity servant of his true identity. Then the butler fell all over himself trying to make amends, accepting back the money he had thrust upon Hunter with a profusion of apologies.

"It could happen to anybody," Hunter assured him with a lazy smile, but wondered just how much Marina had had to do with his ill-treatment.

Still bowing and scraping, the butler showed him into the house.

Hell, this was no simple country manor. It was another mansion, big enough to accommodate the entire population of Sweetwater, Wyoming. For the life of him, he would never get used to such wasteful ostentation nor the people who displayed it with such a shameful lack of appreciation.

Take Marina for instance, flitting about like a butterfly in a field of buttercups. She was beautiful but useless, he decided, just like those little dogs of hers. A woman like her would never make it in Wyoming. Such reasoning did not make him desire her any less, but it did make him more determined than ever to keep his distance.

Whether or not anyone else was aware of it, they were alone in that big, old house except for servants whose job it was to be discreet and keep out of sight. If the rumbling thunder outside were any indication, it could be that way for quite a while.

If he hadn't known better, he would have sworn ol' Dmitri had planned it that way. But even a Russian prince had no influence over the weather.

By evening Marina gave up all hope and pretense that Dmitri would arrive, at least not until tomorrow.

The weather was not his fault, she chided herself. Still it didn't make her feel any less betrayed nor, God help her, any less curious as to how Hunter fared.

"Yakov," she queried the servant who brought in the dogs,

freshly bathed and perfumed just as she was, "Mr. Kincaid? Has he asked for me?"

"The American? *Niét.*" The old man shook his head. "He has sequestered himself in his rooms in the south wing and has asked only for a bath and that his dinner be sent up to him there."

"I see," she said, trying hard to hide her disappointment.

Disappointment with what? she demanded of herself once the old man had departed. She flung herself across her bed, only annoyed when the dogs followed her. Disappointment that Hunter Kincaid did not seek her out? Disappointment that he preferred his own company to hers? Disappointment that she had not had the opportunity to reject him first?

Even Arabesque with his playful antics, pulling on the ends of her wrap ties or nipping at her bare toes and fingers, did nothing to alleviate her petulant mood.

She should practice, she supposed, for she had been quite slack in her *barre* exercises the last few days. Yes, to immerse herself into her work, that would surely take her mind off Hunter Kincaid.

Donning her fleshings and half-skirt and a pair of woolen hose to keep her legs a bit warmer in the country draft, she moved to the window and closed the heavy, velvet drapes. Still, the distant rumble of thunder seeped into the room. She prayed the storm would bypass them, but held out little hope. Automatically, she turned to the small table where she had set her mother's music box.

Inserting the key, she wound it and listened to it play for a few moments before beginning her "frogs," gentle warm-up exercises, while sitting on the floor. For the moment at least, the lively music drowned out all other sounds.

It didn't surprise her when even the dogs settled down to listen. The music, a powerful reminder of her past, had a way of calming even the most unruly beast within.

* * *

Hunter lifted his head and listened.

"That music? Where does it come from?" he asked the servant who brought him his clothes, amazingly clean, and a meal. The dinner consisted of a beet soup he learned was called *borshch* and was considered a staple in Russia as mashed potatoes were in the United States. There were also some kind of meat dumplings that were filling to be sure but strange to the palate and, to wash it all down, a glass of *kvass,* a fermented drink that could not compare to beer.

The old woman looked at him and shrugged.

"Muz'eeka," he stumbled over what he hoped was the right Russian word.

"Ah-h-h. *Da. Muz'eeka,"* she said as if she understood. She said something more, but all he caught was Marina's name.

Marina. Of course. He should have known. Putting down his spoon, he listened once more to the faraway melodic sounds. Such music suited her personality well. He could imagine her dancing to the lively tempo, her long legs and delicate arms lifting with ease and grace into the air, whirling, whirling, dancing only for him.

Pushing away the rest of the strange-tasting food, he stood and began to pace the room, a diversion from the outrageous, downright dangerous, path his thoughts took. In front of the window he paused to watch as yet another storm rolled in, the flashes of lightning illuminating the desolate, already drenched countryside.

For the first time since arriving in this godforsaken land, Hunter Kincaid felt homesick. Homesick for a decent meal; homesick for his ranch; homesick for the sunshine Rainee, his daughter, brought into his life. It was a bad night to be alone.

Making up his mind, he turned to ask the servant to deliver

a message to Marina for him, asking if she would like a little company, but the old woman was already gone, taking the remains of his meal with her.

Perhaps it was better that way.

Hours later the veritable force of the thunderstorm shook the solidly built villa as if it were as flimsy as a soldier's tent.

"Marina!"

Over the cannonade Marina could hear her mother's scream and then her own when the maternal hand grabbed her with an unaccustomed roughness. Then with a kaleidoscope of colors the world— tent poles, heavy canvas, and all—came tumbling down around them. Mama's weight knocked the breath from her little girl's body as it pinned her to the ground.

"Mama?" she whispered softly, tentatively, hiccuping in fear of the sudden darkness, frightened even more of the nasty smell that burned her eyes and throat making it impossible to breathe. When she received no answer, she squirmed just enough to ease the pain when a broken slat of the pretty lacquered fan Mama had been fluttering in rhythm to the music moments before jabbed her in one shoulder.

That's when she realized the music box still played. The lively melody she had been dancing to only moments before, had fallen asleep to every night that she could remember, offered comfort. It assured her Mama was only sleeping and would wake up soon. Finally, after what seemed a lifetime to a child of only five, the music box slowed, plinking out the last notes in staccato. Left in total darkness and now absolute silence, Marina could wait no longer.

"Mama, wake up," she cried, pressing her tiny hands into her mother's soft shoulder, trying to shake her.

Like a shadow, icy terror crept up on her, robbing her of

courage and chilling her to the very marrow of her bones. Unsure just how she knew, she knew for certain Mama couldn't hear her or feel her, that she would never speak to her again.

"Mama! Mama! I'm afraid."

Jarred awake, Marina lay in a cold sweat, the fine linen sheets twisted about her womanly hips. Like the terror clutching her heart, her damp bedclothes clung to her body. Even her hair was plastered wetly to her forehead. Her heart raced out of control. It took her a few moments to realize where she was, but more importantly, where she wasn't.

She had had another dream, one of those recurring nightmares born of reality that sometimes struck even when she was awake, but always in the midst of a storm.

The lightning flashed. Seconds later, the accompanying thunder rumbled directly overhead replicating the dreaded cannonfire that had ripped through her father's army camp, killing her mother. Flopping back and forth on the bed, she couldn't control the tremors that continued to shake her even though now she was awake. The present day fear was as real as her innocence about life and death had been so long ago.

She would get no more sleep, not tonight, not as long as the storm lasted.

"Mama," she moaned softly. Oh, how she missed dear Mama's adoration, her love, so cruelly taken when she needed it the most. Thinking of Mama always made her yearn for the warmth of a loving embrace.

Dmitri loved her. God knew, she never doubted his feelings toward her for a moment, but embrace her? Hold her in his arms until the terror subsided? Due to his age and physical limitations, he never felt comfortable with such intimacy between them.

Unable to remain recumbent another minute, Marina rose. She shivered in the sheerness of her peach-colored peignoir and sought out the bit of warmth the matching thin wrapper afforded her, pulling it tightly about her.

Suddenly the bedroom seemed too vulnerable, too open even with the curtain securely drawn, too isolated and susceptible to the threatening heavens.

Confident the entire household slept and that no one would hear or see her desperate flight, she gathered up her mother's music box, now silent, and headed for the door.

"*Niét,* Arabesque. You must stay here." Ignoring the dog's insistent whines and scratching, she hurried down the corridor that led to the central part of the house. There, with the building all around her, she would be safe, safe from the thunder and the lightning and the inconsolable terror accompanying it.

Hunter couldn't say what it was that awoke him. Perhaps it was the crash of thunder so close he felt the room shake or perhaps it was the rumble in his empty stomach. But whatever the cause, he became instantly alert, and he knew it would be awhile before he would manage to fall back to sleep.

He rose, feeling quite out of sorts in his restlessness. If he were home, it would only be a matter of making his way to his small study and burning a little midnight oil, or better yet the pantry to sate his hunger.

But here in the middle of a Russian forest, it was not that simple. He wasn't even sure where to find the kitchens in the huge maze of corridors in the mansion. Even if he lucked upon it, he wouldn't feel comfortable rummaging in someone else's larder.

Donning his pants and shirt, he moved to the window to observe the storm displaying its power over land and beast alike. It was a sight he never grew tired of watching. Many a night he had spent in a line camp or on the trail of a cattle drive utterly fascinated.

Oddly enough, all he could think of as the storm progressed was Marina Nicolaiev, princess, fleet-footed sprite that had somehow managed to dance her way center stage into his life. It was like a dream come true to find himself alone with a woman like her. So close, yet so out of reach. Still, to look out across the Russian landscape, one would think the rest of the world didn't even exist.

Marina. Hunter took a deep breath, surprised when an uncharacteristic sigh escaped his soldered lips. Fantasy or not, she belonged to another, even if in name only.

And he? Well, he was a man of honor, a man who knew how it felt to be cuckolded. To steal another man's wife was something he would never do, even with permission. His eyes narrowed with self-incrimination when he couldn't shake off a vision of the beautiful ballerina. Or would he stoop so low, he wondered, if the circumstances were right?

What he needed was a good dose of cool night air. A dousing of cold rain wouldn't hurt him any, either.

Pushing off from his vantage point at the window, he made his way to the door of his room, confident no one would be the wiser to his night foray. It stood to reason that the rest of the household, including the princess herself, was sound asleep.

Four

That music. There it was again, only this time much closer. Hunter's ever-alert gaze focused on a door just ahead, off the central foyer in which he stood. The haunting melody came from the other side.

He should ignore it—better yet, pretend he'd never heard it and walk on by. He probably would have done just that if the sweet serenade hadn't stopped the precise moment he chose to make good his escape.

Riveted by the silence, Hunter paused, waiting to see if the music would begin again. His heart raced in a way he couldn't understand or condone.

"Play it, Marina," he coaxed under his breath.

Instead, thunder rumbled closer than before and the door swung open.

Hunter found himself face to face with the very temptation he wished to avoid at all cost.

"Mr. Kincaid, whatever are you doing standing out here?" Her voice sounded as breathless and guarded as he felt. At the base of her throat her hand clutched the gauze of the nightgown she wore. It didn't conceal much from his hungry gaze.

"Evening, Princess." He reached to doff his hat and came up empty-handed. He had left his gray felt Stetson back in his room. Suddenly, he was the one who felt quite naked with only his head uncovered.

"Evening, indeed, sir," she replied, her eyes following the progress of his hand and lingering there. "Is something amiss?" she asked, stepping back from the door. "Perhaps I should call for a servant."

Whether her actions were an invitation or a retreat, he couldn't be certain. He fantasized it was the first, prayed it was the second.

"No, ma'am, that won't be necessary. I just need a breath of fresh air." God knew, he needed more than air. Garnering strength he'd not known he'd possessed, he turned away from the open door and the woman standing just beyond the shadow it cast. He had taken only a couple of purposeful strides when another crash of thunder, so close the hairs on his arms tingled in response, rattled the windows of the mansion.

"Please, Mr. Kincaid, don't go." Hers was a cry from the heart; one, no matter what his convictions, he couldn't find it in himself to ignore.

Knowing it was a mistake, he turned to acknowledge her need as well as his own yearning weakness that he could no longer deny.

"I'm sorry, Mr. Kincaid, I shouldn't have said that."

Wild-eyed, frightened, vulnerable. It was the only way he could describe how she looked.

"That's quite all right. I understand." Immense disappointment shot through him with the force of a wild bullet. "Evening to you, ma'am."

"Good night, Mr. Kincaid. And do be careful. The lightning is very close." Her hand, white against the stain of the door as she moved to shut it, held his rapt attention.

"Yes, ma'am, so it is." He smiled and glanced up when the closest window flashed brightly, noticing she darted a look outside, too. "But it doesn't frighten me." Ambling off, he made his way to the main entrance to the house. The door of the great salon clicked softly as it closed.

And he might have escaped, no damage done, if the inevitable thunder hadn't cannonaded all around them. Turning back around, instinctively he knew what he would find.

As pale as an angel, Marina hovered in the doorway, the barrier between them once again flung open. Her eyes were wide and steady as she watched his every move, yet she never made a sound. He'd never seen anyone so scared.

"What is it, Marina?"

If she noticed that he used her first name, she didn't indicate it in word or action.

"Nothing. It's nothing. Please, do us both a favor." Her great dark eyes implored. "Just go away."

How like a woman. Only moments before she had practically begged him to stay, and now she pointed the blame at him. Maybe he should take her advice, leave before . . . before . . .

Before what?

Before he took her in his arms and kissed those inviting lips of hers soundly? God, just looking at their ruby ripeness left no doubt in his mind a sound kissing was exactly what they needed. If the old prince were to be believed, what they had never been given.

So why did he resist what had been so blatantly offered him? Because he knew it would never be as simple as Nicolaiev might think. Make love to his wife and then what? Just casually get up and leave?

There was nothing casual about a woman like Marina Nicolaiev, nothing casual about the intense attraction he felt for her. Perhaps that was why he fought it so much.

Suddenly, he lost all desire to step outside. To do so would only mean that he must pass this way again, and he wasn't sure he could do it with success. Giving her a barely perceptible nod, he aimed toward the staircase. For all his good intentions, his feet stumbled on the risers as if lead-weighted.

"Mr. Kincaid. Thank you."

"For what, Princess?" At a safe distance now, he gave in to the overwhelming compulsion to glance back at her.

She had followed and stood by the newel post, clinging to it, looking up at him.

"I have met kings who are less of a gentleman than you."

"Is that so." He threw back his head and laughed. "Well, then, that doesn't say much for them, does it?" Even if he refused to show it, he was touched by her compliment.

Two more steps and she spoke again.

"Mr. Kincaid," she asked in a voice trembling with uncertainty, "why *are* you being such a gentleman?"

"Would you prefer that I weren't?" he asked, facing her once more. If she should say yes, then what? he wondered.

"No, not at all. It's just . . ."

From his vantage point on the staircase, he saw the bolt of lightning zigzag toward the ancient birches that lined the circular drive. He couldn't explain what drove him, but he knew he had to be there beside Marina before the thunder hit.

He barely reached her in time. The crash, accompanied by a fireworks of sparks that shattered the tree closest to the house, was deafening. He realized that he might have been standing out there if, for whatever reason, Marina hadn't stopped him. Then he realized she was clinging to him.

Just as he cleaved to her. There they were, the two of them standing at the bottom of the stairs, waiting for the lightning to strike again, their lips only inches apart.

Lightning comes in many forms. It knows no master, no rhyme or reason, merely smites what and where it pleases. Two hearts alone and vulnerable, wounded by life's unfairness, they were no match for such a providential force.

He had only to move a little closer. . . . Instead he pulled back.

"Why, Marina? Why does the thunder frighten you so?"

With a crooked finger he lifted her chin, the better to read her dark, unfathomable eyes. The intense pain, the open honesty he saw in them scattered the last of his resistance.

"I was just a little girl when my mother died. That day, I remember it started so joyously. It had been almost a year since we had all been together, so Mama and I had traveled to Crimea to visit Papa at his encampment." As she related her story, Marina's lips—God help him he was finding them harder and harder to resist—bowed in a small, hope-filled smile, yet sadness glistened in her eyes. "Papa rode off to battle leaving us in the safety of his tent with the promise he would return that evening. To pass the time Mama and I listened to the music box. I was dancing; she was singing." This last came out in a strangled whisper as if she couldn't bear to continue.

"Then your father was in the military?" he prompted gently, hoping to divert her tortured mind.

"Oh, yes." For the briefest of moments her gaze grew hard and angry. She pulled away ever so slightly. "First and always, Papa was a soldier."

Ah, so that meant her father had been less than a desirable parent, might even have deserted her. How could any man—or woman, for that matter—forsake his own flesh and blood? No matter what, he could never do that to Rainee, Hunter swore. He would give up his life, his every ambition, to keep his daughter safe and protected. His heartfelt convictions made him want to track down such a thoughtless father and show him the error of his ways—Wyoming-style.

Instead he pulled Marina close, cradling her against his heart.

"Mama swore the distant rumble was only thunder, so I kept on dancing. I think, at first, she believed her own words."

How soft was the crown of Marina's head lying in dark

repose against the whiteness of his shirt. Reaching down, he cupped his hand behind her head and held her. She trembled. Hunter guessed she was crying; and yet when she looked up at him, her eyes remained dry and steady.

"I don't remember much after the first explosion. Mama was standing in the door of the tent. Then suddenly she was next to me, clutching me so hard I couldn't breathe. She threw herself on top of me, but the bombs kept hitting all around us. The noise. It was so horrible." As she described it, she covered her ears with her hands. "The tent collapsed, yet the music box kept playing. You can't imagine what it was like to lie beneath my mother's broken body in the dark for hours before Papa finally found me. If it hadn't been for the music . . ." She trailed off.

Yes, he could well imagine her terror. He had known his share of battle and death as a grown man, but he didn't tell Marina so. He merely hugged her closer, if that were humanly possible, realizing the importance of the music she had been playing earlier.

Her very real fears were founded in the heart of an innocent child who had been thrust in the middle of a battle gone awry and forced to watch her mother die. How cruel life could be to those who least deserved it. But then, he already knew that from his own life experiences.

"And so, every time it lightnings and thunders, you relive that tragic event." He said it as much to himself as to her; but when she stirred against him in response, he knew he could not leave her as long as the storm raged outside. Perhaps, he could even help her.

Stepping away from her, he caught her by the hand and urged her to follow him into the great salon. To his surprise, he discovered a fire burning in the grate. Although it wasn't really cold, he knew fear could chill even the bravest of hearts. He had to show her a way to calm her anxieties, a way to tame the thunder.

Ah, yes, the thunder. Like the lightning that always preceded it, it knew no bounds. If only he could tame the raging thunder in his own heart.

He spied what must have been the source of the sweet serenade that had drawn him to her. Recognizing the ornate chest from the first time he had seen it stashed in the boot of the carriage, he realized this must be the very same music box she had spoken of. If it had been her mother's, if it had sustained her through so tragic an event, it must truly be very special to her.

With Marina still in tow, Hunter made his way toward the music box.

"This is most impressive. Show me how it works." He ran his hand along the sides and back of this wondrous machine that could produce musical enjoyment for nearly an hour. He paused in his search only when he discovered the empty keyhole.

Marina looked at him strangely, then reaching into a pocket in her gown, she extracted a key, fitting it into the slot.

Unable to stop himself, he placed his fingers over hers as she wound the box and only removed his hand when the music began once more.

"The song it plays—I heard it earlier, but didn't recognize it," he offered in explanation, shoving his traitorous hand into the pocket of his pants.

"A sonata by the great composer Beethoven."

"Bay Tovan. Of course," he replied, but to be truthful, he'd never heard of a songwriter by that name. Having lived in the wilds of Wyoming most of his life, he supposed there were many things he'd never heard of. Still he found this Bay Tovan's melody haunting and memorable.

Leaning forward, he lifted the lid to observe how the insides of the music box worked. When Rainee had been just a little girl, he had given her a music box—nothing quite so fancy, to be sure, but she had loved it, nonetheless. He wondered what she had done with it.

"Look here, Marina." Encouraging her to step closer, he lifted the lid higher so she could get a better look. "Have you ever watched while it played?" he asked, observing her face as she craned forward.

The music, so melancholy, tinkled softly. The tiny pins on the brass cylinder, the largest one he had ever seen, struck the corresponding teeth with a precision that was the work of a master clockmaker.

"My father had it made in Switzerland especially for my mother. The song, Mama's favorite, was a popular one at the time. She claimed it was *their* song." Marina smiled wistfully. "She once told me the first time they danced together this song was what the orchestra was playing."

"It's very beautiful." At the moment, however, he had eyes only for the beauty of this woman who was a romantic at heart.

If Marina noticed, she didn't look up. Instead, she ran one long, tapered finger along the intricate carvings, then turned away nervously when another rumble of thunder drowned out the music momentarily.

In silence, Hunter watched her pace like a hunted mountain lion.

"You know, Marina," he said finally, "our fears can only control us when we allow them to."

"What could *you* possibly know about fear, Mr. Kincaid?" She turned, eyes flashing like the most wary of beasts. "You already declared you have none."

Her accusation could have been construed as a compliment, so he chose to take it that way.

"That's not true, Marina. I said I didn't fear the thunder and lightning."

"What more could there be?" she demanded.

"There is the fear of betrayal, of shattered dreams, of never being truly loved. Those things are much more terrifying than what happens outside on some moonless night." Hunter bit down on his wayward tongue. He had revealed much more about himself than he'd intended.

"So tell me, Mr. Kincaid. If it is so simple, what do you suggest?"

"Let go of the past. Concentrate instead on the here and now." Good advice. So why did he have so much difficulty following it himself? His gaze settled on the slender curves of the woman who stood before him. All he could think of was the past when he looked at her. His own wretched past. The betrayal, the shattered dreams, the lack of true love.

"To the here and the now, Hunter Kincaid," she said in a voice throaty with emotion.

Why she chose that precise moment to begin dancing was a mystery. At first her body merely swayed to the compelling rhythm of the music. The firelight behind her silhouetted the shapely curve of her hips and waist as she moved with an agility he found irresistible. Only then did he become aware of the sheerness of the nightgown she wore and the flawlessness of her body beneath the flowing gauze.

With one last, great effort he tried to pull his eyes away and regroup his honor scattered like a defeated army. It was useless, just as it was useless to deny that she was everything in a woman he had dreamed of finding—and possessing.

Her movements expanded, her arms sweeping wide with an effortless grace that extended to the very tips of her fingers. Then when she lifted one leg, long and arrow-straight, he marveled at the way she bent forward, her outstretched hand and dark, cascading hair nearly touching the floor, her foot high above her head. But it was the fire, glimmering with a golden light of promise along her inner thigh, that made him long for what was just within his reach.

In a helpless trance, he edged forward. The mood of the music changed, turning spirited; and like the enchantress he'd suspected she was from the beginning, she danced away in a whirl of peach gauze and black hair. He followed, and to his surprise, she reached out and took his hand, using it to support herself in a way he had seen her do with her dance partner on the stage.

Her gaze, large and trusting, settled on his face. Then, unexpectedly, she laughed and flitted away again. Even when the thunder crashed, she didn't stop, but kept on whirling and whirling as if she were the apex of the storm.

By God, he realized then that the wish he had made a few days ago had just come true. The beautiful Russian ballerina danced only for him.

With purposeful strides he overtook her, seized her in his arms, and turned her to face him as if she were on a revolving platform. Before she could protest, he brushed away the cloud of wild, dark hair and claimed her lips in a searing kiss that made the thunder outside seem like nothing. It was a two-sided branding iron that burned her mark as deep in his aching flesh as his did hers.

He didn't ask her. There was no need.

Scooping her up into his arms, he made his way up the stairs, the final notes from the music box trailing behind them. He didn't pause until he reached the door of his room.

Since she weighed no more than a feather, it might have been the burden of his own decision that caused him so much anguish. Then and there, he decided it was an agony he was most willing to bear in order to lay claim to the ecstasy.

* * *

More than at the mere threshold to a room, Marina hovered at the brink of a decision that could change the course of her life.

Hunter Kincaid. He was all that she had ever dreamed of in a man. Handsome and strong, to be sure, but more importantly, he hadn't treated her like others in her life who had rejected her, cosseted her, or—worse—attempted to prey upon her. Instead Hunter had taken her and her fears seriously, then shown her a way to beat them. It had thundered and, for the first time she could remember since that devastating event so long ago, she had felt not panic but an exhilaration, a strength like none other. No one had ever given her so much, not even Dmitri, who in his great generosity had unwittingly supplied the crutch to sustain those fears.

Yes, Hunter had empowered her, and his was a gift she wished only to reciprocate. Someone had hurt him—a woman, she suspected. She placed the flat of her hand against his heart and felt it beat against her palm. If she had the ability to heal his wounds in return, didn't she owe him that much?

Such was her logic. Held in his strong arms and waiting for him to open the door, she allowed her passion-driven reasoning to brush aside the last remaining shreds of her resistance.

The room was dark when they entered it. Not a single taper burned. Yet he made his way across the floor without a misstep.

She yearned to ask him to light a candle, for she wanted more than anything to see his face once more—to make sure. In answer, a bolt of lightning illuminated the room, creating a shadowy dance from the bobbing limbs and branches of the trees just beyond the window. He laid her upon the bed.

"Are you still afraid?" His eyes as blue as a Russian sky reflected the fiery fingers.

"No. Not now. Not with you," she replied, although she knew the thunder would soon follow. She thought of dancing to the music, recalling the way he had watched her—mesmerized—as she'd performed a simple series of arabesques and pirouettes. Just as he looked at her now.

To be adored, even revered, was not something new to the Princess Marina Nicolaiev, prima ballerina of Russian ballet. Often enough she saw that in the faces of her audiences. There was something more, so much more to his expression, something intensely personal.

Could it be love?

Foolish heart. Not likely. They hardly knew each other. True love came only with time, the one thing they had precious little of.

As she came to that harsh, unsettling realization, the thunder crashed, rattling the windowpanes, but not shaking her resolve or newfound fearlessness. She would take what little love offered her. Wrapping her arms about Hunter's neck, she pulled him down to lie beside her and kissed him, the first act of passion she had bestowed upon any man.

At first Hunter remained perfectly still, but he allowed her full access to his mouth—not that she knew what to do with it. She savored the feel, the intoxicating taste of her perceived power, for the longest moment before she began to suspect he merely toyed with her.

Panic-stricken, she froze. Could it be she was doing something wrong? Afraid it might make him think her less of a woman, she vowed not to let him suspect her inexperience.

"Marina, what is it?"

"Nothing," she replied, turning her face away in embarrassment and confusion. She struggled to remember everything she had heard the other *danseuses* discussing whenever they gathered and talked about men. But she had caught only snatches of whispered innuendo that invariably grew silent whenever she—princess and prima ballerina—approached. She had no true female friends among the *corps de ballet;* and although she was a married woman in the eyes of her public, sadly enough she knew nothing of what took place in the bedroom.

"If it is nothing, then why do you turn away?"

The feel of Hunter's work-roughened hand against her cheek sent a thrill coursing down her spine.

"Do you wish for me to deny that I want you and have since the first moment I saw you dance?" he asked.

She shook her head.

"Then would you have me go away?"

"Have you forgotten this is your room?" She smiled at him crookedly. "Besides, what kind of hostess would I be to send you out on such a night as this?"

"What kind of guest would *I* be to take advantage of your generous hospitality?" he asked in all seriousness. "Or perhaps I should say your husband's."

"Dmitri? What are you saying?" Her heart began to beat crazily when she thought of how she was about to betray her husband. No doubt, that was what Hunter thought, too. But it wasn't betrayal, not really. For years her husband had encouraged her to take a lover, practically shoved men her way, yet she had refused to succumb. Should she tell Hunter the truth? Could he begin to understand or appreciate the scope of her decision? Or would it be as she had earlier feared and such knowledge would only make him turn away from her? "This has nothing to do with my husband," she declared emphatically.

Hunter stared at her for the longest moment as if weighing the validity of her claim. "No, of course it doesn't," he agreed finally. "This is strictly between you and me."

Before she could utter another word, he kissed her. At first his caress was a gentle exploration, but it unleashed a passion that neither could deny. A physical yearning like none Marina had ever experienced before coursed through her, body and soul. She wanted something more, something she couldn't put a name to or even imagine, and yet she sensed she would instinctively recognize it the moment she discovered it. Buffeted by such powerful sensations, she clung to the source of the brewing emotional storm, unsure who or what she might become if she survived it.

Hunter Kincaid. She had never suspected that any man could make her feel so utterly immersed in a physical act. Not even ballet, the focus of her life, could do that for her. The intimate touch of his hand against her heart. His mouth exploring, tasting, teaching. His words of adoration filling what had been an aching void inside her for so long. Such wonderful sensations left her speechless and reaching out to grasp the wonder of the moment and never let it go. It was like dancing without bounds, with nothing to restrict her movements, as if her feet had sprouted wings; only it was her heart that knew no earthly limitation.

Then he caressed her in a way and in a place that she had always considered taboo. Unable to stop herself, she gasped and stiffened against the invasion.

"Hunter, I don't . . ."

His urgent kiss absorbed the remainder of her protest, turning it into a delighted moan of acquiescence. His hand, a gentle master, coaxed her to open to him even more. To her amazement she found herself complying, responding like the true dancer moving to the music of the maestro. She arched to make the most of each shiver of excitement his fingers evoked. How could she have lived so long without knowing such pleasure existed? How could she go on without experiencing the grand finale?

And so it was, as she had known it would be should she ever give in to the sleeping femininity she had buried deep inside her for so very long. Flirting with the mysterious edges of love was no longer enough.

"I want to know," she whispered. From where did she garner the courage to make such a bold request of a man she hardly knew? From wherever it came, she had asked, and she couldn't back away, not now.

"Are you certain, my sweet princess? What if it is not all that you expect?" Running his finger along the line of her jaw, Hunter smiled down at her with such understanding, it took her breath away.

"Then it will only be better." Committed, she stretched toward him, clasping him in her arms, to reassure him as well as to lay her claim upon him.

"What of tomorrow, Marina?" he asked in all seriousness, disengaging himself from the tangle of her arms and rising to his knees in the middle of that big bed. "What if you should regret your rash decision then?"

"Tomorrow is a long way off. Please, Hunter." She stared up at him with unblinking certainty. Then, rising to her knees to sway before him, she slipped her arms out of her gown, allowing it to puddle around her thighs. "Teach me the dance of love. I may never have this opportunity again."

Uttering a sigh of defeat, Hunter stripped off his own clothing, then pulled her close and took her mouth once more as he molded himself against her naked body. She ran her hand down the length of him, marveling at the solid power of his muscles beneath her fingertips. His was the physique of a man accustomed to hard work. A commoner by the standards of her world, she supposed, but in her eyes he reigned mightier than a king.

Quickly enough she discovered that nothing about Hunter Kincaid was the least bit common. There was nothing ordinary in the way he touched her; it was pure magic. Likewise, there was nothing earthborn in her response. She transcended the self-imposed boundaries of human emotion that she had sworn never to succumb to. Now she found herself eager to reach the next unfamiliar plateau.

The dance of love. How right she had been to call it that, for indeed it was a dance they engaged in, a *grand pas de deux,* an intricate choreography created only for lovers. And like the greatest *danseur noble,* Hunter seemed to know her every move, anticipated her every desire, gently guiding her through the intimate steps of the ballet inspired by God Himself. Placing her complete trust in Hunter, Marina followed his masterful lead, confident her partner in love would allow no harm to befall her.

When he paused, it caught her by surprise. Her first impulse was to think she had done something to displease him.

"Hunter, what's wrong?" She curled her hands about his neck, refusing to let him escape. Not now, now when she was so close to unraveling the secret she had already sacrificed her integrity for.

"I don't want to hurt you."

"You haven't," she assured him with a throaty cry.

"I will if we go any further."

Marina's mind spun in a whirlwind of innocence. "I don't care," she declared.

"But I do. The last thing I want is to cause you anguish."

"Then don't turn away from me now." For if he did, she knew she would never take this chance again but would shrivel up and die a woman never loved.

Later she wondered what he would have done if the clap of thunder hadn't shattered the moment of silent indecision. But the air outside rumbled, spurring her into the wondrous event she had denied herself for much too long.

The pain was sharp but blessedly fleeting, replaced with a glorious sense of fulfillment. Once again she followed his lead, realizing a *tour de force* awaited them at the end of their duet. She wanted to hurry, to get there as quickly as she could; but like the finest of partners, Hunter would not allow her to rush even one step, assuring her that a great finale came only in the perfection of the performance.

That climax was far greater than any she had ever experienced. Greater than the applause of a thousand fans. There was nothing to describe the euphoric feeling that washed over her in delicious waves, nothing to beat it—unless it was the moment she realized he, too, experienced the same wonder.

She had shared something so intimate with this man that never again could she consider him a stranger.

His head rested between her breasts, the golden blondness of his hair darkened with the sweat of exertion. Reaching up, she stroked the damp tendril that curled about his ear.

"Hunter?"

His contented sigh of acknowledgment was as sweet as music to her ears.

"Your Wyoming? Is it truly like my Russia?"

Lifting his head and propping it on the heels of his palms, he stared up at her, the peaks of her breasts like mountains between them.

"I suppose you could find similarities. They are both vast lands, more than any man could dream of taming. The winters are cold and brutal just as I imagine they are here." He smiled at her. "There is thunder and lightning in Wyoming, too."

"Your country estate. Is it much like this one?" She continued her earnest questioning, ignoring his gentle gibe.

"Not at all." His candid laughter puzzled her. "By comparison the house is much smaller, but the land is extensive. To me that is a man's true palace."

"Then you are a landed gentleman?"

"Not at all, Marina. Where I come from some consider me a king. A cattle king."

At that she frowned. Who would wish to rule over simple bovine?

"Someday I would like to see this kingdom of yours."

"You have only to come and I will gladly share my throne with you," he offered with a gentle laugh.

"Someday," she murmured. Pushing up on her elbows, she kissed the tip of his strong, straight nose.

He returned her innocent caress with one much more bold. With his tongue he scaled the slope of one feminine mound, then drew the dark peak into his mouth as he fit himself into the natural cradle her body made for him. Just for him.

A restlessness stirred deep within her with such a force she cried out in dismay. She had thought this need was assuaged, forever dormant. To discover it alive and just as demanding as before . . .

What was she going to do when Hunter left? He would leave, eventually. That was inevitable. Wyoming was so far away. The chances of her ever going there—well, they were very slim. A sob broke free from her aching throat.

"Marina, are you crying?" Lifting his head, he frowned his concern.

"No." She swallowed back the telltale tears, pulling him down to her, wrapping her arms and legs about him, hoping to never have to let go.

They had so few hours. Somehow she must cram a lifetime into one night or, if they were lucky, two. That would be all that she would have to sustain her for eternity.

They made love until exhaustion claimed them, their bodies entwined. Hunter slept. Marina watched him, marveling at the peaceful way he held her as if she belonged to him.

Moments later, the morning sun peaked the forested hills that separated them from the civilized world beyond. Now that the rains were over, the roads would dry out. Then that world they had escaped for a moment in time would come looking for them. A day, maybe two. It was all they would be given.

Once that time had passed, Marina knew who and what she must be once more when reality reclaimed them.

Five

"Your Highness. A carriage has been spotted coming down the road."

They were sharing an intimate breakfast of *blini,* small pancakes served with melted butter and fruited sour cream, in the intimate dining room off Hunter's quarters in the south wing. He had plucked a blood-red rosebud from the centerpiece on the table and tucked it behind Marina's ear. She wore it like a crown.

"Dmitri." Marina rose, gripping the back of the chair she'd vacated even as the loyal servant had made his discreet exit. Her heart pounded. The choice bite of food that Hunter had just playfully fed her from his own plate turned to bitter ash in her mouth. She swallowed it, unchewed. Suddenly she wasn't hungry anymore.

"Marina, you knew this would happen."

How gently his great, work-roughened hand covered hers. She glanced down at it, desperately trying to etch every detail into her memory. The fine-lined scar that ran the hills and ridges of his knuckles. The nails, large and square at the ends of each of his fingers. Her lover's hand.

Even though she knew he spoke the truth, a tremor of disbelief shook her. Yes, eventually their precious moments together had had to end. But why? she wanted to cry out. Instead, she lifted her gaze to memorize his face. Then, accepting what she couldn't change and what she must do, she nodded, slipped her hand from beneath his, and started toward the door.

"Marina!" Although he didn't actually follow her, his body—God help her she would never forget the beauty of his virile body—swayed in her direction.

"I must go. Dmitri will expect me to greet him in a presentable fashion." Grateful for the mist that clouded her eyes so that she couldn't read his expression—hurt, hard, or perhaps hollow—she blindly made her way through the adjacent sitting room into the hallway.

Hunter, too, had known this separation would come, she reminded herself. Whatever his feelings, she could not take responsibility for them.

Only then, realizing that it was truly over when it had barely had the chance to begin, did she pause and allow the betraying emotions their warranted release. Pressing her spine against the wall, her face into her still-trembling hands, she shuddered in silent grief at the unfairness of it all.

Oh, why give her a tantalizing glimpse of love only to snatch it away so cruelly? Whether her God-directed question was a prayer or a blasphemy, she received no explanation.

Hearing Hunter's heavy steps approaching, Marina straightened and, refusing to take even one last glance over her shoulder, she hurried on her way. She dared not allow herself the luxury of his arms even one last time. If she did, she might forget who and what she was.

Above all else, she was the Princess Marina Nicolaiev. She owed Dmitri never to forget her station or all that he had done for her. Nonetheless, at the moment she would gladly exchange her title, her pride, even her career for one more night in the arms of Hunter Kincaid. It was a wish she knew would never come true.

Reaching the privacy of her own rooms, she quickly dressed in a leaf-green foulard gown of soft, cotton twill. Checking her appearance only once in the cheval mirror, she prayed the simplicity of her dress established a look of innocence. She pinched her pale cheeks for a little color, then—scooping up the dogs she had neglected terribly for the last two days—she made her way to the central staircase.

Poised on the top landing, she heard the carriage wheels crunch in the gravel of the drive as the arriving vehicle pulled up before the front door. Knowing it would take the servants a few moments to lift their crippled master's wheelchair to the ground then up the stairs to the portico, she arranged herself to picture-perfection. Then, as the front door opened, she bent and released the dogs.

With the aid of his personal servant, Dmitri came rolling through the door. As she had known it would, the carefully planned tableau of her standing at the top of the staircase, Arabesque and Sissonne barking and bounding down the risers just ahead of her, evoked his ready smile.

"Marinuska," he called.

"Dear Dmitri." In satin slippers that gave the illusion of bare feet, she floated down the staircase. Her sincere affection for this man who had sheltered and protected her for so long propelled her forward. Reaching him, she dropped to her knees before his wheelchair and lowered her head to rest in his lap. He stroked her temple just as he had when she was a child. His simple gesture calmed and reassured her.

"The storm. The downed tree in the drive. I hope you were not too frightened or alone." He lifted her chin with a crooked finger. "I worried about you."

"It was terrible, especially when the lightning struck the tree." She peered back at him in concern. "I was worried about you, as well, Dmitri."

"That wasn't necessary, my dear." His gentle gray gaze followed the sweep of his hand as he pushed a wayward curl from her cheek. "The important thing is that you are safe . . .

and happy." He smiled down at her with benevolence. "You are happy, aren't you, Marina?"

It was as if he knew without being told what had occurred between her and Hunter Kincaid. Like a wary creature pursued, Marina's heart picked up speed. For the briefest of moments, watching him examine her face for some indication of the truth, she wondered if he had even planned for them to be alone together. But that was impossible. Dmitri might be a man of extraordinary abilities, but even he couldn't control the weather. Besides, Hunter was not the kind of man to play along with such a deception.

"Of course I am happy, now that you are here, my husband." She smiled at him with a forced brightness. Then, overwhelmed with guilt for thinking something so devious of a man so pure of heart when she was anything but, she rose to her feet and stepped backward. "You must be exhausted after so long a trip. I think you should rest."

"As should you, my dear. You are trembling. I suspect you haven't slept much of late."

"That's not true. I have slept very well." Again, she sensed he knew of her deception.

"Hunter Kincaid." His graying brows knitted in consternation. "The American is still here, isn't he?"

"M-M-Mr. Kincaid?" She stumbled over the name as if reluctant to say it aloud in the presence of Dmitri. But why should she feel that way when he had repeatedly encouraged her to take a lover in the first place? As foolish as her feelings seemed, she couldn't rid herself of the guilt. She had deceived him and, by not confessing now, made the deception even worse. But she just couldn't find it in her heart to speak aloud of her secret, newfound wonder. To do so would make the affair seem tarnished and truly finished. She wasn't ready to let go of it or the emotions, not yet.

"Of course, he's still here," she blurted. Had she confirmed that too quickly and with too much certainty for so early in the morning? "I greeted him at breakfast just moments ago."

"Good. Good. I will talk with him later. In the meantime, perhaps you are right. I should rest for a while." With a flick of his hand, he signaled for his retainer, who wheeled him toward the mechanical lift tucked beneath the staircase. The unique device had been designed and installed for the sole purpose of carrying the invalid master to the floors above, wheelchair and all.

Once Dmitri was positioned securely in the small car, the mesh door drawn across to protect him, Marina caught the hand of the servant to keep him from working the pulley.

"I do love you, Dmitri." Had the wire barrier not been between them, she would have bent and kissed him on the forehead.

"Of course you do, my dear. I never doubted that for a moment."

Blinking back tears of gratitude, she watched as the elevator rose slowly, taking her husband, a man of rare compassion indeed, out of sight. And so she knew that he was not only aware of what had transpired over the last few days, but that he condoned her actions—did not condemn them. She also knew it would be the last time they would ever speak of the incident.

Hunter had once said he feared never knowing true love. That was a fear she couldn't share with him. For her it was a fear of being loved too much and not being worthy of such gallant devotion.

The pain ran deep, deeper than Hunter imagined that it could. Staring down at his hand, which held the rosebud that had fallen from Marina's hair, he carefully placed the flower on the windowsill. He had thought he had built up an immunity to such humiliation a long time ago. Apparently he had been mistaken. Watching the sudden, irreversible transformation that had occurred in Marina had been as torturous to endure as if someone had cut him open and jerked out a vital organ, leaving him to die slowly.

Marina. He loved the way she rolled her tongue when she said Wyoming, the way her eyes lit up whenever he talked about his way of life, as if she yearned for the adventure. One minute they had been laughing and sharing an intimate meal, talking of the future as if one existed for them. The next, she had fled without a backward glance, without regret, without giving him the chance to . . .

The chance to what? Balling his fist, he smacked it against the sash of the window before him, relishing the physical pain he hoped might dull the emotional anguish. Thank her for a good time? Oh, yes. He could just see himself saying that to her, an insult Della would have readily deserved. But not Marina, not his beautiful, elegant princess, regardless of her actions.

More than anything, he wished he had the guts to reveal his true feelings—that he wanted her, wanted her to become a part of his life, wanted to take her away from her sham of a marriage, a condemnation she didn't deserve either. At that absurdity he laughed aloud. Why not go ahead and make an utter fool of himself? He could always call her husband out. Fight a duel over the lady fair. He could see it now, the big, strapping American cowboy gunning after Prince Invalid in his trusty wheelchair. Such foolish actions would no doubt put an end to any negotiations to sell the Russians cattle.

The damn negotiations. Because of them, there was only one thing he could tell her, if he ever got the chance. Slamming his fist against the sash again, he cursed his own inability to face the ugly truth. No matter what excuse he made for himself, the truth was that he had seduced the wife of another man knowing what it would gain him—a signed contract. It wasn't something he could be proud of, nor was it something he would ever want Marina to know. Perhaps the bittersweet conclusion was best after all, for it had never been his intention to hurt her.

"Ah, there you are, Mr. Kincaid."

The squeak of wheels intruded upon his musings. From his vigilance at the window overlooking the formal gardens, Hunter turned to confront his host. If hell had messengers, then Nicolaiev had to be one of them.

"Your Grace." Caught off guard by the Russian's unexpected appearance, Hunter bowed stiffly. He had never felt comfortable with this royalty thing, and now . . .

With the aid of his ever-present manservant, Prince Dmitri Nicolaiev entered the room. His alert gray eyes took in every detail—the hastily abandoned meal set for two, his guest's casual attire.

"It seems I've interrupted." The prince stared pointedly at Hunter's chest.

"Not at all," Hunter replied, looking down. To his surprise he still sported the napkin Marina had stuffed into the front of his shirt. Removing it, he dropped the white cloth on the table beside his half-eaten meal. "I am finished." The fork he and Marina had been sharing captured his attention. He couldn't help but stare at the silver utensil and remember how beautiful she had looked as he had laughingly fed her choice bites from his own plate.

The momentarily suppressed pain surged once more. He had found the woman of his dreams, and now he must simply walk away from her, forget she had ever existed. Worse, he had to conduct business with her husband and try to act as if nothing out of the ordinary were going on.

"I'm pleased to hear that, Mr. Kincaid. I hope you found

everything—" He gave Hunter a knowing look. "—to your satisfaction."

Hunter bristled at the overt statement. That Nicolaiev knew didn't surprise him. A man would have to be blind not to see the evidence before him. But to speak of it so bluntly, with such utter disregard . . .

"Now, look here, Nicolaiev," he retorted, stepping forward. "It's not what you think."

"Does it really matter what I might think, Mr. Kincaid?"

Hunter stared disdainfully at his opponent. How could any man think so little of his wife's honor? Still he had to agree, he didn't care what some crazed Russian thought. All that mattered was what he thought about himself. At the moment, he had to admit it wasn't much.

"I say, it is only the end results that concern us both. Wouldn't you agree?" the Russian asked.

No, he didn't agree, but he didn't argue.

"Since you have obviously kept your end of the bargain, Mr. Kincaid, it is only fair that I keep mine," the prince continued when it became evident Hunter wasn't going to respond. "Have you the cattle contracts with you here? If so, I will sign them, as we agreed."

Had he been there strictly on his own behalf, Hunter would have turned and walked away. To hell with the Russian's agreement, his money, and his warped sense of right and wrong. But there was more at stake than his own personal pride. The future welfare of every rancher in southwestern Wyoming depended on this cattle deal. He couldn't bring himself to let them down because he had succumbed during a moment of weakness. Why should they pay for his self-indulgent lack of honor?

"I'm afraid I left the papers in St. Petersburg," he lied, unwilling to continue this head-on charade, wanting only to get as far away from it and the cause as quickly as he could.

"Now that the roads are clear, I think it would be best for all of us if I returned to the city. The contracts will be awaiting you in your office."

"Very well. If there is nothing more to say, I will call for a carriage to be brought around to take you back."

"Thank you, Your Grace. I can be ready to go immediately."

"And what of my wife, Mr. Kincaid? Have you nothing final to say to her?"

"I'm sure Ma—" He had almost called her by her first name, but quickly refrained. "I'm sure Her Highness has much more pressing matters on her mind than me. Please make my apologies and express my gratitude."

What he didn't say was that she already possessed his heart and soul, his pride and his honor.

Hunter turned and started for the door. Then, remembering the rosebud he had left on the windowsill, he crossed the room in quick strides to retrieve the precious reminder. He had been right. True love was a fleeting dream that no doubt would elude him to the grave. But in a few short hours of bliss, by God he had come close to claiming it. Close enough to last him a lifetime.

From her vantage point at the velvet-draped bay window in the north wing, Marina watched the carriage pull around to the front of the villa. A few moments later, she saw Hunter emerge, his single bag in hand. He entered the vehicle and never looked back.

The carriage drove away, pausing briefly at the end of the drive, and then it was gone.

Gone. Marina blinked back disbelief and a well of unshed tears.

Gone, never to return.

The loss was more than she could bear.

With a fierce determination, she closed the heavy drapes on the window, shutting out the sight of the empty drive as well as the bright morning light pouring into the room. Still she knew the sun was out there.

It was kind of like love. She could close the curtain on her heart, but she could never forget the wonder of the emotions she had experienced in the arms of Hunter Kincaid. Never again could she hide in the darkness of her ignorance.

Dear Dmitri. Trapped by his own inadequacies, he had been so certain that she needed to know what she was missing. How wrong he had been. Knowledge only made the emptiness harder to endure. But at least now when she danced the *pas de deux* with Sergei upon the stage, she would for the first time truly understand the illusion they created for the audience. Yes, undoubtedly such knowledge would make her a better dancer. What choice did she have but to be satisfied with that, for now?

Hunter Kincaid. She would never forget him. Someday she would find him again. Someday. But it would not be today, or tomorrow, or next year.

Until then, she would simply have to tuck the precious, private memory of him away in the most secret recess of her heart.

It was then that she started to cry—silent, hopeless tears that trickled down her cheeks unchecked. She didn't stop weeping until the pristine beauty in her womanly heart shriveled into an arid wasteland of cynicism. By then the sun had also set behind the line of trees, the beginning of the ancient forest that stood like an army of sentries between the villa and far-off St. Petersburg.

Yes, Hunter Kincaid was gone, and soon more than a mere forest would stand between them. An entire ocean would divide them, as well as cultures and lives so different that they left little room for a future. She would have to accept and be grateful for what she had. She would have to go on even if the joy had been stripped from her life.

He'd forgotten how dusty the dirt streets of Sweetwater, Wyoming, could be.

Hunter stepped down from the train car and, clearing his parched throat, he scanned the anything-but-civilized place he called home.

It was Sunday. His arrival had gone unnoticed; but then, he had planned it that way. Just down the street he could hear the wheezing imperfection of the pipe organ the townspeople had purchased and installed in the church only a week before he had departed. Mrs. Davenport's playing didn't sound any better than it had six months ago. Suspecting it would never improve, he forced a smile he didn't really feel and allowed his travel-weary eyes to move on.

In the other direction, he spotted the dilapidated building that housed the sheriff's office, closed for the day of rest. Only a few doors down from there, his gaze settled on one of three boarded-up saloons.

Shutting down the dens of iniquity. Sweetwater had taken that progressive step almost two years ago. Oddly enough, even though he had owned the buildings that had housed two of the rowdy watering holes, he had approved of the closures, had even helped. Della's death had caused him to agree to such an unwise business decision.

But like oil and water, heart and business concerns shouldn't be mixed. If nothing else, the trip to Russia had taught him that much.

Della. He tried hard not to think about the woman he had married despite all the warnings. He had been like a spring buck, so sure of himself and his abilities to tame the unpredictable ways of a reformed dance-hall girl like Della. At first they had been happy. Rainee had come along; the ranch had prospered. He had never once suspected his wife's growing restlessness to return to her old way of life.

When that East Coast slicker had breezed through town looking for local talent to recruit for some traveling sideshow, he should have been forewarned that things were not what they seemed on the surface. But in those days he hadn't given much thought to Della's increasing complaints about being stuck out in the middle of nowhere with nothing to do. She had Rainee and one of the finest houses in the territory to run—what more could any woman want?

The day he'd rode in tired from a spring roundup, found Della gone and little Rainee squalling and bawling in her crib, wet and hungry, he'd gone berserk. He'd searched everywhere for his missing wife, determined never to give up, had even hired professionals to assist him, all to no avail. Della Kincaid had disappeared, and apparently that was the way she'd wanted it.

"Hunter? Hunter Kincaid? Is that really you? When did you git back into town?"

Damn. Hatty Shackelford. If Sweetwater had a gossip, it was the mayor's overbearing wife.

"Miz Hatty," he acknowledged with a perfunctory tap to the brim of his Stetson. "Shouldn't you still be in church?"

"Why, Mr. Kincaid, surely you didn't think to slip into town without lettin' anybody know, now did ya?" she countered, clucking her tongue like an old biddy who'd discovered a way into the grain bin. "We've all been awaitin' on pins and needles to know how things went with them Russians fellas. Did ya git the deal?"

"Well, yes, but . . ."

She didn't wait to hear his explanation. Like a flash she

darted off, heading toward the churchyard that was just beginning to fill with worshipers.

Bemoaning his fate, Hunter watched the woman hurry toward the gathering crowd, her arms waving and pointing in his direction. Knowing there wasn't a chance in hell of his escaping before the entire town learned of his arrival, he made his way toward the livery stable anyway.

He never reached his destination. In minutes he was surrounded by well-meaning friends and neighbors.

"So, tell us, Hunter. Them Russies gonna buy our cattle?"

Someone took his bag; someone else slapped him on the back.

"They've agreed to our terms," he replied.

The roar of approval that went up drowned out the chiming of the afternoon church bells. Gunshots ricochetted in the air, followed by flying hats and several pairs of ladies' gloves. Then, before he could protest, Hunter was bodily lifted by several of the townsmen and hoisted on their shoulders to be carried down the main street in an impromptu parade.

"Daddy? Daddy?"

"Rainee, honey." He looked down and spied the upturned face of his daughter, more beautiful and endearing than he had remembered it to be. Her eyes reflected the unwarranted adoration of all those around them.

Although he had tried to avoid it, he'd received a hero's welcome. He didn't deserve it. But there wasn't a damn thing he could do to change what was happening or the reason he felt so unworthy.

"Lift, Marina, lift. I need a lot more lift in your forward leg."

Feeling as if she might pull a muscle, Marina nonetheless complied with the demands of Marius Petipa, the master of the Royal Ballet. Then, as he tapped his cane to set her pace, she whirled off, completing the *assemblé* with a final, exhausted dip. There she stayed until the director thumped his cane again, allowing her to rise.

"Adequate," the aging dancer, once one of the greatest of the century, announced. He surveyed the assembly of performers standing before him on the stage. "Tomorrow I shall expect perfection from each and every one of you." He gave Marina a pointed look.

Slumping her aching shoulders, Marina sighed relief as Petipa walked away. She felt anything but adequate. But then nothing gave her pleasure anymore, nothing had since . . .

She lifted her chin, refusing to indulge herself and think even for a moment about Hunter Kincaid.

"You know how Marius is a few weeks before an opening, Marina." Sergei Bozzacchi, her dance partner, her friend, put his arm about her sagging shoulder and bolstered it with a squeeze. "You were perfection already, my dear."

"No, Marius is right, I need more lift, more enthusiasm."

"You are tired, just as we all are."

"Lack of rest is no excuse, Sergei; you know that." It seemed she always had to remind him that discipline was half of what talent was made of. "Please, I would like to go over the *pressage* lift once more."

"Very well, Marina," he said with a sigh. "If you are determined."

They were on the third run-through and she was already planning to demand a fourth, when Sergei simply quit. He walked off the stage, insisting, "Enough for one day, Marina. We'll begin fresh tomorrow."

Biting back an angry retort, something to the effect that he was immature and undedicated, she instead had to admit he was right. Her compulsive need to always give a perfect performance was a reflection of the dissatisfaction she felt in her personal life.

Picking up a small towel, she dabbed at the back of her neck and along her moist collarbone. Compulsive or not, it was all she had. She would tackle the task tomorrow and do better.

"Marinuska?"

Deeply engrossed in her thoughts, Marina startled at the unexpected summons. She turned, and at the foot of the stage she spied Dmitri, a prisoner of his wheelchair as much as she was of her unhappiness. Her heart began to hammer at the strange, uncertain look in his normally assertive gray eyes.

"Dmitri. What is it?" It had to be something. Otherwise, he wouldn't have come all the way down to the theater. He rarely made an appearance and never during rehearsals.

For the longest moment he sat there, staring at her as if he thought never to see her again.

"What's wrong, Dmitri?" Forgetting her tired, aching muscles, she scooted off the stage.

"There are some things we need to discuss immediately."

"Of course. If you think it cannot wait. Just let me change my clothes and we can . . ."

"No. Please sit down." He indicated one of the wooden chairs next to him in the gallery.

Stunned, Marina sank into the uncomfortable seat, her eyes wide with alarm.

"If anything should ever happen to me, Marina, you must promise . . ."

"Happen to you?" she cut in. "Dmitri, are you in some kind of trouble?"

"All of Russia is in trouble, my dear. Five years ago there was an attempt to assassinate the tsar."

"Yes, but it was unsuccessful; and if I remember correctly,

the university students responsible were caught and tried. It was an isolated incident."

"That was the popular consensus. However, there has been another attempt." He leaned forward. "Just last night in the tsar's private quarters. The would-be assassin escaped. We believe he was an aristocrat." Dmitri looked up and scanned the empty theater as if he suspected someone might be eavesdropping. "However, we've managed to keep the entire affair a secret."

"Dmitri, why are you telling me this here and now?" Was his life in danger, too? Never once in all of her unhappiness had she ever truly considered her future alone. He had always been there for her, to love and protect her. She couldn't begin to imagine life without him.

"Because, if anything should ever happen to me, it's important that you be careful whom you trust."

"Nothing is going to happen to you, Dmitri," she cried as much to reassure herself as him. She grasped one of his aging hands and held it tightly.

"No, of course, it won't." He reached out and patted her trembling fingers. "Nonetheless know that you can trust Olga."

Olga. Her personal servant. It was true. She could trust the old woman with her life if she had to. But would she have to? Nothing was going to happen to Dmitri. How could it? He was a prince of the realm, a man of great power. Nonetheless, she would indulge him.

"If necessary you must be prepared to go and leave everything behind," he insisted.

"Not everything, Dmitri. I would never leave my mother's music box." It was an impulsive, no doubt trivial, declaration to make at the moment, but it was the truth. She went nowhere without that music box. She would be lost without its comfort and reminder of that wondrous two days in the country with Hunter Kincaid.

"Of course, my dear, I wouldn't expect you to leave so precious a possession behind. Now, get dressed, and I will see you home."

"Dmitri," she protested. There were so many questions he had left unanswered.

"We'll discuss this later, my dear."

But she knew her husband well. No matter how much she insisted, it would be the last he would ever speak of it.

Six

After a while, one would think the details of a memory would fade. For Hunter, the vision of the lovely Russian ballerina, watching her dance just for him and then making love to her . . . The recollection of that stormy night grew more vivid, more intense, and more exciting with each passing day. If only he could go back. If only . . .

He tucked the dried rosebud, the one that had fallen from her hair, back into his shirt pocket. *If only* wasn't possible. In fact, the chances were Princess Marina Nicolaiev didn't even remember him; and if she did, he doubted it was with the same unfulfilled passion that possessed him. The specialness of that oh-so-brief affair was his own invention. Like so many memories, he told himself, the bad ones eventually faded. However, the good ones became even stronger, deepening into something that perhaps had never been.

The cherished memories of Russia and the woman who evoked them, were best left undisturbed. To go back would only risk ruining what had become perfection in his mind.

Marina. It hurt so much to accept the validity of his reasoning. No memory could ever replace the taste of her lips, the softness of her skin, the perfume of her dark hair, the way she trembled when frightened or aroused.

"Mr. Kincaid, did ya hear me? I said the last of the late calves are all rounded up and branded."

Hunter tore his distracted gaze from the distant horizon where a brewing black cloud warranted watching and focused on the insistent voice that demanded his attention. Spying the half-Indian, half-Mexican cowhand that worked for him, he realized the much-younger man had been sitting before him, talking to him for some time.

"All right, Paco. Then I suppose we should wrap it up for the day. Looks to be a storm coming our way."

"What about those mavericks? Don't ya want 'em branded and cut as well, Mr. Kincaid?"

"Of course," Hunter replied with undisguised annoyance. "See to it and hurry."

"Yes, sir." The cowhand rode off in a cloud of dust.

Like everyone in Sweetwater, Paco Santana probably thought his boss had contracted some strange foreign disease while in Russia that had caused him to lose his mind. Still, like everyone else, the sometimes overly practical boy chose to indulge the crazy ol' loon. And why not? Kincaid hands were the best paid in the territory. Wyoming cattle fetched the highest prices in the market; the success of the Wyoming Cattlemen's Association was the envy of every other like organization in the West. As a result, Sweetwater was growing by leaps and bounds.

Folks continued to treat him like a decorated war hero. If they only knew the truth—what he had done to cement the Russian cattle deal which had made it possible for them all to live high on the hog—they might not think so highly of him.

He could just see Hatty Shackelford's face if he ever told her the only reason she wore ready-made dresses ordered from the catalogs was because he'd slept with another man's wife. The thought made him smile. Miz Hatty would be horrified, but he couldn't imagine her giving up a single luxury or possession to exonerate herself or him.

By what right did he criticize others, especially the mayor's industrious wife? He hadn't exactly turned his back on the good life either.

He watched as his men lassoed and wrestled down the last of the full-grown steers that had managed to escape previous branding. The angry, bawling beasts were finally released along with the other penned stock, his contribution to the success of the Russian venture. Next week, along with all of the other ranchers' marketable animals, they would be driven to the stockyards, loaded on train cars and eventually onto ships in Houston, Texas, headed across the ocean.

Russia. Even as he thought of that faraway place of fantasy, the first bolts of lightning cut a jagged pattern across the leaden sky. As always when it stormed, his willful imagination conjured up a haunting vision of his beautiful ballerina. Did the thunder still frighten her? Did she continue to dance? At moments like this did she ever stop and think of him? Had she taken another lover? Knowing that the answer to that question might be *yes* caused him great pain.

Relentlessly hounded by questions to which he never received answers, he made his way toward shelter to wait out a storm that promised to be violent. Princess Marina Nicolaiev no doubt continued to live her life of luxury. What need would she have to hang on to fleeting memories of an ordinary man like Hunter Kincaid?

"Where is that driver and carriage?" Marina murmured, glancing out the side door of the theater to give the darkening sky a worried look. Exhausted after a long day of rehearsal, more than anything she would like to be home before the impending rain hit. She had never gotten over her restlessness during thunder and lightning. Storms still made her nervous, but worse, they reminded her of people and times better forgotten.

Despite her determination, the unbidden memories swept over her like a gale. She fought desperately not to validate them or give them a name, but the image of a man, strong and tall, managed to slip past her defenses. Hunter Kincaid. It would be best if she wiped him from her memory, for it served only to remind her of what she would never have. No matter how hard she tried, she couldn't find the strength to give him up, even if she did manage to keep her longings to herself.

"There it is," she said to no one in particular when she spied the black carriage coming her way, traveling fast down the narrow lane. Pursing her lips and glancing around to see if anyone else had noticed, she vowed to give the thoughtless driver a stern talking-to about his recklessness when he finally decided to stop.

Several of the other *danseuses* were congregated around the exit waiting for rides, most from male admirers willing to pamper the unattached ladies of the ballet. As usual, her cohorts ignored her. So, without a backward glance or a farewell, she stepped through the door, careful not to open her umbrella until she was all the way outside. She had heard that to do otherwise brought bad luck.

Absorbed in the struggle to release the stubbornly steadfast clasp, she paid little heed to the approaching carriage or the group of chattering women who followed her out of the theater. Then the catch relented and snapped open and, just as suddenly, a great gust of wind caught the flimsy frame, turning the umbrella inside out.

Just what made her look up, she couldn't be certain. But when she did, she couldn't believe her eyes. The vehicle had jumped the curb, the wheels closest to her bearing down on her with incredible speed and disregard. There was a man inside. She could see him staring at her through the unshuttered window, but she couldn't make out his features.

"Look out, Marina."

Frozen in place, the shouted warning seeming to come from far away, she was helpless to do more than watch in morbid fascination as the carriage came toward her in what seemed like slow motion. The umbrella, inverted and broken, dropped from her immobile fingers and clattered against the sidewalk.

She followed seconds later.

That someone had pulled her out of the way in the nick of time didn't occur to her until she opened her eyes against the splatter of raindrops and realized she was uninjured and that the vehicle had never stopped. Instead, it had careened on around the corner and disappeared. Sergei stood over her, his handsome face a mask of frantic emotions. Thank God for his quick thinking. Otherwise, she might be dead. Gratefully, she threw her uninjured arm about his strong, familiar neck.

"You saved me," she cried.

"Marina, what happened?" he demanded, lifting her and carrying her back through the side entrance of the theater. The curious crowded about her when he sat her in a chair near the door to examine her left arm where it had struck the sidewalk.

"I-I-I'm not sure," she stuttered, flinching when he forced her to bend her bruised and scraped elbow. "Did you see who was inside that runaway carriage?"

"No." He looked at her worriedly. "Did you?"

She shook her head.

"Well, at least you seem relatively unharmed." Satisfied she was uninjured, he released her and backed away. "Your arm will not be a pretty sight, and it will probably be sore for a while. You'll have to cover it with makeup until it heals. You were very lucky, Marina. Very lucky, indeed."

"Did any of you recognize the man in the carriage?" she demanded of the mute spectators pressing in around her.

They only shook their heads. Then, realizing the excitement was over, they moved off.

"Marina, you have to be more careful. An accident like that could have broken your arm or, God forbid, one of your legs."

"Sergei, what if this weren't an accident?" she asked thoughtfully, dabbing at the scrapes with a damp cloth some-one had stuck in her hand. The strangest feeling coursed through her as she recalled what Dmitri had said to her not so long ago.

For months he had insisted on personally picking her up each day after rehearsal; and during performances of *Don Quixote,* he had come with armed guards to protect her from the crowds. Only recently had he sent the conveyance unat-tended. That carriage had looked like Dmitri's; but, now that she thought about it, there had been no royal emblem embla-zoned on the door. In fact, it had had no identifying coat of arms at all, which was quite unusual for such a fine vehicle.

"Of course it was an accident." Sergei's laughter challenged her seriousness. "Who would want to run down the *prima ballerina* of the Royal Ballet?"

"I can think of a few people." She glanced toward the tight-knit group of ballerinas, all of whom coveted her posi-tion.

"To be honest, so can I." Sergei's amused gaze followed hers. "But be serious. Not one of them is the type to have you murdered on the streets."

"No, I suppose not," she agreed, forcing a smile she didn't feel.

"It was a freak accident, Marina, nothing more. You must

believe that." With a reassuring hand he smoothed back her tumbled hair.

"No doubt, you are right, Sergei." She smiled up at him wistfully.

But she wasn't certain that he was correct and she was unsure what, if anything, she should tell Dmitri. If he learned of the accident, he would once again treat her like a helpless child unable to take care of herself. He would restrict her movements. Besides, she didn't like to see him worry, especially about her. As it was, he seemed to have enough on his mind lately dealing with the crisis that had taken place at the Summer Palace and the events that had followed.

"No harm done, so why not just forget about it, Marina?" Sergei urged, helping her to her feet and brushing off her rain-splattered cape. "Come on, I'll see you home."

Still hesitant, she glanced up at her dance partner, her friend. Of course, Sergei was probably right. It was best to forget about this isolated incident and consider herself lucky. Furthermore, she made up her mind, she wouldn't breathe a word to Dmitri about what had happened.

"I would appreciate your company."

At Sergei's insistence, they took a public carriage, a rare experience for Marina. Dmitri never allowed her to travel in so common a manner, and she found it daring to move about incognito. With Sergei as her protector, she felt confident.

By the time they reached the gates of her mansion, she was thoroughly enjoying herself. Sergei had her laughing at his stories of his latest paramour. He was never without an entourage of women—always in high places—who fell head over heels in love with the handsome *danseur*.

Countess Anna Petrovsky was the wife of the very man who had pursued Marina several months back. According to Sergei, the count had some strange fetishes for one who seemed so stodgy.

As the hansom cab navigated the circular drive, Marina was surprised to see many official carriages parked before the front door.

She sighed regretfully. No doubt Dmitri had already received news of the accident behind the theater. Not that it surprised her, for she knew her husband had ears and eyes planted all over the city.

"Shall I come in with you?" Sergei asked, taking in the commotion with wide-eyed wonder. Handing her the broken umbrella, he stepped out of the carriage to assist her down.

"No, that won't be necessary." She smiled brightly as she urged him back inside, a gesture he did little to resist. "I'll see you at the theater tomorrow." Through the open window they clasped hands.

"If you need me, you know where to find me," he assured her. Then he called for the driver to proceed.

From the protection of the mansion's portico she watched the cab pull away as the drizzle turned into a deluge. Sergei was truly a dear friend, one she could depend on and couldn't imagine ever being without. With a sigh, she turned toward the front entrance, prepared to face the smothering good intentions of her husband.

Stunned, Marina sank down on the damask-covered couch. Although the room was crowded with strangers and servants, she saw no one, not even the commissioner who had given her the unexpected, shattering news.

Dmitri was dead.

Her heart twisted with a feeling of such loss she couldn't catch her breath. She glanced down at the mangled umbrella she clasped in her hand, wondering why she still had it. Turned inside out, it was dripping wet and broken beyond repair. Just like her life.

"How did it happen?" she asked in a voice that sounded much calmer than she felt.

"One of his secretaries found him slumped over his desk. It appears he died of apoplexy."

Impossible. Just that morning at breakfast he had been so full of life.

"Are you certain it was natural causes?" That question popped out of her mouth before she had time to consider the implications.

"Is there a reason to suspect that it wasn't natural, Your Highness?" The man, one of Dmitri's most trusted assistants, scrutinized her through his monocle. Taking a kerchief from his pocket, he mopped at his brow.

"No, of course not," she replied hastily to cover her impulsive query.

However, it did seem strange—considering Dmitri's warning not so long ago at the theater—that on the very day he was found dead, she would nearly get run over by an unmarked carriage, but she didn't mention it.

"If you are concerned for your safety, I can see to it that police are stationed outside."

"No, no. I'm not worried." It was just the storm that made her feel so skittish, nothing more, she assured herself. Besides, she recalled Dmitri's warning to be careful whom she trusted. She glanced about. The house was crawling with strangers. "I would prefer it if you and your men would simply leave now."

"I'm sorry, Your Highness. That is impossible."

"Just what are all these men looking for?" she demanded, suddenly realizing they were everywhere, going through everything.

"Your husband was at work on several important projects." The commissioner continued to squint down at her through that single lens as if deciding how much—or more likely how little—to tell her. "There are vital papers that can't be accounted for. Papers entrusted to his discretion. The tsar has ordered that at all cost they be found."

"And you think they are here in my home?" she demanded. What she didn't ask was whether these missing papers had something to do with the attempted assassination of the tsar. She suspected they did.

"We won't be much longer." He bowed stiffly and formally. "It would go much faster if you and your people would simply leave us to our work. I promise you will not be disturbed in your private quarters."

In other words, he was ordering her to her room. Although a princess, she had little choice but to obey. If Dmitri were still alive no one would dare to treat her in such a shabby manner. But Dmitri was dead. She had to accept that. Confusion caught in her throat, a lump that refused to go down.

With inborn grace and dignity, Marina rose and, refusing offers of assistance, made her way out of the great salon into the foyer and up the winding staircase.

At the top landing she paused, the full impact of what had happened hitting her hard. She was a widow. Suddenly, the thought of facing the raging storm of her life without protection seemed more frightening than ever before.

Yet, what choice did she have but to proceed, alone and vulnerable?

Hunter Kincaid. That she should think of another man at the moment she learned of her husband's death was an atrocity, but she couldn't stop herself. What she felt for the American had nothing at all to do with what she felt for Dmitri. The emotions could not be compared, for they were two different kinds of love. Love. She couldn't define love, except to say it had something to do with security and the guarantee of forever, neither of which she had at the moment. Neither of which Hunter Kincaid had ever offered her, she reminded herself.

She headed for the safety of her room, hoping the intruders would find what they were looking for with expediency, then leave her alone to cope with her grief. She wanted nothing to do with Dmitri's world of government and intrigue. Nor at the moment did she have room for the unknown world of Hunter Kincaid. All she wanted was peace—and to be able to dance.

The shouts and whistles of the experienced cowboys loading the bawling cattle up the walled gangplank of the ship, then down a long chute to the small pens constructed on the lower decks was sheer cacophony. To be in the middle of the fiasco was nothing short of chaos. Hunter was the boss and had done more than his fair share of such backbreaking labor in his time, so he couldn't resist the urge to add his know-how to the others.

Cattle, no doubt the stupidest beasts God had ever created, were as unpredictable as women. If even one of them should decide to make a break for it, they could all—steers, horses, and men alike—end up in Galveston Bay, the venture busted before it ever got off the ground or, better put, out to sea.

So far, the loading had gone without a hitch. So far. There was still one last group working its way down the incline to the loading docks.

Hunter reined his dependable cow pony toward the final herd, whistling sharply as he beat his coiled rope against the saddle to keep the restless animals moving forward. One snorting beast caught his attention. Its glazed stare promised trouble.

Unrolling his lasso, Hunter prepared himself. However, he moved a moment too late. The half-crazed steer, just looking for a reason to go berserk, spun about sharply, aiming for him and the wooden railing that separated them from the bay.

True to their bovine nature, the entire herd turned to follow the troublemaker. Hunter saw them coming, red eyes glaring and nostrils flaring. Many a good cowhand had lost their lives to just such a stampede. He wasn't about to be the next fatality.

The pinto mustang he rode no doubt was thinking the same thing. Settling back on his haunches, the horse leapt forward, charging the head steer. Shouting and flaying his rope, Hunter bent to the task at hand, praying for heavenly intervention. If they were lucky, they might deflect the cattle before the moving wall of flesh and hooves ran them over and plunged headlong into the water.

Snorting and puffing, the herd charged straight ahead. The brave horse never faltered, although Hunter admitted, if only to himself, he experienced a moment of uncertainty; but he kept on shouting and slapping the side of his saddle. The moment came when he could feel hot, fetid breath bearing down on him.

Damn! He'd misjudged the enemy. Preparing himself for the impact of the wall of flesh, he opened his mouth and shouted.

At the last possible second, the herd turned. Twenty minutes later, they were safely aboard the cargo ship, milling and mooing in the makeshift corral set up on deck to hold them until they could be moved to permanent quarters.

Wordlessly, Hunter wiped the film of sweat from his face and breathed relief that he had passed yet another test. That had been close. Too close for comfort.

Even so, the next few weeks would determine the worth of the entire undertaking. He had assigned his best hands to see the project through to success. None particularly looked forward to the long ocean voyage—they were men of the earth not of the sea—but they would do everything in their power to make sure that the livestock arrived in Russia fat and healthy.

As always, whenever Hunter thought of Russia, his thoughts turned to the woman he had loved so briefly yet intensely and left behind. Obsessively he dreamed of her, but this time it was different. Struck by an overwhelming certainty that Marina was in trouble, he fantasized about how he would go to her and save her from the direst of threats.

But it was only the threat of his own mortality that had brought such thoughts to mind. Heroes and grand rescues. Such notions were pure foolishness, he assured himself. Marina Nicolaiev didn't need him to save her from the lap of luxury, not now or ever.

"Daddy, please, are you ready to go yet? You promised me an hour ago we would leave."

Rainee. How like her mother she sounded when she wanted something. Hunter glanced over to the sidelines where his daughter, just barely fourteen, perched on the rail guard looking as pretty as a cowboy's dream of heaven on earth. When had that womanly transformation taken place in her? Or had she always been that way?

No, it was only a recent occurrence. He glanced at his men, who were eyeing her with interest. One youngster in particular, Paco Santana, was drawn to her like a bee to nectar. He would have to keep a tight rein on that boy.

"I'm sorry, honey. We're going." Spurring the mustang to where she waited with such feminine impatience, he smiled at his young daughter, dismounted, and tossed the reins to Paco. He had promised to take Rainee shopping in Houston, a bribe that had readily convinced her to accompany him on this trip.

Yes, indeed. Rainee was growing up. To have left her back home to her own devices wouldn't have been wise. He dared not leave her alone, not anymore. The thought of her turning out like her mother, yearning for things that weren't good for her, didn't set well with him. Therefore, as long as *he* saw to it she got everything she wanted—the dresses, the schooling, the companionship—then, if he were lucky, she would never have the opportunity to be exposed to those things that had lured her mother away. Then she would be safe. And he would be safe.

They would be safe together, which was just how he'd planned it and would make sure it remained.

Settling first the girl and then himself onto the seat of the dogcart he had hired to take them back to town, he took up the reins, snapping them across the horse's back. Reaching their destination, he couldn't help but notice how Rainee's water-blue eyes sparkled, soaked up everything like a blotter on ink as they rode through a town that made Sweetwater look like the backwoods. From now on, to ensure their safety, he would see to it that they both stayed home and learned to be satisfied with what they had.

By damn, he had every right to protect his only daughter. And protect her he would, no matter how much she might come to despise him for doing what he thought was best for her, as well as for himself.

Never would he allow Rainee to turn out like her mother, to run after false dreams. And never would he chase after a will-o'-the-wisp in a far-off country.

As expected, Marina had been instantly relieved of her duties with the Royal Ballet, her coveted roll of Dulcinea in the current production of *Don Quixote* given to another, less competent dancer. Not that she blamed Marius Petipa, the director. He had little choice. The Princess Marina Nicolaiev was in mourning and must remain out of public view for a year.

In a year she would undoubtedly grow stiff and flabby, never to regain her limberness or grace. In a year, she would lose her status as *prima ballerina,* ending her illustrious career prematurely.

Then what would she have left? Nothing.

Pacing in her frustration, she ignored the plate of *blini,* normally her favorite treat, that a servant had brought upstairs to her. She didn't want to eat, so she picked up the plate and put it on the floor.

Arabesque and Sissonne did not suffer from her lack of appetite. With little pink tongues they licked the bone china dish clean in a matter of moments, pushing it into a corner and underneath a drapery panel. She didn't bother to retrieve it.

"Excuse me, Your Highness."

Marina whirled about guiltily, wondering how long Olga had been standing there. Had the old woman seen her mistress's disregard for her late master's possessions? Everything, even the bed Marina slept in, belonged to Dmitri's estate. Nonetheless, she knew she could count on Olga's loyalty.

"You have a visitor, madam."

"Send him right up," she said with undisguised relief, certain it must be Sergei, the only person who came to visit her on a regular basis.

A few moments later the old woman escorted a stranger into her private sitting room. The moment she saw the man, sized him up for his official capacity, Marina sensed he brought bad news.

"I'm sorry to have to be the one to tell you this, Your Highness." The stockily built man cleared his throat before he continued. "Your husband's estate has been confiscated."

"Confiscated?" How absurd. "By whom?" she asked.

"The tsar."

"Why would he do that to me? My husband was loyal to his cousin," she insisted, knowing full well Tsar Alexander was capable of doing many things without explanation. It could be as simple as one of Dmitri's enemies having petitioned the crown and discredited the crippled prince. But why? Did it perhaps have something to do with the unspecified papers the men had been searching for but had never found?

Wordlessly, he handed her an official-looking document, the wax seal stamped with the Romanov emblem of the two-headed eagle.

Breaking open the seal, she skimmed the papers quickly, much of the grandiose language meaning nothing to her, but the crux of the royal decree was perfectly clear.

"This orders me to vacate my home immediately."

"It is within my jurisdiction to give you until tomorrow morning. Pack only personal possessions and none too tightly. I must go through everything before it leaves the premises."

"Just where do you and the tsar expect me to go on such short notice?" she demanded.

The unemotional look on his face made it apparent that he, at least, didn't particularly care. She didn't expect much more from his royal master.

Well, she would just see about that. As a princess of the realm, she would demand an audience with the misinformed tsar. Surely once he heard her side of the story, he would change his mind.

"Leave me now." Marina rose with all of the commanding dignity afforded her title.

The tsar's messenger bowed stiffly and departed without a backward glance.

However, the moment she was alone, her shoulders slumped and her head dropped into her open hands. What was she going to do? Where was she going to go? Especially if her pleas fell on more deaf ears.

As always when she was at the ebb of her strength, her

thoughts turned to Hunter Kincaid and the promise that was America. Hunter? Did she dare try to find him? Would he even remember her? Once he had said he would welcome her and share his kingdom with her. Had he meant that or had those words simply been the hollow promises of a man's desire?

"Daddy, look at those ladies sitting over there." Rainee leaned forward at the table in the dining room of the elite Houston hotel to speak in soft, excited tones. "See how beautifully they're dressed. They must be very important."

"Rainee, honey, you gotta quit gawking at other people," Hunter chided. "It's rude." Nonetheless, he had already noticed the group of women the girl had indicated and had come to his own conclusion.

He didn't want her to be influenced by what she saw—not the opulence of the hotel in which they were staying or the people who frequented it. Maybe it had been a mistake to bring her along on this trip as the "ladies" she found so intriguing were anything but. He had seen their type before—performers of some kind, no doubt—all gussied up in clothing meant to flaunt not just flatter their feminine attributes.

"Don't you think they look pretty, Daddy?"

Hell's blazes, why did the girl insist on pursuing the unsavory subject?

"It's all a matter of what you're lookin' for, honey," he tried to explain without sounding testy. Then seeing she had no intentions of dropping the matter until it was thoroughly discussed, he abandoned all attempts to finish his dinner. Were all little girls as difficult and trying as his? "You see, there's pretty like you, and then there's pretty like them." He tilted his head toward the table of women.

"In other words, you don't think I'm all that pretty." The girl lowered her head, dejected.

"To the contrary, Rainee." He reached across the table and lifted her pointed little chin, so like her mother's. "Your kind of sweet, innocent beauty is what every man hopes to find in a wife someday, someone to be the mother of his children."

"I don't want to be a wife or a mother. Their lives are dull and boring," she stated matter-of-factly, her gaze steady with certainty.

"That's not true, Rainee. Whoever told you such non-sense?" he demanded.

"Nobody. All you have to do is look around. Married women are always complaining."

"Rainee, don't talk like that. It's not becoming in a young lady," Hunter scolded, shocked, his fork clattering to the floor when he accidentally hit it with his out-flung hand.

"Wives and mothers never get to dress the way they want or be what they want. They must look and act old and frumpy. You never let Momma dress pretty, did you?" She continued without a pause. "You never took her places she wanted to go." She looked at him pointedly to see if he would deny it.

"That's not true," he declared. But it was the truth, even if he refused to admit it. "Who told you such lies, Rainee?" Someone had to have told her. How else would she have known how things had been between him and Della? She had been just a baby when her mother had disappeared.

"I hear things, Daddy. You can't keep me from finding out the truth about my mother forever."

Her statement, blunt with accusation, caught him by sur-prise. He had never told her much about her mother, only that she had died. At the time, it had seemed the safest way to spare the girl undue grief. Besides, he reasoned, the less she knew about Della, the less likely she was to turn out like her. No matter what, he had to keep his daughter from making Della's fatal mistakes.

So what did he say to her now? How did he wipe away

that look of anger and betrayal from her face, a look that reminded him of how Della used to glare at him.

"Look, Rainee, there's an old saying: The grass always appears to be greener in the other man's pasture. But appearances aren't everything. I loved your mother and tried hard to make her happy. And I love you. Would you like a new dress, honey?" he asked, hoping to change the subject. "If that would make you happy, we can look for one tomorrow."

"Daddy, don't you understand? I don't want a new dress. I want you to let me be who I want to be." Righteousness suffused her blue eyes.

"You're only fourteen, Rainee. You can't possibly know what it is you want to be at this age," he insisted, certain that he was right.

Rainee burst into tears.

Hunter threw up his hands in frustration.

It was a dinner never meant to be completed, nor forgotten. Rainee's pain reflected his own. He had buried his anguish so deep he had thought he had let go of it, but that kind of betrayal could never be forgiven.

Quickly he called for the check and paid it. Then he took Rainee, still crying, upstairs to the suite they shared, wishing that he could take her home instead.

Once they were alone, he sat her down and stared at her while he gathered courage. She was only fourteen, but he knew she was entitled to more than parental ultimatums. Still, he wasn't sure what to say about men and women and growing up.

This was a talk a young girl should be having with another female, with her mother. But he was all she had. In turn, she was all he had, and he didn't want to lose her.

Taking a deep breath, he began to speak, awkwardly at first, about life and all its expectations.

Hunter could remember only one other action that had been

as hard for him—walking out the door of Marina Nicolaiev's villa and forcing himself not to look back.

Even as he began to warm to the subject of marriage and commitment, he found himself wondering just what kind of wife Marina would make. In some ways she was a lot like Della, but she was also totally different.

She had been loyal to an invalid husband. Or had her fidelity been something less than noble? Had her determination to remain with Dmitri been no more than the desire to hang on to her social status? Hell, Della would have slept with a tumbleweed to have obtained just a few of the career opportunities Marina no doubt took for granted.

It was all so damn confusing and inconclusive. If he had half a brain in his head, he would listen to what he was telling Rainee about women and their aspirations and he wouldn't even think about Marina for another moment.

Yes, he would take his own advice and go home. There he could immerse himself in his work and forget about his brief affair with Marina. For in truth, that was all it had been or ever would be, a memorable affair that had been fated to end as quickly as it had begun.

Marina did as instructed, packing only personal effects, and very little of that. There was only one possession she refused to be parted with—her mother's music box. Exhausted by the utter turmoil of the last few days, Dmitri's funeral—far below the caliber of his rank and status in the government—and the sudden desertion of many of the servants once they'd learned she was being evicted, she dropped down across her bed still fully clothed, ignoring the golden lights of yet another sunset streaming in through the break in the pulled curtains.

In that twilight state she realized she hadn't seen either of the dogs all day long, not since morning when she had fed them her breakfast.

She should get up and call them, make sure they were all right and not into mischief. But then what did it matter what they might tear up? It didn't belong to her anymore. Any damage they might do was now the tsar's problem.

Still, poor darlings, she should make certain that they received something more nutritious to eat.

Unable to master her leaden eyelids, Marina stifled a yawn. She would see to the dogs' needs after she rested her eyes for just a few moments. Just a few and not a second longer, she swore, giving over to a feeling of utter defeat and hopelessness.

"Your Highness, you must wake up."

Someone called her name and shook her rudely, but it took awhile to register in her sleep-laden mind. Instead of the golden light of sunset she'd had to shade her eyes from what had seemed only moments ago, a single candle shone in the darkness just over her head.

"Olga? Is that you? What time is it?" She blinked the haze from her eyes, the muddle from her mind.

"You must get up right away, Your Highness, and come with me."

"Olga, what's wrong?"

The old woman didn't answer, just signaled for her to hurry. Knowing Olga would only have her mistress's best interest at heart, Marina didn't question the servant's authority. Rising from the bed, she followed.

Olga led her into the small, private dining room just off the bedroom. Wordlessly, the woman lifted the candle high, illuminating the far corner near the curtained window.

The white furry ball could have been many things, but Marina instantly knew what it was.

"Arabesque!" she cried, rushing forward. Dropping to her

knees, she reached out to stroke his tangled fur and discovered him still and cold. A few feet away lay Sissonne, just as dead. Why? What had killed them? With questioning eyes, she stared up at Olga.

The woman bent and pulled something out from beneath the curtain. A bone china dish, licked clean by the dogs.

"The *blini*," Marina murmured, gathering up the bodies of her pets and pulling them into her lap. "This morning they ate what was intended for me." She couldn't stay the tears that gathered behind her eyes, but she managed to keep them from overflowing her lashes, already spiked with guilt.

"That happened yesterday morning, Your Highness. The sun will rise in less than an hour. I found the dogs on my pre-dawn rounds, just after I discovered the kitchen fires stone-cold. It seems the cook left in a hurry without notice."

"Then someone tried to poison me. But why?"

If the loyal servant knew the answer, she didn't share it with her mistress. Nonetheless, Marina had a good idea it had something to do with the missing papers. Had Dmitri hidden them on purpose? Quite possibly, for she had never known her husband to accidentally lose anything. And if the tsar were looking for them . . .

That could mean that the orders to have her murdered might have come directly from Alexander himself. But why? What was in the documents that made them so deadly? Anything was possible, she finally concluded; and if the tsar wanted her dead, then she would be safe nowhere in all of Russia.

"I must get away." That thought was as frightening to contemplate as the certainty of the chain of events if she stayed.

"I agree, Your Highness." Olga sighed with obvious relief, even though the worry in her old eyes looked anything but alleviated. "As fast as you can."

"Even if you are right, I cannot go alone."

"Again I agree. Have you no one you can trust."

"Besides you, Olga?" She stared at the woman hopefully, for she could think of no one who would make a more trustworthy companion to her than the old peasant.

"Your Highness, you know there is nothing I wouldn't do for you. Please, do not ask this of me." Olga's great eyes clouded with tears of helplessness and exhaustion.

"It's all right, Olga. Really." She placed her arms around the weeping servant to whom she owed her very life. It was then that Marina realized just how old the more-than-kind woman must be. How fragile. How much she had given over the years, without questions, without asking for anything in return. Olga deserved to live out her final years nestled comfortably in a rocker before a fire, grandchildren running around her feet, not running for her life. As hard as it was, she let go yet another symbol of security. If not Olga, then whom to trust?

"Sergei," she murmured aloud.

"Whom, madam?" The old woman sniffed and looked up at her through her shield of tears.

"Sergei Bozzacchi, my dance partner. I think I can convince him to go with me." Especially once she had told him where she planned to go.

"Are you certain he is trustworthy?" Olga studied her with the worried eyes of a faithful hound.

"Of course," she replied, warming to her plan. "Don't you see? It is the perfect solution. I have trusted dear Sergei every day for years, and he has always been there for me." Although she spoke of their relationship upon the stage, she perceived that in life his stalwartness would be no different.

"I'm so relieved, Your Highness, but where could you possibly go to assure your safety?"

"America." Marina smiled at the servant with glowing confidence. Her mother's homeland was the most logical place in all the world for her to go. America and Hunter Kincaid. They were her destiny.

Once she reached the golden shores of the promised land, how difficult could it be to make her way to a city called Sweetwater in a province called Wyoming?

Seven

April 1874
Sweetwater, Wyoming

Life was good. In fact, by all rights, it couldn't have been
better. But then, Hunter always felt that way come spring with
its promise of renewal and hope. The change of season sig-
nified a fresh beginning that all ranchers considered the new
year.

Come spring, a man counted his cattle, projected his annual
profits, and made his plans. For Hunter and his fellow Wyomingites the calves were plentiful, the herds healthy. The profits
promised to be enough to set aside money for leaner years.
As far as plans for the future . . .

Hunter frowned at the inevitable hitch in his euphoric
dreams. God knew he was lonely. All the money in the world
couldn't fill the void, a gaping chasm left in the wake of
Della's desertion and widened in those few fleeting days spent
in Russia, a time and place that seemed as distant as the
moon.

Distance, however, wasn't necessarily a bad thing. He
took up the dried rosebud that sat on his desk and ran his
thumb over the dark, curled edge of one petal. Distance offered safety. From far away he could explore his feelings,
even mold them to his liking, without the fear of being hurt
again.

Through reliable sources he had learned that Dmitri Nicolaiev had died suddenly a few months back, but they could tell him nothing about the mystery surrounding his death or what had become of Marina. She had simply disappeared. At first he had hoped to hear from her, but with time he had come to accept that it was better that he hadn't. Women like Marina lived a lifestyle foreign to what he knew or could ever provide. She had family on her father's side, no doubt. If he remembered right, he had been of nobility. A woman like Marina never looked back or regretted. And she never waited foolishly for something as elusive as love.

After that brief indulgence in morose contemplation, Hunter shook himself both mentally and physically, put the shriveled flower aside, and sat back from his figuring, his arms folded over his chest. He was satisfied with what he saw in the ledgers before him.

By damn, he had dandy plans all worked out for himself and Rainee. Plans that didn't include pining away for what he could never hope to have.

Hearing a commotion in the hallway outside his office door, he edged his chair away from his desk, cupped his hand about the desk lamp, and blew out the pulsing flame. Rainee was home late from her weekly excursion into town. Knowing that she would be a pot of information—name it for what it really was, gossip—just ready to boil over, he ambled down the corridor into the main room of the sprawling ranch house and paused in the archway to watch her entry.

So like her mother. God, he could still remember how alive and happy Della's face had always appeared whenever she returned from town.

Peering through a fog he refused to give a proper name—to do so would make him seem less of a man—he stared at the ceiling to regain his control.

Although well-constructed of massive hand-hewn beams and lumber, by some standards the building would be regarded as crude in structure. But here in Wyoming his home was considered a mansion with its three separate bedrooms, office, and kitchens with a well pump right inside the house—a house any man could be proud of.

But more important to him was the sight of his daughter's beaming face as she swept into the room and turned to greet him. His pride swelled, blotting out his trepidation.

"Daddy, Daddy!" Rainee cried, pulling off her kid gloves and tossing them on the table as she hurried past it, ignoring the dinner he had ordered left out for her. "You won't believe the wonderful news I have to tell you." As soft and spry as a playful kitten, she fell into his arms.

Whatever it was, it had to be important, for she was atremble with excitement.

"Calm down, honey," he said with a chuckle, "unless you aim to tell me a twister's about to rip through town."

"Not a twister, Daddy." Her eyes sparkled with joy. "Something bigger and a whole lot better."

Bemused, he watched as she battled with her beaded purse, pulling out a piece of folded paper. Spreading it open, she held it up for him to see.

It was a handbill. He read it slowly.

His heart dropped to the pit of his belly.

"Where did you get this, Rainee?" he asked in a low, purposely controlled voice.

"Isn't it just the most wonderful news, Daddy?" Dreamy-eyed and smiling, the girl whirled on feet as light as thistledown.

"Who gave you this?" he demanded.

This time his tone of voice caused her to pause and take stock.

"Why Mrs. Shackelford is posting them all over town. What's wrong, Daddy?"

Not bothering to reply, Hunter refolded the handbill and stuffed it into the pocket of his shirt. Gathering up his Stetson and jacket, he put them on and strode out the back door.

"Daddy, where are you going so late?"

He didn't tell her, but he'd be damned if he'd let it happen all over again.

In all this time, Marina still had not grown accustomed to the never-ceasing clackity-clack of the train wheels both day and night. Twisting on the hard bench, she tried to find a more comfortable position. It was impossible. Nature never intended for man or woman to sleep in such cramped quarters. Nor were they meant to stay in a place for only a few days at the most and then move on to the next location to give yet another round of half-hearted performances. Still and all, to do so served her purposes.

Giving up all attempts to rest, she sat up and glanced around at the other occupants in the train car with envy. Sergei's lithe frame was stretched out on a seat across from hers, his head pillowed on his long coat. He slept peacefully, as did the rest of the small troupe of dancers and musicians they had assembled in New York and brought with them on this "Tour of the Great American West."

The great American West? Hah! It was anything but. Issuing a sigh, she shifted in her seat and propped her elbow on her mother's music box, staring out the soot-hazed window.

The pale light of a full moon cast its eerie illumination over the unfamiliar landscape in this country known as Wyoming. She had learned that the craggy juts of rock and mountains were called buttes, but to her they looked more like demons frozen in a ritual pagan dance. They were just stones, she reminded herself, nothing more—as hard and unyielding as life had suddenly become what seemed a lifetime ago. Hopefully, that was all about to change.

Pulling the thin quilt closer about her shivering shoulders, Marina brushed aside her apprehensions. As was often the case with middle-of-the-night worry, she was not successful.

Hunter Kincaid. She could see his face, and she remembered the way he had looked at her as if she had betrayed him in their last few moments together. His face was so dear and clear in her mind she could have reached out and touched it. Just as she should have that day long ago in Russia so that he could have understood that she'd had no other choice but to walk away. Now, he was only a few performances and fewer days away . . .

"Marina, are you at it again when you should be sleeping?"

Startled, Marina glanced up at the speaker, then fidgeted nervously on the seat. Shaking her head in denial of the truth, she tried hard to suppress the apprehension that compressed her lips into an expressionless slash across her face.

"You aren't asleep either, Fanny," she pointed out, scooting over to make room on the seat.

"So share." Petite and pixie-pretty, the girl dropped down beside her and grabbed the unclaimed end of the quilt, tucking it about her slender shoulders. They sat in silence, nestled comfortably under the cover together. Listening to the clatter of the wheels beneath them, they clasped hands in unspoken sisterhood.

Fanny Stuart was the only real female friend Marina had ever had. She remembered the first time she had seen the other woman during the auditions for the *corps de ballet* she and Sergei had danced with when they had first arrived in New York. She had stopped to watch Fanny's performance and immediately recognized the American dancer's extraordinary but undeveloped talent. She had seen to it that Fanny was hired as a *corypée* and had dedicated her own time to teaching her first protégée many of the techniques that she had learned during her years of rigorous training at the Imperial Academy in Russia. She had found her initial experience as an instructor most fulfilling and had been glad when Fanny had agreed to accompany them on this tour across America.

"It's nothing." Marina shrugged her shoulders and closed her eyes, pretending to succumb to the yawn she faked.

"You're thinking about him again. Admit it," Fanny insisted.

"So what if I am?" Marina stubbornly continued her window-side vigilance, but she clung to Fanny's hand and friendship. She had every right to indulge herself with thoughts of Hunter Kincaid and how her life would change for the better once she found him.

She could see it. Once again running through the chain of events as she pictured they would be, she smiled with romantic contentment. His surprise at discovering her would be no greater than his joy. They would have two whole days together. Not nearly enough time, of course. He would protest, even beg her not to go; but once she explained her need to fulfill her obligation to complete the rest of the tour, a month, maybe two at the most, he would understand. But more importantly, he would vow to wait for her to return, to share his life and kingdom with her. It would be the princess's fairy tale come true.

And so she clung to promises Hunter had made long ago and her dreams of how they would be fulfilled. They were the only reason she had agreed to this madcap excursion by train across the American West.

When Jack Yancy, the promoter, had approached her and

Sergei with the idea, she had made only one stipulation. He must see to it that they danced in Sweetwater, Wyoming.

"Why Sweetwater, Your Highness?" the fast-talking little man had asked.

She had been vague in her answer for she had not wanted Sergei to know the truth. He might have laughed at her romantic notions.

Eventually, once they were on the road, she had confessed her fantasies to Fanny. Her friend had been supportive if somewhat skeptical. But what others might think didn't matter to her. Finding Hunter, coming face to face with him at long last, telling him how she really felt, and knowing that he reciprocated, were essential for her own peace of mind. Sweetwater and Hunter had been her primary goal from the moment she had reached the safety of America.

Upon her arrival in New York, she had naively thought to make her way to Hunter's home in a few short days. Secure in her ignorance, she'd had no concept of the vast diversification of the American population and lifestyles. Her patrons had wasted no time telling her the frightening stories about the "wild West."

People who lived "out there" were regarded much as the Cossacks were in her native Russia. Tough, wild, a breed all of their own, the Cossacks battled to tame the Siberian frontier. They were respected and feared, yet at the same time ostracized by those considered more civilized.

In America, "cattle barons" fought to claim an equally uncivilized land. But she had learned that more than severe weather had to be conquered in places like Wyoming. There were savage Indians and armed bandits. In fact, most men walked with guns strapped to their hips, or so she had been told, and apparently there were no laws to stop such barbarism.

So went the stories. However, in her personal travels she

had seen only a few Indians and cowboys. None had seemed particularly savage, but once again she had been warned not to be deceived by the five-and-ten-cent variety she had run into thus far. She refused to believe such nonsense, especially when it came to Hunter Kincaid. She maintained she knew him well. In Russia he had acted perfectly civilized, if a bit arrogant at first. Surely she had no need to worry about Hunter.

"Fanny," she whispered, desperate to sort through the jumble of her emotions. "I cannot believe it might actually happen. What do I say to him after all this time?"

"There's no doubt in my mind you'll know what to say when you see him." Her friend squeezed her hand with earnest affection. "Just don't get your hopes up too high, sweetie. Expecting too much from any man can set you up for a giant fall. There's always the possibility that he's not even in Wyoming anymore. How can you be certain he hasn't remarried in all of this time? It's possible, you know, Marina. Only in fairy tales does love manage to conquer all."

No, no. Fanny had to be wrong. The dear woman had simply forgotten what it meant to be in love.

"Fanny? Where the hell are you?" The gruffly muttered query issued from the bench three rows back. John was the troupe's piano player and Fanny's beau.

"Prince Charming calls," she said with an exaggerated sigh and a roll of her doe-brown eyes. "Don't worry, sweetie. I'm just a cynic by necessity. Not all men are to be judged by the likes of John Carey. If ever there were a fairy princess to find a knight in shining armor, it's you." She patted Marina's hand before letting it go.

Fanny's well-meaning words offered her anything but encouragement.

* * *

Just as Rainee had said, Hatty Shackelford had posted her handbills on every available location. On the announcement board in front of the telegraph office, along the porch railings of the general store, even at the doors of the church.

Hunter saw the stark-white fliers fluttering in the darkness. The silhouette of a row of women dancers caused his jaw to tighten with determination.

Never mind that it was past the polite visiting hour. He headed straight for the tiny house on the other side of town where the mayor and his wife resided.

Never mind that not a single light shone in the windows when he arrived at his destination. He pounded on the door, demanding an answer.

"Mr. Kincaid. Is something wrong?" Blinking like a sleep-deprived owl, Mayor Shackelford greeted him in his ridiculous nightshirt.

"You might say that, Jonas," Hunter replied. "Where is your wife? I want to talk to her now."

"Mrs. Shackelford?" The mayor glanced over his own shoulder into the darkness with the look of a harried capon. "Why she's abed like all decent folks should be at such an indecent hour."

It was a none-too-gentle hint Hunter chose to ignore.

"Then I'll be glad to wait here while you rouse her." Folding his arms over his chest, he gave every indication of staying put on the Shackelford front porch as long as it took to get his way.

He waited only a few moments. Smiling at the impatient sounds of henhouse cackling coming from the interior of the house, he suspected Hatty Shackelford was anything but glad to see him. He had to admit the moment he caught sight of her, it was anything but pleasant for him, too.

He knew plenty of women could look a fright when they went to bed, but he had never personally confronted such a phenomenon. With her hair rolled on green rags and white cream smeared on her face, the mayor's wife could make any man swear off marriage.

"Well, what is it, Mr. Kincaid, that you felt it necessary to so rudely disturb my beauty sleep?"

Beauty sleep? Until she voiced her irritation, Hunter had had no idea he had been staring so long at the anything-but-beautiful apparition. Reaching into his open jacket, he extracted the flier from an inner pocket.

"This." He waved the sheet of paper under her long, cream-tipped nose. "I want it stopped immediately."

"Stopped? Whatever for, Mr. Kincaid?" If the woman had sported hackles around her neck, they would have risen with her indignation.

"Whose harebrained idea was this, madam? Yours?"

"Mr. Kincaid," the mayor interjected, "there's no need to be so—"

"There's every need, Jonas," Hunter cut in, silencing the henpecked man.

"Look here, Hunter Kincaid." True to her nature, Hatty barrelled forward, shoving her hapless husband aside. "This 'harebrained' idea was the decision of the Sweetwater Ladies' Committee. We got together and decided, rightly so, that this town needs a little cultural influence."

"Cultural influence? Is that what you think you're going to get by bringing in some traveling band of disreputable entertainers? Hatty, how could you and your ladies have forgotten so quickly where such foolishness leads? How could you have forgotten what happened to Della?" Hunter demanded.

"It's not at all the same thing. These people are reputable. They're European royalty, for goodness sake. Besides, it's too late to cancel the performances even if *we* ladies decided *we* wanted to, which *we* don't." Hatty stubbornly planted her meaty fists on her ample hips. "They will be here the day after tomorrow on the train from Cheyenne. Get used to it, Mr. Kincaid. There's nothing you can do to prevent it."

Maybe he couldn't stop them from coming, but by damn he could see to it that the unwelcome vagabonds were sent packing the moment they set foot in Sweetwater. Only then could he be certain that Rainee was safe from making the same terrible mistakes her mother had made.

Wordlessly, he spun on his heels and marched back to his horse. Mounting up, he spurred the paint mustang toward home. Yes, he would be waiting to head off disaster the minute it arrived in town, no matter what tempting form it chose to take.

Finally. At last. She held the direction her future would take in her own two hands, in a tangible form. Breath held, Marina fanned out the train tickets, one for each member of the troupe, on the counter of the front desk of the Cheyenne hotel and mouthed the name printed on them in big, block letters.

Sweetwater.

"Well?" Standing behind her, Fanny tapped her foot with impish impatience.

Turning to face her friend, Marina nodded. Nothing needed to be said.

"Oh, sweetie, I'm so happy for you." Fanny enveloped her in a brief hug before flitting away, no doubt to pack a few last-minute items.

Marina smiled. She, too, had some packing to do. Folding up the stack of tickets as if they were a deck of playing cards, Marina tucked them into her reticule for safekeeping and followed in Fanny's footsteps.

Sweetwater, Wyoming. It had seemed so far away, impossible to reach. Now, she would be there tomorrow. Bless Jack Yancy. Once again he had come through at the very last moment, sending her tickets and instructions for the troupe's next engagement just hours before their departure. But that didn't matter now. What mattered was that he had kept his promise to see that they performed in Sweetwater, the one stipulation she had insisted on from the beginning. Yes, there had been times when she had doubted the fast-talking promoter's sincerity and honesty. Now was not one of them.

Still smiling, she walked as she read the personal note that accompanied the packet containing the tickets, giving detailed instructions as to whom to contact once the troupe reached their destination.

Hatty Shackelford. The wife of the town's mayor. How very bourgeois. Marina crinkled her brows. As ridiculous as it was, disappointment dampened her newfound joy. Just whom had she expected to find waiting for her on the boarding platform? Hunter Kincaid himself?

Only in her wildest dream could that happen, she assured herself—but with little real conviction.

Hunter. She tried to envision how he would look. Of course he would be wearing that crisp felt hat and those polished leather boots that had seemed so foreign when she had first seen him, exotic and exciting. Now she realized such attire personified the American West. Would he flash his crooked, endearing smile at her. Would he embrace her, perhaps even kiss her? Her heart, empty for so very long, fluttered at the mere thought of what might happen.

"Marinuska, my satin-lined cape. Where is it? What have you done with it?" Looking more aristocratic than he ought to, Sergei swept through the hotel lobby, confronting her before she even had the chance to close the door behind her, and presented his problem without consideration for her needs, or for that matter, anyone else's.

Dear temperamental Sergei. Not so long ago she, too, had been just as demanding and inconsiderate. Circumstances and responsibilities had forced her to change, to grow, to take on real responsibilities. She could only hope she would never act that way again.

Sergei, however, she excused. He had done so much for her since that terrible night of terror when he had fled Russia with her without question, without once expressing regret. Then, on the long trip across the ocean, he had worked day and night to learn English. He had never once complained about the total upheaval he willingly suffered for her. In return she would find it in herself to better tolerate his occasional fits of ill-temper.

Smiling patiently to cover up an ever-increasing sense of frustration, Marina tucked Jack Yancy's note into her purse.

"Sergei, think," she urged softly, stepping forward to lock arms with him. She guided him toward the stairs. "You wore your cape just last night after our final performance. Only you know where you left it."

"Me? Have left it somewhere?" His brows furled in a perplexed frown that seconds later relaxed. "Of course. Silly me." Kissing her exuberantly on one cheek, he shot off, making as much noise and fuss as a misfired cannonball.

Just how, Marina wondered as she watched her exasperating dance partner make his way back up the stairs of the hotel, had she become mother to thirteen capricious entertainers?

Hunter's intention had been to confront the band of unwanted vagabonds at the station and not allow them to even disembark from the train. He was even prepared to pay them

for their "inconvenience" if he had to, knowing full well
monetary compensation for doing nothing was not likely to
be turned down by that kind of people. The health of one of
his prize bulls foiled his plan.

The bull, an Aberdeen Angus he had imported all the way
from Scotland to improve the dressing percentage of his hardy
but sometimes lean herd, went down suddenly and mysteri-
ously. Had he lost that bull, years of planning and considerable money would have been forfeited. Fortunately, he
managed to save the valuable beast.

However, not in time to meet the train from Cheyenne.

Not bothering to stop at the house to change out of his
soiled jeans and chaps and still smelling of cattle, Hunter
rode straight into Sweetwater in hopes that the train had arrived later than usual. But of course, true to the laws of nature, the train had chugged into the depot and deposited its
passengers on schedule for the first time all year.

Cramming his dusty Stetson back on his flattened, sweat-
streaked hair, he made a beeline to the hotel. There was nowhere else in town for strangers to stay.

Reminiscent of the days when no less than three saloons
vied for customers, the crowd spilt out of the front doors of
the Addison Hotel. However women and children made up a
good majority of the craning bystanders trying to see inside.
To his relief, Rainee was not among them.

European royalty, my behind, he railed inwardly, catching
sight of a poster clutched in the hand of a woman in front
of him as he tried to make his way through the mob of on-
lookers. He'd had plenty of experience with the likes of people who claimed such status during his years of searching for
Della. Invariably they turned out to be confidence artists,
nothing more, looking to separate fools from their money.
These entertainers would be no different.

"Excuse me," he said, attempting to sidle his way into the overflowing hotel.

When politeness didn't serve his needs, he pressed harder, unmindful that he stepped on a toe here or that his elbows bumped against others there. His disagreeable scent seemed to work to his advantage, for people looked back with wrinkled noses and immediately moved out of his way.

Once in the lobby he heard the tinkling of a piano—that sound too reminiscent of saloons—in what had once been the main dining room of the hotel. Music and dancers, all kinds, went hand in hand. He aimed in that direction.

Word of his arrival had spread through the crowd. With little effort he made his way to the forefront of the gawkers pressed in the doorway of the dining room as if someone had drawn a line prohibiting them from going any farther. He stepped clear of the imaginary boundary and paused to assess the situation.

All the tables had been cleared from the large room, the chairs stacked in one corner for later use. A makeshift stage, no more than a rough-plank platform, took up nearly half the available space. Several women dressed in short skirts that revealed calves and ankles covered with colorful leggings milled about, lifting their legs on backs of chairs and bending over them to stretch. A piano, manned by a male player of considerable talent, stood to one side.

But it was the couple on the platform that captured Hunter's undivided attention and caused his breath to snag in his chest like driftwood in a spring flood. He couldn't be certain of the man's identity as he had only seen him once at a great distance. But the woman . . .

"Marina?" he murmured through a throat constricted by shock.

Her face was turned away, but her hair, long and gently waved, hung clear to her slender waist in dark familiar curls.

He could see them spilling over a lace-covered ivory pillow. He could feel the silky strands sliding through his fingers and around his bare wrist, could smell her exotic perfume. No. He had to be mistaken. Not only was it unlikely, it was impossible for Marina Nicolaiev to be here in Sweetwater. He had to be seeing something that couldn't possibly exist with a mind influenced by wishfulness.

In spite of the logic he tried so hard to accept, he continued to follow every move the dancing couple made, oblivious to the people standing in the doorway watching them. The woman turned and spun on the toes of one foot as if it were the most natural thing to do. Hunter craned to make out her features, but her hair whipped about her face, concealing it from view, so he still couldn't be sure. However, the emotions ripping through him couldn't have made him more certain.

He thrust aside his purpose for being there, once so all-fire important, like so much discarded litter. He only knew he had to confirm the ballerina's identity.

Once more, he stepped forward until he stood only a few feet from the edge of the platform, his head tilted up. He was so close to the woman he could see the fine blue veins that ran down the soft length of the inside of her arm, the delicate shape of her hand resting lightly on the shoulder of her partner.

Blue blood. A princess. It was all that he could think as he watched the pulse at her wrist pump gently.

At that moment the male dancer glanced down at him from the high stage. He paused, the expression on his face, much too handsome to be considered manly, was one of alarm as he pinned Hunter with glaring disapproval.

"What are you doing in here, mister?" The dancer, his accent undeniably foreign, let go of the small woman and stepped in front of her. "It is forbidden," he warned. "Now, get out." He pointed toward the exit.

But Hunter refused to be sent away by the likes of a pretty boy in tights. What did the fool think? To shield her from the bad American? He had no intention of hurting her. He just wanted to get a good look at her face.

As if in response to his need, the woman whirled, her dark eyes meeting his.

"Marina?" Her name rushed out of his mouth on a breath of startled emotion.

She looked not a day older. In fact, if it were possible, she appeared even younger. Her hair, which had grown much longer since he had last seen her, hung long and loose to her supple waist.

"Hunter," she said. She smiled, the expression aristocratic and unrevealing. The body he remembered so well swayed toward him, then quickly drew away.

Briefly he thought she was about to descend from the platform and run to him, arms open. Instead she held her ground, proud and straight, her hands calmly resting at her sides.

Try as he might, he couldn't decipher how she felt about seeing him again. Nothing in the way she looked, the way she said his name, or in the manner in which she held herself gave him a reliable clue.

"Marina? What are you doing here?" he asked rather gruffly and immediately felt like a bumbling fool.

"Why, I've come by invitation to dance," she replied. "And you?" Her smile at last reached her dark, exotic eyes, so full of hope and promise. Undisguised joy radiated from their depths.

He should be glad to see her too . . .

Instead, a steadily rising panic undermined any pleasure he might have felt. Marina. Here in flesh and blood, so close he could reach out and touch her. So close, she could lay claim to his love-battered heart as yet still hurting and unhealed from a past he had yet to resolve. How easily she could completely destroy him if he allowed her to. Just as important, he had Rainee to think of, so vulnerable and easily influenced.

No matter what dreams he might have harbored, no matter what his heart might cry out for, Marina's unexpected presence here and now threatened to destroy the last bit of security in his life.

"Me?" he answered, pinning her with a level stare generated by self-defense and a memory of that day in Russia when she had walked out on him without looking back. "I've come to put a stop to all of this culture nonsense. There will be no dancing in Sweetwater, not if I can help it. These people aren't ready for it. So you and the rest of your motley group might as well not go to all the trouble to unpack. The next train out of here leaves in the morning. If you're smart, you'll be on it."

Having stated his position just as he had originally planned, even though he felt his heart breaking in the process, Hunter turned and headed for the door. As much as he wanted to, he knew better than to look back. If he did, he ran the risk of changing his mind.

Changing his mind was the worst possible thing he could do.

Eight

"Hunter, please, wait."

At first Marina thought he would simply ignore her heart-felt plea and continue to walk away. Just before he reached the door, he stopped, but he didn't look at her. Shoulders hunched, he remained stiff and unyielding like a man facing a blinding rainstorm.

Dumbfounded, she struggled to understand his angry reaction, to find the right combination of words to change how he felt. Only on rare occasion did she find herself lacking in communicative skills. Now, facing a barrage of the doubts and fears she had kept at bay for so long, she couldn't think of a single thing to say. However, thoughts were plentiful, terrible and naked. Had Fanny been right? After all this time, could there be another woman in his life?

If so, if he were the one now encumbered, her struggle to reach him, her dream of rekindling the torch of passion that had burned so brightly, had been all for naught. In a blink of an eye, the last of her world crumbled beneath her feet, her hopes dissipated into bitter ashes.

"Please, Hunter. Don't I at least deserve an explanation?"

"Yes, I suppose you do," he replied, his stance still un-compromising.

She closed her eyes, as prepared as she could be for what he would say.

"I'll come back later. We can talk then without an audience."

Marina's eyes snapped opened. The audience he spoke of still congregated in the doorway, gawking. In her misery, she had forgotten about them. Reluctantly the crowd parted just barely enough to allow him to pass through their midst.

"Marina? That was your cattle baron, wasn't it? Hunter Kincaid." The gentle concern laced with awe in Fanny's whisper jerked her back to reality.

"Yes," she murmured. "That was Hunter all right, in the flesh and blood." She lowered her gaze when he disappeared into the crowd. How could he walk away without once looking back? Had he truly forgotten those intimate moments in Russia and the promise he had made to share his life with her? His whispered words of passion apparently meant nothing to him, not then and not now. The blade of harsh reality ripped through her with a painful, eye-opening stab.

"You never told me he was such a handsome devil."

Devil, indeed. That described Hunter Kincaid most appropriately. Still, Marina stepped toward the doorway and tried to see around the unruly, uncooperative crowd of strangers filling it, hoping to catch a final glimpse of him, something to prove her wrong.

But he was gone. The mob surged toward her, forcing her to stumble back into the safety of the makeshift theater. Then Sergei was there, insisting in his most arrogant manner that she immediately return to the stage and their practice.

"In a moment, Sergei," she responded, squeezing her eyes closed to hold back an onslaught of emotion. Still she clung to her need to believe that all was not lost. Sure, there might be pieces of the puzzle missing. But once she found them she could put her hopes back together and . . .

Whom did she think to fool? Surely not herself?

"Marina."

"Yes, yes, Sergei, I'm coming," she said with an exaggerated sigh.

No matter what happened or what anyone said, foremost she was a professional and the show must go on. Hunter must never suspect how she really felt, what dreams she had come there hoping to fulfill.

One thing she knew for certain, no matter what he might say, she remembered how enthralled he had been whenever he'd watched her dance. If she accomplished nothing else, she vowed, she would leave Hunter Kincaid with a lasting memory and longing of the same caliber he had left her with in Russia.

Hunter waited until the curious grew bored and went home. Using his time wisely, he'd bathed and changed clothes in the hotel. The manager, always willing to accommodate someone of his stature in the community, provided him with the necessary facilities, for a fee of course, and Hunter always kept a clean change of clothing in his saddlebags, just in case he might need them. Perhaps not Sunday-go-to-meeting attire, but it would do.

He decided not to approach Marina until everyone had left, including Sergei. The long wait gave him plenty of time to gain control of his maverick emotions.

Marina did deserve an explanation. However, he could not tell her the truth. At least not the crux of it. Their time together so long ago in Russia had been too short to develop even a little trust for a man who trusted so few. Della and her deception would remain his secret, for now. So would his fears regarding Rainee.

"Marina." He called softly to her from the dark threshold of the dining room–theater.

"Hunter, is that you?" Still on the stage, she straightened at the sound of her name.

In spite of his efforts to maintain discipline, he felt his traitorous heart lurch at the undisguised tremor in her cultured voice. The sweet smell of her perfume wafted around him, filling his head with memories. He struggled to disguise his feelings.

"Who else?" he replied, opting out of desperation to use arrogance as his main defense. Stepping out of the concealment of the shadows, he propped himself against the door frame. "Expecting someone different?"

"No, of course not," she answered just as arrogantly.

He'd forgotten that she could give as good as she got when it came to hauteur. Against his better judgment, he smiled.

Dropping down from the stage, she picked up a small towel flung across the back of a chair. She patted at her face and neck, then down her arms with a mindlessness that suggested her actions were commonplace. He found them anything but. Instead, he found them oddly disquieting.

Finally, she noticed him watching her intently. Pausing, she returned his stare for a moment before tossing the towel back on the chair.

"So. We're alone now," she said matter-of-factly.

"Yes, yes, we are," he agreed.

Tension bled the air of any chance of true intimacy. Hunter resorted to twisting his Stetson round and round in his hands.

"You said you had something you wanted to tell me." Marina settled casually into one of the empty chairs.

She looked so damn cool sitting there. She had managed

to turn the tables on him and take control of the moment, and he didn't like it.

"Yes, I did." Straightening, he cleared his throat, then his mind of any hesitation. Flinging down his hat, he moved toward her with purposeful steps.

She flinched at his sudden aggression. Stubborn, little witch, she refused to yield, crossing one leg over the other with a casualness he suspected was a ruse.

Grabbing her by the arm, he pulled her up, intending to hold her at arm's length and shake a little respect, and perhaps even fear, into her. Instead he found himself crushing her slender body to his own.

She didn't resist. In fact, she yielded so easily that the satisfaction he had sought not only wasn't there, but had turned into an emotion that made him feel powerless and desperate. Staring up at him, she remained calm, cool, so damn collected.

Needing to make certain he wasn't alone in his struggle, that she, too, at least fought to maintain control, he lifted her bodily beyond the point where those strange shoes she wore made it possible for her to dance on her toes.

"Put me down," she gasped, wiggling in the tight noose his arms made about her slender waist. But with her legs swinging freely and her body pressed hard against him, eventually she had no choice but to cling to him.

His victory short lived, Hunter found himself staring down into the dark, liquid pools of her eyes only inches from his own. He didn't mean for it to happen, but suddenly he was kissing her, her mouth a sweet receptacle for the passion he had kept under control for too long. Now it bubbled up from deep inside and overwhelmed him.

Snared in a trap of his own making, Hunter cursed himself for his carelessness. Only a greenhorn or a fool got tangled up in his own lasso. But there he was, wanting more, unconcerned as to what it might cost him, be it pride or possession.

"Marinuska, are you coming? I got worried when. . . . Hey, you. You're the man from this afternoon. What do you think you are doing? Let go of her."

Saved by the intrusion and the masculine hand that gripped his shoulder, Hunter released Marina and swung around to confront his opponent.

He stared at the handsome Russian dancer, too damn handsome to be taken seriously. But at least here was a familiar situation he could handle easily without fear of bungling the job. He curled his hand into a fist.

"No, Sergei." Marina stepped between them, focusing her full attention on her fellow Russian. "It's all right."

"Are you sure?" Sergei asked protectively.

"I'm sure." Still she refused to look at him. "Besides, Mr. Kincaid was just leaving."

Oh, he would leave all right, but not before he had said what he had come to say.

"Marina, you made a big mistake coming here. This town isn't ready for the likes of you." He blurted out the words. They sounded more like a threat than the explanation he'd intended. It was too late to take them back, but he tried to soften them. "They lead settled lives," he went on, thinking of his own innocent Rainee. "The young people don't need someone like you breezing in and out, making them long for something they can never have."

"If anyone is making a big mistake, mister, it's you if you do not go," Sergei interjected, stepping forward menacingly.

"Butt out, Pretty Boy," he warned, finding the dancer's tactic laughable. The fool didn't stand a pig's chance in hell of beating him when it came to a brawl.

"Sergei, please, I can handle this," she insisted, placing a restraining hand on the Russian's arm, as if he were the one needing it. As sudden as a dust storm can descend on the high plains, she whipped around to face him. That cool, collected expression still dominated her aristocratic features.

"Look, Hunter, I came to Sweetwater strictly to give my two performances then move on. Contrary to what you might think, I'm not some crazed gypsy come to steal your children. But if you're so worried, perhaps you had better lock them up. Otherwise their safe lives might be shaken," she warned with biting sarcasm. Her dark gaze never wavered, never showed even a second of regret for striking him where he was most vulnerable. "Don't worry about your precious town—or yourself for that matter. I just thought it might be nice to stop in and say hello, thought you might feel the same way. Otherwise, I expect nothing more from you. I never did. So, don't make me out to be more than I am."

Latching onto Sergei's hand, she marched off, taking him with her and leaving Hunter alone.

She was right. From the very beginning, she had never expected anything from him. *He* had been the one, as foolish as it had seemed even then, who had sought something more out of a moment of contrived intimacy. Nevertheless, he had walked into that one with eyes open and heart exposed. There had been no deception, at least not on her part.

This time, he would not be so naive. He refused to take any chances, not with his emotions and not with Rainee's welfare. "Locking them up," as Marina had so aptly put it, might not be such a bad idea for both his heart and his daughter.

"Marinuska, how do you know that uncouth cowboy?" The way Sergei spat out the words, he made it sound like anything but a manly pursuit.

Marina had tried to extract herself from his interrogation with little success. She tried even harder to give no credence to what he had said about Hunter. However, she had to admit he had looked ill-kempt in his peasant attire. And that gun he had been wearing, strapped right to his hip—it had been so big and . . . uncivilized. Was that how cattle barons dressed and acted in the American West? She shuddered.

However, she did not wish to discuss the matter any further with Sergei. To her exasperation, he followed her up the stairs, down the hallway, and even into her room, repeating his question over and over. How did she know him? As much as she wished to avoid answering him, she knew if she didn't reply, he would never go away.

"What does it matter, Sergei?" she asked, trying to shove him toward the door. "I met him very briefly in Russia."

"In Russia?" Planting his feet, he refused to budge. His thick blond brows furrowed, then he shot her a look of accusation. "The American. The one with whom Dmitri negotiated," he commented in recognition. He did not seem pleased. "You have kept in touch with him all of this time?"

Unless she was mistaken, she detected a touch of resentment in his voice. He was beginning to sound more like a guardian than a friend.

"No, Sergei. I haven't kept in touch with him."

"But you knew he was here," he persisted.

"No. I am as surprised to see him as you are."

She lied, barefaced, without a twinge of scruples, and made no attempt to take it back. She had a right to her privacy and a need to terminate his endless questioning.

"Stay away from him, Marinuska," her dance partner warned, but he allowed her to show him out. "He is trouble."

"I'll try," she promised.

Once she closed the door, she sighed and leaned against it for support.

"Oh, Sergei," she whispered. "You have no idea how right you are."

Trouble or not, she had Hunter Kincaid in her blood. It would take more than a promise to expel him.

"Rainee, get down here." Hunter bellowed from the bottom of the stairs, demanding his daughter's presence. Fear not anger put a razor's edge to his voice.

"Daddy, what is it?" Dressed in peacock-blue and looking much too saucy, she tripped down the steps, her hand gliding easily along the polished railing.

By God, when had his little girl become such a beautiful woman? He felt even more distressed.

Since the night she had come home with the flier, they had not spoken of his angry reaction. There had been no time for discussion. They had hardly seen each other in the last few days.

Reacting to his stern words and rigid stance, Rainee paused on the next-to-last step, her hand gripping the banister until her knuckles bleached white.

"Daddy, what is it?" she repeated, her eyes wide and darting, just as her mother's had been whenever he had confronted her.

"We need to talk, Rainee. Now." Without giving her the chance to dispute him, he whipped about and made his way to the spacious main room of the ranch house.

He pointed to a chair. The girl settled into it, her face uplifted, anxious concern marring her pretty features—so like her mother's—so damned much like her mother's it made his heart squeeze with a pain he'd thought himself incapable of ever feeling again.

"Rainee, I don't want you going to town for the next two days."

"But, Daddy," she protested instantly, springing to her feet.

"No buts, Rainee. You are not to go into Sweetwater for any reason unless I tell you differently."

He saw the hurt leap into her water-blue eyes only to be quickly replaced with defiance. Just like Della.

Restricting her might be the wrong approach. No, damn it, he was doing the right thing. This was an impossible situation.

"Rainee, if I discover you've disobeyed me, I swear to God I'll drag you home kicking and screaming if I have to."

That was exactly the vow he had made to himself when he had gone looking for Della.

Why in all of His infinite wisdom did God feel the need to put him through this nightmare again?

"The stage, madam. It must be widened." Sergei spoke in an authoritative tone of voice.

"Widen it, Mr. Bozzacchi? Impossible on such short notice. You will have to modify your dance steps." In spite of the mayor's wife's lack of sophistication and shorter stature, the woman confronted the temperamental dancer with the pluck of a brooding hen.

"Impossible on such short notice." He echoed her uncompromising sentiments.

Marina stood in the doorway of the converted dining room, watching. With the first performance only hours away, nothing and no one, it seemed, was prepared for it.

Not even herself. After the terrible confrontation with Hunter last night, nothing really mattered anymore. This morning, when Sergei had offered, she had been more than glad to let him take charge of making the final arrangements.

But as she observed their interaction, it became more and more apparent Sergei lacked the necessary negotiation skills. If she allowed him to continue, the mayor's wife might even cancel the performances and demand back the guarantee money the town had paid Jack Yancy. That was a problem she didn't need, one that could lead to other cancellations if word got out. So whether or not she cared about these particular performances, she had to weigh the future of the entire troupe against her personal feelings.

Clearing her throat, she stepped forward, determined to save the situation before it was too late.

"Sergei, Mrs. Shackelford, please," she implored, closing the door behind her to avoid an unwanted audience.

The crowd had yet to return, thank goodness, but the morning was still young. A ragtag boy, no doubt an employee of the hotel, shuffled unenthusiastically about the room setting up chairs in uneven rows. Considering him no threat, Marina skirted his progress and stepped upon the makeshift stage.

"It *is* a bit small," she said to appease Sergei, "but we can cut the *jeté* to three steps instead of four."

"But, Marinuska," her dance partner protested.

"I'm glad you're in agreement, Sergei." She focused her attention on the townswoman before he could contradict her. "As for you, Mrs. Shackelford . . ." She smiled brightly, much more brightly than she felt ". . . I look forward to seeing you at the performance tonight."

"But of course," the woman gushed. "Everyone who is anyone, will be here," she assured her. "I cannot tell you how pleased we all are to have you here."

Not all of you, Marina thought but kept it to herself. However, according to Mrs. Shackelford, Hunter might well be in the audience tonight—whether he wanted to attend or not.

Marina reminded herself of her goal to make him regret his cold, cruel reception. Yes, she would give the performance of her life in that backwater American town, one Hunter Kincaid would never forget for as long as he lived.

In the dimness of the makeshift auditorium, the music started. The piano tinkled softly, soulfully accompanied by a lone violin. The two instruments comprised the ballet troupe's entire orchestra. Nonetheless, the crowd, captivated, grew quiet. The overture of *Le Papillon,* the story of a beautiful girl turned into a butterfly by a sorceress and rescued by a prince, built to a crescendo, the signal for the stage lights to come on.

Dressed as the wicked, old sorceress, Fanny held center stage, primping at an imaginary mirror. The audience's silence indicated their immediate fascination with the ugly, animated character the beautiful girl played so well. That was a good sign.

Marina relaxed, releasing the stale air she had held deep in her lungs for so long that her heart thundered in protest. Stage fright, Fanny labeled such nervousness. That was ridiculous, of course. What she felt had nothing to do with being afraid of the stage and everything to do with concern for the viewers' reactions. One viewer and one reaction.

The music played her introduction. In flowing gauze, Marina moved automatically onto the stage, as light as the butterfly-girl she portrayed. She paused in arabesque, arms folded to her heart, head lowered, waiting for the cue to begin her solo.

On the first note, the spotlight burst upon her statuesque figure, a pose she had perfected in front of mirrors. Opening like a blossom to the rays of the sun, she began her first steps, dancing on the tips of her toes. Quickly enough, she fell under the spell of the sensuous rhythm and the movement of the choreography.

Deep in concentration, she nonetheless heard the audience gasp and smiled to herself, interpreting their initial reaction as delight and approval.

At first the whispers were mere murmurings, nothing to be alarmed about and yet . . . Ears cocked, she danced on, evading the pursuing sorceress with agile leaps and bounds that normally elicited applause. Not a single pair of hands offered encouragement. She tried to suppress her growing concern, even when the buzz of voices continued, growing louder and pervasive. When she danced close to the edge of the stage, she could have sworn someone tried to touch her. But of course, that was impossible. No one of manners would take such improper liberties.

But there was no mistaking the mood of the audience when Sergei joined her on the stage dressed as the prince in a traditional billowing shirt and tights. Someone started laughing.

What was the matter with these people? For the first time in her professional life, Marina paused center stage. She turned, fists on hips, to face the obvious ridicule. The stage lights blinded her. The room, filled with nothing but darkness, came alive with the restless sounds of shuffling feet and chairs scraping against the wooden floor—and unsettled voices.

"Marina, what do you think you are doing?" Sergei hissed in her ear. Taking her hand, he squeezed her fingers so hard she flinched. His jarring actions forced her to remember who she was and that, no matter what, the performance must go on.

As they went through the motions of the first in a series of *fouettés pirouettes*—and quite well, she thought, under the circumstances—she managed to sneak a quick glance out over the audience while dangerously teetering on the very edge of the too-small stage. What little she could see of the first few rows of spectators confirmed that they were like no audience she had ever performed for before. Nothing like the patrons in New York or St. Louis or even Cheyenne.

These people—uncouthly dressed—looked identical to the unruly rabble who had crowded in the doorway to watch the troupe practice the previous day. Even in a quick glance she could have sworn one man actually spit on the floor beside his chair.

What kind of place did Hunter Kincaid live in? Were these peasants truly his friends and neighbors? As she performed the final steps of the *pas de deux,* she recalled with growing alarm just how unkempt Hunter himself had been, how crude he had acted.

What had ever made her think she should come to Sweetwater? What had she hoped to find? A miracle? Perhaps she had come seeking something much more impractical. As laughable as it was, she had hoped to find the happy-ever-after conclusion to the fairy princess's story.

Somehow, she got through the rest of the performance. The splattering of applause they received was hesitant and for the most part unenthusiastic.

Never again. She made a mental note. She dipped a ballerina curtsy, the tips of her fingers resting lightly in Sergei's, who bowed alongside of her. She must make sure that Jack Yancy never again booked them in such an unreceptive, uncultured place. But then, the promoter had tried to warn her it would be a mistake and she had refused to listen.

At least if Hunter Kincaid were in that audience, she tried to assure herself, the degradation that she had been forced to suffer would not have been in vain. For in truth, this night's performance was no doubt the most difficult she had ever given in her entire dancing career.

Nine

Hot, dusty, and hungry, Hunter slid out of his saddle and tossed the reins over the pinto's head. Just as bone-tired, his cattle dog, Rowdy, flopped on the ground near the water trough, his tongue lolling to one side. Leading his horse, Hunter walked toward the corral gate. It had been a long day of dogging stubborn strays, then a longer ride back in the darkness to the main house.

"I'll see to 'im, Mr. Kincaid." Emerging from the bunkhouse, Paco caught up to him, matching his saddle-weary strides.

"That's fine, son. See to it he gets plenty of oats. He deserves it," Hunter ordered, patting the mustang on the neck before gratefully turning the loyal beast over to the young cowhand to be cooled off, fed, then turned out with the rest of the milling horses.

Now to see to himself and Rowdy, but more important to make sure Rainee had obeyed his orders. Marina gave her first performance that night. In fact, it was probably already in progress. All day he had worried about his daughter and had meant to get home in plenty of time to head her off if she attempted to sneak into town. Once again the pressing demands of the ranch had foiled his plans.

"Wait a minute, Paco," he called out.

The kid paused.

"Have you seen Miss Rainee tonight?"

"Yes, sir. Earlier. Just before supper. She was hanging out around the corrals."

"She didn't leave, did she?" Hunter asked, alarmed.

"No, sir. Not that I saw."

"Thanks, son," he said, whistling softly and slapping his leather gloves against his dirty chaps. "Come on, Rowdy."

The dog rose and padded behind him obediently.

Entering the back door, Hunter slung his hat and gun belt on the rack in the mud room. Out of the habit he had developed when Della was still with them, he shook himself just like the dusty trail dog did before proceeding further into the house.

In the kitchen he paused long enough to accept the cloth-covered plate from his housekeeper, Sierra, Paco's Indian mother. She placed a bowl of scraps on the floor for Rowdy. The dog instantly began to wolf down his dinner.

"Rainee's already eaten?" he asked, uncovering a slice of fried ham with biscuits and gravy that smelled heavenly. His empty stomach growled in anticipation of the feast.

"Several hours ago, Mr. Kincaid. Then she went up to bed. She said she was tired."

"Good," he mumbled and, without bothering to take a seat, devoured his dinner.

Once he had finished, he deposited the dishes on the hutch and made his way wearily up the stairs. Passing Rainee's room, he paused, lifted his hand, and knocked to make sure she was really there.

"Rainee, honey?" He frowned when he got no answer.

Opening the door, he peeked inside. In the darkness, he saw the outline of a form under the quilt. Satisfied she was safely tucked in for the night, protected at least for the moment, Hunter continued down the hallway to his own room.

Although exhausted, he couldn't stop thinking about the ballet performance going on at the hotel even as he stripped off his sweaty clothes and prepared to go to bed. Marina. Did she truly dance as provocatively as he remembered? If so, what had been the town's reaction? He doubted any of them, Marina included, would get what they expected.

That thought made him smile. Whatever happened, they all would get what they deserved, and he refused to feel responsible. Had he not warned them, one and all? Yet no one had bothered to listen to him.

None of that really mattered as long as he kept Rainee out of the middle of it. As for his own foolish, rebellious heart . . . it was only for a few days. Surely he could manage to keep it under thumb as well.

"Excuse me, Your Highness. May I speak with you, please?"

Normally after a performance Marina refused such inquiries. After tonight's disaster she felt even more disinclined, but something about the young woman standing before her, dressed in a refreshing stylishness, looked hauntingly familiar. She felt drawn to her.

"I suppose I could give you a few moments," she said warily.

"Oh, thank you," the girl effused.

Marina realized then she *was* merely a girl, fifteen, maybe sixteen at the most.

"I just wanted to meet you. I've always wanted to be able to dance as you do. They don't appreciate you." The girl wrinkled her pert nose and glared at the other people rushing to get out of the hotel and ready for gossip. "But I do. No matter what they may be saying."

"And what are they saying, Miss—"

"Kincaid. Rainee Kincaid," the girl offered without hesitation.

Marina froze. Had she heard the girl's last name correctly? If so, what was her relationship to Hunter? Surely she was much too young to be his wife.

"They don't understand ballet," Rainee explained. Her face flushed as she glanced over Marina's shoulder. "I find it wonderful and very . . . exciting to watch," she murmured, speaking to someone standing behind Marina.

Marina turned, knowing whom she would find there.

"Sergei," she said by way of an introduction. "An admirer, I believe. Miss Rainee Kincaid. It is 'Miss,' isn't it?" she fished.

"Oh, yes." Rainee's adoring gaze never left the Russian dancer's handsome face. She flexed her knees awkwardly. "Mr. Bozzacchi, I am honored to meet you. I live just outside of town," she rushed on. "My father owns one of the largest cattle ranches in the territory."

"Indeed. I assure you, Miss Kincaid, the pleasure is all mine."

Rainee blushed an even brighter shade of red when he lifted her hand and pressed his lips to her knuckles with such high drama that Marina shot him a warning look. Sergei was always such a rapscallion with the ladies, with the pretty ones—and more often with the rich ones. But this one was much too young. Besides, she was Hunter's daughter; and after their confrontation yesterday, the last thing she needed was for him to accuse her of trying to abscond with the child.

Hunter's daughter. She should have seen the resemblance right away. The girl looked just like her father, especially in the proud tilt to her chiseled chin. Curious. She had not even known he had a child, much less one so old. Now more than yesterday, his unwarranted accusations stung. Had it been his own child who had prompted his concern?

"We really must be going now, Miss Kincaid." The resentment she harbored for the father found its way into her voice.

"Of course. You must be exhausted. How thoughtless of me." However, the pain Marina felt was reflected in the girl's unguarded eyes as they flickered over her. "I shouldn't have bothered you." Rainee turned away, rejected.

"Not at all, Rainee." Marina caught the girl's arm, unwilling to punish the innocent child for her father's foolish misconceptions. "Perhaps, if you come by tomorrow morning, you could watch the practice. I might even have the chance to show you the basic positions, enough to get you started."

"You would do that for me?" the girl asked in wide-eyed appreciation.

Marina hesitated for a moment, mulling over the things Hunter had said to her. He was wrong. What harm could come from showing the child a thing or two about ballet?

"It's nothing really," she said. "Be here by nine. I will leave instructions at the front desk that you are allowed to come in."

She watched the starry-eyed girl waltz away in a visionary's cloud of dreams.

"Marinuska, why did you do that?" Sergei demanded once they were alone. "Because she is Hunter Kincaid's daughter and you want to get even?"

"No," she defended. Her generous actions, and they had been generous, had had nothing to do with Hunter. She had seen something in the girl, a spark that had reminded her of herself. She knew how it felt to want something so badly and fear never to achieve it.

Besides, it was all in innocence, a few moments taken to show the girl the basic steps and that would be the end of it. No harm done.

Hunter was wrong. A girl deserved the chance to explore her hopes and dreams—even if someone like him eventually came along to crush them.

* * *

"Rainee, where are you going so early this morning?" Hunter looked up from his coveted, week-old copy of the Cheyenne newspaper and pinned his daughter with a pointed stare as she tried to sneak past the dining room.

The girl jerked to a halt.

"Going? Why nowhere, Daddy." Framed in the doorway she gave him an innocent look reminiscent of Della at her guiltiest.

"Then you have plenty of time to join me for breakfast." Shaking out the wrinkled paper, he returned to his reading.

Wordlessly, she slid into the chair nearest to the exit and farthest from him.

"Eggs?"

"What?" She jumped in her seat at his monosyllabic inquiry.

"I asked if you would like some eggs," he repeated, folding back the edge of the paper to shove a platter of egg and sausage her way.

"No. No. I'm really not that hungry." She squirmed with impatience, her eyes looking very tired for someone who had gone to bed so early the night before, darting now and then toward the door. Did it offer escape?

"Didn't you sleep well last night?" he inquired.

"I slept just fine," she defended.

Yes, indeed, Rainee was up to something. But what? He eyed her cautiously over the top of his newspaper.

Again she smiled, so innocuously it made him grit his teeth with worry. Whatever it was, he prayed it had nothing to do with Marina.

How could it? he assured himself. The girl had had no opportunity to pursue that vice. Still, he was determined to take every precaution.

"Honey, why don't you get dressed and come riding with me today?" he suggested. Rarely did he offer her the opportunity to accompany him on the range. He didn't consider it a ladylike pursuit, but today it was his ace in the hole. Under the circumstances he didn't hesitate to press his advantage, knowing full well she always jumped at the chance to ride out among the cowboys and make them all vie for her attention. Right now that seemed a whole lot safer than leaving her, unattended, to her own devices.

To his surprise, a look of indecision crossed her pretty face, but only momentarily.

"Do you mean it, Daddy?"

"Of course, I do."

Rising from the table, she darted off.

"Wait, Rainee, you didn't eat anything," he called after her when he saw her plate still clean.

But she was already gone.

It was only one day, he reminded himself. If nothing worse happened to them than forgetting to eat, he would feel relieved. Tomorrow it would be behind them both.

When Rainee didn't show up that morning, Marina experienced a spurt of disappointment, but she didn't allow her feelings to show. Already enough raw emotion crisped the air to melt butter or the strongest constitution.

Practice went as usual, without a single misstep, without disturbance. But then she had made a point to see that the rabble didn't intrude upon them.

By curtain time she had herself, as well as the rest of the nervous troupe, convinced that the night before had been only a fluke. The audience tonight would be different, she said with assurance. Finally, even temperamental Sergei agreed to go on with the show.

She had no idea just how right her intuition was until the bombardment of rude catcalls, whistles, and unidentified objects thrown upon the stage gave them no choice except to halt the performance before completing the first act. Immediately, almost as one, the few women in the audience quickly stood and forced their protesting escorts to take them to safety, callously abandoning those on stage to the rowdies determined to be disruptive.

"Stop. All of you," she cried, angered by the desertion of the very people who had invited them to come there in the first place. In response, an object whizzed past her. Realizing it was an empty whiskey bottle, she turned to warn those behind her. To her horror, the well-aimed missile struck Sergei on the knee.

Clutching his injured joint, the *danseur* stumbled backward, knocking down part of the portable, irreplaceable scenery. As valiantly as Marina tried, she was powerless to stop the disaster.

There was to be no stopping anything except for the music, which ended abruptly when an ill-kempt hooligan jerked poor John off of his stool, took his place, and began pumping out an ear-splitting, teeth-grinding rendition of a barroom ditty.

"Yahoo." Another man shouted, doing a jig in a row of chairs." Hey, girlee," he called out. "How about flipping up them skirts and showing us some more leg?" The jig dancer fell from his perch to the delighted howls of his comrades.

"This is the best damn thing to happen to this town," cried another wheeling cowboy, "since they closed up all the saloons."

How could this be happening? How?

Before Marina could answer her own earnest plea, a whoop to put a raiding Cossack to shame rang out. It was as if someone had opened a floodgate on a steppe.

From all sides they poured onto the stage, as motley a group of marauders as any outlaws she had ever envisioned. Worse than wild Indians. Spurs jingled. A fight broke out right next to her, and she had to scoot sideways to keep from being hit.

A man grabbed her, led her in a rib-crushing, toe-stomping gyration. All around her, Sweetwater locals invaded the *corps de ballet*. Someone screamed. Thinking Fanny was in trouble, she struggled to escape the arms of her torturer. Finally succeeding, she turned to comfort her friend, to protect her with her own body if she must, only to discover that the repeated sounds had issued from her own raw throat. To her relief she saw Fanny on the floor, huddled in a corner with John, both safe, at least for the moment.

Quickly enough she discovered it wasn't just the women the mob of ill-kept cowboys came after. Not at all.

"Nancy boy," one of them shouted, pointing at Sergei, still trapped in the scenery rubble. "We don't want to see his ugly legs anymore, do we boys? Hell, we're red-blooded men. Let's git 'em."

Almost as one, they converged on her hapless dance partner.

"Sergei," she screamed, fearing the unstoppable rabble would tear him from limb to limb right before her unbelieving eyes.

What was she to do? How was she ever going to save him short of throwing herself bodily in the middle of it all?

The answering gunfire cut through the confusion like a beacon through a fog.

Fearful of what would happen next, that they might all be shot dead, Marina whirled to confront the worst possible disaster. All of the horrible things she had been warned to expect in the wild West, showdowns and gun battles, ran rampant through her mind.

Except for the stage, the room remained in pitch black, but the figure framed in the open doorway surrounded with the light from the lobby behind was as familiar as her own. Feet braced wide apart, he held a smoking gun above his head.

"Hunter," she whispered, an immediate sense of relief rushing through her. He had saved her, saved them all.

He spoke with the voice of authority.

"You've done enough damage for one night, boys. Now go home."

"Aw, Mr. Kincaid, no harm meant. We was just havin' a little Saturday night fun," insisted the man who had terrorized her by dragging her around the stage.

"That's all right, Jake. Now apologize to the lady."

His head ducked in submission, Jake turned to face her.

Instinctively, Marina backed away, fearing he might try to grab her again.

"Sorry, ma'am. Didn't mean to upset you none. You was right fine entertainment." He found his hat on the floor, crammed it on his head, and grinned at her as if all were forgiven. "Maybe we can do it again sometime."

Again? Did that gross caricature of a man really think she would forgive him and his cronies for wrecking her performance? And what of Sergei? What if his knee had been seriously injured? He could be crippled for life.

"I think not," she replied.

The man actually looked deflated, as if she were the one being unreasonable. In silence he climbed down from the stage and followed the rest of the subdued band of hooligans out of the room.

To her surprise, Hunter said nothing more to them, didn't even try to stop them as they shouldered their way past him.

"Aren't you going to have them arrested or something?" Marina demanded.

"What for?" Hunter asked. With a show of fancy fingerwork, he slipped his gun back into the holster slung low across his hip.

"For assault, malicious damage." The list could go on and on. "If we were in Russia . . ."

"Let me remind you, you aren't in Russia. You're in Sweetwater, Wyoming, now. In case you haven't noticed, things are done differently here. There are no tsars or secret police at Your Highness's beck and call. Here we take care of ourselves in our own way." He glanced around. "From what I can see, no real harm was done. But lucky for you, darlin', I got here in plenty of time."

"Plenty of time?" Her mouth flopped open. "We could have been maimed, or even killed."

"I think not," he mocked her earlier words. Then he chuckled as if he found her accusations completely preposterous. "To suffer a little humiliation was about the worst of it." He stepped forward and offered her a hand in assistance.

She stared at that hand, rough and calloused, the very hand to draw a gun and shoot it right there in the building with little regard for the damage that might have been done. Ignoring it as well as the man to whom it was attached, she whirled and made her way to Sergei, who still sat on the stage floor clutching his knee and rocking.

"Let me see," she offered with the patience she would use with an injured child.

"What if I can't use my leg ever again, Marina?" Sergei lamented. "What am I going to do?"

"Please," she repeated, "let me see," until he finally removed his hands and let her exam his knee. Even though his blood-stained tights had been ripped beyond repair, the wound itself wasn't that bad, not much more than a scratch that would heal in a few days.

"You don't need to worry about permanent damage," she assured him. "Can you walk?"

Sergei made a dramatic show of gaining his feet. At her prodding, the musicians helped him from the stage and aided his limping progress to the exit. When forced to go past Hunter, he issued a silent challenge, one that might have been formidable if she hadn't taken into account for whom it was intended.

But Hunter didn't find Sergei's dramatics amusing. His returned hostility made her shiver with dread.

"Aren't you coming, Marinuska?" Sergei demanded, breaking eye contact in the wake of Hunter's cold look.

"Right behind you, Sergei," she assured him, fearful of taking her eyes off Hunter, even for a moment.

Allowing all the other performers to precede her, including Fanny who looked as shook up as she felt, Marina descended from the stage, making her way across the room with as much dignity as she could. Hunter allowed them each in turn to pass him. All except Marina. He grabbed her by the arm when she tried to brush past.

"Marina, are you going to be all right?" Fanny asked, darting a concerned look first at Hunter and then at her as if unsure whether to leave them alone.

"I'll be fine, Fanny," she assured the other woman even though she wasn't that certain. After all, this was Hunter Kincaid.

"I tried to warn you, Marina," he said the moment they were alone. His eyes, the color of blue ice, raked her just as they had Sergei. "You made a mistake coming here."

"You're the one who made a mistake. A gun is not the answer to everything. What you did is unconscionable."

"What I did is rescue you."

Cold look or not, the feel of his fingers crushing her flesh sent fire coursing through her veins. Unwanted fire. Unwarranted fire. He didn't deserve to be the only man to ever make her feel so flushed and out of control. In utter frustration she tried to pry herself loose.

"Perhaps what I neglected to do, Your Highness, is to point

out you aren't ready for Sweetwater." In spite of her struggle, or perhaps because of it, he grasped her that much harder.

"Let go of me." She clawed at him.

"If that's what you really want." His mouth lifting in a cynical smile, he released her so suddenly and unexpectedly she stumbled backward.

The stampede of emotions that rushed through her—relief, disappointment, disbelief—trampled the last shreds of her composure.

"I'm glad we're leaving on tomorrow's train," she cried, rubbing her arm. It still stung from his rough treatment. "In fact, I truly regret ever coming here in the first place, Hunter Kincaid." Her statement erupted as a sob although she tried hard to prevent it. "This is a mean town with nothing but uncouth rabble-rousers for citizens. And you, sir," she accused, her voice breaking on the strength of her convictions, "you are no better than the rest of them."

"Whatever made me doubt even for a moment that you might feel that way, Marina? I shouldn't have expected more from a woman like you." He smiled, a bitter driven expression that ripped through her like a knife. "I'm just glad to have heard you admit it before I made a bigger fool of myself." He touched the brim of his hat, a gesture of farewell. Then he spun on his heels, heading for the door.

If he walked away then it was over, over before the love she had dreamed of had truly had a chance to begin. If he left, she would get on the train headed west in the morning never to return, never to know what it was that had divided them. She didn't want that to happen.

"Hunter, wait," she implored, wanting to run after him but unable to take that all-important first step.

From a safe distance he faced her, his expression hard and unreadable. "I'm sorry I didn't get the chance to see you dance again."

Just when she thought he would say something more to her, would open his heart and his arms to her, he turned away and disappeared through the doorway.

The storm of tears she expected never came. They lodged in her throat, the stillness almost more than she could bear. With a crash as frightening as the loudest thunder, her heart broke into a million pieces.

As soon as she felt certain no one would see her, she fled for the stairs and the comfort she knew she would find in the music box beside her bed.

Hunter reached the livery stable, two buildings down and across the street from the hotel, never quite certain how he had made it there. But by the time that he did, he had managed to tuck his pain and disappointment so deep inside of himself they would never see the light of day again.

Marina had been no better than Della except in one respect. At least she had been honest with him from the beginning.

"I'll have your horse saddled and ready for ya in just a few minutes, Mr. Kincaid."

"Thanks, Virgil. I'm in no rush."

In truth he was in a great big hurry to get as far away from the Addison Hotel as he possibly could before his heart managed to change his mind and point his errant feet in the wrong direction.

Even now his mind played tricks on him. He could hear the music now, the soulful melody that had drawn him to her long ago in Russia. When he had seen her dancing, all alone . . .

"Right purdy music, ain't it, Mr. Kincaid?"

"What?"

"That music." The smithy pointed. "Comin' from the hotel

for the last two nights. Them Russies, they're strange people. Ain't never heard nothin' like that music before."

Hunter stopped to listen. His gaze traveled from window to window of the hotel seeking the source—the open window, third from the left and Marina's music box.

"Virgil, did you know that the man who wrote that music was deaf. His name was Beethoven." He knew now what he hadn't known then because he had made a point of finding out.

"Bay Tovan. Deaf, was he? You gotta be wrong, Mr. Kincaid, beggin' your pardon. Cain't hardly understand how he could make music he couldn't hear. It would be like me havin' no eyes to see what I was doin'. Cain't make a horseshoe fit iffen you cain't see it."

A man who made music he couldn't hear. Hunter smiled wistfully. It was hard to believe, like a cowboy with no feel for a horse trying to head off stampeding cattle. Or a preacher without faith telling others about God. But the comparison that came closest to how he felt was that of a bitter man with a shriveled-up heart trying to find love.

Claiming the reins to his mustang, Hunter mounted up and rode out of town, determined not to return until Marina Nicolaiev had departed.

Ten

Early the next morning found a sleep-deprived Marina and her equally exhausted troupe of dancers and musicians—bags, wardrobe cases, and scenery boxes—waiting at the train depot. Packed and ready to go only because she had badgered them into it, the grumbling group arrived long before the ticket clerk made his morning appearance. By the time the man presented himself for work, Marina's patience had worn as thin as her nerves.

"Good morning," she offered, trying to sound cheerful as she followed him through the train station.

The man said nothing in return, merely nodded.

In silence she watched him insert his key into the lock on the door to the wire-cage booth from which he conducted all railroad business. After a moment of scrutiny, she could have sworn he was the same man she had seen spit on the floor at the disastrous performance two nights before.

"Now, ma'am. What can I do for you?" he asked, taking in the milling group as if he didn't know who they were. But he had been at the first performance. She remembered him clearly. Had he attended the second as well and been one of the ruffians to storm the stage?

"I'm here to pick up a packet of tickets for Marina Nicolaiev. The *Princess* Marina Nicolaiev," she stressed as a reminder even though she believed it unnecessary.

"Nick-o-la-iff," he repeated, distorting her last name with

his awful American twang. He absentmindedly sorted through a stack of papers, then turned to her empty-handed. "Could you spell that name please?"

"Nicolaiev." She corrected his pronunciation, unable to hide the condescension in her voice as she slowly said each letter.

"Nick-o-la-iff," he said again as if she had not bothered to speak. "Nope. Sorry. Nothin' here for that name."

"Check again. Perhaps you overlooked something. There have to be tickets purchased in my name for fourteen," she insisted, spreading out her arm to indicate the troupe. Then leaning forward on tiptoe, she tried to see beyond the clerk to his stack of disorganized papers. "I'm looking for a rather large packet from a Mr. Jack Yancy."

"Like I done told you already, miss," the clerk stated without bothering to search again, "there's nothin' here for ya."

Marina was stunned. In the past, the promoter had always seen to it that tickets to their next destination, along with instructions as to whom to contact and where to go, were waiting for them at the train station. True, the packet sometimes arrived at the very last moment, but the tickets were always waiting for them on the day of their departure. Only then did she learn the name of the town in which they would give their next performances. By the same token, when they reached each destination, Yancy would have made the necessary arrangements ahead of time to pay for the troupe's hotel expenses for the designated number of days they stayed. He always remained several steps ahead of them, promoting the troupe and scheduling arrangements. Not once had Yancy failed to come through like clockwork. Until now.

What if the tickets were lost? Worse yet, what if he had

never sent them? What if he had abandoned them here in the middle of nowhere?

Such a notion was ridiculous, of course. Jack Yancy would never have abandoned them. Not unless word had already leaked out about the disastrous performances in Sweetwater. What if he were unable to schedule more? Might he then consider himself no longer obligated to fulfill a contract she had broken?

She had never really been comfortable with the way Jack Yancy had handled the business affairs, but the fast-talking promoter had insisted it was the manner in which things were done in America. Arrangements were best kept flexible in order to take advantage of opportunities as they presented themselves. When she had insisted on personally being responsible for the finances, again he had shaken his head. For her, a woman, to carry a purse full of money across the American West would have been asking for someone to rob them. Finally, she had agreed to carry only enough for unforeseen incidentals along the way.

Fool that she had been, she had willingly put herself at a disadvantage in order to get to Sweetwater and Hunter Kincaid. Look at the mess her trust in men had gotten her into.

Panicking, she dug into her purse, scrambling to come up with a ready solution. If she had enough money to at least pay for tickets out of Sweetwater . . . to anywhere. At the moment she didn't care where as long as the name Hunter Kincaid meant nothing.

"How much for fourteen tickets to the next stop after this one?" she asked, carefully counting her meager funds. So pitifully little.

"Ten dollars apiece," the clerk informed her.

"That much just to get to the very next town?" she protested, knowing full well that the price of a straight-through ticket from St. Louis all the way to San Francisco was only two hundred. Ten dollars or two hundred, it was still more than she could afford. Her heart skipped several beats in hopeless defeat.

Whatever was she going to do?

She refused to yield to panic. Surely the tickets from Yancy would arrive any minute. Even as the thought crossed her mind, she heard the whistle of an approaching train from the west. Of course, the anticipated packet would be on board and in her hands in moments. Her worry would have been all for nothing. It had to be. Otherwise . . .

"Marinuska, is something wrong?" From his superior height, Sergei stared down at her, frowning. Earlier, he had been the biggest complainer and the last one packed when she had rushed the sleepy troupe to the station.

"It's nothing, Sergei. Just a little delay," she assured him, managing to hide her own rising fear.

"Well, it had better not be for too long," he grumbled, readily showing his temperamental annoyance. "I don't want to stay in this town a minute longer than we have to."

Although she didn't say it aloud, Marina, too, fervently prayed the unbearable waiting to escape would be over quickly and painlessly.

Regrets. Hunter had more of them than he cared to admit, especially when it came to women.

"Step it up there, son," he murmured, setting spur to horseflesh. At his command, the pinto's muscles bunched and leapt forward beneath him. Too bad a man couldn't run his personal life like a cattle ranch. With a knowing touch to the reins, he positioned his horse between a particularly determined steer and freedom, watching calmly with satisfaction when the uncooperative animal, snorting in protest, veered back toward the herd, Rowdy nipping at his heels.

Too bad a man had to have feelings at all. Emotional decisions involved risks. Invariably, whenever he allowed his to take over, he always made the wrong choices.

As a prime example, just look at what had happened last night at the hotel. Only a fool or the mayor's wife and her Ladies' Committee would have scheduled such a performance on a Saturday night. Every randy cowboy within twenty-five miles had shown up. Letting his emotions get the best of his logic, he had ridden to the rescue and, regardless of what he'd said to Marina, he had put a stop to what could have turned into a real disaster. Had she shown the least bit of gratitude? Not at all. Instead, she had found fault with his methods and even more fault with him. But had he really expected anything different from her?

Settling back in his saddle and giving the surefooted mustang his head to pick his own comfortable pace, Hunter glanced up at the roiling sky and the gathering clouds. It could mean rain, or maybe not. Lifting his Stetson, he scraped his hair off his face, then squared the hat on his head with a determined tilt.

Too bad women were like the weather, always taking a turn for the worst when a man least wanted them to.

"Hell, who needs them?" he grumbled under his breath.

"I'm sorry, Mr. Kincaid, what was that?"

"Nothing, Paco. Absolutely nothing." He shot a frustrated look at the young cowboy who had ridden beside him in respectful silence.

"It's that woman, the pretty dancer, ain't it, sir?" The kid, much too serious for one so young, frowned. "I know how it is to be distracted by a woman."

"How could you possibly know, boy? You're still wet behind the ears. Besides, I don't care to talk about it." Applying his spurs, he rode on ahead.

"I'm not a kid, Mr. Kincaid, and I can tell you this much:

Avoiding a problem doesn't make it go away." The boy's words of wisdom, shouted to be heard over the thunder of hooves, trailed him like an unrelenting horde of disturbed hornets.

Paco didn't know what he was talking about. Ignore anything long enough, especially a woman, and she went away. Della had taught him that much. Marina would be no different. He kept telling himself her imminent departure was the best thing that could possibly happen.

If that were so, why did he have so much difficulty convincing himself?

By late that afternoon Marina had come to grips with the realization that the tickets were not coming. For whatever reason, Jack Yancy had abandoned them, leaving them ill-prepared to face the dangers of the wild, uncivilized American West. She fully understood now what people had tried to tell her all along.

Of all places! Marina groaned inwardly. *Why did it have to be Sweetwater, Wyoming?* Had the promoter picked that particular town on purpose because she had shown such desire to get there in the first place? No amount of wondering would solve that mystery.

"What are we going to do, Marina?"

Three people had asked her that same question in the last five minutes. How unfortunate for Fanny that she chose that moment to make her inquiry.

"How am I supposed to know?" Marina snapped in anger, flailing her arms, then instantly regretting that she had taken out her frustrations on her one true friend. The truth was the responsibility did belong to her. After all, it had been her idea to blithely dance her way into the American West against all advice, presumably into Hunter Kincaid's loving arms.

What a fool she had been to think he would want her, would be willing to wait for her to complete her tour and return to him. "I'm sorry, Fanny. Truly I am." Her shoulders sank with defeat.

"It's all right, honey." Fanny's pixie-sized hand gripped her elbow and guided her toward a bench. "Don't blame yourself. You're just hungry like the rest of us."

Hungry? Marina looked up, acknowledging the gnawing hollowness in the pit of her stomach. Thirteen trusting faces stared back at her expectantly, waiting for her to do what she always did—see to their immediate needs. But hunger was the least of their problems. The little bit of money she had on her would last them maybe a day or two.

How were they going to survive then? What would they eat when there was no money to pay for food? Where would they stay when their funds ran out all too soon?

The answer lay out there somewhere. At the moment, however, exhaustion and hunger blinded her ability to recognize it. Regardless, she could no longer see a point to remaining in the train station. They were traveling nowhere, at least not today.

"Come along, everybody," Marina instructed, insisting everyone gather up their bags and boxes and follow her. "We're going back to the hotel for the night."

Giving the troupe the opportunity to collect themselves, she approached the ticket clerk one last time.

"If the packet of tickets should arrive, would you please send them over to me at the hotel?"

"I'll be glad to—if they arrive," the agent qualified with no conviction in his voice.

Feeling like a Russian goosegirl, Marina herded her noisy, flapping flock out of the depot, across the street, and down the block past the general store and the livery stable. No one in the group questioned her decision, even if they grumbled about the execution. No one that is except herself.

The last place in the world she wanted to be was Sweetwater, Wyoming.

"What do you mean, they're still here?" Hunter's brows knitted as he pinned Hatty Shackelford, sitting primly on his couch, with an accusing glare.

"It's just as I told you, Mr. Kincaid. I have it directly from the ticket clerk at the train depot and the manager of the hotel." The mayor's wife fussed and fluttered in her seat like a biddy in a dust bath. "Oh, they packed and went to the station early this morning, all right. However, they claim their tickets never arrived. So late this afternoon, they returned to the hotel. That woman had the audacity to demand their rooms back."

By the way Hatty said "that woman," he knew without a doubt she meant Marina. His frown deepened at this unexpected turn of events. Marina's immediate departure had made it easy for him to avoid dealing with the personal war waged between his conflicting desires. Now, if she stayed, he would be forced to face them.

"So why are you telling me this?" he demanded of the little woman who had instigated all this misery in the first place. He quirked his brow like a question mark.

"I thought . . ." She stuttered to a halt before his unwavering scrutiny, then began again. "Since you were the one who opposed them initially . . ." She flashed him a pleading look. "Quite frankly, the committee hoped you would be willing to do something about this intolerable situation." She glanced down at her hands, then back up when he didn't immediately reply. "Please, Mr. Kincaid. It has happened just as you warned us it would. A disaster, total and complete.

Men and woman dressed like *that,* doing *that* on a stage in front of decent people."

"*That,* as you call it, Mrs. Shackelford, is culture," he told her flat out, oddly enough compelled to defend the nature of ballet. Or was it that he felt a need to protect Marina's reputation?

"If that's the case, sir, then Sweetwater is much better off without culture," she confessed. "The next thing you know, our impressionable young daughters will be talking about a life on the stage or, worse, making sheep's eyes at that vulgar-clad Russian man."

"That vulgar-clad Russian as you now call him is the same man you thought so highly of when you heard he had a title." At least he had managed to keep his own impressionable daughter away from such bad influence.

"You mean to tell me Mr. Bozzacchi is an aristocrat? I thought it was just the woman who claimed such honor. But then how would you know?"

"I know," Hunter declared evasively. "He's a count or something along that order," he said, vaguely recalling that to be the case with everyone in Russia associated with Marina. What possible difference did it make? "So what is it that the Ladies' Committee wants me to do?" he asked abruptly, growing tired of the way the woman beat around the bush.

"The committee decided you would be the best person to see that the unwelcome dance troupe leaves on the next train and never comes back."

For the longest moment Hunter simply stared at the mayor's wife making no effort to conceal his disgust. Even though they shared a common goal, he refused to be a party to railroading people out of town—especially if they had no means of fending for themselves. If he took part in the expulsion, then Marina's accusation would be right, not only about him but about the entire town.

"Please, Mr. Kincaid," the woman pleaded without a shred of dignity.

"I'm sorry, Mrs. Shackelford, but I'm the wrong man for the job. Perhaps it's time the Ladies' Committee realized that when a mistake is made, it has to be seen through to the end." He stood in dismissal.

"Don't think this is the end of it, Mr. Kincaid." Hatty rose, too. "The real men in this community will see to it that the right thing is done."

"Perhaps." He smiled sardonically. "But right now they have much more pressing problems."

Without further explanation, he turned on his heels and, in spite of the rattle of thunder from the impending storm, he left his gaping guest to find her own way out of his house and her self-made problem.

God knew, he had enough of his own to contend with now that Marina would most likely be staying in Sweetwater awhile longer.

From the window of her hotel room, Marina watched with agitated anticipation as the sky roiled and churned like molten lead. She paced and wrung her hands, her actions reflecting the certainty of the violent storm to come. Regardless of all that had happened in her life, how hard she tried to change it, thunder and lightning still took their toll upon her nerves.

Sending the others down to eat and put the charges on the hotel bill she had no earthly idea how to pay, she had chosen not to join them, wishing instead to be alone. Now she wished she'd not been so hasty. With the approaching storm, a little company would have been nice. But it wasn't really social contact she wanted, only consolation.

Turning her attention to the pile of boxes and bags she'd not bothered to unpack in hopes it wouldn't be necessary, she knelt to search for her prize possession, the one constant in her life to offer her the comfort that she needed. Her mother's music box.

Finding it nowhere in the pile, she sat back on her heels to think. Odd, she could have sworn she had packed the precious heirloom, could have sworn she'd seen it earlier that day, if not at the train station then just before they had left the hotel. Confident she had simply overlooked it, she sorted through the jumble of luggage once more. This second, much more thorough, search was no more successful than the first.

Where could it be? she wondered with growing alarm. Straightening, she scanned the small hotel room, the same one she had occupied before, trying desperately to recall where she might have put the ornate wooden box too large to be easily overlooked. The first clap of thunder sent her scurrying, digging fervently through the contents of each piece of luggage, hunting even in impractical places too small for the music box.

In a matter of moments she had scattered all of her possessions helter-skelter on the floor. Still no music box. A flash of lightning precipitated an infusion of utter panic. She had to find it, needed to immerse herself in the familiar melody it played. How else would she manage to survive the debilitating fear that always overtook her and stole every ounce of courage she possessed? God help her, but she had so little ability to control it no matter how hard she tried. As shameful as it was, the fear always won out over her rationale. The storm became more than just a storm, and she relived that terrible night her mother had died.

Only once, for a little while, had she conquered the memories and the fear they evoked. Only once, so long ago. She closed her eyes, remembering how it had felt to be held and loved and protected.

The second crash of thunder, so close she covered her ears, sent her racing down the stairs to the dining room below. She didn't care that her unbound hair flew out behind her in wild disarray, that the terror that made her heart pound might show on her tear-streaked face.

"My music box? Have any of you seen it?" she demanded of the room of startled diners, fortunately mostly members of the troupe. Everyone shook their heads, but their eyes, round and curious, left no doubt that they thought she had lost her mind.

"Sergei?" She turned to her partner, not caring what any of them thought. Since he knew of her attachment to the music box, surely he would understand her need. "Perhaps you picked it up with your things in our haste to get out this morning?" She didn't intend to sound accusing, but she did.

"Sorry. I haven't seen it, Marinuska." The Russian sounded faintly annoyed. She couldn't blame him. Still, making an effort to help her, he abandoned his meal and put his arm about her shoulder.

"Marina, are you sure you didn't leave it in the depot in the confusion to get out of there this afternoon?" Fanny asked, she, too, rushing to her side to comfort her.

"Of course, I'm sure," she snapped defensively. But she couldn't be certain of anything anymore except that if she didn't find her music box . . .

Marina struggled to take a deep breath, to calm herself. These were her friends, after all, her only friends in the whole world. True friendship might be a new experience for her, but that did not give her the right to abuse it. Fanny was right. She had only to retrace her steps since this morning and she would find the misplaced music box.

But if she didn't find it? Then she would simply have to make it through this one storm on her own volition. There was no one else to turn to, no one who could possibly understand. No one except . . . no, she thought vehemently, there is absolutely no one.

In the midst of her denial, the storm rattled the windows and shook her resolve. Fighting down the terror, she whirled and ran.

"Marina, wait. Where are you going?"

Ignoring the concern in Fanny's voice, she sprinted through the lobby. She couldn't stop now. She had to find the music box. If she had carelessly left her most precious possession in the train station, someone could have stolen it by now. What if she never got it back? She had no one to blame but herself. Anxiety left little room for such luxuries as hope and self-worth. She had an immediate need, a need beyond such rationale.

Against every vow she had made to stay away from Hunter Kincaid, she found herself wishing she would see him striding through the front door of the hotel. No matter what had passed between them, he would understand her fear. The storm had brought out that side of him once. If only it could do it again! What she wouldn't give to have him wrap his protective arms about her, to have him assure her everything would be all right! To have him once again drive away the childhood terror that she could not seem to conquer on her own.

To her disappointment, he did not appear.

Once outside the hotel, she paused in the middle of the street, whirling to get her bearings. Only vaguely did she recall the way back to the depot. Spying the tracks meandering off into the distance, she sprinted toward them.

By the time she reached the train station, she had convinced herself that the missing music box would be just inside the door, waiting for her to retrieve it. Then the first fat drops of rain splattered the front of her gown and the wooden sidewalk on which she stood. She glanced up. The sky, dark and ominous, threatened to spew forth a deluge at any moment. So she darted through the depot door.

The building was empty except for the stationmaster, who didn't bother to acknowledge her entrance. In the dim light of dusk, she took a quick look around the depot, pausing to search more thoroughly the spot where she remembered the troupe had stacked their piles of luggage. Determined not to be daunted when she didn't immediately find the music box, she made her way with purposeful strides toward the ticket clerk who looked just as obnoxious behind the security of his wire cage as when she had left earlier.

"Excuse me, sir. I'm sure you must remember me."

His fleeting glance at her suggested that he didn't.

"It seems I have lost a piece of my luggage. Did anyone find or turn in to you an ornate music box—so big?" Using her hands, she indicated the approximate size.

"Cain't say that they did, miss."

"Are you sure?" she demanded.

"Like I told you, lady, I don't know nothin' about missin' luggage." Only then did he make an effort to really look at her, which he did with undisguised irritation. "Now if you please, leave. The depot is closed."

He lied, of course. Of that she felt quite certain. But realizing it and proving it were two different things. Stumbling backward, she retreated, bumping into the open depot door.

Turning, she began to run. Only when biting slivers of rain mingled with her tears did she realize she was once again in the streets of Sweetwater. Pausing only long enough to get her bearings and to brush the hair from her eyes, she sprinted down the street.

Her destination? She had no idea until she got there. Finally, feet soaked, hair damp and frizzing around her face in dark tendrils, she found herself standing before the livery.

Earthy odors wafted around her, rich and faintly sweet. A stable, no matter where it might be, Russian countryside or American West, always smelled the same. She remembered her mother scolding her father whenever he returned reeking of horses and sweaty leather. But she had always liked the smell. It had been such a vital part of her father. Its presence had meant he was home for a few short days before going off to yet another distant battle, but Mama had always seemed at odds with that side of his personality.

Struck by the strangeness of her mother's actions, that she might have been repulsed by the very thing that attracted her, Marina paused to explore the importance of her discovery. Mama had loved Papa. Everyone had said theirs was a match made in heaven. So then why had she been so intolerant of him?

Love and hate. Were they so interchangeable? Had her mother, too, felt the same conflict of emotions she experienced whenever she thought of Hunter Kincaid?

Had it not been his straightforwardness, the undaunted way he had faced a situation and conquered it fearlessly, that had attracted her to him in the first place? He had tried to warn her of the differences when she had first arrived in Sweetwater, but she had rejected his honesty. And he had been right. She had not been prepared for what she had had to face, and now she was even less capable of confronting her fears alone.

Hunter. Once before it had been her vulnerability to the storm that had stripped away his reservations and revealed the man inside, as gentle and loving a person as she could ever hope for. Could it happen again? If they recaptured the wonder of what they had shared in Russia, even if only for a fleeting moment, the spark of a more lasting relationship might be rekindled.

Such meager hope. Was so little enough to sustain her? Perhaps not, but it could be the only chance she would have.

"P-please, I need a horse," she blurted out, determined to find Hunter.

The burly man bent over his anvil. He wore a dirty leather apron, and his face was burnt red from the heat of his smithy fire. He stopped his ear-splitting pounding and stared fixedly at her as if she'd asked for something unreasonable.

"A horse," she repeated, thinking perhaps he hadn't heard her request correctly the first time. "You do rent horses, don't you? How much?"

"Well, ma'am," he said in that slow Western drawl that, even when she wasn't in a hurry, drove her to distraction. He wiped his smutty hands on the bib of his apron and eyed her suspiciously. "You're that dancer woman, aren't ya?"

"Yes, I am. Marina Nicolaiev." She smiled with relief that someone finally acknowledged her.

"Well then, Miz Nik-o-la-iff, iffen I had a horse to rent ya, which I'm not sayin' that I do, only a dang fool would take it out on a night like this."

"You don't understand. I'm an excellent horsewoman," she assured him, "and I must find Hunter Kincaid." There she had said it aloud. Having voiced her innermost desire, nothing was going to stop her from fulfilling it. Not if she could help it. "Have you a horse to rent me or not?"

"I suppose I could let you have that ol' mare in the far stall. At least if she dumps you, she'll come back home on her own." The liveryman snickered.

"I'll take her," Marina agreed. "You can rest assured, sir, she will not, as you put it, 'dump' me." However, even as

Marina boasted, the animal in question began kicking the
walls of her enclosure.

Once under saddle, however, the mare seemed quiet
enough.

"But I need a lady's saddle," she insisted. In Russia no
woman would ride astride.

"Lady's saddle," the liveryman scoffed. "Here, a saddle is
a saddle. If you want the horse, you take her as she is."

Given no other choice—after all, nothing that happened in
this godforsaken town could surprise her—Marina paid the
outrageous rental fee from her meager funds. Taking the reins,
she pulled herself up into the uncomfortable saddle, refusing
to face how low she had finally sunk.

"The Kincaid estate. How do I find it?" she asked, reining
the horse with an excellent hand that the liveryman couldn't
possibly help but notice.

"Estate?" he asked, scratching his head with dirty fingers.
"I don't know about no estate, Miz; but iffen you're wantin'
Hunter Kincaid's spread, then take the road north outta town.
'Bout four miles out, you'll run across the road that leads to
the main house. Cain't miss it. The Kincaid ranch is the big-
gest in these parts."

Of course, she should have known. King Kincaid. Once
Hunter had boasted to her of his great wealth and influence
in Wyoming. It did not surprise her that he had not lied about
that.

Oh, Hunter, Hunter, I'm coming, she cried inwardly, confident that he would not turn her away, not when she needed
him so.

Once they had left the outskirts of Sweetwater far behind,
she pressed the nervous horse to pick up speed. Love and
hate. The two conflicting emotions vied equally for a place
in her confused heart even as she battled to keep her mount
under control. Perhaps she was making a mistake chasing af-

ter such a man; but like a horse that runs back into the burning stables, she raced toward the one thing familiar and comforting left in her life. She yearned for the security offered
by the loving arms of the only man to ever show her the
ways of love, no matter how fleeting the display might have
been.

A flash of lightning struck the ground just ahead of her,
illuminating the winding road. The frightened horse reared,
its front hooves pawing the air. True to her earlier words,
Marina held steady, wrestling the animal back to all fours,
calming it with a gentle stroke of her hand that trembled as
well.

In that moment of brightness she had seen what looked
like a pile of boulders blocking the way. Before she could
decide for sure, the rumble of thunder echoed around
them.

Whinnying in terror, the horse grabbed the bit between its
teeth and darted forward, out of control. No amount of
strength or horsemanship could stop its headlong race. All
Marina could do for the moment was hold on for dear life
and ride it out. If she had made a mistake, it was too late
now to turn back.

Something hidden among the rocks—another animal, perhaps, trying to find shelter from the storm—spooked the already terrorized horse. Veering suddenly and unexpectedly,
Marina found herself flying over the horse's head and through
the air for what seemed an eternity.

She hit the rocky ground with such force that the sparks
of pain before her eyes blinded her with the fury of a bolt
of lightning. Tumbling over and over, she came to a stop next
to a large boulder. Dazed, she lay gasping for breath with
battered lungs.

Just before she lost consciousness, she wondered if the liveryman had been correct. Would the wretched beast that had just thrown her truly head for home?

She prayed so. Otherwise, what reason would anyone have to come looking for her?

Eleven

The annual spring meeting of the Wyoming Cattlemen's Association always proved a boisterous yet tedious affair. Held in the vacant building that had once housed the Songbird Saloon, one of the few buildings in town large enough to accommodate such a large, rowdy get-together, the debate often went on for hours. The subjects argued could range from prediction of the weather to the goings-on in other such fledgling associations across the West.

Tonight, however, the subject was much more vital to the welfare of each and every rancher in the association. For the most part, the members were in accord. Everyone agreed that the pickings were getting mighty slim when it came to the Russian deal. Each year the foreign order for prime beef had dwindled. This spring it had reached the point where it was barely enough to sustain the cost of production and transportation.

Hunter had tried to warn them, but like miners with gold fever who thought the vein would never run out, most of the other ranchers had failed to listen to him. Now they blamed him and, like everybody else in the community, they expected him to fix the problem.

"Listen to me. There are plenty of other foreign outlets for our cattle. We have to explore them," he shouted from the stage above the din of angry protest that made the drumrolls of thunder outside seem far away in comparison. Lifting his hand, he once again demanded silence from a group rarely known to be quiet. Trying hard to contain his impatience at the lack of cooperation and the overall tendency to point fingers and do little else, he glanced around the dilapidated room of the once-grand saloon his father had owned and been proud of, but that he, the ungrateful son, had willingly sacrificed, all in the name of Sweetwater's best interest.

An unsettled feeling he couldn't shake off mantled his broad shoulders, causing him to look toward the window when a flash of lightning illuminated the deserted street beyond. It was nothing, he assured himself, just a restlessness brought on by the greedy dissatisfaction of others. He returned his attention to the important matter at hand.

"Who among you can deny that his profits have been good up until now?" he asked, finally accepting that the low roar of grumbling was the best he would get from his peers. "You, Jeb Granger." He pointed at one of the loudest objectors. "You've made more than enough to build that brand new house of yours."

"That may be, Kincaid," the rancher retorted, "but it still seems to me them Russies have taken unfair advantage of us. Hell, I'd even go so far to say there's a spy among us. How else do you account for them obtaining Wyoming know-how so quickly when it comes to raising cattle?"

A murmur of agreement circulated the room.

"What are you saying, Jeb?" Hunter demanded, forcing his temper to remain under control, his face unreadable. "That other people don't have a right to better themselves?"

"Not iffen they're stealin' it outta my pocket."

Hardy approval trailed the rancher's mercenary comment.

"So what are you suggesting, Jeb?"

"From what I can see, Kincaid, your profits haven't been hurt none lately. In fact, they seem to get better while all of ours get worse. Some of us tend to believe that maybe you got in real tight with them Russies while you were over there, that you're gettin' some kind of special consideration."

"I made a damn fine deal for this association, Jeb Granger." God knows, he had sacrificed his very honor for their profits, but he'd be damned if he'd ever tell them that. "I tried to warn you it wasn't a bottomless pot of gold that you could just keep dipping into and never replenish. There are other buyers out there; we have to seek them out," he said again.

"You're a liar, Hunter Kincaid." The rancher stood, his hand resting threateningly on the butt of his pistol. "And a no-account cheat."

In a subtle response, Hunter stepped back from the edge of the stage, allowing his hands to drop to his sides.

Chairs scraped against the plank floor. The group of men parted like the Red Sea and, for once, grew deadly silent.

"Everybody knows them Russies all take a shine to you like ducks to water." Granger continued his accusations. "Just look at that crazy dancer woman, that Princess Nicolaiev. Ain't hers the same last name as that Russian you contracted with to sell our cattle?"

"That's right, Hunter," someone said, showing support for Jeb Granger.

Hunter glanced over the mute crowd. He had wondered how long it would take them to put two and two together and turn on him. Much longer than he'd given them credit for. Still, Marina's presence in Sweetwater had nothing to do with cattle contracts. He had done everything in his power to prevent her arrival and had done nothing to encourage her to stay.

"Why don't you explain her reason for racin' off in the middle of this storm to go lookin' for you."

"You don't know what you're talking about, Jeb," Hunter declared in all honesty, certain that the last action Marina would ever take was to go out in the midst of thunder and lightning looking for him or anybody else. Only too well he knew how much storms terrified her.

"Don't I? Half the town saw her lookin' stark-starin' mad in the hotel dinin' room babblin' on about some lost music box. Then Jake over at the livery stable said not long after that she whirled in there like a dervish demandin' a horse and directions to your spread. Hell, Kincaid, don't deny it. Everybody knows you got a thing for fancy females like her."

Hunter's fist curled, hovering just above his pistol. The last thing he wanted to hear was the truth about himself. Besides nobody said such things about Marina, especially a loud-mouthed son of a bitch like Jeb Granger.

Then the real impact of the rancher's words filtered through the red haze clouding Hunter's brain. The music box. He knew full well its importance to Marina, especially during a storm. Its loss would devastate her. Was she frightened even now, out on a strange road thinking to find him at the end of her wild ride?

Suddenly his palms began to sweat, his heart to melt. Good for him or not, he couldn't turn his back on her, not when she needed him.

Remembering what she had said, that guns were not the answer, he wordlessly lowered his hand and turned his back on the challenge issued by Jeb Granger. No doubt, it was an act that would eventually label him a coward and a liar in the eyes of these men. At the moment he didn't care what others thought of him, not even when the group of ranchers began to murmur derogatory comments.

He had to find Marina and reclaim what they had experienced in Russia. If nothing else, even if it lasted for only one night, at least he would have a fresh memory to sustain him over a lifetime of lonely nights.

As he gathered up his slicker and slammed his Stetson on

his head, another streak of lightning zigzagged it way across the bit of sky framed in the window. Thunder followed quickly, indicating its closeness, rumbling with the promise of nature at its wildest.

"Kincaid, where do you think yer goin'?" Granger taunted. "This meetin' ain't over. Beside I ain't done with you yet."

"Perhaps not, but I'm done with you for the time being. And as for this meeting, gentlemen, I can't see that it's going anywhere. If you decide you want to take my advice and look for a new, untapped market for our beef, then let me know and I'll do my best to find one. In the meantime, please be kind enough to lock the doors behind you when you leave." Having stated his opinion, he left, but not before hearing the group's parting sentiments.

"I told you Kincaid was as loony as a bedbug."

Standing on the porch of the deteriorating building, Hunter sloughed off the stinging comment as he would the biting rain. He supposed they were right about him. No man in his right mind settled for less than all by chasing after some dang-fool woman in a storm, especially one who could never commit to him or his way of life. But then he had never considered himself the same as other men, especially after two passion-filled nights spent in the willowy arms of a Russian princess.

Lowering his head against the onslaught of hard, driving rain, sharp as needles as it slashed him in the face, Hunter mounted his pinto and rode off in the direction of his ranch.

Marina, I'm coming, darlin'. The cry came from his heart left bared and vulnerable by a need he could no longer deny.

Hunter saw the still form sprawled beside the road. He knew who it was long before he actually got close enough to identify her. Marina. His heart thundered like a herd of stampeding cattle, catching in his throat with fear.

God, please, don't let her be dead.

Before the surefooted pinto came to a complete halt, he vaulted from the saddle, running. Kneeling beside her, he lowered his head to rest his ear against her heart. Steady and strong, the sound of its pounding reassured him.

She lay in a puddle, her lovely gown soaked and ruined. Her dark hair spread across the muddy ground, its once-glorious sheen dulled. A damp frizz framed her china-doll face, alarmingly pale in comparison.

"Marina?" he called to her softly, gently brushing a thin streak of dirt from her temple with the pad of his thumb. Beneath the smudge glowed the telltale shadow of a large bruise. When she had fallen, she must have struck her head on one of the many rocks littering the road.

She moaned softly. Her right arm twitched as she tried to move it. A small whimper slipped past her ghostly lips, then she grew still and silent once more.

He had to restrain himself. He wanted to shake her, hard— do anything to bring the color back to her wan face, to make her eyelids open so she could see that he was there to protect her. No matter what, he would protect her, he vowed vehemently. Instead, stubborn fool that he had been, he had almost let her slip away from him all because of a misplaced sense of pride.

Carefully he checked her arms and legs looking for fractures. Relieved when he found none, he was nonetheless concerned about the bump she had received on her head. Regardless, he had to move her and see to it she got warm and dry as quickly as possible. Slipping off his weatherproof slicker, he covered her, then slid his arms beneath her shoulders and knees and picked her up, unmindful of the mud that smeared the front of his shirt.

"Hunter," she moaned softly. "Please, help me. I must find Hunter Kincaid."

"Shh. Shh. You have found me, darlin'," he whispered back, doubting that she heard him. "Thank God, I found you."

It was no easy task getting back up on his horse with Marina in his arms. However, the wiry mustang was accustomed to his rider mounting and maneuvering with arms filled, his usual burden consisting of squirming, bawling calves that had been separated from their mothers. With her head cradled against his heart, the slicker securely around her, Hunter held the spirited animal to a walk.

With their backs to the storm, they plodded steadily ahead. It would take them some time to reach town. Not too long, Hunter prayed. When Marina's teeth began to chatter and her hands turned icy cold in spite of the slicker tucked around her, Hunter feared they might not make it back to town before . . .

Refusing to think about what might happen, he concentrated on getting her inside and out of the storm quickly. He could think of only one place to go, but it was not the kind of place to take a woman like Marina. Desperately he tried to come up with another solution, but nothing came to mind. Finally, he accepted he had no other choice.

A mile outside of town he turned his mount down a well-traversed trail already turned to mud. When they reached the dilapidated two-story house, long in need of a good coat of paint, he stopped at the hitching rail running the length of the porch.

He didn't have to wait long. Several women, scantily clad, burst out of the front door to greet him, stopping short of actually getting wet.

"Hunter Kincaid, is that you?" one of the women cried. "You ain't been around in such a long time."

The group giggled like innocent schoolgirls. They were anything but.

"It's not what you think, Ellie." Dismounting, he carried his precious burden to cover, using his own body to shield the shivering Marina from the waterfall of rainwater running off the eaves. "Tell Chloe I'm here and that I need her help. Tell her to hurry," he ordered the woman whose lush body was barely concealed by the white-lace chemise and red corset, the sum total of what she wore.

Without further invitation, he shouldered his way into the house. He glanced around at the red-velvet drapes and wallpaper that had seen better days. God help him. He couldn't begin to imagine what Marina would think when she came around and discovered he had brought her to recuperate in a not-so-fancy parlor house.

Marina woke up with a start. She glanced around the strange bedroom, noting the lace canopy and curtains. A woman's bedroom. But whose? she wondered. The last thing she remembered had been hitting the hard, rain-soaked ground. Well, whomever it belonged to, at least she was safe from the raging storm that even now pounded on the window across the room. She lay there glorying in the long-forgotten luxury of silk sheets, focused on an unkempt bush at the mercy of the storm, beating itself against the panes of glass.

Finally she took another assessment of her surroundings, the finely carved furniture, the quality needlework of the eyelet coverlet, dresser scarves and doilies covering everything, making the room look homey and lived in. Still, there was nothing tasteful to be said of the decor. Once again, she wondered whom it belonged to.

She pushed herself up onto her elbows. Her hand flew to her temple, which throbbed so viciously a wave of nausea swept over her, forcing her to drop back against the lace-encased pillow with a groan.

"Take it easy, honey. You've got a nasty bump to your noggin."

Startled to discover she was not alone, Marina glanced up at the hovering woman who had spoken to her. Dressed in a thin wrapper, none too clean and hastily repaired at one shoulder, the older woman smelled of cheap lilac-water. The familiar odor brought back unpleasant memories of the common women who, for the most part, had made up the *corps de ballet* in St. Petersburg. Those women had never been kind.

"Where am I?" she asked hesitantly. With a shaky hand she explored her forehead, wincing when she fingered a bruise as big as a plum. "How did I get here?"

"You're at my place, honey. I'm Chloe LaRocca." The woman reached over and patted Marina's hand reassuringly. "And I brought you here, darlin'."

"Hunter," Marina cried, instantly recognizing his voice. Ignoring the throbbing pain, she slid her gaze to the open door.

He was leaning against the frame, his familiar arms crossed over his broad chest. He smiled at her, easy and wide, as if nothing adverse had ever passed between them, as if oceans and time and circumstances had not separated them.

But all of those things had happened. Besides, who was this woman who seemed so at ease around him dressed so— she looked Chloe up and down—casually? Marina's hungry search, initially filled with hope, melted into wariness.

"Just where is *here?*" she asked, lifting the covers enough to peek beneath them and discover that she wore a most revealing nightgown of red satin and black lace. The flimsy garment didn't belong to her; no *lady* would be caught dead in it. Whose was it? How had it gotten on her body? And what had happened to her own clothes?

"Chloe is an old friend of mine," Hunter volunteered.

"Just how old?" Marina demanded, dropping the covers when she suspected he was looking beneath them right along with her. She narrowed her eyes suspiciously.

"Old enough, honey, for you not to have to worry about it," Chloe interjected, chuckling throatily. Again the older woman—much older, Marina realized now that she looked at her closely—reached out and brushed the back of her hand, which was clutching the coverlet. "Now you just rest and get better. You can stay here as long as you need to."

Chloe rose. With a private exchange of glances that Marina found most disquieting, the woman slipped past Hunter.

Except for a lemon-yellow canary in a wire cage in one corner of the room, they were now completely alone. Hunter continued to watch her, unnerving her. She felt stripped and bare.

She pulled the covers up to her chin, but that did nothing to relieve the intensity of his stare or the depth of her discomfort. Marina felt more trapped than nervous, like the caged songbird darting back and forth between its two perches. Determined not to reveal her feelings, she stared back, unwavering, the regal Princess Marina Nicolaiev at her best.

"Word has it you were looking for me." Pushing off the door frame with his shoulder, Hunter stationed himself at the foot of the bed, so close he could have touched her if he wanted to.

"I wasn't," she lied, laughing nervously before she could prevent it. Intimidated by his sudden nearness, his towering height, his confident stance, she glanced away.

The edge of the mattress sagged, and she found him sitting beside her on the bed. She tried to scoot away, but he prevented her by reaching across her and planting his hand in the middle of the bed. Grasping her chin between his fingers, he forced her to look at him, his face only inches from her own.

"Have you forgotten how well I know you, Marina? Or have you learned to overcome your fear of storms?"

"I'm not afraid." Even as she said it, a burst of rain pattered against the window, almost as if the frightening weather mocked her attempt to defy the truth. In reaction she leaned forward, away from the window. Her movement, ever so slight, nonetheless brought her lips so close to his they brushed.

"I can see how brave you are."

She tried to pull back.

His hand, still holding her chin, prevented her. "Have you forgotten everything I taught you about taming your fears?"

"No, I remember," she defended. Did he think she would ever forget? she wanted to ask him, but couldn't find the courage. She closed her eyes and covered his hand with hers, then pressed her face into his palm, which suddenly relaxed into a comforting cradle. She sighed, reveling in the warmth of his touch, breathing in the smell of well-oiled leather that lingered on his masculine skin. "I remember," she repeated on a much softer note. "But how am I supposed to dance without music?"

"Don't worry, my sweet princess. We'll find your missing music box." His caressing hand moved down the side of her face, along her neck, his fingers lingering in the indentation of her collarbone. "But until we do, we can simply make our own music. Do you trust me?" he asked, a crooked smile lifting one side of his mouth.

Her gaze darted up; her heart grew still, her blood igniting into liquid heat that raced like wildfire through her veins. Trust him? Did she dare? Should she allow herself to be persuaded by the prelude of a passion she had experienced only once in her life? She had to admit, if only to herself, that what she had come looking for was arms of love to shield her from her fears. Now that she had found them and they had opened to her, she didn't have the will to turn them away.

Nor did she question that he knew about the disappearance of her music box. It only mattered that he had cared enough to find out, that he alone truly understood the importance of her loss, that he had promised to help her find it. Still, there remained one important unanswered question.

"Tell me, Hunter. When the storm and this moment together is over, what then?" she asked.

There was no denying the guarded expression on his handsome, rugged face. His eyes, as blue as a cloudless sky, shifted and stared over her head before he replied.

"It can be whatever we wish. Whatever we are both willing to make it."

She searched hard and swore she saw sincere longing in the look he gave her. Clinging to that hope, she wound her arms about his neck, tugging until his head came down and their lips brushed tentatively. At first he held back. Then, like a thirsty man discovering an untapped wellspring, he pulled her to him, drinking of the pure, unsullied waters of her surrender.

To her it was more than mere surrender. That first kiss represented freedom, and she savored the glorious feel of giving herself up to this man, the only one to ever show her the power and wonder of physical loving. Nothing—no one—could come between them, not now that Dmitri and her life in Russia no longer bound her.

Dmitri. Her heart, so full of sudden realization, slammed to a halt. Could he be the reason Hunter had turned away from her when she had showed up so unexpectedly in his life again? It all made perfect sense. He was a man bound by honor. Of that she was quite certain. Did he mistakenly

still think of her as a married woman? Someone he had no
right to put his claim on?

"Hunter," she gasped, reluctantly dragging her mouth from
his.

Hungrily he sought her mouth once more.

"No, Hunter, wait. You must listen." She pressed her fingers against his lips. It was important to her that he realize
that their coming together would no longer be considered
adulterous—not by God, or state, or man.

"Whatever it is, it can wait," he murmured. "Unless you
plan to change your mind."

"No, it's not that at all."

"Then it can wait." Curling his hand around hers, still
pressed to his mouth, he took one finger between his lips,
alternately nibbling and sucking gently.

The studied effect of that simple caress drove her wild with
need. A delightful need that freed her mind of thoughts other
than exploring the glorious way he made her feel.

His mouth covered hers once more—seeking, robbing her
of the last bit of strength to hold him off for even another
moment.

Sighing softly, she gave herself up to the all-powerful sensations that swept through her, overtaking her body that had
somehow survived this long without the tender, knowing
touch of a man's love.

His touch was truly knowing. The way his hand, big and
rough and calloused, cupped her breast as if he feared he might
crush her made her feel like the most precious china doll. Ever
so gently, he teased the nipple into a hard nodule that strained
against the confines of the scandalous nightgown.

Then at just the precise moment when that initial intimacy
no longer sufficed, he freed her aching flesh from the binding
black lace, encompassing it with his warm lips. The gentle
tug of desire exploded into a desperate yearning that had been

suppressed for too long. It robbed her of all reason and any
lingering doubts.

This was Hunter, the man who had taught her everything
that she knew about passionate love between a man and a
woman. Hunter, whose image had sustained her through the
most crushing crises, the man who had given her hope and
a dream to pursue when life offered her little else.

In return she strove to provide him with all that he wanted
from a woman. Perhaps it had been a glimmering princess
that had attracted him in the first place, the prima ballerina
of the Russian ballet, the prize that he had pursued and won.
Now, she was none of those things.

She feared he might find her no longer desirable. Could
he ever be satisfied with a woman willing to forego the riches
of the world and the acclaim of an adoring audience to have
the simple, earthy pleasures a man like him could provide?
The prospects frightened her, not for what she must sacrifice,
but for what he must be willing to give up. Therefore, she
knew she must work harder to compensate for his loss.

"Tell me, Hunter. What pleases you?" She felt shy, even
naughty, for asking; but if thinking first of his happiness
made her a bad woman in the eyes of the world, then bad
was what she wanted to be.

"You, darlin'. Don't you know that whatever you do
pleases me?" he answered.

Brazenly, she unbuttoned his shirt, shoving it off his shoulders. Then she rubbed her hands against his manly chest,
threading her fingers through the swirl of hair that covered
the broad, tan expanse. To her delight, his nipples hardened
like smooth pebbles against her palms. If so simple a gesture
pleased him, then what else would he find exciting?

She moved her hands lower, marveling at his physique, that
of a man accustomed to hard physical work. His stomach was
so flat, his hips narrow and tapered, as solid as rock. Reach-

ing for the buttons on his pants, she hesitated only a moment before tackling the challenge they presented. She had never unfastened a man's trousers before, but she didn't find it difficult; she did find it exciting.

"What do you think you are doing, woman?" he asked in a low, throaty voice. He lifted one eyebrow in amusement. Covering her industrious hands with his own, he rolled to his side to lie next to her.

Why must he tease her when she sought so hard to make him happy? Suddenly overwhelmed with embarrassment and self-doubt, she pulled away, presenting him with her back.

"Whoa, darlin'. Where're you going? I only asked what you were doing, not that you stop." Reaching over her shoulder, he gathered up her balled fists, bending over her to kiss them until they unclenched. Then, urging her to roll back over, he returned them to his torso.

Miraculously, the unbuttoning had already been accomplished.

"Please, don't stop."

Gladly she would continue, but, even if courage hadn't failed her, she didn't know exactly what to do or what would pleasure him.

This time when his hand captured hers, it served as a guide, gently leading the way, finally revealing the most intimate secret desires of his all-male body. To discover she had such control over him, that he was so willing to trust her with that power, strengthened her commitment to reciprocate with her own body, with her heart—God help her, with her very soul if he asked it of her.

But just as she had known that he would, Hunter demanded nothing, except that she share with him the glorious joy of their reunion. In those precious, yearned-for moments of togetherness, nothing else mattered—not where they were or what terrible injustices life had thrust upon them. They were united here, and now, and always.

Always. Her heart, so happy it could have burst and she wouldn't have cared, slammed against the pressure of his chest as he covered her. How well they fit together, as if they had been designed only for each other, their uniqueness special above all others. Yes, their love was truly special.

And so was this coming together.

His hand felt so right as it slid along the length of her thigh, raising her knee so their bodies fit like interlocking pieces of a puzzle. His mouth molded perfectly to her own. When he trailed a fiery path along her neck with his lips and tongue, tracing the hollow just beneath her ear, exploring the slope of her shoulder, collarbone, and more, she could not have asked for anything else.

And was it not true that her hand had sheathed him perfectly as well, as did that most womanly part of her when he thrust deep within her? A perfect match—as perfect as the love that bubbled up inside her, filling every nook and cranny of her once-empty heart.

They moved with the grace of dancers, their bodies meshing, moving apart, and meshing again to a melody composed just for them and that only they could hear. The music grew louder, the tempo faster and faster. Caught up in the uncontrollable emotional storm that swept through her, she clutched Hunter's shoulders, clinging to him and the total trust that carried her along on the wild abandonment of the moment.

It came with a crash, the wonder of more thrilling and fulfilling than any performance she had ever given.

Still spinning on the pinnacle's magic whirlwind, she heard him cry out.

"Marina. Marina. God help me, but I cannot get enough of you."

His was a cry straight from the heart, pure and uncensored.

She cherished it then as she would for all eternity. As she would always cherish him.

He fell against her, his gasping breath stirring the wisps of hair that curled about her face. Reaching up, she traced his cheek, his jawline, then his lips with a fingertip. Pressing his face into her hand, he suddenly rolled.

"No, Hunter," she cried softly. "Don't let it be over."

"It's not over, my sweet princess," he promised.

But much to her disappointment, he severed the precious union of their bodies before she could stop him. He pulled her close, cradling her head against his heart, which still hammered out of control. His protective arm staked his claim to her; his hand, cupping the curve of her thigh, reassured her.

Marina sighed and listened quietly as his heartbeat slowed to a steady thumpity-thump. It felt good to belong. Safe and warm and incredibly good.

Confident that bliss and Hunter would be hers forevermore, she closed her eyes and surrendered to the sated tingle of fulfillment. Soon she slept, more deeply than she had in years, at ease in the promise of his unwavering devotion.

"It's not the same thing, Hunter."

"How can I be sure?"

He watched the crochet hook in Chloe's fingers whip in and out of the yarn making lace doilies. It had always seemed such a strange pastime for a woman of her profession. But then Chloe had never been one to do the expected.

"You want to be sure?" She snorted, her hands pausing in their busywork. She pinned him with an unsympathetic look. "So tell me something we all don't want, honey. I'd like to be sure that after I've grown too old and ugly to make a living, I'll have done something with my life to make me more than a worn-out whore with nothing better to look forward to than death."

"I won't let that happen, Chloe. You know that. If you would just let me set you up in Denver . . ."

"No, Hunter." She placed a restraining hand over his mouth. "Like I've told you from the beginning, I gotta do this for myself. And you have gotta stop looking for the bad in every woman you meet."

Chloe LaRocca had always been a woman of independent spirit. He remembered how she had looked the first time he had seen her. His daddy had pretended not to notice when, as a mere boy, he had sneaked into the saloon to watch the line of barroom dancers kick up their heels, show their legs clear up to the thigh, displaying the fancy garter belts strapped to them. Then they had turned and flipped up the backs of their skirts revealing their posteriors. Chloe had possessed one of the finest posteriors he had ever seen and one of the sharpest tongues he had ever heard. She'd taken flack from no one, not even his father.

As he'd sat gaping at the pretty saloon girls, it had been Chloe who had protested to his father that an innocent boy of thirteen didn't belong there.

His father had only laughed. "Hell, there's nothing like the sight of a good whore to make a sapling sprout new limbs," he'd declared.

Hunter smiled. Yes, indeed, Chloe had met Mac Kincaid's challenge head on. That day, to spite his father and the apparent feelings she'd harbored for him, she had seen to it that his sapling son had indeed grown a new limb.

"You're wrong, Chloe. I'm just trying to keep from getting stung again," he said.

"Hunter." She put aside her needlework and peered sternly at him over the rim of the glasses she now needed to wear for doing close work. "It's not fair to judge all women by Della's betrayal."

"That's not what I'm doing."

"Aren't you? Haven't you automatically assumed that this woman will eventually desert you just as Della did? Hunter, you're wrong about her."

"How can you be so sure? You just met Marina."

"A woman like me knows these things. From the very beginning didn't I tell you that Della could never give you the support you needed, that she would demand to hold center stage all the time?"

Chloe spoke the truth. Repeatedly she had warned him in his impetuous youth that Della DeAngelo would never be happy in the secondary role of a rancher's wife. To make matters worse, he'd struggled each year just to make ends meet and couldn't give her the material things she'd craved. Perhaps if he had spent more time with her, she would not have left him. More likely, Chloe had been right; it wouldn't have mattered. Nevertheless, he'd refused to listen to her then.

And now?

How could he be certain he could trust her instincts now? Too much was at stake. More than his best interests, or Marina's, for that matter. He had to think of the possible consequences to Rainee if he allowed a woman like Marina to waltz in and upset his daughter's carefully structured life.

"Chloe, it's not that simple."

"Yes, it is." She smiled, her expression a gentle form of coercion. "Marina Nicolaiev is a real lady; and once they commit, ladies always keep their word."

"If that's what it means to be a lady, then that makes you one of the finest." He touched her shoulder affectionately.

"Oh, bosh, Hunter Kincaid. Don't try to change the subject. You know as well as I do, Marina came to Sweetwater just to find you. She's no Della looking to line her nest with easy pickings and then move on."

Having heard enough, but no nearer to coming to a decision, Hunter rose from his seat.

"Please, Hunter, give her and yourself a chance."

Forcing himself to smile, he nodded at the only woman to have ever earned his trust. He would have gladly paid a king's ransom to feel as confident as Chloe about Marina and what the future held in store for the two of them.

Give her a chance? Better yet, he could put her to the test.

"Hunter, where did you go? I've missed you," Marina cried. Propped up on a pile of pillows, she smiled widely when she spied the man she had pinned all of her hopes and dreams on walking into the room.

She'd panicked when she'd awakened and discovered herself alone in the bed, certain that Hunter had deserted her. No doubt he had thought he still had no claim to her. But she planned to lay those fears to rest when she told him the news that she was now a widow.

Not that her feelings for Hunter diminished for a moment how important Dmitri had been to her. Her relationship with a crippled husband who had been much older had been an interim in her life, preparing the way for what she would eventually have with Hunter. Even Dmitri had seen it and been glad of it.

Smiling graciously at Hunter, she patted the bed beside her, urging him to sit down.

"Marina, we need to talk." Along with a somber expression, he held his ground, keeping distance between them.

Alarmed at first, she told herself he needed space to keep from doing what she wished to be doing. Finding it hard to resist made her giddy and happy in a way she had never felt before.

"I know," she agreed, holding on to her bright smile and the knowledge that soon he would be smiling, too. "I have something to tell you. I'm a widow now." She blurted it out, unable to contain herself another moment. "Dmitri died—"

"Two years ago. I know." He cut her off.

It took her a moment to weather the impact of his abrupt confession and unchanged expression.

"How long have you known?" she asked, forcing herself to continue to smile. Of course, he would tell her he had just found out. If that were so, why did he show so little enthusiasm?

"Not long after it happened," he replied, crushing her hopes.

What was he saying? That he had known all along and never attempted to reestablish their relationship? Why wouldn't he have at least tried? Did it mean that he didn't care?

"If you knew, why didn't you contact me?"

He must have tried, she assured herself. She had fled Russia so quickly, he must have missed her.

"Why didn't *you* bother to contact *me*?"

"I did," she defended. "Why do you think I'm here, Hunter. I came looking for you."

The desire to tell him of the terrible nightmare of her final days in Russia, the mystery surrounding Dmitri's death, and her escape from Russia hovered on her lips, but she held her tongue. She needed Hunter to want her for the sake of their love, not merely out of sympathy.

"You told me you came here strictly to dance."

"That's not true." She had said just that when she had first seen him, but only because she had felt uncertain of her reception.

"Admit it, Marina, you would have left if a little bad luck hadn't prevented you."

"You're right. I would have," she admitted truthfully, lifting her chin with dignity, "but only because I felt I had an obligation to continue with this tour."

"Your career," he said with a sneer. "It's everything to you, isn't it?"

"I won't deny that it's important, Hunter. Just as your ranch is important to you."

Without further explanation, he turned and walked out of the room.

"Hunter, wait." Bewildered, Marina tried to rise out of the bed and follow him.

When he didn't stop, she realized with a sinking heart that she'd lost him. But why?

"Oh, Miss LaRocca," she cried when the kind woman hustled into the room with determined strides. "I don't understand."

"I do. Hunter Kincaid is as stubborn and bullheaded as his father was," the woman declared, her eyes narrowing. Then she turned, insisting that Marina lie back down. "And call me Chloe, honey." She fluffed the pillows beneath Marina's head. "All my friends do and, after what he just said to you, I have a feeling we're gonna be close for quite a spell."

"Then you were listening?"

"Just say I was passing by and couldn't help but overhear."

"Oh, Chloe. What am I going to do?"

"I'll tell you exactly what *we're* going to do. First, we're gonna see to it you get well."

"We?" Marina asked, uncertain why the woman would be so willing to help her.

"Of course," Chloe insisted, tucking the covers around Marina's slender shoulders. *"He* may not be able to see what's good for him, but *I* can; and I'm not going to let him make another mistake. It's simple. After you're back on your feet, all we have to do is prove to him that he's wrong about you."

Marina shook her head doubtfully. In a matter of moments everything had changed again, and somehow she had to figure out a way to make it on her own—without the support of Hunter Kincaid.

Twelve

"Chloe, are you certain this is the best way to go about proving our point?" Standing on the sidewalk before the boarded-up building, Marina mustered every scrap of dignity she could find within herself to confront what she didn't feel ready to face.

" 'Fraid so, honey." The older woman gave her a sympathetic look accompanied by an encouraging smile. "This is the only place in town that meets your needs."

"But there were other saloons in town, weren't there?" Marina asked. Over the last few days she had heard the stories about the notorious cleanup of Sweetwater, Wyoming. Although Chloe had never once mentioned her part in the strange affair, Marina sensed her newest friend had somehow been more deeply involved than she cared to admit.

"Yes, but none so grand as the Songbird Saloon." That wistful, telltale look returned to Chloe's face. "It was the only one with a real, honest-to-God stage."

The presence of a stage held great importance in the success of their plan.

"Then I suppose I have no choice but to face him," Marina conceded.

Him was none other than Hunter Kincaid, the owner of the building.

It had been nearly a week since she had last seen that most infuriatingly complex man, five days since he had walked out on her, leaving her in the hands of strangers, without explanation or a chance to defend herself. Not that she owed him anything, much less an apology. After all, he had made no effort to locate her after Dmitri's death.

If it hadn't been for Chloe, she would have given up hope. God knows, the entire troupe would have been destitute by now if the kind woman hadn't taken them under her wing and given them a temporary place to stay until Marina had recovered from her head injury. Now, with a clearer, if not total, understanding of what made Hunter Kincaid tick, she knew what she had to do and why.

She must prove to him that she had no intentions of leaving Sweetwater, now or ever, with or without his support.

"Here he comes now," Chloe whispered, squeezing her arm and pointing down the street.

Yes, there came Hunter, all right. She would have recognized that arrogant saunter of his a mile away. He was dressed in clean nankeens, his knee-high boots polished, his checkered shirt freshly starched. Of course, he wore one of those gray felt hats called a Stetson. Obviously he had taken care to make a good first impression.

Pulling back her shoulders, she clung to the knowledge of who she was, a princess, once the prima ballerina of the Russian Royal Ballet, a woman of world influence. She prayed she had the strength to maintain her grace and dignity no matter what took place in the next few moments.

"Afternoon, Chloe," he said. If he experienced surprise to see Marina there, he gave no indication, merely tipping his hat at her.

She nodded in return, trying hard not to think about the intimacy they had shared only a few days before, wondering if he simply dismissed it as a night's entertainment and nothing more. She had to forget his towering height, the way he shifted his shoulders that invariably sent a thrill rushing through her. She would not think of him kissing her or . . .

She closed her eyes to the vivid image, instead trying to envision what he had thought when he had received Chloe's message informing him she had a prospective tenant for his empty building.

"Is this who wants to rent the Songbird?"

This of course, was her. Marina. She notched her chin and said not a word even when his blue eyes raked her with suspicion.

"Does it matter as long as it's put to a proper use?" she demanded.

"No, I suppose not," Hunter replied, then, ignoring her, he turned to Chloe. "As long as no town ordinance is violated. She does know that town statutes prohibit saloons and dance halls?"

Why did he insist on talking about her as if she could not speak for herself?

"I know of the law, Mr. Kincaid," she interjected. "Rest assured, I have no intention of opening a saloon or dance hall, or any other kind of disreputable business. I'm sorry, Chloe," she instantly apologized, fearing she might have inadvertently hurt the other woman's feelings.

"No need, honey. The law's the law."

Apparently satisfied, Hunter inserted the key into the padlock on the front entrance, shook it loose, then opened the double doors which were in need of a good oiling. Then he waited for the two women to enter ahead of him.

Such gentlemanly behavior. How unlike him of late, Marina decided, entering first. Stationing herself as close to Chloe and as far away from Hunter as she could, she contained her nervousness as she waited in the darkness for him to strike a light.

"This way, ladies," he said, blowing a film of dust from

the oil lamp's chimney before replacing it over the flame. Automatically he took the lead.

The building was larger than its facade suggested. She noted the stage, small but more than adequate for her needs. She discovered plenty of chairs stacked in a corner. Although dusty and in need of repair, there were still enough to accommodate a good-sized audience.

She continued her exploration. The dilapidated piano she found under a tarpaulin had definitely seen better days. Running her hand over the black and white ivories, she played a simple three-octave scale. Two keys stuck and some of the others sounded out of tune. Hopefully John could take care of that problem.

However, the bar would have to go, as would the atrocious painting of a near-naked woman.

Suddenly aware that Hunter watched her every move, especially when she stopped to stare at the picture, she cast her eyes in the opposite direction. A flight of steep stairs led to another floor above them.

"What's up there?" she asked.

"Bedrooms. Ten to be exact. Care to take a look?" he asked, his gaze never faltering.

Of course there would be bedrooms in what once had been a notorious saloon.

"No, thank you. I'll take your word for it." The last place in the world she intended to be with Hunter Kincaid anytime in the near future was a bedroom. Turning in the opposite direction, she checked out several closed doors, discovering two smaller rooms and plenty of storage for props and wardrobe trunks.

As much as she hated the idea of renting a place from Hunter Kincaid, she had to admit the building fit her needs to a tee, even if the circumstances did not.

The entire dance troupe had been cooped up at Chloe's

place for too long. Dear Chloe. Marina glanced at her new-found friend. Never once had she complained, making light of the fact that her business suffered because of the over-crowding. For several days after she'd regained her feet, Marina had stubbornly hung onto the belief that they would hear from Jack Yancy and be obligated to move on; but a week later she had come to accept that the promoter had truly abandoned them.

The one positive event in all of the confusion had been the unexplained reappearance of her music box. She had found it among her personal effects when they were delivered from the hotel. It had been there all along, Sergei had sworn, when to her delight and relief she discovered it. At the time she did not question the mystery further.

But now, remembering Hunter's uncanny knowledge of her loss, she wondered if he'd had something to do with the return of the music box. Should she thank him or blame him? She only knew she preferred not to deal with him directly. Glancing at Chloe with a prearranged signal, she nodded.

"We'll take it, Hunter," the woman said, conveying Marina's decision. "How much a month are you askin' for it?"

"For you, Chloe, it's free."

"It's not for Chloe, Mr. Kincaid," Marina piped up. "It's for me, and I don't want it for free, not from you. How much?"

"Why are you doing this, Marina?" he asked, glaring.

"I have to make a living—like everyone else who lives here, don't I?" She held her chin high with pride.

"Very well then. Twenty-five dollars a month. Is that fair enough?" he asked.

She looked at Chloe, wanting to make sure he hadn't tried to take further advantage of her.

"That's fair," the woman assured her with a nod.

"Rent's due at the end of the month."

"I prefer to pay you now." Reaching into her reticule, she took out the last of her money. She handed him all of it and quickly pulled back her fingers.

He, too, looked uneasy. Did his discomfort stem from touching her hand or taking her money? Finally, as if sensing her determination, he folded the wad of bills and jammed it in the front pocket of his shirt.

"In return, Mr. Kincaid, I expect prompt services from my landlord. I expect you to see that those chairs are repaired. As for that . . . that art behind the bar," she said, pointing at the image of the half-clad woman," I insist you remove it from the premises immediately."

"Is that all, Your Highness?"

"For now," she replied haughtily. Then realizing that he mocked her and that he stared at her with a condescending look that made her itch to slap it off his handsome face, she turned away. "Thank you," she murmured.

She heard him drop the key on the end of the bar. Only after the front doors had slammed closed, did she look up.

He was gone. And he had taken his despicable painting with him.

"Well, now, honey," Chloe said, propping her hands on her hips, "thanks to Hunter Kincaid, you're the first legitimate independent businesswoman in Sweetwater. I will thoroughly enjoy seein' what the close-minded, tight-assed citizens think about that."

"This is abominable!"

The Ladies' Committee rarely invited a man to one of their meetings. Whenever they did, the "guest" faced worse than a firing squad. In Wyoming, women had the right to vote and could even run for public office. The ladies of Sweetwater had allowed such freedom to go to their heads.

It came as no surprise to Hunter when he received his summons. He'd known the moment he'd turned over the keys to the Songbird to Marina that he sat smack-dab in the middle of a controversy. It also came as no surprise that Hatty Shackelford led the crusade against him. Not to do something Hatty's way was the same as declaring war against her and, consequently, against the entire Ladies' Committee.

"You owe us an explanation, Mr. Kincaid," the mayor's wife continued. "What were you thinking when you rented your building to that woman?" she demanded.

He'd been thinking he wanted to believe Marina truly wanted to stay, that a possibility existed for her to be happy in a place like Sweetwater, that he wasn't a fool for letting hope override his cynicism. Regardless of what Hatty and her cronies thought, Marina had done nothing to deserve their contempt—unless they found her guilty of being too beautiful and gracious, a lady through and through. But he didn't say any of that now.

"It's my building. I can rent it to whomever I want as long as I don't break the law."

The ordinance stated no saloons or whorehouses. It said nothing about theaters.

"Well, we'll just see about that," Hatty said in a huff, sticking her biddy-like beak high in the air. "Laws can be changed, you know."

"Yes, ma'am, they can. But until then, it's my building to do with as I see fit." Having said his piece, he could see no point in remaining another moment. So Hunter rose from the wooden pew and started down the aisle of the church, where the ladies had chosen to hold their impromptu meeting.

"You of all people, Hunter Kincaid. After what Della DeAngelo did to you, I would think you would know better," she shouted, bombarding his retreating back with her cackling.

Hatty Shackelford had a vicious tongue that needed more than simple curbing. He turned to confront her and a situation that quickly was becoming no better than a witch hunt.

"Ladies, if any of you had a Christian bone in your body, you'd give her half a chance."

Ignoring the pointed stares, he left the church, pausing only a moment in the vestibule before proceeding through the door and into the dusty street.

Still, in spite of what he thought of Hatty Shackelford, she could well be right. After Della, he should have known better than to even consider trusting another woman with his heart. But, oh, how he wanted to!

As hard as he tried to block them out, his mind overflowed with memories of Marina making incredibly sweet love to him. What he should have remembered instead was that a woman like Marina Nicolaiev, a woman born to a life of luxury—a dancer, by God—would never be satisfied for long with what little he or a place like Sweetwater could offer her. Eventually she would get her fill of them both and move on.

He paused in the middle of the street, his heart stretched nearly to its limit, to consider how it would feel to suffer such disappointment again. The darkness made the brightly lit building at the far end of the street appear even more like a beacon than it had years ago when he had been barely more than a child. Only now his need sprung from more than innocent curiosity. It was the product of pain, a longing that ran so deep it twisted him up inside and left him feeling battered. He wanted to believe her, wanted to open his heart and his life to her, wanted to experience the joy without fear of regret that only she could give him.

As if they had a mind of their own, his feet moved in the

direction of his desire. On reaching the stoop, he paused on the first step, trying to convince himself to go home, to forget about her. The woman simply didn't warrant the risks.

Then, through one of the windows, he caught sight of her and her surprisingly industrious efforts. The Songbird Saloon had never looked better. Everything sparkled, clean and polished, even the two chandeliers his father had had shipped all the way from St. Louis. Someone had artfully arranged the chairs in an arc at the foot of the stage. The piano, not so long ago a haven for mice, looked restored and shone from hours of hand-rubbing. He had always loved that damned piano, had wanted to learn how to play it, but his daddy had insisted that real men didn't pursue such pastimes.

Dressed simply in a becoming green gown with a high neck and stiff collar, Marina sat on the edge of the raised platform, dejected. Sergei paced behind her. Hunter noted that the dance partner had elicited her instant disagreement, for her lovely head with her glorious dark hair piled high upon it whipped back and forth.

As much as he wanted to go to the door, to enter the building and tell her that he wanted to trust her, he hesitated. He had a spare key and as her landlord he had every right to come and go on his own property as he pleased, but Hunter fought down the urge to be with her, shoving his hands into the pocket of his jacket.

Unaware of his presence, Marina slid off her perch on the stage and came toward the window. He ducked back. From the protection of the darkness he could see her forlorn expression as she stared past him into the Wyoming night. Whatever she needed to prove, he doubted her motives had a damn thing to do with him.

Walking away, he wished her well. Truly he did. But realistically, he didn't think she'd make it to the end of the month.

"You're wrong, Sergei. They will come." Frowning, Marina strained to see beyond the edge of the porch. From the corner of her eye she caught a slight movement, a flash of what could have been a checkered shirt. Filled with hope and longing, she focused on the void until she was forced to accept that she had seen nothing except what her imagination had devised.

"*A Night of Cultural Exchange,*" Sergei read, picking up one of the hand-printed fliers. "What makes you think these people even know what a cultural exchange is?" Carelessly, he tossed down the paper square, unconcerned when it fluttered to the floor.

"It's explained right here," Marina said, moving away from the window to retrieve the precious handbill and dust it off. She and Fanny had worked hard all day, first designing then making a dozen of them.

"I won't be a part of such nonsense." Sergei rose haughtily. "Besides, I refuse to put myself at unnecessary risk again."

"Sergei, I promise there will be little risk involved. Chloe has even agreed to lend us one of her doormen to keep out riffraff, and I am targeting the wholesome sensibilities of the women of the community. I plan on reciting a selection of works by the English poetess Elizabeth Barrett Browning. Fanny has agreed to sing an ensemble of Irish ballads, and John is brushing up on several classical pieces by an array of international composers—Beethoven, Chopin, even our own Tchaikovsky. The members of the *corps de ballet* have decided to put on a display of folk dances from around the world to the accompaniment of the violinist."

"What did you have in mind for me to do, Marinuska?"

Knowing Sergei had never been one to be left out of the limelight for long, she smiled at him. Taking him by the hand, she led him back to the stage. "I thought you might like to perform the traditional Russian sword dance."

"The *Zaporózhets?*" Sergei's handsome face lit up with Slavic pride. "It is very difficult, you know. Only the most athletic dancer can perform it."

"Very difficult, indeed, and most impressive to an audience, especially a paying audience. That is why it would be perfect for you. Besides—" She added the crowning touch to her persuasive argument. "—I'm sure the female population of Sweetwater would find it irresistible."

"Really? You think so?"

"I'm certain of it."

Well, if not certain, then pretty sure, if she could believe what Chloe had told her. According to some of the madam's more influential customers, their wives had gotten the false impression that Sergei had a title. It was all they talked about day and night, the men complained, Count Sergei this, the handsome Count Sergei that. Dying to get to know him better, they were unsure how to go about it.

"A public performance, something more along the lines of their expectation of hearth, home, and wholesomeness. Give their idol top billing, then them access to him afterward. It might just do the trick," Chloe had asserted.

"I don't know, Chloe." Marina had voiced her reservations to her well-meaning friend. "To use a lie . . ."

"Only a little, insignificant one. What possible harm could it do?"

None that she couldn't make right once they had gained acceptance in the community, Marina assured herself, fighting down a recurring twinge of guilt. Without public acceptance, an inner voice argued, how could she ever hope to convince Hunter of her sincerity in wanting to stay?

Watching Sergei, full of his own preeminence, prance about the soon-to-be theater, she wondered how her partner would feel if he knew about her decision to stay. She had yet to find the courage or the right time to tell him. He, along with the rest of the troupe, thought that they worked toward a mutual goal of making enough money to pay for their way back to New York.

She had every intention of seeing to it that anyone who wished to return did so. As for Sergei and the loyal way he had stuck by her . . .

She gnawed on her lip guiltily.

"Marina," Sergei called to her, emerging from the prop room, his arms laden with an assortment of costumes, his demeanor one of self-importance. "You must help me decide what will look the most authentic."

Authenticity? What did it really matter? The people of Sweetwater wouldn't know the difference even if he wore peasant's garb. More importantly, he must look irresistible.

"I'm coming, Sergei," she called out sweetly, praying she hadn't underestimated any of the participants in the risky game she played.

"Daddy, it's simply a night of cultural exchange."

"Just what does that mean, Rainee?" Hunter asked, wondering how in the hell she had gotten yet another handbill when he had ordered her to stay away from town. But just as importantly, he wondered what new stratagem Marina had devised now.

"Poetry reading, classical music, traditional folk dances."

"Sounds boring to me."

"Please, Daddy. Even Annie Shackelford's parents are going to allow her to go tonight."

"Hatty Shackelford? Are you sure?" He lifted one brow in

surprise, unable to imagine what could have possibly changed the incredibly opinionated mind of the mayor's wife regarding Marina and her group. He doubted it could have been anything he might have said. Whatever had influenced her, it had to be something monumental indeed, something Hatty thought advantageous to her own well-being.

"Please, Daddy," Rainee pleaded prettily when it appeared he had stopped to consider her request.

"I'm sorry, Rainee, but I have good reason for not wanting you exposed to such an unhealthy influence." At least not until he'd had a chance to check it out for himself first.

"You are mean and cruel, and I hate you, Daddy!" Rainee cried, racing back up the stairs.

The door to her room slammed so hard he felt the angry vibration in the banister beneath his hand.

Tomorrow, once his daughter had calmed down, he could only hope she would feel differently. Clamping his lips together in determination, Hunter spun about, departing the house as if a pack of annoying coyotes nipped at his heels.

The night of cultural exchange arrived long before Marina felt prepared to give the all-important performance. It was one thing to execute a difficult combination of steps, quite another to recall the intricate words of a poem. Even if she did succeed in remembering her lines, what if nobody came?

She peeked around the curtain drawn across the stage. It was only a half an hour before they were to begin, and less than a quarter of the chairs were occupied. Then, to her relief, she saw the mayor and his family enter and take seats close to the front. Fifteen minutes later, the theater had filled to capacity.

Rushing into the wings to report her findings and bolster the uncertain spirits of the performers, she spotted a young man, a cowboy judging by his dress, standing to one side, looking totally out of place. How had someone unauthorized managed to get not only past the doorman but backstage? Fearing a repeat of the disaster of their last performance, Marina approached him, determined to send him away as quickly as possible.

"You are not allowed back here," she stated with authority, taking the boy by the arm and whisking him toward the outside entrance to the stage. To her relief he didn't resist.

"Please, I'm sorry," he said instead. "It's just that I've been asked to deliver this message to a Mr. Bozzacchi. Could you see it gets to him?"

"A note for Sergei? Of course." Taking the folded piece of paper from the messenger's hand, she shoved him through the exit into the alleyway. Shutting the door, she locked it for good measure, making certain no one else could find such easy access. She started to unfold the note when the lights inside dimmed in the traditional warning that the performance was about to begin.

As the opening act she only had a few moments to prepare, so Marina tucked the missive into her pocket with the intention of delivering it to Sergei as soon as possible and hurried to take her place center stage.

The curtain rose. She took a deep breath.

" 'How do I love thee? Let me count the ways,' " she began the first line of her recitation.

What little she could see of the stone-faced audience over the bright stage lights, they stared back at her with little encouragement or understanding.

* * *

Marina had only just begun when Hunter heard the restless rustle of programs opening. Sitting in the very last row of chairs, he stared down into his own playbill. He had no idea who this Elizabeth Barrett Browning might be, but her poetry clearly made little sense . . . unless Marina intended to speak directly to him. Still, the rich, lyrical quality of her cultured voice was pleasing to the ear. Closing his eyes, he listened and pretended.

Too soon, at least in Hunter's opinion, she finished, followed by a smattering of polite applause. However, the robust exhibition of folk dances received a much more enthusiastic reception from the audience. Many of the steps and quadrilles were similar to the lively dances performed by the citizens themselves at Saturday-night shindigs. Next came a songstress, who, although she had a sweet-enough voice, could hardly be heard since she sang so softly.

By the time the piano player had begun his recital the audience's restlessness had turned to boredom. Once again Hunter glanced at his program. He recognized the name of Beethoven among the several composers listed and nodded approvingly. Still, by the time the musician had finished and stood to receive his applause, many of the men in the audience had fallen asleep. The women, stoically attempting to feign an interest, clapped halfheartedly.

Had the entertainment, such as it was, ended there, no doubt everyone would have gotten up politely and left, grateful to be set free of the trappings called culture. But, to everyone's surprise, the lights dimmed suddenly except for a narrow spotlight on the closed curtain across the stage. When it opened, the Russian exploded onto the stage with a fierce, bloodcurdling yell that made an Indian war whoop seem tame by comparison.

"What in the hell's going on?" muttered Jonas Shackelford,

nearly falling out of his seat when rudely jarred awake from his sound sleep. "Are we under some kind of savage attack?"

Unfortunately, he was the only one "under attack." As usual, Hatty's henpecking could be merciless.

Ignoring the disruption, the dancer continued. Hunter had never seen anything like it. Dressed in a costume garish enough to blind a man, the Russian slashed the air with three wicked-looking swords that made every male, including himself, tense with discomfort. Then the man proceeded to dance, leaping and jumping, doing things with his feet and legs that seemed humanly impossible as he defied the laws of gravity. At the same time, the glistening weapons flashed around him in such a dangerous manner that every man in the audience couldn't help but admire his fortitude if not his foolishness.

Even Hunter had to admit he was in a cold sweat and ready to get out by the time the Russian had finished, jumping down from the stage only feet from the first row and emitting another savage yell. The women, however, seemed totally entranced, clapping with undisguised enthusiasm.

Every man in the place had the same idea he had. Hunter had seen cattle stampede with more consideration. Not until they were all outside did they realize that the womenfolk hadn't followed their lead.

"Where the hell are those damn-fool women?" bellowed Jeb Granger, always the first to complain when something didn't go his way.

Curious, even though he had no womenfolk to contend with himself, Hunter peered back through the open door. If he had thought the male stampede to get out had been something, then he had another think coming.

Incredibly, the women crowded around the Russian, oohing and aahing, holding out their programs for him to sign as if he were a truly grand celebrity. All he could think as he watched them make fools of themselves was, thank God he had the foresight to leave Rainee at home. The last thing he would ever tolerate was for her to make cow-eyes at some dang-fool Russian dancer.

Apparently the other men felt the same way about their wives and daughters. In the same manner in which they had hurried out of the building, they pushed their way back in.

"Jonas Shackelford, let go of my arm," Hatty raged as he pulled her along, courageously avoiding the sting of her rolled-up program as she hit him with it repeatedly.

Elvira Granger followed her husband in obedient silence, but if looks had been bullets, an unsuspecting Jeb would have taken a cylinder full in the back.

Finally the makeshift auditorium cleared, husbands with temporarily subdued spouses and daughters in tow. Left standing alone in the doorway, Hunter stared at the self-glorified Russian glaring back at him from across the room as if goaded by a personal vendetta. But how could that be? He hardly knew the other man.

However, he did know that the once-happy community of Sweetwater, Wyoming, was now split by a rift as wide as a canyon, the men on one side, the women on the other. Neither side had yet to flex the muscles of their full potential to do battle. Whether any of them knew it or not, including the Russian himself, Sergei Bozzacchi could very well be the catalyst that could spark a full-fledged war.

Did Marina realize the dangerous game she had choreographed? If she did, did she care whose lives it might affect? His gaze drifted to where she stood, her attention focused on the mousy woman who had sung the Irish ballads.

As if she sensed him staring at her, she glanced his way. An uncertain smile lifted her sensuous lips; her dark eyes searched his face. For what? Approval?

The one thing he felt incapable of giving her.

Looking away, his gaze clashed once again with that of her partner. With an automatic—yet guarded—gesture, Hunter touched the brim of his hat, acknowledging the other man's presence and open hostility.

Turning his back on a newfound enemy, he left the building, closing the door behind him.

Thirteen

"Marinuska, I demand to know exactly what that man, Hunter Kincaid, means to you." Following Marina down the upstairs hallway, Sergei claimed her arm with uncharacteristic high-handedness that caught her by surprise.

"Means to me?" She laughed, wondering if her attempt at nonchalance had succeeded or if she merely sounded nervous. "Why nothing, Sergei. He means nothing at all to me." Expecting him to accept her statement, she turned away to continue toward her room.

Instead, he shook her roughly.

"You would not lie to me, would you?"

They stood alone in the hallway, no one else within hearing range. So why did she hesitate to tell him the truth? Perhaps because she couldn't be certain yet of the outcome that hinged so much on Sergei's cooperation. But she would tell him, eventually, as soon as she could, as soon as she was sure.

"Sergei, let go of my arm," she demanded, staring down at his bruising fingers with an imperial air that rivaled his. "You are hurting me."

He obeyed immediately, of course. Just as she had known that he would.

"I'm sorry, Marinuska," the Sergei she knew so well and considered a friend quickly assured her. "It's just that I don't trust him."

"Then at least trust me." Again she turned from him.

"How soon will we be leaving?"

"Leaving?" Her heart skipped a beat when confronted with the fact that once again she must lie to him.

"Of course. Since tonight's performance was a big success, surely we made enough money to purchase train tickets out of here."

"We did well," she agreed, seeking a way to put him off, at least until she'd had a chance to formulate a better answer, "but I doubt we made enough for everyone in the troupe."

"Everyone? Look, Marina. Perhaps it's time you stop assuming responsibility for *everyone*. I know we must have made enough for you and me to get back to New York."

"Sergei!" she exclaimed with genuine shock. "Surely you aren't suggesting that we abandon the rest of the troupe?"

"Abandon? Good God, Marina, they're not children. They are quite capable of taking care of themselves." Reaching out, he grasped her hand. "You must simply look at it as a necessary parting of the ways."

"No, Sergei." She struggled to push away the fingers that had suddenly clamped down on hers. "I could never do that, not to Fanny or John or any of them. But if you wish to go on, I understand." Perhaps such a "necessary parting" was inevitable. As much as she needed him, she would not stand in his way.

"No, I can't leave you behind, Marinuska. You wouldn't want me to, would you?" His pleading look radiated a desperation she'd never noticed before.

"Of course not, Sergei," she reassured him. "But I have never forgotten the reason we came to America in the first place, why I was forced to flee from Russia. What's so wrong with Sweetwater, Wyoming? It's isolated, far away from the mainstream of life. I feel safe here. At least it offers us a place to rest for a while," she pointed out. Until she could decide otherwise, until she knew whether she'd won or lost Hunter Kincaid, that was as close to the truth as she dared come.

"Marinuska." In a gesture of exaggerated gentleness, he touched her face. "Remember how it was in New York. Wouldn't you like to go back?" He stared at her as if he wanted to say more. "Oh, very well," he suddenly conceded with a dramatic sigh. "We can stay here for a little while. But you must agree to consider our inevitable day of departure."

"I agree." She smiled in gratitude, shoving her hand in her pocket when he released it and started down the hall toward his own room.

Her fingers curled around a piece of folded paper. The note the young cowboy had asked her to give to him.

"Sergei, wait." Catching up to him, she pressed the missive into his hand, waiting for him to open and read it.

"From one of your many ardent admirers?" she asked half-jokingly.

"As a matter of fact, it is," he replied after scanning it quickly. Smiling secretively, he tucked the message into the pocket of his shirt.

As he swaggered away, Marina wondered what the note had said and who had written it. Perhaps she should have read it before giving it to him. But of course, how perfectly ridiculous! Sergei Bozzacchi was one of the few people she should completely trust. The fact that she didn't, no doubt indicated a need for her to examine her own shortcomings.

Long after all the lights were extinguished downstairs, then slowly, one by one, upstairs as well, Hunter waited outside the Songbird. Only it wasn't the Songbird Saloon anymore. Overnight it had become Marina's theater, a place that now reflected her elegance and cultured style, or at least a facsimile, the best Sweetwater could ever hope to offer.

Should he go or should he stay? Not a man normally prone to fence-straddling, he felt like a petty thief in the night standing before his own property trying to decide whether to enter the building or not. However, this need that possessed him to feel close to Marina, to let his guard down and take the risk of allowing her into his heart, was certain to backfire on him. One way or another, he was bound to lose her.

But make up his mind he must or else continue to stand in the middle of the street like the worst kind of fool until the sun came up.

Reaching into the pocket of his jacket, he fished out the key to the front door. At first he just stared at it—a small metal object lying in the palm of his hand—trying to convince himself that he had no idea how that key had gotten into his pocket. But the truth was, he had put it there on purpose with every intention of using it.

At last, his mind made up, Hunter let himself in. The silent stillness washed over him with a dignity that had never been a part of the Songbird. Once again it reminded him of Marina, of what they had shared all too briefly, and he wondered if he might be throwing away something precious in the name of self-preservation that would leave him weighted with regrets for the rest of his life. Regrets not for what he had done, but for what he *hadn't* done.

Moving forward as if in a trance, he sat down in the first seat of the front row of chairs. Watching the stage, he halfway expected the curtains to part, the show to begin, the lovely ballerina of his dreams to dance only for his eyes to see.

* * *

Something woke her. A sound? No, she hadn't heard anything, even though she strained in the darkness to catch the slightest unfamiliar noise. All remained quiet except for the soft, mournful warble of an unfamiliar night bird outside her open window.

Then it must have been a disturbing dream. Why else would her heart still be racing out of control? As hard as she tried, she couldn't recall even a fleeting glimpse of a nightmare. So it wasn't a dream, good or bad, that caused her to lie there, wide awake, filled with an overwhelming desire to get up and go downstairs.

The scrape of a chair sounded from below.

Cautiously, she threw off the covers, pushed her always-cold feet into the waiting pair of warm, woolen slippers, her arms into the sleeves of the wrapper she kept at the foot of the bed. Taking up the lamp from the dresser, she lit it before quietly leaving her room to investigate.

Once she reached the second landing, she paused, spying one of the swords that Sergei had so carelessly left there after the performance. She lifted the lantern high enough to cast its halo of yellow light over the makeshift auditorium on the first floor, empty now and silent.

Sword raised, she let her gaze run along the front row of chairs until it collided with the sky-blue eyes of Hunter Kincaid.

"Hunter? What are you doing here?" she asked in a voice breathless with a hodgepodge of emotions. Abruptly, she lowered the sword.

"Funny, Marina, that you should take the words right out of my mouth." He made no effort to rise or to look away.

Or to explain the meaning of his statement. Instinctively she sensed his sarcasm held the key to understanding him.

"I live here, or have you forgotten that?"

"You don't live here, Marina. At least, not for very long. A woman like you never does."

"You have no right to be here." Fear that he'd changed his mind and now planned to evict her before she had the chance to prove herself gave her the courage to speak up.

"I have every right. I own this building, or have *you* forgotten that?"

"Not at all, Mr. Kincaid. You'll get your rent money at the end of each month. And as long as you do, you can't make me leave."

"Make you, darlin'? Oh, I don't think I'll have to make you. After tonight's performance I can't imagine what you have planned next. You know, you can read only so many poems and expect people to pay to listen to them. This town has yet to accept you."

It wasn't as much what he said that hurt as what he didn't say. *He* had yet to accept her.

"Get out!" Infuriated by the realization, she pointed at the door.

To her surprise he not only did as she told him, but didn't bother to even once look back.

For the rest of the night Marina tossed and turned in her lonely bed, the encounter with Hunter making it impossible for her to sleep.

She couldn't continue to ignore reality. How many performances *could* they hope to give before they simply ran out of paying audiences? Two? Three? A dozen, if they were lucky? Even Sergei's newfound popularity couldn't carry them forever. Then what?

It took money to feed and house so many, a steady influx of money. Maybe she should listen to Sergei. Maybe she should take what they had earned tonight and leave while she still had the chance. No, she refused to do that, not now, not ever. Even if she had not wished to stay for her own selfish reasons, she would never abandon those who depended on her. Such nobleness, however, did nothing to bring her any closer to a solution.

As the sun peeked into her window, her thoughts drifted to a safer time when she had been a child first learning ballet at the Royal Academy. Would she have shown such enthusiasm and determination if she had realized then where her talent would eventually lead her? Recalling the many instructors who had pounded their batons and worked her until quite often she collapsed with exhaustion in tears, she wondered from where she had garnered her stamina and determination never to give up. Of late, she had felt anything but the strength to carry on.

As for her dance masters, what had driven them to devote their lives to teaching others? Maybe they, too, had succumbed to a need to eat and keep a roof over their heads.

A teacher? At first the idea buzzed in her mind like an evasive bee. Grasping hold of it to examine it more closely, she finally concluded it might actually work.

Brimming with enthusiasm, she rose, quickly changed her clothes, and made her way to Fanny's room. She knocked softly on the door.

"Who is it?" came the sleepy inquiry.

"Fanny, it's me," she whispered, not wishing to awaken anyone else at the moment, not until she'd had the chance to discuss her idea with the only person she had ever taken the time and opportunity to teach. If anyone would know if she had what it took to be a good instructor, Fanny would. "I need to talk to you."

After a few moments, the door cracked opened. Fanny stuck her sleep-tousled head out.

"What is it?" she asked.

"Please, get dressed and come downstairs as soon as you can."

Downstairs Marina waited, alternating between stillness and pacing. Glancing over the empty theater, she continued to formulate the details of her plan, which was beginning to look better and better. At last, Fanny, accompanied by John, joined her.

"So, what's so important this early in the morning?" Yawning, Fanny plopped into one of the theater chairs, slouching down and throwing one slender leg over the back of the seat in front of her.

"I have an idea about how to make money. Steady money," Marina began, not bothering to contain the excitement that bubbled up inside her.

"All right. Let's hear this one," John interjected. "After last night, which was a bust except for Sergei as far as I'm concerned, it had better be good." The piano player folded his arms over his chest.

"Fanny," she asked, ignoring John, "do you think I would make a good ballet instructor?"

"The best," her friend readily admitted. "Look how much I have learned from you. What do you have in mind?"

"We can open a school of ballet."

"We?" Fanny asked.

"Of course, we," Marina replied, launching into a detailed explanation of her plan. Even as she spoke, she heard a noise on the stairs. Sergei.

"Marina, what are you thinking?" he demanded. "Teaching is a waste of your superior talents. Besides, whom would you have as students?" He laughed. "Chloe's whores?"

That was exactly where she intended to start. Several of the "ladies" who worked for the madam had expressed their admiration for the sensuous moves incorporated in dance. Even Chloe had once mentioned the correlation between lovemaking and a *pas de deux*. Perhaps those women would be willing to pay to learn ballet. In time, Marina might even attract some of the more respectable citizens of Sweetwater.

"And why not? Money is money, and we will have lots to earn if we ever want to get out of here," she added, flashing Sergei a look she hoped would remind him of their conversation in the upstairs hallway. "Unless you think you can do better," she baited him sweetly, assuming he would concede when he had no ready answer.

"Better? Of course, I can," he said, puffing up like a game-cock duly challenged.

"You can?" Marina exclaimed, surprised by his unexpected response.

"Yes, Marinuska. I know who might wish to be our very first student."

"Who?" she asked, not missing the fact that he had said "our" student, unconsciously including himself in this latest venture.

Reaching into the pocket of his shirt, he pulled out the crumpled note she had given him earlier. "Who else but Miss Rainee Kincaid?"

"Hunter's daughter?" Why did it alarm her so to learn that Rainee had written Sergei a note? Remembering the concern Hunter had shown when the troupe had first arrived in town, something about bad influence and gypsies if she recalled, she wondered if he knew what his daughter was up to.

"Of course." Sergei smiled in that secretive way he had of late that always made her worry. "She's already asked me if I could show her a few steps."

"That's all. She wants you to teach her to dance?"

"What else would you have me do with one so young?" he retorted.

"Nothing, Sergei. This is wonderful." Perhaps more so than

she had first realized. It was apparent that the girl was important to Hunter. Perhaps if she could gain the daughter's trust, the father's would soon follow. But that was not the only reason she would look forward to teaching her. There was something special about Rainee, something that reminded her of herself. "You must let her know right away about our plans for a dance academy."

"Then you approve of my writing her back."

"Absolutely," she agreed readily, her mind a whirl of happy plans. All they needed was to get one of the younger female citizens involved, someone respectable like Rainee Kincaid. Once that happened, the others would eventually follow.

In the meantime, she had every intention of following up on her original idea to invite Chloe's girls to dance classes.

To Marina's relief, her plan was an instant, if somewhat modest, success. Chloe's enthusiasm, if not that of all of her employees, brought in an influx of students, more than enough to fill Marina's and Fanny's agenda and maintain the impression among the troupe members that she was working hard to earn the money necessary to take the entire troupe, including herself, back to New York. With any luck, to the town, including Hunter, she would appear more determined than ever to stay.

Although it was frustrating, Marina quickly learned to accept that not all her students, practically none to be honest, showed even an inkling of talent. Oh, she had to admit they had an inborn sense of rhythm. It was little enough to work with, but for the most part all she had.

"First position," she instructed the group of women lined up along the makeshift exercise *barre* John and Sergei had constructed from the old foot-rail of the saloon bar. This was at least the dozenth time they had gone over the five basic positions of ballet. Only half of her students got it right or were reasonably close. The rest . . .

Fanny, working as her assistant, demonstrated the stance as Marina went down the line adjusting feet and knees and hips that swiveled too much to suit her. She could do only so much.

"Plié," she said as Fanny showed them the simple-yet-graceful movement so essential to good form. "Now, you do it," she requested.

Clearly she recalled Marius Petipa, her dance master, comparing her once to an ostrich attempting unsuccessfully to bury its head in the sand. At that moment as she watched her students bob and duck and strain, she could truly understand his meaning.

"Again," she instructed with unfailing patience.

This time the procedure was even more painful to watch. One of the girls practically fell on her face.

"All right," she said, stifling a frustrated sigh. "I suppose that's enough for today. I want all of you to go home and practice. Practice, practice," she insisted in a lyrical, school-room voice.

Her words were not met with much enthusiasm. Perhaps Sergei had been right in the first place. She wasted her talent.

"It's not as bad as you think, Marina."

Attempting to keep the weariness out of her smile, Marina turned to Chloe, who sat watching from the sidelines like a stage mother.

"Oh, Chloe, I don't know. It seems so hopeless."

"Take heart, honey. They'll learn."

"I don't know why you want to waste your money."

"It's not wasted. These lessons will give my girls something to do besides lie around and eat all day." She leaned confidentially toward Marina. "In my business, it's a proven fact. Increased activity goes hand in hand with increased productivity."

In spite of herself, Marina laughed.

"Talking about productivity, the Ladies' Committee had a meeting the other night." She said it with such pretention, with her nose in the air, her pinky lifted in an exaggerated crook, that Marina couldn't help but laugh.

"It was all about you."

"About me?" Marina's heart began to hammer with alarm.

"Yes. It took place just a few days before you gave your last performance."

"How do you know? Were you there?"

"In a pig's eye." Chloe snorted merrily. "But I got my information from the most reliable of sources." She leaned forward. "Mayor Shackelford, no less, told me he heard it from the old biddy herself." She studied Marina for a moment before continuing. "Hunter attended it, though."

"I'm sure he did." Crossing her arms, she looked away to conceal her sour expression. "No wonder he threatened to evict me."

"Evict you? Not likely. He stood up for you against the good ladies of Sweetwater."

"Hunter?" Marina asked incredulously, breathless with the hope that surged through her. "Are you certain?"

Chloe nodded, her green eyes conveying the pride normally reserved for mothers.

Marina wavered. Did Hunter's unexpected support mean that he'd finally begun to accept her?

More likely it meant nothing, she cautioned her incredibly naive heart, remembering the cruel things he had said the night after their last performance, after he had attended that meeting. Chloe must have gotten her information wrong. But even if he had stood up for her, like any good businessman, he could have done so simply to protect an investment. Why wouldn't he want his tenant to stay—as long as she paid the rent on time?

"Thank you, Chloe, but I think you give him more credit than you should," she insisted, determined to maintain her dignity and grace, at least in the presence of others. Although sometimes she couldn't help but wonder if such strength of character didn't do her more harm than good, she struggled that much harder to control her flagging spirits and a feeling of helpless defeat.

"Look, honey." Chloe touched her arm as if she truly understood what Marina felt, as if maybe she, too, had gone through a similar battle in her life. "I've known Hunter Kincaid a long time. You've gotta believe me. He's a good man—about as honorable as they come. Just give him a little more time to see that you are worth trusting. He'll come around."

"Oh, Chloe, I can only hope that you are right."

Indeed, only time would tell. However, Marina had learned that hopes quite often fell short of achieving goals.

The next morning renewed Marina's faith in the merit of hope.

Marina preferred to practice in the early morning hours; she always had. Here in Sweetwater she might not have a cup of hot chocolate to accompany her exercises, but she did have several hours of quiet to work at the *barre* undisturbed.

Dressed in tights and leggings, unaware of anything but the familiar melody played by her music box and the exhilarating feel of every muscle in her body stretched and limber, she was in the middle of practicing a series of *fouettés pirouettes* when she felt as if someone watched her.

"Yes, what is it?" Perturbed at the interruption, she dropped from *pointe* to face the intruder.

Discovering the familiar face of Rainee Kincaid pressed to the front window, Marina went to the front door and opened it.

"I'm sor-r-ry, Your Highness," the girl stammered, stepping back with a guilty look. "I didn't mean to be a Peeping Tom. I only wished to watch. Maybe it would be best if I came back later."

"Instead, why don't you come inside, Rainee?"

"You don't mind?" Rainee cast her a concerned look.

"Not at all. In fact," she said, taking the girl by the arm and leading her into the building, "I was disappointed when you didn't showed up for our rehearsal."

"Believe me, I wanted to be there more than anything." Rainee's brows worked with worry. "I really did, but circumstances . . . out of my control," she hedged, her blue eyes as piercing as her father's when they finally settled on Marina, "prevented me."

"I know what you mean. Out of your control puts it mildly." Marina offered a little laugh of encouragement, assuming Rainee referred to the unreceptive attitude of the good citizens of Sweetwater. "With any luck, maybe we can all put that behind us now."

"Do you really think so?" Rainee asked, her expressive eyes aglow with hope. That's where the similarity to her father ended. Hunters eyes never revealed anything he felt or thought.

"I'm banking on it," she said, then added under her breath as she steered the girl toward the stage, "now that you are here."

"I'm sorry. I didn't catch what you said," the girl confessed as she sat down. She stared up with open trust, waiting for Marina to repeat herself.

"Nothing, Rainee. Absolutely nothing." Marina smiled sweetly to cover up an ever-increasing sense of guilt. Was it wrong of her to use this innocent child as a means to get to her father? No, she reassured herself. She had no ulterior motives, merely a wish to gain his trust the way she had his daughter's. Someday, if she had her way, Rainee might be like a daughter to her as well. She wanted to get to know the girl better, wanted them to become friends, wanted to give her the chance to follow her dreams. "So, what can I do for you, Rainee?" Marina asked.

"Please, I would like very much to take lessons. I want to learn to dance, to be beautiful just like you," she pleaded.

If one could truly think of eyes as *starry,* then that best described the look in Rainee's. Once again, Marina was reminded of herself so long ago when all she had wanted to do was dance.

"Rainee, you are already very beautiful. But surely your father must tell you that."

"He does." Rainee shrugged. "Sort of. But Daddy says there are two kinds of pretty. The marrying kind and the other kind."

"Other kind? And what kind is that?" Marina pressed, confronted with a growing suspicion of what Hunter considered the "other" kind.

"Pretty like you. Daddy says it's not the way a nice girl should want to be, but he's wrong. I want to be just like you."

"Your father said that?" Marina exclaimed. So Hunter Kincaid didn't think of her as the marrying kind, did he? Well, she would show him just what kind of woman she was. "Well, Rainee, I think perhaps I can find the time to teach you ballet."

"Oh, thank you," the girl said. Then she glanced about as if not quite satisfied, as if there were something else.

"Is that not what you want, to learn how to dance?"

"Of course." She looked down at her hands as if embarrassed. "It's just that the count . . . in his note he promised *he* would teach me."

"The count? Oh, you mean Sergei. He will. Eventually," Marina promised, knowing full well she would have to deal with this misconception with every new student. Whether she liked it or not, it was Sergei's popularity that would bring them. And she was truly grateful for it and for him. "However, he is not an early riser. Besides, in the beginning I think you will find my instruction more beneficial. Now, when would you like to get started?"

"As soon as possible."

"Shall we begin now?"

"Now? Right now?" Rainee glanced around nervously and giggled. "I didn't think . . . I'm unprepared. I don't even have on proper clothing."

"That's not a problem. There's a dressing room through that door." Marina pointed toward a small room that had once been a liquor closet. "There you will find tights and slippers that should fit you." Castoffs of the dancers of the *corps de ballet,* their contribution to the business endeavor.

Not that Marina complained. Not at all, for everyone in the troupe pitched in and did their fair share. The musicians had all worked hard to turn the building first into a theater and then into a dance studio and now provided the music for the lessons. Fanny cooked the meals. The other girls willingly divided up the chores—cleaning, dishes, and laundry—among themselves. They were truly pulling together like a family.

A few moments later, Rainee emerged from the dressing room appropriately dressed and stood before Marina.

"Don't be embarrassed," Marina instructed as she carefully assessed the girl's body potential now that it was more clearly defined in the unrestrictive clothing.

She had lovely arms and legs, graceful and expressive. Her long waist, set off by a high rib cage, offered an excellent degree of flexibility. Without a doubt, Rainee had been built to dance; and if Marina hadn't known the girl's father, she would have sworn the child had been born to it. With only a little talent, and Marina suspected she possessed more than a little, Rainee might even someday be a prima ballerina.

Marina could hardly suppress her rising excitement. At last, a worthy student, untouched clay for her to mold and form to her own visions of perfection. She imagined all dance instructors must feel that way whenever they discover raw talent. It gave her new insight into the great masters—including her own, Marius Petipa, who had demanded so much from her.

"Shall we get started?" she asked, clapping her hands.

She spent the rest of the morning showing Rainee the five basic positions of both hands and feet. Then she drilled the more-than-willing student until the girl could do them adequately with little reminding.

After several hours they were both exhausted. Reluctantly, filled with glowing elation, Marina declared the first lesson over. Her feeling of accomplishment was contagious, and Rainee fell into her arms. They both began to laugh, and the moment was special.

"What's so funny?"

At the same time they both looked up. At the top of the stairs stood Sergei, sleep-tousled and irritated.

"Your lordship." Rainee dipped a less-than-respectable curtsy.

Marina found her attempt charming. Would Sergei? she wondered. He studied the girl, still dressed in tights and leggings, intently.

"Oh, yes, Rainee Kincaid. I'm glad you could make it." He turned and went back up the stairs.

Rainee's crestfallen look told her the girl was disappointed. Marina would have to talk to Sergei about showing more enthusiasm when it came to the students.

"Don't let his early-morning ill-humor alarm you, Rainee. He's always grumpy when he first gets up," Marina assured her.

"Oh, yes, I suppose you would know, wouldn't you?"

What a strange look the girl gave her! Uncertain, Marina put her arm around Rainee's shoulder and gave her another encouraging squeeze.

"When shall we make your next lesson? The same time next week?"

"No, I would like to make it later in the day, if we could."

"Later, of course." She suspected the request had something to do with Sergei. "Say around eleven."

Rainee gave her a questioning look.

"Not to worry, Count Sergei will be up by then."

Again, they both laughed.

Awhile later, once Rainee was dressed in her street clothes again, Marina, filled with an astonishing sense of pride, watched her slip out the front door.

Rainee Kincaid. Given enough time, she could come to care as much about the girl as she did her impossible father.

Hunter Kincaid. An infuriating man with his theory of two kinds of beauty. Well, she would show him only one kind was worth reckoning with.

"Afternoon, ladies."

Marina nodded in response to the storekeeper's salutation.

Once a week on Fridays, she and Fanny did the necessary shopping at the general store. Shopping. Such a quaint custom, one she had always relegated to servants when she had lived in Russia. Persons of distinction never visited the stalls and shops of the marketplace in St. Petersburg.

St. Petersburg was a long way off, as was the life she had lived there, she reminded herself. In Sweetwater, everyone, rich or poor, came to the general store to make their purchases.

The general store. An interesting place, Marina readily admitted, if somewhat unusual. Old men sat around cracker barrels playing cards or dominoes. Children eyed the glass jars of candy, and women fingered bolts of gingham cloth while the men checked out the latest in sidearms, leather goods, and ranching equipment.

She still found it incredibly difficult to believe that, in America, men openly toted loaded pistols on their hips as a proud symbol of their masculinity. Never would she forget the fiasco of that night of the troupe's second performance when Hunter had worn a gun in just such a manner and then had used it to stop what could have turned into a riot. Although she did appreciate his interference, she nevertheless felt only repulsion for such an uncivilized custom.

But that was only one of the few aspects of staying in Sweetwater she found difficult to accept. There were also hardships, shortages, and a definite lack of sophistication, but with time she felt she could live with those.

Winding up the last of her shopping, she handed Fanny the first load of packages the clerk had wrapped in brown paper.

"Go on ahead," she instructed. "I'll finish up here and be right behind you." When Fanny hesitated, she urged her to go. "Chloe and the girls will be there soon. I need you to get them started with their warm-ups."

"Very well, Marina." Arms full, Fanny departed.

Once she had paid for the purchases, Marina gathered up the remaining bundles. She could barely see over her burden as she started for the door. Concentrating on not dropping anything as she juggled her precarious load, she did not see Hunter until she practically ran into him.

Like a gentleman he opened the door for her but never said a word. He didn't have to, his dour expression said it all.

Wrong kind of woman.

She supposed she should have thanked him, but the words never found their way through her constricted throat for all she could think of was that label he had placed on her. And then it was too late. The door swung closed, leaving her on the outside, him on the inside, so much unsaid between them.

Fighting back tears, she turned to leave. Chloe had no idea when it came to Hunter Kincaid. It was only too obvious that he would never care for her the way she cared for him. Perhaps it was time to give up.

Armed with the truth, no matter how painful, Marina headed toward a place she could never consider home. Nonetheless, she was determined to get there as fast as she could.

The moment had been too brief, the feelings too strong for him to continue to ignore them much longer. She looked out of place, the once gloriously regal princess in her simple blue-gingham dress struggling to carry an armload of packages like everybody else.

Hunter straightened, forcing himself to turn away from the closed door and the woman on the other side. He had to remember not only who he was but where he was.

Russian ways didn't hold water in Wyoming. A woman like Marina Nicolaiev, no matter how hard she tried to change, didn't belong here. Eventually she would grow tired of it all and yearn to return to the genteel life she knew best.

Unfortunately, as of late, he had more and more trouble

convincing himself of that likelihood. He found himself wanting it to be different, actually believing it might be.

No, damn it. He only kidded himself. She didn't belong here; she never should have come. No matter how hard she tried, she could never be the proper wife for him, or mother to Rainee. Not that he would ever dare consider marrying her. Not at all. But even as he chided himself for being the world's biggest fool, he found himself wishing, wondering if perhaps this time . . .

He took one last look at her through the storefront window.

Marina hurried down the sidewalk—her arms laden clear to her stubborn, little chin—not bothering to watch where she was going. A man, unrecognizable in a dark, concealing coat and hat, brushed against her, shoving her out of his way.

Even as Hunter watched in horror, she tumbled headlong into the street, her purchases flying every which way. Jeb Granger tried to swerve his wagon, of that he felt certain, but there wasn't enough time.

She disappeared beneath the vehicle like debris in the roaring wake of floodwater.

"Marina!" Putting his shoulder to the door, Hunter crashed through it, unmindful of anyone else on the other side. He pushed his way through the cluster of women standing on the sidewalk and began to run, not caring who saw him or what they might think. By the time he got down the street, a crowd had already gathered. Why did people always stand around and gawk?

The huddled heap in blue gingham lay still, and yet he could swear he heard her calling to him. He couldn't move fast enough, almost as if lead weights in his shoes impeded his progress.

When finally he did manage to reach her, he threw himself down beside her, gently rolling her over.

Dirt crusted one pale cheek; her eyes were closed. Blood trickled from one side of her mouth.

Whatever you do, God, he thought, *please don't let her be dead.*

Fourteen

The nightmare. Why was it happening again?

Racked by the excruciating pain, Marina fought valiantly to control it. But more importantly, she tried to escape the unforgettable terror of a similar experience. But how could she ever block out the memory of standing before the Maryinsky Theater in St. Petersburg, as an unidentified carriage careened toward her? Someone had tried to kill her in Russia? And now, here in faraway Wyoming, had someone tried again?

If so, the implications crushed her already shaky sense of security.

"Sergei?" she moaned, certain that the strong arms lifting her from the hard ground had to belong to her staunchest friend and no one else. In spite of his temperamental, often self-serving ways, Sergei had always been there for her, never labeling her right or wrong, good or bad. Sergei considered her worthy. Yes, Sergei. Resting her head against his heart, she knew she could always count on him to continue to be there whenever she needed him.

Filled with an overwhelming sense of guilt for having lied to him, Marina forced her eyes open, attempting to focus her fuzzy vision on the man who carried her through the front door of the dance academy and toward the stairs that led to the floor above.

"Someone get the doctor and hurry," her valiant rescuer ordered.

Recognizing that voice—which certainly didn't belong to Sergei—she stiffened, realizing just who held her. Surely her ears deceived her, as did her heart, thudding with such foolish optimism.

Settled on her own bed, she tried to protest as Hunter Kincaid quickly stripped her of her shoes, stockings, and even her torn and muddied dress. By what right did he treat her so disrespectfully? By what right did he label her the wrong kind of woman? He didn't care about her, at least not in the way she wanted him to care.

"My packages? What happened to them?" she mumbled deliriously.

Her dress still clutched in his hand, he stared at her incredulously.

"Your packages? My God, Marina. The fate of a sack of flour is your biggest concern when you might have been killed?"

"And what would you care?" she groaned, the pain in her leg, her head, in every part of her body leaving her defenseless to hide how she really felt.

"I care," he snapped. "Probably too damn much for my own good."

Lying there, she blinked back the desperate need to believe him. But before she could respond, to try and draw another reluctant confession from him, a breathless Fanny rushed in, the doctor in tow.

"Here she is, Doctor," Fanny explained with little fanfare, pushing Hunter out of their way.

When he didn't resist, in fact, almost seemed relieved by the interruption, Marina lifted her hand to send them away with an imperial gesture, wanting only to know what Hunter had meant by his biting statement. But the pain was much too intense and she succumbed to the physician's poking and prodding. Still, she continued to watch Hunter, looking for another indication of concern. To her disappointment, he turned away.

"Does your arm hurt?" The doctor forced her to flex her elbow.

"No," she denied, trying to lift her head, which fairly exploded with agonizing pain behind her eyes. Dropping back down against the pillow, she whimpered before she could swallow the sound down. "Well, maybe just a little."

If Hunter noticed or cared about her discomfort, he said nothing. He continued to stare out the window, his shoulders taut and rigid.

"What about your leg?" The doctor repeated the painful process with her knee, flexing—straightening, flexing—straightening.

"It's fine. Really," she insisted through gritted teeth. But even she could see the big, ugly bruise forming above her kneecap.

"You're lucky, young lady." The physician sat back, reaching into his little black bag. "A tad higher and a smidgeon harder, and your kneecap might have been shattered, you permanently lamed."

"Lamed?" Goaded by a ballerina's worst fear, she reached down and carefully ran a finger over the injury, shuddering to think how close she had come to losing her career.

Once again, she glanced at Hunter's rigid back. Would he feel differently about her if she could no longer dance?

"As it is, Miss Nicolaiev, you suffer from a serious concussion and there still might be a small fracture. It is necessary that you stay in bed and off your leg for several weeks, just to be on the safe side."

Weeks? No, she couldn't afford that kind of setback. She

had students to teach, a business to run; so many depended on her.

She tried not to think of the fact that someone had intentionally pushed her in the way of that oncoming wagon. But who would have done such a thing? And why?

Perhaps the good citizens of Sweetwater had decided to get rid of her any way that they could. What other explanation could there be? Only by coincidence, she assured herself, had it been another vehicle to run her down. The threats from Russia were too far away to be considered a concern here in the wilds of Wyoming.

She glanced around at those crowding in her doorway— dancers, musicians, friends—looking for a clue. Yes, the town had banded against her, determined to run her off. No other motive made sense. If she were lucky, they had only meant to frighten her. And if not . . .

Her gaze searched the room, frantically seeking Hunter. To her dismay she discovered he had left without saying goodbye or offering her an explanation.

Hunter pushed his way through the crowd in the familiar hallway of what had once been the private quarters of the Songbird Saloon. He knew the layout well, well enough to know which room he wanted. A man like Pretty Boy would want the largest one. Reaching his destination at the end of the corridor, he pounded on the locked door without hesitation.

"Sergei, open up," he demanded, not bothering to conceal the angry certainty in his voice.

Silence greeted him.

With growing impatience, he knocked once again, a little longer, a little harder, determined to ascertain the man's whereabouts.

Sergei Bozzacchi, count, confidence man, whatever. Hunter had not trusted him from the first time he'd met him. Everyone else in the troupe had either immediately crowded into Marina's room or congregated in the doorway. It had been Sergei's name Marina had called out when Hunter had scooped her up in the street. Had she seen who had pushed her? Had it been her dance partner? He didn't ask himself why. Who knew what drove such a self-centered bastard to do the things he did?

"He's a sound sleeper," one of the troupe members informed him, a pretty girl with blonde hair and pale blue eyes. She assessed him curiously from the fringes of the crowd.

"And does he always sleep this late?"

"Usually."

Not to be thwarted, once again Hunter beat his fist against the door. At last his insistent summons received an answer.

"Go away and leave me alone."

"Open the door, Sergei, or I swear I'll bust it down."

When at last the Russian dancer complied, Hunter had to admit he did look as if he had just risen from his bed. Still, he wanted more proof. Pushing the man out of his way, he stepped through the doorway, giving the room a quick once-over.

The bed was a shambles, the pillow on the floor. In one corner near the uncurtained window, clothes were heaped on a chair. Without asking permission, Hunter crossed the room and sorted through the pile, looking for the dark clothing Marina's assailant had been wearing; but he found nothing.

"What do you want?" Sergei demanded, rather nastily for someone who had nothing to hide.

Hunter paused in his search and looked the Russian up and down.

"Marina's been hurt."

"Marinuska! How?" Sergei immediately aimed for the doorway showing the proper amount of concern.

Hunter wasn't that easily deceived. Grabbing Sergei by the arm, he swung him about, discovering an amazing amount of strength in the other man.

"A few minutes ago, a wagon nearly ran her over in the street. But you wouldn't know anything about that, would you, Sergei?" He stared steadily at the man trying to read the play of emotions on his too-handsome face.

"How would I know? I've been asleep. Now let go of me, sir. Marina needs *me.*"

Hunter watched him go, wondering. Sergei seemed genuinely concerned about Marina's welfare. Still, he would leave nothing to chance and, alone in the room, he renewed his search, starting with the pile of clothing. Finding nothing there, he stooped to check beneath the bed, but then realized he had an audience. The fair-haired ballerina, who had watched him so intently earlier, stood in the doorway.

"Ma'am," Hunter murmured, touching the brim of his Stetson as he shouldered past her.

At first glance, it seemed he had been mistaken about Sergei. If so, whom did that leave as a suspect?

The doctor departed, leaving instructions and a packet of powders to help alleviate the pain. And indeed they did. Feeling strange, almost as if she floated on the pillow, Marina closed her eyes, giving up to the euphoria.

"Oh, Marina. I'm so sorry. I never should have left you; I should have waited so we could walk together." The woman settled beside her, anxiety marring her pixie-like features.

Without opening her eyes, Marina searched the top of the coverlet blindly, discovering Fanny's hand.

"No. You mustn't blame yourself. How were either of us

to know something like this might happen?" She smiled weakly. All the same, she should have been better prepared, Marina chided herself. "Besides, in a few days I'll be up and back to normal."

"Oh, no, Marina. You must do as the doctor says. I can handle everything, including the lessons. There's nothing for you to worry about."

What Fanny said made perfect sense. She could handle anything . . .

"Out. Everyone out." Sergei's imperial command cut through the tranquility and was not to be denied.

Anything except Sergei. Marina opened her eyes. A few moments later, the room was cleared except for Fanny.

"You, too," Sergei demanded, pointing toward the door. "Out."

"It's all right, Fanny. Go on. I'll be fine." Sighing, Marina resigned herself to Sergei's presence. She would have to deal with her dance partner whether she felt up to it or not, and do so with compassion, for he could often be difficult in times of crisis—his way of showing his concern, no doubt.

"Is anything broken, Marinuska?" Sergei asked when at last they were alone. "Are you in pain?" He looked so worried when he knelt beside the bed and took her hand, she found it hard to feel anything but gratitude.

"It's all right, Sergei." She patted his consoling fingers. "In a few days I'll be just fine."

"What happened?"

She considered lying to him once more, but too many people already knew what had happened. The most she could do was minimize it for the present; eventually he would ferret out the details from the others.

"Someone ran into me," she explained, making light of the situation. "I fell into the street, right in front of an oncoming wagon."

"Did you see who shoved you?" He frowned, his gaze settling on her with genuine concern.

"I didn't say anyone shoved me." She studied him, wondering why he would make such an assumption. "No," she finally answered his question. "Whoever it was, he was behind me," she confessed.

"He? Are you certain it was a man?"

"Well, no. Whoever it was, he or she was very strong." Once again, she closed her eyes, fighting down the rising panic. Someone had tried to hurt her! Thank goodness for the medicine. It helped her remain calm.

"Marinuska, don't you see what this means? You and I have no choice now but to move on."

"No, Sergei." She glanced at him, unwilling to give up. "You're wrong. I told you. It was an accident, nothing more. For now, we are going nowhere." She was emphatic.

"Sometimes, Marina." Sergei issued one of his famous dramatic sighs, "I think you are the most stubborn woman I've ever met."

"And you, my dearest friend," she replied, smiling to cover her own unassuaged fears, "worry too much."

"Mr. Kincaid, what you're suggesting is preposterous!"

"Is it, Mrs. Shackelford?" Hunter demanded, slowly scrutinizing every member of the Sweetwater Ladies' Committee. Most of the women looked away or down when his gaze pinned them, but not all. "Everyone knows you ladies are determined to run Marina Nicolaiev out of town."

"No more so than you once were, sir."

"Perhaps." He smiled caustically. "However, *I* haven't asked the town council, which includes many of your husbands, to change the ordinance so that you can accomplish your dirty deed legally."

"As the wife of the mayor, I refuse to be interrogated like a common drifter." Huffing, Hatty popped up and pushed back her chair. "For your information, Mr. Kincaid, the committee voted against trying to have that ordinance revised."

"Oh, really? And what changed your minds?" he asked.

"I and several of the other ladies have decided to allow our daughters to take ballet lessons from Count Bozzacchi." She lifted her pointed chin.

"Ballet lessons? You're going to allow them to take ballet lessons?" he asked, filled with a sense of foreboding. Sergei Bozzacchi, a dance instructor? That wasn't exactly the image he had of the man.

"Yes, we've decided we want them to stay. So why would we arrange to have someone shove the princess underneath the wheels of a wagon?"

"It's true, Mr. Kincaid," piped up Elvira Granger, a timid woman by nature. "I plan to enroll my Sarah. Besides, it was my husband's wagon that hit Miss Nicolaiev. I'm surprised you aren't blaming him."

"It seems I've made a mistake. I hope you ladies haven't made one as well."

Hunter turned and walked away, feeling worse than when he had burst unannounced into the middle of the meeting. If someone had intentionally pushed her and it wasn't the ladies or Sergei, then who the hell wanted Marina out of the way?

Whoever the culprit was, Hunter made up his mind then and there to do everything in his power to keep them from succeeding.

The throbbing in her head and leg awoke Marina. Lying in the darkness of her room, uncertain of the time or how long she had slept, she wondered where Fanny had put her medicine. She could use another dose.

Reaching out, she blindly groped the top of the night table, searching for the packet. Her fingers brushed against the music box and a book she had left spread open. It slid off the table, clattering to the floor.

The shuffle of feet not far away startled Marina.

"Fanny? Is that you?" she called out in relief, assuming her friend had decided to stay with her through the night.

The dark stillness answered her.

"Sergei?" she spoke to the only other person who might have decided to sit with her. "Please, if you are there, I could use your help."

Again, no response. Only foreboding silence. Yet she knew she was not alone.

Why didn't the person answer her? Then it dawned on her. Whoever it was didn't wish to be discovered.

"Hunter?" she whispered almost hopefully, knowing he had a key to the building.

When once again she received no answer, her heart began to pound in fear.

What if the intruder were the same person who had shoved her underneath the wagon earlier that day? Had her assailant returned to finish an uncompleted job?

"Whoever you are, I know you are there."

The loud crash as the invader tripped over something unseen in the darkness reverberated through the room. Marina screamed. The door flew open. The light from the hallway illuminated the hulking silhouette for an all-too-brief moment before the figure raced away.

Her heart still hammering in a terrified staccato, she tried to put a face to the shadowy presence. Although she could not actually identify the person who had been in her room uninvited, she knew for certain the intruder had been a man.

* * *

"Mr. Kincaid, how did you get in here? And where do you think you are going?" Fanny demanded. Standing in the doorway to the kitchen tucked beneath the stairwell, a tray of food suspended between her petite hands, she watched him mount the first steps leading to the rooms above.

"It's okay, Fanny," Hunter assured her. "She is awake, isn't she?" True, it was a bit early for a visitor, but he knew Marina not to be one to sleep late. After a long night of agonizing, he had to make sure for himself that no further harm had come to her.

If anything should happen to Marina . . .

"Well, if I can't stop you, then save me a trip and take her breakfast to her." She thrust the tray of food at him.

Grinning, he gladly accepted the task.

Reaching the door to Marina's room, he juggled the tray, balancing it in one hand, and knocked softly, trying to contain his impatience.

"I already told you, Fanny, I'm not hungry."

How lethargic Marina sounded. Not at all like her usual self. Without bothering to announce his intention, Hunter charged into the room.

"What do you mean you're not hungry?" He deposited the tray on the night table. Standing over her, he stared down at her. "If you don't eat, darlin', how do you expect to regain your health?"

"Hunter!" She jerked the covers clear up to her little, aristocratic chin. "Who said you could come in here?"

"I did, and it's a good thing. Otherwise, you might just waste away."

Urging her to sit up, he ignored her attempts to maintain modesty. He fluffed her pillows, straightened her covers, then stationed the tray across her lap. For several moments he watched her pick at the stack of flapjacks.

"You know, those aren't so different from what you served me in Russia."

"Blini?" She looked up at him, her dark gaze steady, searching his—for what he could only guess. Hopefully she remembered the positive aspects of that shared memory. He was trying to. "They're not at all the same," she murmured. "What do you call these?"

"Flapjacks."

"Flapjacks," she repeated. The way she said the word made it seem like food for the gods.

"Sure they're the same," he insisted. "Not so delicate, perhaps, but flour and water and . . ." He wasn't sure of the other ingredients, but he didn't really care. Watching her place a bite between her beautiful lips made him wish he were a flapjack instead of a man, at least at that moment. He cleared his throat. "They'll stick to your ribs."

"Why would I want them to do that?" She quit chewing and dropped her fork, her hand flying up to press against her bosom in a protective gesture.

Her actions, but mostly her innocence, made him laugh. Perhaps that was what he loved about her best. That, and the lovely way she blushed.

"What did I say that you find so funny?" she demanded.

"They don't actually stick to your ribs, darlin'," he explained, forcing back a chuckle. "It's just a saying that means you won't get hungry again for a while."

"In other words, if I eat now, you won't bother me to eat later."

"Marina, think what you will about me," he said in all seriousness, "but it *is* important to me that nothing happen to you."

Their eyes met and held. He leaned toward her, unable to stop himself.

"Hunter, were you in my room last night?"

"Last night?" Surprised by her question, he shifted backward, alarm furrowing his brow. "No. Why do you ask?"

She shrugged, refusing to look at him.

"Did someone enter your room last night?" he asked, forcing her chin up so that he could read her reaction.

"No, of course not." She tilted her lips in a perfunctory smile.

The door opened. Fanny bustled in.

"Well, now, Mr. Kincaid, I see you were no more successful than I was."

"What?" he mumbled, glancing up in annoyance at the untimely interruption.

"At getting our patient to eat."

"Oh, but I am, Fanny," Marina assured her. Retrieving her fork, she resumed picking at her food.

To Hunter's disappointment she looked relieved to no longer be alone with him.

Could there be something she wasn't telling him? Realizing the moment to ask had passed, Hunter rose.

"I guess I'd better get going, but I'll be back, Marina," he promised.

"I would like that, Hunter. Very much." This time she smiled genuinely.

Hours later, Marina had another surprise visitor.

"Oh, Marina, I was so worried about you."

Like a refreshing spring day, Rainee Kincaid filled the room with her sweet essence. Thoughtfully, she had even brought an artfully arranged bouquet of wildflowers to help brighten the cheerless room. But it was her sincere concern that brought a ready smile to Marina's lips.

"I'm sorry I won't be able to teach your lesson today."

"So am I." Rainee settled in the chair beside the bed and

took up Marina's hand with easy familiarity. "But don't worry. Fanny is a wonderful instructor." She leaned forward. "And Sergei has even promised to help me personally with my *arabesques*. I cannot wait." Her eyes, so like her father's, gleamed with excitement.

"Why, it sounds like you won't miss me at all, Rainee." Marina feigned jealousy.

"Oh, no, Marina, that's not true," Rainee assured, the poor child—taking what she had meant to be harmless teasing much too seriously. "I have looked forward all week to this lesson with you. You must get well quickly so that I don't have to miss any more."

"As quickly as I can." Marina gratefully accepted the affectionate kiss the girl planted on her cheek. Reluctantly, she let her go.

Rainee glided as gracefully as a swan across the room. How had the girl claimed such a special place in her heart so quickly? Marina wondered. True, she was Hunter Kincaid's daughter. But that factor only played a small part in her feelings. More importantly, Marina had found a kindred soul in Rainee, a spirit whose hopes and dreams she shared. If she ever had a child of her own, she would want her to be like Rainee.

"Rainee," she called softly just as the girl started to close the door.

"Yes, Marina?"

"Please, be careful. It's important that foremost you listen to Fanny."

"Don't worry. I know what to do," she replied with a dreamy-eyed smile.

Minutes later, listening to the music and the sounds of a lesson in progress coming from the floor below, Marina again felt an overwhelming need to shelter Rainee from a brewing storm of disaster.

But that was silly, of course. Nothing threatened Rainee, not here in Sweetwater, her home.

Nonetheless, Marina pushed herself up and turned to the music box, for so long silent, sitting on the table beside the bed. Turning the key, she wound it up, then let the familiar, comforting melody drown out the music from below and the premonitions that accompanied it.

"Rainee, where have you been?"

"Nowhere, Daddy," the girl replied, slipping out of the saddle rather gingerly. Casting him a dubious look, she led her horse toward the corral, turning the gelding over to Paco without even glancing at the youth.

That look was all too familiar. He had seen it many times on Della's pretty face. He also knew better than to accept his daughter's statement at face value. With his own two eyes, he had seen her come from town, just as he had the week before.

A terrible sinking feeling invaded the pit of his stomach. It had begun again. The pattern was the same as it had been with her mother. Now, as then, it had started with denials regarding trips into town.

Then it had progressed when Della had not even bothered to come home one night. He had been wild with worry, beginning his search for her at the first light of dawn, but had been unable to find her.

Della had turned up a few hours later, declaring she had stayed with a friend. Oh, her story had been corroborated by another woman in town all right; and, fool that he had been then, he had honestly believed her. Three weeks later, his lying wife had packed her bags and left while he had been busy with a spring roundup. It had been the last time he had seen her alive.

He didn't want something like that to happen to Rainee.

"Look, honey, as soon as I get through the breeding season, would you like to take a trip somewhere?" he asked, hoping to console his daughter. "San Francisco, maybe. Or even St. Louis, if you would like. I understand they have all kinds of theaters there. We could go see a performance." He put his arm around her slender shoulder and walked with her toward the house, feeling he had made a big concession. Hopefully, one she would appreciate.

"Sure, Daddy. That would be nice." She smiled at him with an indifference that left him feeling deflated and even more frustrated.

Rainee. He watched her walk on without him and slip through the back door of the house. Did he do too little, too late?

This time he refused to leave anything to chance.

Fifteen

"Marina, you should still be in bed."

A week had passed, seven long, dreary, pain-filled days. But the worst part of her confinement was that Hunter had not come back as he had promised.

"If I lie there another moment, Fanny, I swear I'll lose my mind."

Dressed for the first time in days, she was attired in the loose-fitting, wide-necked blouse that peasants often wore back in Russia tucked into a simple calico skirt that at one time would have appalled her. But for once free of the pain-medicine the doctor had given her, Marina slowly descended the stairs leaning upon a most unusual cane with a beaten-silver handle. It had been presented to her by one of the dancers who had chanced upon it stashed and no doubt forgotten in a back storeroom.

While Cecilia had given her the walking stick in jest, a gesture meant to cheer, Marina had instead taken it as a serious sign that she should and could get up. Getting up meant continuing with her life, and that meant dancing. She couldn't imagine existing any other way.

More determined than ever, she made her way to the *barre*. Resting her hand on the brass fitting, she assumed fifth position and attempted a simple *plié*. The movement hurt so much she had to bite her tongue to keep from crying out.

Accepting Fanny's unbidden support and I-told-you-so look

without comment, she limped toward a nearby chair and gladly sank down, easing the weight off her injured leg. But just for a moment, she assured herself. Then she would get up and try the exercise again.

"No, no. Sit back down," Fanny insisted when she started to rise.

"I have to. There are lessons to teach and . . ."

"That's only an excuse, Marina. You and I both know it. Besides, Sergei and I have taken care of all of that. In fact, we enrolled three new students yesterday and have a promise of even more to come."

"Oh, Fanny. That's wonderful." If she truly meant what she said, then why did she feel like crying?

"Come on, honey." Taking her hand, Fanny urged her to her feet. "We could both use a little fresh air."

"I don't want any fresh air." Swallowing the painful lump in her throat, she wiped at eyes that kept on misting no matter how hard she tried to prevent it. "At least not the kind available in Sweetwater, Wyoming," she added peevishly.

"You don't mean that. Come on," Fanny insisted. "Even the grimmest circumstances always look better in the sunshine."

Appreciative of her friend's unrelenting support, Marina allowed Fanny to help her limp out the front door to the porch. To her delight, someone had placed a trio of chairs beside the railing, a lovely place to sit and observe all that went on along the main street of town. Taking a seat, Marina closed her eyes and lifted her face to the healing heat of the late-morning sun. And, indeed, she did begin to feel a little better, but not enough to eradicate the nagging doubts.

What had ever made her think she could deny her birthright? Instead of feeling more at home in Sweetwater, each new day only served to show her how wrong she had been to come here in the first place.

"What am I to do?" Although she expressed her fear aloud, Marina spoke mostly to herself.

"If you mean about that rascal Hunter Kincaid, I think you're doing about all that you can."

"Oh, Fanny." Encouraged, Marina straightened and twisted in her seat. "Do you really think so?"

"He doesn't make it easy, I'll admit." Fanny smiled mischievously. "But I consider myself a fair judge of men. Just keep your chin up a little longer and he'll be asking you to stay. That is why you came here, isn't it? To stay in Sweetwater?"

After a moment of hesitation, she nodded with a sigh. "I'm so sorry I got you mixed up in this. Nothing has turned out the way I planned."

"Don't be sorry. I don't blame you. I might envy you a little, perhaps, but I don't blame you."

"Whatever happens, whether I decide to stay or not, I never intend to abandon you or anyone in the troupe," she declared.

"Of course, you wouldn't."

"That's why these lessons are so important now," she continued. "With the money we earn, I'll see to it everyone will have the means to return to New York."

"I know that, honey. John and I figured that was what you intended to do. Have you told Sergei yet?"

"No," she replied guiltily. "I was afraid he would get upset."

"That's best, I suppose. Quite frankly, I don't think he'll be happy about leaving you behind."

"I know, but he would be even more unhappy stuck here." Marina took a deep breath and let it out slowly. "To be honest, I'm not so sure Sweetwater, Wyoming, is the right place for me, either."

"It's right." Fanny patted her hand reassuringly, then she

glanced down the street. "Speaking of Mr. Right, here he comes now."

"Hunter? Are you sure?" Marina stiffened and followed Fanny's gaze. When she spied Hunter driving a wagon headed in their direction, her heart began to race—her mind as well. "Quick, Fanny, help me get back inside."

"Whatever for?"

"I don't want him to think I'm sitting here waiting for him."

"But you're not." Fanny chuckled softly. "Marina, sit still. Don't let him rattle you, or at least, don't let him see it. Otherwise, you'll never accomplish what you've worked so hard for."

Knowing Fanny's advice to be sound yet hoping he would drive on by and she wouldn't have to face him, Marina relaxed in her chair, trying to pretend she didn't notice his steady approach. But she did. How could she not be aware of him as he came closer and closer?

He didn't seem to be slowing down, not even a little. Did he really intend to just drive on by? she wondered with panicked indignation when it seemed she would get her original wish. Unable to stop herself, she watched him with hopeful eyes.

With the skill of a Russian sleigh-driver, he brought the buckboard to a calculated halt in front of the building only a few feet from the edge of the porch where Marina sat. She immediately looked away, keeping tabs on him only from the corner of her eye. As if unaware of her slight, he dipped his head, touching the brim of his hat with a gloved hand, the standard greeting Wyoming-style.

"Morning, ladies."

"Morning to you, Mr. Kincaid," Fanny replied in the wake of Marina's stubborn silence.

Even when the other woman nudged her ever so subtly in

the side, Marina refused to speak. She was afraid to talk, afraid of what she might blurt out—something like, why hadn't he come to see her sooner? Or why hadn't he warned her he might drop by so that she could have dressed in something more flattering? She no doubt looked like the lowliest peasant in her thin slippers and the shapeless blouse that kept falling off one shoulder.

"It's a mighty fine day to be up and out enjoying the sunshine."

Although he directed the casual comment to Fanny, Marina knew to whom he really spoke. Unable to stop herself, she darted a quick look in his direction.

He was looking back, grinning at her as if he'd caught her doing something reprehensible like filching coins from the royal coffers.

"In fact," he continued, pushing back his brimmed hat from his forehead in a lazy gesture she recognized as calculated, "I figured this might be the perfect day for a picnic. You wouldn't know of anyone who might like to join me, would you?"

"Are you asking me, Mr. Kincaid?" Her voice sounded calm and cool, thank goodness.

"Why, yes, Princess, I suppose I am."

Why, whenever he called her by her rightful title, did it make her feel anything but royal?

"Then, I suppose I could," she answered, mimicking his nonchalant attitude. "However, I'll need time to throw together a quick meal and—"

"No need." He reached behind the wagon seat and lifted up a lidded basket. "I've already taken care of that."

"I see." She struggled to stand with the aid of her cane. "Then give me a few moments to change my clothing—"

"No need for that, either." Hunter jumped down from the

wagon seat and quickly scooped her up. "You look just fine to me."

Before she could utter a protest, he carried her around to the other side of the wagon and swung her up onto the seat. Then he joined her, gathering up the reins.

"Mr. Kincaid, wait," cried Fanny, bounding out the door toward the wagon, clutching a large straw hat. "Protection from the sun." She handed the bonnet to Hunter.

"Why, thank you, Fanny," he said, still grinning. Then he turned and plopped the hat on Marina's head.

Without warning, he snapped the reins over the backs of the horses and the wagon lurched forward.

Hanging on to the hat, the side of the wagon, and her dignity for dear life, Marina suspected sunburn would be the least of her problems.

Hunter chose a grassy slope beside Bitter Creek where a great aspen spread its mighty limbs, offering shade. Not far from a deserted line shack, this was one of the few places along the river where the bank inclined gently to meet the water's edge instead of forming high, dangerous cliffs. He unharnessed the team, staking them out on a lush knoll a few yards away to eat their fill. Finally, he returned to the spot where he had deposited Marina on the blanket he had brought with him.

As he watched covertly she debated a moment before lifting the top of the basket to inspect the contents. The minute she realized she had an audience, she jerked her hand back, allowing the lid to flop shut. He liked the way she looked just now—pretty and flushed—and the simple dress that kept sliding off one shoulder was about the sexiest damn thing he'd ever seen. He could almost believe she was a woman who could be happy with the ordinary things in life.

"My, you packed enough to feed an army," Marina observed with a valiant smile that trembled ever so slightly on the ends. To his dismay, she straightened the lopsided neckline of her blouse.

"I was hungry." He shrugged, suddenly awkward. "I guess my eyes were bigger than my stomach."

"You Americans say such odd things." She laughed, the spontaneity of the sound a tinkling melody that shot through him like an unexpected bolt of lightning. It was the kind of joy he just didn't have the heart to live without but had been too damn spooked to accept. For the moment, he couldn't remember why.

"Marina," he said, dropping to his knees on the blanket beside her, so near to her he could have reached out and scooped her into his arms.

As much as he wanted to, he didn't. Like some wild, young thing, she stared at him with uncertainty, yet wanting to trust. God knows, the last thing he wanted was to scare her off. If he tried to get too close, he feared the reprisal. She would soon realize that she didn't really want what little he could offer her.

Therein lay the crux of his dilemma. He didn't doubt that he wanted her; he questioned how long it would be before she discovered her own dissatisfaction with him.

Like a fool, he sat unable to make the next move, unable to reverse what he had already done.

"Perhaps it would be best if we ate now." The sweetness in her voice flooded him with relief.

"That's a good idea." He scooted to the very edge of the blanket and watched her unpack the basket. "Since that's why we came here . . ." he explained quite unnecessarily ". . . to eat."

Without comment, she handed him a plate. Then she unwrapped a square of cheesecloth, offering him a selection of cold chicken and ham slices. When he stared at them in indecision, she picked out several of the choicer pieces for him, taking only a wing for herself. She repeated the process with cheese, bread, and fruit, each time heaping his plate and taking very little for herself. Finally she poured them both a drink from the earthen jug.

Sitting back against the trunk of the tree, she took a tentative sip of the cool cider. What a picture she made, cozily curled on the blanket, the neckline of her dress once again drifting toward her shoulder.

"That building we passed near the falls, does someone live there?"

She asked only out of a need to start a conversation, he suspected, so he answered her in kind.

"No, just an old line camp." When she didn't seem to understand, he explained. "A place for cowboys to get out of bad weather when out checking on the herds."

"Oh, sort of like a peasant's hut."

"Something like that. We used to run our cattle along this river, but we lost too many to accidents around the cliffs, so we don't bring them up here much anymore."

"So no one is there."

"No. If you're worried about someone seeing us . . ."

"I'm not worried," she defended rather quickly. She smiled. Hunter did, too.

"This is good," she offered after another moment of awkward silence. She stared into her cup as if trying to decide just what she drank. "Not quite as strong as *kvass.*" She took another drink. "But tasty."

Although *kvass* was a common Baltic drink fermented from rye bread, it was not the choice he expected of a Russian princess.

"And when did you ever try *kvass,* Your Highness?" he asked boldly, setting aside his untouched plate, suddenly realizing he hungered, but not for food. Instead, he wanted to know everything about this woman—past, present, and future.

She looked at him guiltily, then started to laugh. "I didn't think you would catch that."

"Darlin', nothing about you ever slips past me."

"Then I suppose I'll have to be much more careful in what I do and say around you." She pinned him with that same confident look she had given him the first time he had seen her so long ago in Russia, standing at the top of the stairs in a gown of shimmering silver.

"No, Marina." Finally, unable to stop himself, he reached out and grasped her arms, wanting to put his brand on her, to claim her as his, only his. "You don't ever have to be guarded around me."

Like dancers caught in a musical interlude, neither moved. Oh, God, how he wanted to kiss her; and had she given him even the slightest indication that she wanted him to, he would have. Instead, she gripped her plate, keeping it firmly between them, holding him at bay.

"I'm sorry," she murmured.

"So am I." Reluctantly, he released her. His heart twisted when she edged away.

"I don't think I'm really all that hungry." Following his earlier lead, she discarded her food.

"Then I guess this outing was a mistake." He started to rise.

"No, Hunter, that's not what I meant."

As gently as she plucked at the sleeve of his shirt, it was as if the dam of his resistance gave way to the flood of his desire. Dragging her to him, he held her tightly, determined never to let her go, no matter how hard she struggled or how loudly she insisted that she wanted her freedom. Somehow he would figure out a way to hang on to her, to calm her, to keep her happy, to make her forever his.

Their mouths met and molded to one another, the hot arrows of need shooting through him, piercing his heart. After a moment he realized she offered no resistance, but clung to him as readily as he clung to her. Only then did he relax his embrace, allowing his hand to explore the gentle slope of her bared shoulder, fragile and feminine beneath his calloused palm.

God help him, above all others, he needed this particular woman in his life, wanted her and was more than willing to throw all caution to the wind.

Whom did he think to kid? It would be much easier to master the elusive wind than a free spirit like Marina Nicolaiev. Even as he came to that unhappy conclusion, a cool breeze stirred the air around him like a whispered warning. Like a tease, it seemed to laugh at him.

Pulling back, he looked down upon her tilted face, so beautiful in its naked translucence. Her eyes were closed, her lips parted in anticipation. At the moment it would be easy to believe that there was nothing she wanted more than him. And for the moment, that was probably true.

But could he take what the moment offered him and not look beyond it? Take it? Yes. Be satisfied with it? Never.

Placing his hand beneath her head, he slowly lowered her onto the blanket. Hovering above her, he buried his face in her thick, abundant hair. The smell of wild mint crushed beneath the blanket rose to greet him and seemed a natural part of her, of them, of that moment. He tucked the memory away for another time when perhaps it would be all he would have left—the memory of making love to Marina in a field of wild mint beside the river.

Yes, this would be the fulfillment of the perfect fantasy he would take with him to the grave.

Confident they would not be disturbed—after all, they were on Kincaid land—he stripped the skirt and loose-fitting blouse from her body, amazed to find she wore nothing but a plain, cotton chemise beneath. In his heart he knew no matter what she wore, Marina would always be a princess, regal even in such simplicity. He didn't want her to be any less, but he needed to feel equal in her eyes. Not superior, only equal.

He could not say exactly what she did that granted his wish. Perhaps it was the way she reached up and ran her fingers through his tousled hair with such reverence. Or maybe it was the way she offered up her vulnerability with such a calm, self-assuredness when he kissed her that made him feel like a king. Whatever it was, he knew he must never squander so precious a gift, but must cherish it, nurture it, put it on a pedestal, and worship it. But more important, in exchange he must offer her his own heart for safekeeping.

The kiss that had begun with such tameness gave way to a wild, Wyoming passion more uncontrollable and earth-shaking than the stampeding of a herd of cattle. To his delight, Marina found the caress as exciting as he did. Her hands tore at the buttons of his shirt and pants, her mouth demanding more as she kissed him back.

Covering her naked body with his own, he sought to unite them as quickly as he could, for she made it evident in the way she clung to him, her hips lifting to meet his with equal fervor, that that was what she wanted as well. In that union they were truly equals, a man and a woman seeking to consummate not only the coming together of their bodies but of their hearts so long, too long, alone and unloved.

Caught up in the urgency, Hunter suddenly realized that unless he did something to prevent it, the glory of their lovemaking would be over all too soon. Wanting the day to be special, for her as well as himself, he paused, trembling as his needs, the physical and the emotional, battled to conquer one another.

She whimpered unhappily. He kissed away her distress, assuaging his own in the process as he gradually regained control, allowing the gentleness, that allow-it-to-happen-not-struggle-to-conquer-it rhythm to take over once again.

"No need to rush it. We have all day, darlin'." Urging her to look at him, he smiled.

"All day," she agreed in a passionate murmur, wrapping her willowy arms around his neck and drawing his mouth to hers to initiate another kiss.

When she relaxed beneath him, offering him her trust without questioning his motives, he gave himself up to the passion.

He moved against her slowly, making the most of each thrust, each silken wave of ecstasy that washed over him more thrilling than the last. Almost mindless in the wonder of the gradually building excitement, he clung to that uppermost height of sensation for as long as he could, feeling as if he would explode if he didn't let go. But he didn't let go, not until he felt Marina join him at the precipice then slip over the edge. Only then did he gladly follow her down into the whirling vortex of physical fulfillment.

But it was more than the physical he experienced, his body satisfied, yes, of course, but it was his heart that sighed with contentment as he held her tightly, kissed her gently, reassuring her with words meant to comfort.

"You're mine, Marina." He kissed her gently, clung to her fiercely. "Say you're all mine. Promise me that I'm all you need to be happy." He showered her with kisses on her face, her neck, her shoulder.

In the wake of her silence, he opened his eyes to find her watching him with wide-eyed indecision.

"What is it, darlin'?" he asked, trying to ignore that old, familiar sense of uneasiness.

"I-I . . ." Slipping her hands between them, she splayed

them on his bare chest. "It's just that I'm not sure what you're asking of me."

"What's there to understand? It's simple. I just want to know if I'm going to be enough to make you happy or will you want more?"

"Are you asking me to forfeit everything else that is important to me in my life? My friends, my dancing . . . my responsibilities?"

"That depends. Do you consider Pretty Boy an important part of your life?" Jealousy or inadequacy?

"You mean Sergei? Are you suggesting . . . Hunter, if you're jealous of him, there's no need to be."

That teasing look of amusement tainted with defiance. He had seen it before, knew what it meant.

"I'm not jealous," he denied quickly, shifting so that, head and shoulders, he loomed over her. Then he pressed her down against the mint-scented quilt. It wasn't jealousy, but a fear of his own inadequacies that made him want to isolate her, to keep her from temptations, to have her swear fidelity.

But no matter what she might promise aloud, he knew there was still a good chance she would eventually leave—if not with Sergei, then with some man like him who had more in common with her than he, Hunter, did.

The pain was like a knife cutting through him to the very quick. Oh, God, how it hurt, and yet he should have been prepared, never should have expected her to be any different. But he refused to let her see how easily she had wounded him. So he smiled back, lazily, pretending not to care.

The kiss was short and bittersweet. Then he rose, aware that her gaze lingered on his naked body with appreciation. But it was a hunger that could never hold her. For a day, a month, with luck maybe even a year. That was not long enough for him, much too short a time to risk his fragile heart.

He noticed then that she winced when she tried to sit up.

"Your leg. It still hurts." He found himself devouring the beauty of her perfect body.

"Only a little."

She lied about that, too.

Tearing his eyes away from what he could never have, not completely, he presented his back and quickly donned his clothing. Then he set about harnessing the horses.

When he returned, to his relief, he discovered her dressed as well, calmly sitting on the edge of the blanket.

Wordlessly, he knelt to pick her up.

"No, please. If you will just hand me my cane, I can get up on my own."

He found the walking stick lying in the crushed mint. Picking it up, he stared at it for a moment, instantly recognizing it.

"Where did you get this?" he demanded.

"I found it in a back storage room at the academy."

"It was my father's." Studying it for a moment longer, he then flipped it in his hand, presenting it to her silver handle first. "After his death, I couldn't find it. I figured he had lost it in a poker game."

"I'm sorry. I didn't mean . . . If you want it back . . ."

"No, no. It's yours now."

Taking it, she struggled to her feet and slowly, and no doubt painfully judging by the look on her face, made her way toward the wagon.

Unable to watch her struggle so, he ignored her earlier request and picked her up and deposited her on the buckboard seat.

"Thank you," she said.

"You're welcome."

To his disappointment she didn't say another word, didn't bother to protest the sudden end to a day that had come so close to being perfect.

Gathering up the picnic supplies, he balled up the blanket. Just before he tossed it into the back of the wagon, he brought it to his nose and inhaled deeply.

Wild mint, sweet and tangy. It would always make him think of Marina—and what might have been—for as long as he lived.

Sixteen

"Lift, Rainee. Give me more lift," Marina demanded, tapping in rhythm with the silver-handled cane that she had decided not to discard even though, after several weeks, she now managed quite well on her own. Somehow, knowing it had belonged to Hunter's father made it special to her.

Hunter. Recalling the last time they had spent together evoked a rush of jumbled emotions. That day had been almost perfect. She had felt closer to him than ever before; and then just as she had come close to trusting him, to confiding in him all her fears and concerns, he had suddenly withdrawn. Yes, she had come so close to telling him about all that had happened in Russia, how she had come looking for him with such hope and expectation. If only he had pressed her, insisted that she speak her mind, she would have. But he had turned away instead.

"That was better, Rainee," she said when the girl finished going through the steps. "But I want even more lift," she insisted.

The girl tried to do as asked, striving wholeheartedly to please her dance instructor. Marina found her an infinite joy to watch and to teach; during their hours together, a unique, fulfilling bond had formed between them. In fact, Marina was only too willing to admit that the girl stirred strange new emotions in her heart, something akin to maternal feelings that had nothing at all to do with the fact that Hunter was her father.

"Oh, Marina," Rainee cried, dropping her elevated leg with disgust. "What am I doing wrong?" Sighing, Rainee slumped her graceful shoulders.

"First of all, you're setting limitations on yourself by giving up, Rainuska," Marina scolded, softening the reproof with the Russian endearment of the girl's name. Propping her cane against the base of the risers, she joined the girl on the stage. Grasping Rainee's knee, she positioned it at the proper angle, allowing for the lift she looked for.

"There," she instructed. "See how simple it is?"

"But it hurts."

"Of course, it hurts. That's how you know you are doing it right. Nothing comes easy that is worth having." Perhaps she should heed her own words of wisdom, especially when it came to Hunter Kincaid. But winning a man's heart and pursuing a dream to dance weren't the same. Not at all, she assured herself, returning her attention to the latter.

Living up to Marina's expectation, Rainee continued to do it right from that point on without uttering another complaint.

"Good. Good." Marina clapped her hands in approval. "Keep it up, and I promise you a very special surprise," she told the girl after another grueling twenty minutes.

"Oh, Marina, what is it?" Rainee demanded, laughing, dropping down into a graceful heap on the stage floor.

Even as the girl begged to be told, Sergei sauntered down the stairs dressed in tights. Since Marina had taken over the lessons once more, the *danseur* only made occasional appearances during them. The moment Rainee saw him dressed for dancing, she stood up, her face aglow.

"How would you like to start learning a *pas de deux?*"

"Marina, do you mean it? I can begin to dance with Sergei? Do you think I'm ready?" the girl asked breathlessly, her eyes watching the lithe *danseur* with undisguised adoration.

"I think you've earned the opportunity to try."

It was evident from the way Rainee looked at Sergei as he guided her through the intricate steps of a *finger fouetté* that the girl had developed special feelings for him. Marina smiled. It wasn't unusual for young ballerinas to grow attached to each and every one of their dance partners, especially their first. She remembered hers, Ivan Berditchev. He would always hold a special place in her ballerina-heart. And Sergei. They had become as close as a brother and sister over the years.

The relationship between Rainee and Sergei was perfectly innocent, and she had no doubt that he was too much of a professional to allow feeling for a young, inexperienced girl to progress beyond stage presence.

"Rainee, you must relax and trust Sergei," she insisted over the music as the *danseur* picked up the girl in a *pressage* lift. "I promise you, he will not drop you."

Filled with a longing to dance again, she watched her partner lower the girl with the ease and skill of a man twice his strength. But then Sergei was one of the best male dancers alive. It was truly a shame for him to waste his extraordinary talents in Sweetwater, Wyoming. No matter how he might feel or what she chose to do, it would be for his own good to return to New York.

For the briefest moment, when Sergei held the girl about the waist a little longer than seemed required and Rainee leaned into him a little closer than necessary, Marina experienced a jolt of real concern. Concern? About what? That Sergei might do something foolish? When he released Rainee, who danced away in a series of well-executed pirouettes, she decided she had made too much of a strictly innocent embrace.

"That's enough for today," she said, calling the lesson to a halt on a moment of success.

Still, it might be best to remind Sergei he had to be very careful not to give others the wrong impression. While it had been important to use his popularity to gain initial acceptance in the community, it was just as important not to do anything that might create the spark that could ignite the fuse of a potential powder keg.

The next day, for the first time, several of the mothers of students chose to remain during class and observe their daughters' progress. Marina concealed her nervousness, much worse than any she had felt during an onstage performance, by tapping to the music with her silver-handled cane and counting out the rhythm in a loud, clear voice.

"One, two, three. One, two, three." Out of the corner of her eye, she watched the skeptical parents, wondering just what they whispered about among themselves. She could only hope they liked what they saw.

But the real intent of their visit didn't make itself evident until the moment Sergei made an unscheduled appearance, gracing them with his regal onstage presence. The students vied for his undivided attention, flirting outrageously. True to his nature, Sergei flirted right back, dancing with each of them in turn, making them feel special.

Marina worried that the mothers might frown not only on what he said to their innocent daughters but on the way he handled them with such familiarity and ease, especially after the troupe's disastrous performances in front of some of these same ladies. Marina shot the group of parents a concerned look. Her worry was for naught, it seemed, for they acted just as giddy as their gushing daughters.

"Is it true he's a Russian count?" she heard one of them

ask another when the hour was over and the students were in the dressing room donning their street clothes. "He's so handsome—and single, I understand. He is single, isn't he?"

So that was it. Matrimonial interest. Marina chewed her bottom lip wondering just who would have told them such . . . embellishments. She couldn't actually call them lies, for Sergei's father did hold the title of count. On the other hand, Sergei as the fifth son, claimed no peerage, only a promise that if his older brothers should die without issue the position would eventually go to him. However, that possibility didn't seem likely. What did seem probable was that Sergei had been making false claims to impress his young fans.

"Excuse me, Your Highness."

Unexpectedly, Marina found herself face to face with Hatty Shackelford.

"Saturday night there's to be a town barbecue and dance held at the church," the mayor's wife said. "I have been asked by the Ladies' Committee to see if we could hire your musicians to play. Do you mind?"

"Mind? No, of course not, but you will have to ask them." She turned to go, fully expecting that to be the end of the polite conversation.

"Wait. Please." Mrs. Shackelford touched her arm tentatively. "We, the ladies of the community, would very much like it if you, *all of you,* would consent to join us Saturday night at the church." With a look she made it quite clear that her interest lay mainly in Sergei's participation.

But Marina didn't mind. As outsiders, the troupe had at last attained a chance of acceptance, at least with the women.

"Of course. We would *all* be delighted," she answered graciously. "Thank you."

Once the students and their mothers departed, she confronted Sergei, who was still practicing.

"Just what stories have you been telling those gullible

women?" she demanded, standing center stage so that he had to either pause or run over her.

"Only what they wanted to hear, Marinuska." Laughing, he took her by the hand and led her into their favorite *pas de deux,* the climax of "The Little Humpback Horse." "Besides, I didn't tell them anything. They told me."

"Sergei, it's wrong to perpetuate lies," she chastised, remembering the steps easily but, to her chagrin, finding them embarrassingly difficult to perform. "This is not St. Petersburg or Paris or even New York, but a small American town where it is important that we fit in."

"Why?" he demanded, whirling her to a crashing stop against his chest. "Tell me why must we fit in where we do not plan to stay, Marina?"

"It just is," she replied lamely,

"You have to admit that my little, innocent lies have gained you the acceptance you crave, Marina. Without me, where do you think your precious dance academy would be?" he asked with a condescending laugh.

While she couldn't deny that he had achieved what she wanted, she didn't like that he had lied to the townspeople with calculated deliberation. Give credit where credit was due. How could he ignore that she had sacrificed much to get what she wanted. Already she had given up most of her own practice time. Sadly enough, she feared it was beginning to show.

Even as the dreadful thought passed through her mind, she miscalculated her step. Stumbling, she fell to her knees in the middle of the stage.

"Marinuska, are you all right?" Rushing to her side, Sergei hovered over her, then attempted to haul her up by the armpits.

"I'm fine, Sergei. Really I am," she snapped, pushing him

away. She was embarrassed to have done something so amateurish and foolish.

Pulling herself up, she heard the boards beneath her squeak. She glanced down in concern. To her surprise she discovered that the wood panels had given way. Ominous nails stuck out, a clear and dangerous threat. Had she landed even a little closer to the protruding projectile . . .

She sat back on her haunches, thinking herself extremely lucky to have avoided yet another accident.

Accident? She reexamined the damaged floorboards. Odd that the nails would work loose on their own all at the same time. Was it possible that someone might have tampered with them?

But why would someone do such a thing?

She glanced up at Sergei, wondering if she looked as pale on the outside as she felt within.

"Marina, what is it?"

"Nothing," she whispered, but in her heart she knew this incident—like all the rest—had been no accident. Now that the people of Sweetwater didn't resent her and the dance troupe's presence, whom did that leave who might wish to harm her or her students? One of the troupe members? An unidentified man had pushed her into the street. A man had entered her room. The only men were Sergei, John, and the violinist. She couldn't believe her pursuer was one of them.

But who could he be? No one came to mind—except for faceless, nameless enemies far away in Russia. Could they have actually followed her to Wyoming? She had nothing, knew nothing that could possibly be a threat to them. So why did they evoke a fear as debilitating as what she experienced during the worst thunderstorm?

Inevitably, whenever overwhelmed by the need to seek shelter from the turbulent storms wreaking havoc on her life, she made her way to her room and the solace waiting there. Sitting on the edge of her bed, she wound the music box and listened to it play. Her thoughts turned to Hunter Kincaid. He would know what to do, how to protect her. More than anything, she needed to talk to him; but she couldn't go running after him, not after the way things had been left between them the day of the picnic. On the other hand, she doubted he would seek her out.

If only she could make it appear that she had simply run into him!

But, of course. The Saturday-night dance planned by the ladies of Sweetwater. That event was only two days away. She felt certain she would see him there.

Hours before they left for the party, it was apparent to Hunter that Rainee didn't want to go. How unlike his vivacious daughter not to jump at the chance to attend a social function, especially a Saturday-night dance.

Even now she fidgeted on the seat beside him in the buckboard, her slender hands nervously picking at an imaginary thread on the skirt of her apple-green gingham dress.

"What's the matter, Rainee? I thought you liked to dance honey."

"I do," she replied guardedly. "I just don't feel like it tonight."

"Well, I'm sure you'll feel differently once we get there." Issuing a sharp whistle, Hunter lifted the reins and slapped them against the backs of the team that pulled the wagon. Frankly, he did not want to participate in a town social any more than his daughter did. He didn't particularly care to rub elbows with the bigoted citizens of Sweetwater. Still, in light of the unfair accusations he had made against Hatty Shackelford and the Ladies' Committee, he felt it necessary to make amends.

Things had been more than a mite edgy in town, the women openly declaring their support of the dance academy, the men threatening to draw up a new ordinance to outlaw the group's presence and close down the entire operation.

The men wanted to drive Pretty Boy out of town. The women were equally determined that their Count Bozzacchi stay.

Every day their battle gathered more steam, like a runaway train, the women spending more and more time away from their wifely chores to poke their noses in traditionally male concerns. In the Wyoming Territory, women had the right to vote, seek office, even be appointed justices of peace. Rumor had it that Hatty Shackelford had considered running for mayor against her own husband, and the women claimed they'd back her so they could pass their own ordinance.

Another impromptu meeting of the Wyoming Cattlemen's Association made it clear that the men of Sweetwater felt by necessity that steps needed to be taken to assure that the matter didn't turn into a political heyday. And so, reluctantly, Hunter had agreed to attend the dance and make amends.

At times like these, he could truly feel glad he no longer had a wife. Otherwise, his own household, including Rainee, might have been thrust into the middle of it all. He shot his daughter a searching look. No matter what, he would continue to see to it that she remained outside the controversy.

The festivities were already in full swing by the time they reached the church. Hunter parked the buckboard beneath an aging aspen and came around to assist Rainee down. He still couldn't believe how grown up his daughter looked, how lady-like.

"You're awfully pretty tonight, honey," he complimented, hoping to spark a little enthusiasm on her part.

"Thank you, Daddy." She blushed so becomingly, he couldn't help but smile with parental pride even if he did find it hard to accept that his little girl would be a woman all too soon.

Swinging her down, he folded her gloved hand in the crook of his elbow and patted it. Enough said, he led her toward the back door of the church house where the sound of music wafted toward them on the gentle summer breeze.

Inside the building, a colorful crowd milled about, some people hanging around a food-laden table, others dancing or listening to an elaborate rendition of "Sweet Betsy From Pike." Such music was a rare treat in a town the size of Sweetwater, yet Marina's accomplished musicians seemed to belong.

"Isn't that Jeb Granger's boy over there trying to get your attention?" he asked, indicating a towheaded lad not much older than Rainee standing alone in a corner. Elation lit the boy's youthful face when Hunter acknowledged him.

"I don't like him." Wrinkling her nose, Rainee turned to stare at the hapless kid who looked ready to crumple to his knobby knees under the intensity of her disapproving scrutiny. "He's so immature."

"Since when is it a crime to be young and show a pretty girl interest?" he demanded playfully. "You could do a whole lot worse than Jeb Granger's boy."

"Oh, Daddy." She rolled her eyes impatiently. "You don' understand these things." Before he could stop her, she flounced away in the opposite direction from her disappointed suitor.

Issuing a parental sigh, Hunter watched his daughter join a group of her contemporaries. The girls giggled and whispered behind the screen of their hands. Rainee, he assured himself, was the prettiest one of the bunch.

So she thought he didn't know about things, did she? He frowned. Hell, he'd been young once and in love with her mother. If only he'd known then what he knew now. He glanced at the Granger boy, feeling sorry for him but knowing the kid had to learn for himself, hard knocks and all.

Thinking Rainee safe for the moment and no doubt happy to be here even if he had forced her to come, he turned his attention to the rest of the crowd, thinking to do his duty and be done with it, a fixed smile plastered on his face.

To his amazement, he spied several members of the dance troupe clustered together. They no more fit in than muleys in a herd of cattle. Such hornless steers invariably found themselves ostracized and ignored. The New York dancers fared no better, it seemed. Then he noticed a group of local women, older for the most part, gathered about Sergei Bozzacchi, gushing over him like cow-eyed girls. The Russian dancer was trouble, just the kind of man to turn the head of a foolish woman. Who in the hell had invited him?

He glanced around to confirm Rainee's whereabouts, although he was certain she would have had no opportunity to become acquainted with the man. Still surrounded by her friends, she didn't seem aware of the Russian's presence, but he decided it might be best if he made his amends with the ladies and took Rainee home as quickly as possible.

His eyes continued to scan the crowded room, seeking the mayor and his wife. Up until that moment, he had managed, quite admirably, to maintain his wooden smile. Then his heart stopped and his expression instantly inverted.

It wasn't possible. What was *she* doing here?

Yet there she stood. Marina, a vision of regal beauty in blue, chatting with a group of women who not so very long ago would have had nothing whatsoever to do with her. Did she see him? If she did, she gave no indication.

His heart, that wicked beast, as unruly as an outlaw mustang, took up an uneven tempo he found impossible to control. Still, always the protective father, his gaze once more shot to the spot where he had last seen Rainee. The girl had disappeared. Where had she gone?

Perplexed, he frowned and glanced around, but his search was interrupted when he caught a glimpse of Marina staring at him. Then she smiled at him, and he couldn't help himself.

His feet started forward without once bothering to consult his will, powerless to stop him. *Smile, damn it, smile,* he told himself, *and whatever you do, slow down.*

He did his best to do both.

Marina thought she had more-than-adequately prepared herself for this moment, but nothing armed her for the intensity of the need that shot through her upon seeing Hunter again. It was not just a physical need, but an emotional yearning to be near him, to share her life, her hopes, and her fears. For a minute she'd feared he would simply ignore her, leaving it up to her to make the first move. Then he had donned one of those lazy, irritating smiles of his and sauntered toward her.

It's only an expression, and looks can't bite, she reminded herself, reciprocating with her best, most confident smile. She held her ground, letting him come all the way to her when what she really wanted to do was throw caution to the wind and race toward him with open arms.

"Hello, Hunter," she said in a deceptively calm voice when at last he stood before her. He looked so ruggedly handsome that her heart did flip-flops. For the life of her, she hadn't the slightest idea how she managed to speak with her throat so dry and her tongue thick and useless in her mouth.

"Princess," he replied. Leaning one broad shoulder against the nearby doorjamb, he glanced about the whole room before his gaze finally settled on her. "You're looking most lovely tonight."

"And you exceedingly handsome," she replied quickly.

Much too quickly, it seemed, for his blue eyes sparkled with amusement before lifting again to ignore her.

How irritating. She scrambled to think of something to say to regain his attention; otherwise she might lose this one-and-only chance to talk with him without sacrificing her pride any more than she already had. Thank goodness the musicians had struck up a slow-paced waltz!

"Would you care to dance, Hunter?" she blurted out.

He looked at her so strangely, she instantly regretted her boldness, fearing he would decline.

But after another thorough scan of the crowd he took her by the elbow and led her onto the dance floor. Just what or whom did he look for? Another woman perhaps? Feeling foolish, she waited for him to finish his perusal and take her in his arms

When finally he did, it wasn't enough. She yearned for him to hold her close, but he maintained the proper distance as he whirled her in the three-step rhythm of the song.

The first time they had danced together had been in Russia. She had been so sure of herself then while perceiving him as awkward. Then she had been confident of not just her identity but the path her life would take. How wrong she had been, how innocent of the knowledge that life could change quickly without warning. Now, here in his world, she took the role of outsider. How much easier it would be if she could count on the certainty that soon the pendulum would swing in her favor once again. Unfortunately, life offered no such guarantees.

"Are you looking for someone, Hunter?" she asked, unwilling to share his attention with anyone else.

"My daughter, Rainee. I'm worried about her."

"Rainee?" She laughed lightly with relief. "I wouldn't worry. I'm sure she's quite capable of taking care of herself."

"You don't know Rainee. She's very innocent and young."

Oh, but I do know her, she almost said, but something cautioned her to maintain her silence. The look in his eyes perhaps? This was a side of Hunter—the overprotective father—that she understood the least. What did he really think could happen to the girl here in a church surrounded by friends and neighbors?

"Do you think we could talk for a few moments? It's rather important." The request tumbled out of her mouth before she could reconsider.

"Talk? What about?" Brows furrowed, he looked down at her. Then he brought them to a standstill in the middle of the dance floor, unmindful of the other whirling couples, even when several bumped into them.

She realized then that he held her in a bone-crushing embrace against his chest, so close she could feel the thunderous rhythm of his heart. Her own, much more timid, thudded with renewed hope, for it seemed she had his undivided attention at last.

"Perhaps we could go somewhere a little less crowded," she suggested, smiling sweetly.

"Very well, if you wish," he agreed but made no effort to lead her to the sidelines. In fact, he appeared even more distracted than before.

"Hunter, please." She tugged on his arm.

"In a moment, Marina. Did you see where that damn Russian Pretty Boy went?"

"If you're referring to Sergei Bozzacchi, my *friend,*" she answered indignantly, "no, I have no idea where he is. And quite frankly, I don't care." Pulling out of his arms, she made her way through the whirling dancers to the opposite side of the room, unmindful of the curious stares she received along the way.

"Marina, wait."

That she refused to do. Instead, she picked up speed, dashing through the vestibule to the door leading outside. Once she reached the freedom of the churchyard, she sucked in great gulps of fresh air and fought down the rising self-chastisement. What had ever made her think she could turn to Hunter?

He caught up with her before she could master her raging emotions.

"Leave me alone." Prompted by his touch, as searing as a bolt of lightning striking her shoulder, she darted away.

"Marina, what in the hell is going on?" He trailed her footsteps, following her around a parked wagon to a clearing beneath a giant spruce. Chinese lanterns hung on the limbs of the tree, meant to add an atmosphere of gaiety to the party. Instead the undulating light created an eerie shadow-dance, an uneasiness that caused Marina to pause and not relish the idea of venturing into the darkness beyond.

"I came to you for help, Hunter," she cried. Feeling trapped, she whirled to face him. "You didn't even have the decency to hear me out."

"I'm listening now."

"Well, I'm not talking now." Fueled by her need to get as far away from him as possible, she kept moving deeper and deeper into the woods, the darkness suddenly presenting less of a threat than the man.

"Stop, Marina." He caught up with her in the shadow of another giant tree, grasping her by the arm to keep her from escaping again. Then he forced her to face him. "I'll not let you run away."

"What would you care if I did?" She swayed under the intensity of his stare, the pressure of his work-roughened hands on her bare arms, the fear that she meant nothing to him.

"More than you know. More than I should." He pulled her

into the circle of his strong arms and tucked the top of her head beneath his chin. "Oh, Marina," he said with a sigh, "if only I could be certain you wouldn't want to run away."

She leaned against him, listening, enthralled by the sound of his heart thudding so reassuringly in his chest.

Run away? She preferred to stay there in the circle of his arms forever. Closing her eyes, she permitted her own arms to curl about him. The longer the embrace lasted, the more real the possibility became. Yes, remaining forever in the arms of Hunter Kincaid would suit her just fine.

She heard a muffled sound in the distance, but thought nothing of it, assuming it to be the twitter of some night bird. Smiling in the contentment of the moment, she nestled against the hard plane of Hunter's chest.

When the noise, which now sounded more like human laughter, rudely invaded her consciousness again, she felt Hunter stiffen in her embrace.

"What do you think it is?" she asked, looking up at him for an answer.

"I don't know for sure. Shall we find out?" Keeping his arm about her, he led her deeper into the woods behind the church.

"Hunter, wait, maybe we shouldn't interfere," she cautioned, pressing herself against his back.

"Interfere? Why not? Are you afraid of what we might find?" Just as she had hoped that he would, he angled about, taking her once more into the protective circle of his arms.

"Never, as long as I'm with you." Lifting her face, she didn't resist his advances; she encouraged them, straining toward him with as much eagerness as he displayed. Their lips brushed, ever so tentatively, but then it was too much for either of them to endure.

As with all Hunter's kisses, the embrace quickly turned passionate, demanding, giving, making her forget everything except her need to experience love at its fullest. She clung to him shamelessly, wanting the intimate moment to go on forever and ever.

A bush rustled behind her.

"Oh," she gasped in alarm. Her eyes flew open to discover that Hunter, too, was alert and looking over her shoulder even as he abruptly ended the kiss.

"What is it?" she asked in a frightened whisper. "A wolf, perhaps?" In Russia, wolves ran rampant, often attacking villages and people foolish enough to wander into the woods unprotected.

"Maybe," he warned, tucking her safely behind him. "But I doubt it this close to town. Unless it's the two-legged kind."

"A wolf with only two legs?" she asked incredulously, peeking around his solid frame, trying to imagine how such an unusual beast could possibly get around, much less attack them. "How dangerous could it be?"

"Trust me, they're the worst kind. Now be quiet."

Accepting his words as fact, she clutched the back of his shirt and matched his steps as he crouched and moved forward, ducking underneath the low limbs of a tree.

A short distance away, they emerged into a small clearing checkered with patches of deep shadows.

The sound issued again and appeared to be human, reminding her of a young girl's giggle. What followed stunned her.

A man's voice, speaking Russian.

There was only one other person besides herself in Sweetwater who spoke Russian.

"Sergei?" Marina stepped forward, calling loudly, truly relieved to discover no wild animals lurked about. "What are you doing out here?"

The noises instantly ceased. Only silence answered her. And then she saw him emerge from the shadows.

"Don't you know there are dangerous two-legged wolves roaming out in these—"

"Marina, be quiet," Hunter interrupted her. He had moved to stand in front of her again. "Who is that you have behind you, Pretty Boy?" he demanded, on a note of deadly quiet.

Marina gasped in surprise when Rainee Kincaid stepped into the light.

Seventeen

"Rainee, get in the wagon."

Amazed at the calmness in his own voice, Hunter recognized it for a sham. The nightmare had begun to happen all over again just as he had feared that it would, only this time he would lose his precious daughter.

"But, Daddy . . ." She looked so young, so innocent, so very vulnerable—and yet so determined.

"Shut up, Rainee, and do as I tell you. Now!" he ordered briskly, pointing at the buckboard.

Throughout it all, Sergei never moved, never blinked an eye, never even glanced at Rainee. Yet the girl didn't respond to the parental demands until the Russian dancer released her hand and waved her away with an imperial gesture. Then, unquestioning, she sprinted off, her face buried in her hands.

Rainee was crying, but, more importantly, judging from her still unruffled appearance, she remained intact. Tears were temporary. He would deal with them later.

However, he would damn well deal with the two-legged Russian wolf who had caused all this misery now.

"You son of a . . ." Fist clenched, he stepped forward, menacingly.

"No, Hunter!"

His mind a red haze of righteousness, Hunter glanced down at the hand that gently restrained his arm. His first instinct? To shake it off and complete his all-encompassing mission to protect his daughter. Had it been anyone but Marina who tried to hold him back . . .

Damn it all. Why must her mere presence make his life so complicated? Why did he have to care when he would be far better off unaffected? Why did he feel that all too soon he would be forced to make a choice?

"Please, Hunter," she pleaded softly.

"Very well, Marina." He lowered his fist to his side, yet continued to keep it balled tightly. He might not give the man who had dared to try and violate his sweet Rainee what he deserved, but he'd be damned if he'd forgive him. "You ever come near my daughter again, Pretty Boy," he warned in a low, unemotional voice, "I promise you, you won't have anything left to tuck in your tights."

His point well made, Hunter turned and marched away.

"Hunter, wait. It's not what you might think."

He glared down at the woman clinging to his sleeve, attempting to match his anger-driven footsteps as best as she could. His heart lurched. God only knew why it always did that whenever he looked at her. Whenever he even thought about her, it did crazy flip-flops in his chest that he was powerless to control. He might not be able to stop them, but he didn't have to succumb to them, or to her, any further.

"How could you possibly know what I think, Marina? Just keep your fancy man away from my daughter." At last he found the strength of will to shake her off.

Free but hurting more than he cared to admit, he continued on, out of the woods and into the clearing where he had parked the buckboard.

Rainee sat on the wagon seat, her head held high in discernible defiance. More than ever, she reminded him of her mother the last time he had seen her. But it didn't matter what the girl thought or how she felt about him at the moment. He cared only for her safety.

Wordlessly, he climbed onto the seat beside her. He released the hand brake and, issuing a soft whistle, snapped the reins, setting the wagon in motion. He couldn't get out of the churchyard fast enough.

By damn, he would take her home and never let her out of his sight again. Even as he made the vow, he knew no matter how hard he tried he would never be able to keep it. Oh, in the beginning he could watchdog her, but eventually she would find a way to sneak out, to defy him, to break his heart just as her mother had. He only wanted the best for his one-and-only daughter. Was that such a crime?

From the corner of his eye, he glanced at Rainee. Predictably, she had scooted as far away from him on the seat as she possibly could. Arms folded over her chest, she glared at him with eyes that glittered like those of a wild animal, as if he had wronged her instead of the other way around.

"Look, Rainee," he said, hoping to initiate a conversation that would make her see reason.

Instead, he might as well have opened up the floodgate of a raging river.

"Daddy, how could you have done something so humiliating to me?" she cried.

"Me?" he retorted. "You're the one who has disgraced yourself and the Kincaid name. What were you thinking, Rainee, to go off in the woods with that . . . that dancer? Or did you bother to think at all?"

They stared at each other. He could see how much she hurt. Why couldn't she recognize the same in him?

"Oh, you're one to talk, Daddy." She snorted. "Just what were *you* doing out there in the woods with *your* dancer?" she demanded.

Her blunt accusation caught him completely offguard.

"My actions have nothing at all to do with this, young lady," he defended; rather lamely, he realized.

"Don't they, Daddy? Don't they have everything to do with it?" she cried.

"What do you mean?" He found himself shouting back, but as much as he wanted to stop himself, he couldn't. The truth made a powerful enemy, one he had no ammunition to combat.

"Did you honestly believe I wouldn't find out all about you and Marina Nicolaiev? Do you think the whole town doesn't know and think you're making a fool of yourself? 'Another dancer,' they say," she mimicked. " 'You'd think he'd have learned his lesson with the first one.' " She glared at him, her eyes brimming with more unshed tears. "The first one, Daddy? That was Mother, wasn't it? My mother, the dancer, who ran off and left me because she didn't love me enough to stick around." Her young voice broke on a note of pure despair.

So did his love-scarred heart as he endured the sound of his cherished daughter weeping uncontrollably. It ripped him apart to think that she took on such unwarranted responsibility for events completely out of her control.

"No, no, Rainee." He pulled the team to a halt, wrapped the reins around the brake handle, and gathered her trembling form into his arms. "It wasn't like that at all, honey. Believe me." He brushed the hair from her tear-streaked face. "Your mother loved you. The inadequacy rests on my shoulders, honey. I simply couldn't give your mother what she wanted."

Yes, he supposed it was high time he faced the truth. He had only himself to blame for Della's desertion. Only a fool expected a woman accustomed to the high life to ever be satisfied with his simpler wants and dreams.

Rainee and the rest of the town were right. He should have learned his lesson the first time around. Only a fool would think that Marina might be different. That she might love him enough to stay.

Oh, for a while she might be happy. But, like Della, she'd grow tired of the mud and the cows, and the isolation. Marina would never fit in here.

As for Rainee. He hugged her fiercely. She presented a whole different set of problems. In her case, he had time on his side. She had grown up on the range. The vastness, the freedom, the land itself, were an inescapable part of her, as much as they were a part of him. Once she got a little older, she would acknowledge her love of their lifestyle. In the meantime, he was damn well determined not to lose sight of it himself.

"It's all right, Rainee. Trust me. Everything will turn out all right." He listened patiently until her sobs subsided into little sniffles and hiccups. Then, still holding her, wishing only to protect her—and himself as well, he supposed—he gathered up the reins in his free hand and set the horses in motion once more.

Although at the moment Rainee seemed complaisant enough and silence prevailed between them instead of a barrage of angry words, Hunter knew he still had a long row to hoe when it came to shielding his daughter from the pitfalls of life.

"It was all in innocence, Marinuska. I swear it. We were merely talking. I was telling her what it is like to be the *premier danseur* of the Royal Russian Ballet, what it could be like for her to become a *prima ballerina* if she set her mind and heart on it."

Above all else, Sergei loved to talk about himself and his accomplishments. But Rainee didn't need to have her head filled with faraway dreams. America was nothing like Russia. Dreams were different here.

"Why did you have to sneak into the woods just to *talk?*"

"She didn't want her father to see me talking to her."

"That's only an excuse, Sergei. Promise me it wouldn't happen again. Promise me you'll stay away from all the young girls in town."

"All of them?"

He looked so forlorn and confused, she reconsidered the harshness of what he no doubt believed to be undeserved punishment. But no. It had to be that way.

"All of them," she insisted.

"You expect too much, Marina. I am only a man, not a saint like you," he said with obvious sarcasm.

She took no offense at his cutting remark. It was Sergei's way of getting back when admitting defeat. She stared at him patiently, waiting for the proper attitude and response.

"Oh, very well, if you insist. I will stay away from the little witches. All of them." He sighed dramatically. "I suppose you even want me to stop attending your precious classes. But that might not be good for business, for it will not make the mamas very happy, you know. And what will you do without their approval?"

"The mamas will get over it. Their daughters are here to learn to dance, not flirt." Reaching up, she stroked his face as she would an obedient, if somewhat petulant, child.

Clasping her hand in his own, he pressed his face against her palm, kissing it with an intensity he had never displayed with her before.

"Thank you, Sergei," she said somewhat guardedly as she pulled her hand from his grasp. "I promise you, it really is for the best."

"Whose?" he muttered, frowning when she refused to let him take her hand again. "Not mine to be sure." He turned and walked away.

Uncertain what to think of Sergei's strange behavior, Marina decided it might be best if in the future she kept a close eye on him.

The next few days Marina tried hard to put the disaster of Saturday night firmly behind her, no easy task considering that the events, thoroughly discussed and embellished, became the focus of the town's gossip.

Rainee didn't show up for her Tuesday afternoon lesson.

Marina thought little of it. Under the circumstances, the girl's absence could be considered excusable, she supposed, although she would have never allowed mere gossip to keep her away from something as important to her as dancing.

When Rainee missed yet another lesson without sending word, Marina grew first concerned, then upset. After the fiasco of Saturday night, it was obvious to her whom to blame for her prize student's continued absence.

Hunter. How like him to overreact. Perhaps it was time someone pointed out to him the error of his ways. When Chloe arrived with her girls for their lesson, she turned to the older woman for help.

"Why do you think he will listen to me?" Chloe asked.

"Because he trusts you and you understand him better than anyone else," Marina replied confidently.

"When it comes to Rainee and his version of what is in her best interest, believe me, he won't listen to anyone. Maybe it's better this way, Marina."

No, Marina refused to accept defeat. Rainee deserved the opportunity to make such decisions for herself. Someone had to talk to Hunter. If Chloe wouldn't, that left only Marina.

With the rest of her afternoon free, Marina hired a rig and headed for the Kincaid estate. Since the night of the terrible storm, when she had raced off ill-prepared to search for Hunter, she had not once considered visiting his domain.

However, she had never been invited. Hunter's slight stung. That in all of the time she had been in Sweetwater, he had not wanted to show her his kingdom, to share with her his hopes and dreams revealed more about him than she cared to acknowledge.

The lack of invitation would not stop her now, now that she had a mission. It was high time someone took the bull by the horns. Pleased to no end that she had expressed herself in Western terminology, she slapped the reins against the horse's back, urging it to pick up its pace. Yes, someone had to make him realize that his daughter, a bright and talented young woman, deserved his encouragement and support to make the very best of what life offered her.

An hour later, she came to the fork in the road that the liveryman had described to her as the way to the Kincaid estate. Without hesitation, she reined the horse down the rutted lane.

Imbued with excitement at finally seeing the place Hunter had described as an empire, she paused on a hill to take it all in. The ranch consisted of a quaint collection of crude buildings and enclosures nestled in the small valley below. Comprised of a main house along with several outbuildings of different sizes and shapes, the Kincaid kingdom, to her disappointment, was not impressive.

And yet, she felt herself drawn to the picturesque setting. It fit Hunter Kincaid to a tee—rugged, solid, a fine home, even if somewhat rough around the edges.

A barking dog greeted the buggy as she brought the horse to a stop in front of the main house. The rather odd-looking beast, a far cry from her own dear, little pets so tragically lost in Russia, flattened it ears and bared its glistening fangs at her. It reminded her more of a wolf, the four-legged kind, than a domestic canine. So much so, that she hesitated to step down from her rig.

She waited patiently. However, no one came to her assistance; no servant arrived to take charge of her conveyance.

Americans were truly a strange breed.

Finally, she spied a stableboy, if one could judge by dress, emerging from one of the outbuildings.

"Excuse me," she called out, expecting to receive immediate assistance. Instead, she discovered a wide-eyed Rainee dressed in boy's clothing.

"Marina? What are you doing here?" the girl asked in a choked whisper. She grabbed the barking dog by the collar, holding it back.

"I was about to ask you the same thing." Tying off the reins, Marina descended from the buggy. "You've missed your lessons all week, Rainee," she scolded gently. "I came here to find out why."

"Please, you must go away." The girl glanced about worriedly.

What was she so afraid of? Hunter?

"Look, I'll be glad to talk to your father. Surely he doesn't intend to stop your ballet lessons because of what happened Saturday night."

"What ballet lessons?"

Marina whipped around to discover Hunter Kincaid in the doorway of the house. He looked anything but pleased to see her.

"Daddy," Rainee gasped, releasing the dog, who began barking at Marina once again, especially in light of its master's hostile attitude. The girl, however, began backing up as if she considered running.

"Rowdy, git," he commanded sharply. "Rainee, you stay put," he demanded with equal ferocity.

Without question, both did as they were told. The dog lay down on the far end of the porch under a swing, eyeing Marina as if only waiting for permission to tear her apart. Rainee looked scared half out of her wits.

Next she expected him to order her off his property. He didn't, but he didn't invite her inside his home, either. Although his rudeness hurt, she chose to ignore it.

"Honestly, Hunter," she said, fearlessly stepping onto the porch to confront him. "Do you really think it's fair to keep Rainee from something that she enjoys simply because of one innocent mistake?"

"Just how long has she been enjoying these lessons?" he asked, but he wasn't looking at her. No, she decided. He didn't dare face something unafraid of him. Instead he chose to stare pointedly over her shoulder at the daughter who quaked in her shoes.

Prompted by a sense of loyalty to Rainee, Marina did not instantly respond to Hunter's question. Instead, she turned, looking to Rainee for a clue. The girl's resentful look directed at her father offered evidence enough. Apparently, she had never even told him about the lessons. But why would Rainee keep them secret from him? And what could she now say to minimize the blundering damage already done?

"She's good, Hunter." Marina whipped back around to face him. "She really has talent and ability. You will be proud of her. I know that you will when you see how much—"

"Rainee, get in the house," he ordered. "I'll deal with you later."

Before Marina could protest, the unhappy girl darted around first her then Hunter's imposing figure.

"I'm not sorry, Daddy." Rainee flew up the interior stairs without looking back.

"Really, Hunter. Was that necessary?" Marina planted her fists on her hips for emphasis. Rainee might be intimidated by him, but she was not.

"Stay away from her, Marina."

To her surprise, he turned and entered the house as well. Did he plan to just leave her standing there, her many questions left unanswered? Her gaze shot to the dog, who began to growl softly. Did he plan to leave her at the mercy of that cur of his who looked ready, willing, and able to rip her to shreds?

"Wait a minute," she demanded, stepping forward to prevent him from shutting the door.

Although he paused and looked back at her, he said nothing to encourage her.

"You may not realize it, Hunter, but Rainee is very talented and deserves the chance to make something better out of her life."

"Better than what, Marina? Better than I can give her? Well, if that something 'better' is to become a dancer and sashay across a stage every night," he said, glaring at her derisively, "I think not."

It took her a moment to realize the full implications of his words and that he mocked her identity and accomplishments.

"What's so wrong with devoting your life to the stage?" she demanded.

"Nothing, as long as you aren't my daughter or my . . ." Without finishing his declaration, he clamped his mouth shut.

"Or your what?" she demanded, but he refused to answer. He didn't have to. It was easy enough to fill in the blank for herself. And so there she had it, whether she particularly wanted to hear it or not. The truth according to Hunter Kincaid. He treated her greatest accomplishment in life as if it were something for which she should feel only shame, for which he held nothing but contempt.

Before she could tell him what she thought of him and his prejudice, Hunter took her by the arm and led her back to her waiting buggy. He picked her up, plopped her on the seat, and inserted the reins into her unwilling hands.

"Hunter, I don't know what you think you're doing; but when it comes to Rainee, you're making a terrible mistake. You can't isolate her against her will and think that will stop her from becoming who she is meant to be. One day, when it's too late, you'll discover you've lost her. Is that what you are afraid of, Hunter, of losing her?" she asked softly.

For a moment, encouraged by the naked emotion on his face, she thought he might actually confide in her; but then he pressed his lips together with determination, and his eyes grew hard and expressionless.

"I'm not afraid of anything, least of all you and your crazy notions about what it takes to make my daughter happy. I know what's best for Rainee. And if you know what's best for you, you'll stop trying to fill the innocent female minds of this town with foolish thoughts of stardom and nobility. You and Mr. Fancy Pants, Count Sergei, are only headed for trouble."

"What are you saying?"

"I'm saying Rainee was lucky. Sergei didn't have enough time to ruin her. But what about the next innocent girl he sets his cap for? Her father might not be as lenient as I was."

"You're wrong about Sergei," she insisted, knowing herself right. "He would never compromise Rainee or any other young girl." Sergei's interest had always run to older, more experienced women who controlled fat, enticing purses. "How stupid are the fathers if they can't see he's simply being kind in showing their daughters attention? The mothers of this town are not so thickheaded, in fact, they encourage it. And if Rainee had a mother—"

"Rainee doesn't have a mother. She doesn't need a mother. She has me."

He cut her off so quickly, Marina opened her mouth to protest. But then she saw the undisguised agony in his sky-blue eyes. She had never seen such pain in another human being. Then the door to his soul—the door that had exposed that glimpse of vulnerability—slammed closed. A look of uncompromising distrust took its place.

She knew without a doubt that pain had been inflicted by a woman, an uncaring woman. Rainee's mother, perhaps? As distressing as that seemed, at the same time such insight offered a glimmer of hope. The only hope she had left to cling to. If he concealed intense pain so well, perhaps he hid his love for her just as easily.

"Hunter," she whispered, searching for the right words to convey her understanding, her willingness to believe in him, to be patient.

Before she could formulate her thought, she saw him lift his hand.

Whack!

Slapped on the behind, the unsuspecting horse lurched forward, dragging the buggy behind it. Even as she scrambled to gain control of the reins, Marina came to a decision. She had to face the truth, all of it, had to find out just what scarring memory kept him from trusting her, even if it were the love for another woman. She knew exactly who could tell her what she wanted to know.

"Della. Her name was Della." Chloe stared at Marina for a moment as if sizing her up, but whether for sincerity or stamina, she couldn't be certain. "Are you sure you want to hear this?"

"I have to find out, Chloe. I cannot combat what I do not know."

"I suppose you're right," the madam conceded with a sigh. "But promise me, you'll never let him know I was the one to tell you."

"Of course." Marina leaned forward with expectation and

more than a touch of apprehension. She had felt the same sitting in the buggy outside Chloe's, uncertain if she should go inside or drive away. But only the truth could prepare her for the battle ahead.

"Della had the face of an angel, innocent and sweet to look at; but inside, she possessed the heart of a demon. She could sing, dance, seduce an entire audience of men in a matter of moments."

No wonder Rainee had such talent. She got it from her mother.

"That's what she did to Hunter," Chloe continued. "Seduced him because she thought he could give her what she wanted."

Marina tried not to look at the bed in Chloe's private quarters, the bed where she and Hunter had once made love—tried not to think of him with another woman. But it was hard.

"Did he marry her?"

"Two days after she hit town. Mac, his father, was furious. Told him no man in his right mind married that kind of woman." Chloe's mouth turned down sadly, as if the memory of Hunter's father claimed a special place in her heart, feelings comprised of tender poignancy. Had she loved the man? Had he refused to marry her because she was "that kind of woman"?

"I'm so sorry, Chloe," Marina offered softly.

"Don't be, honey; it's not your fault." Chloe smiled with false brightness. "None of this is your fault, but it seems you have to pay the consequences."

"Was he happy with Della?"

"Like a blind man in a braille factory. But I could tell, after the newness wore off, she grew restless. Della always had to be in the limelight. She couldn't play second fiddle to anyone or anything else. Then Rainee came along. Della couldn't stand the attention Hunter showed the baby; and the ever-increasing demands of the ranch occupied him more and more. The people of Sweetwater never accepted her; and—not that she ever tried—she had no real friends. A year later, she was gone. She took off with a high-rolling gambler, leaving the baby and Hunter without any warning."

"So Hunter still has a wife?" The irony, after all that they had been through because of Dmitri, caught her by surprise.

"No, Della's dead. Hunter found her two years later in a hovel in Denver. She died in his arms, cursing him for ruining her life and her career. She never once asked about Rainee."

"Oh, Chloe, I had no idea. No wonder he's so fiercely protective of Rainee. He's afraid she'll follow in her mother's foolish footsteps. And as for me . . . Oh, Chloe, how am I supposed to fight such a powerful enemy?"

"You can't fight it, at least not with conventional weapons. You've just got to show patience and prove to him you're not Della, that you're not going to run out on him when he least expects it."

So much of what Hunter had said to her, his every reaction, now made sense; but knowledge didn't make her job any easier. Patience. Hers ran thin of late, but she had to find more, enough to show him and all of the skeptics in town that she and her troupe were trustworthy.

No, it wouldn't be easy to become everyday and ordinary. But if that were what Hunter wanted her to be, she could do it.

"Thank you, Chloe, for telling me the truth." Taking a deep breath, she stood, feeling anything but prepared.

But at least she knew her next step. Sunday was just around the corner. How much more ordinary could one be than to go to church?

Sunday morning church services. Hunter didn't particularly look forward to them, but he attended them out of necessity, for Rainee's sake.

Already the day promised to be a scorcher, and the minister had yet to begin. Hunter slipped a finger beneath his collar and hames, thankful that he only had to wear his Sunday-go-to-meeting neckwear once a week. An annoying fly buzzed about. He shooed it off, and it landed on Hatty Shackelford, who occupied the pew in front of him. Then it moved to the hat of the woman sitting next to her before darting off to parts unknown. He knew that like any pest, it would be back—if for no other reason than to aggravate him.

Rainee sat beside him. Bored, she stirred the air with a fan she'd fashioned from a hymnal. He understood her lack of enthusiasm. Nevertheless, church was good for her. It had to be. Della had always refused to attend.

At last the Reverend Endicott climbed to the pulpit. Hunter took a deep breath, resigning himself to the long hour ahead. He tried hard not to think about the work he'd much rather be doing, the more important tasks that needed his attention than sitting on a hard bench listening to a sermon from a man who knew as much about real life as a tenderfoot knew about cattle. Ranches didn't run themselves, he thought resentfully, but the minds of young girls did if given half a chance and exposure to the wrong kind of influence.

He wasn't alone in his sentiments. Just this morning Jeb Granger had pulled him aside before they had entered the church to confirm the events of Saturday night and express fatherly concerns about his own daughter's possible involvement with such an unsavory sort.

Hunter felt more than justified in what he had said to Marina yesterday. Indeed, the presence of the dance troupe in Sweetwater was the wind stirring up the dust. It would not settle until Marina and her cohorts left.

The pump organ wheezed out its first ear-grating notes. Mrs. Davenport's playing still hadn't improved. It took him a few moments to recognize the tune she played, an off-key rendition of "Rock of Ages." When he thought he couldn't take another note, the music stopped. At the same time, the door of the outer vestibule swung open, allowing a blinding blast of sunshine to streak through the darkened church.

Along with everyone else, he turned to see who had entered at the last moment. If it hadn't been so amazing, it might have been laughable. It was almost as if he had conjured them up out of his own thoughts.

Marina and her troupe made a colorful picture clustered in the back of the church. He recognized several of them, including Fanny, but her piano-playing boyfriend wasn't present. Although they said not a word, they caused quite a commotion as they breezed down the aisle in single file. Marina led the way to the only seats available, a pew right up front, her head held high, no doubt pretending not to see him.

It took the newcomers a few moments to get situated, skirts and purses arranged and rearranged. Pretty Boy stood and removed his jacket. As he did, he flexed his muscles and glanced over the congregation. His gaze settled on several of the young ladies, including Sarah Granger, who sat right behind him; and he grinned, evoking little unchurch-like giggles from his victims.

Looking extremely uncomfortable, the preacher stood at his podium, politely waiting for Sergei to sit down and the required solemnness to return. When it didn't happen, he cleared his throat.

"Oh, I'm sorry." Glancing up at the clergyman, the Russian paused in his showboat display. "Are you waiting for me?" he asked in his heavily accented English.

At Marina's insistent urging, the obnoxious dancer finally sat down.

Obnoxious. In Hunter's mind that described the Russian perfectly. He glanced at Rainee and then at several of the other calf-eyed girls. What could they possibly see in such a man?

Escape? A way out? That had probably been what Rainee had seen in him. The grass had looked greener on the other side of the fence. It had been the promise of a better life, not the man who had offered it, that had enticed her, just as it had her mother. Instinctively he draped his arm in a protective gesture along the back of the pew where Rainee sat.

"I see we have several visitors today. I would like to welcome you," Reverend Endicott began. This greeting was standard when, on rare occasion, someone new attended services. However, ignoring the customary ritual, no doubt out of concern for where it might lead, he didn't ask them to each stand up and introduce themselves.

Everyone noticed the slight, except for those snubbed, of course. No one said a word, thank goodness, for even one innocent comment could have sparked the underlying tension into an uncontrollable brush fire. To everyone's relief, the preacher launched right into the services. Today it seemed even he was in a rush to get it over with.

Hunter relaxed a little, thinking the worst over, allowing his mind to wander to other things, thoughts most inappropriate in church. But with a woman as attractive as Marina sitting only a few feet in front of him, what man in his right mind could focus on the preacher's droning voice?

Instead he heard music, beautiful music. It swelled in his heart like an overwhelming emotion. Then he saw her dancing, Marina, a gypsy woman in shimmering, provocative gauze, lighter than air, whirling, whirling, right into the arms of her partner. That partner? Not Sergei. Oh, no. Instead he envisioned himself with her.

He was the one there to catch her, the one to lift her high above a cruel, destructive world. She trusted him above all others. But more importantly, she was satisfied with him, with what he could offer her. If only he could prove that.

The buzzing of that irritating fly in his ear pulled him from his reverie. Resentfully, he jerked back to reality. He sat in church, the preacher droning in harmony with the fly. Instantly alert, he fought down a sense of rising anxiety.

Suddenly Reverend Endicott's voice took on a decided note of urgency as he spoke of God's forgiveness. Wondering if God would indeed forgive him for his indulgences, if the preacher had the power to read another's mind and spoke directly to him, Hunter took careful inventory of his surroundings.

Irreverence seemed to be on the minds of the entire congregation. In fact, unless he missed his guess, all hell was about to break loose in church.

Eighteen

` "Why you low-down son of a bitch. You deserve to be pistol-whipped. Keep your filthy hands off my daughter."

Something jerked Sergei from the seat beside Marina.

"No, Father," a young female voice screamed.

Alarmed, she turned to investigate. Yelping in pain, the *danseur* hit the floor, his head smacking against the pulpit where the clergyman stood. Blood spurted from his nose, obscenities from his mouth. Thank God, he spoke Russian.

Subsequent events happened so fast she couldn't be certain how they actually got started, or even exactly what occurred; but after his earlier demonstration, she suspected Sergei somehow had instigated the fiasco.

Why hadn't she listened when Hunter had warned her something like this might happen?

"Please, Mr. Granger." Rising, she stepped between Sergei and the angry father, putting her hand out to stop him.

"You no-account count," the man bellowed. If he saw or heard Marina, he gave no indication. "We'll see if blue blood runs as freely as red." Pushing up his sleeves, Jeb Granger leapt over the pew, practically knocking her out of the way. Although he still clenched his fist, a piece of paper fluttered out of his hand.

"No, Jeb," his wife screamed. In just as futile an attempt to stop him, Elvira Granger grabbed him by the back of his shirt. Her efforts barely slowed the irate rancher down.

Sergei, covering his blood-splattered face, crawled toward the only safety offered to him by the reluctant feet of the Reverend Endicott, who was trying hard to reclaim control of his wayward congregation.

"People, people. Please, sit down," the preacher cried, pounding the podium with his splayed hand.

No one listened to him, either.

In the meantime Marina retrieved the piece of paper, opened it, and read the incriminating note. She glanced at Sarah Granger. The foolish girl. What had she been thinking?

But then, as if things weren't bad enough, Mayor Shackelford came flying down the aisle toward them, waving his fist high in the air.

"Let's get 'im, boys," he shouted, calling his fellow fathers to arms with the passion of a Russian revolutionary. "Are we going to continue to allow some Nancy boy and our womenfolk to make fools of us?"

He barely took three steps before his wife, using the only weapon available to her, hit him over the head with the Bible she clutched in her hand. The little man reeled, stumbled into a crowded pew, practically into another lady's lap. That woman screamed and whacked him in the face with her purse. Dazed and cowed, the mayor didn't resist as Hatty dragged him back to his seat.

Unfortunately, it didn't end there. Instead, it turned into a free-for-all with husbands pitted against wives. One woman even resorted to chasing her spouse around the church with the ornate candle snuffer used to put out the wicks at the end of each service.

"Stop this," Marina cried, but no one heard her, or if they did, they ignored her. Marina realized she had made a big mistake coming to the church and especially to have brought Sergei with her.

She had meant well, wanting only to prove that she belonged in this community as much as anyone else. But Hunter had been right all along. There was no place for her, or any of her people, in Sweetwater. Their presence had turned this dreadful little town upside-down and inside-out. She had no one to blame but herself.

From across the room she saw him. He had Rainee firmly by the upper arm, his hands full preventing the fretful girl from dashing into the middle of the melee. Yet through it all he looked so calm, so utterly in charge, so devastatingly handsome. If she hadn't known the depth of his pain, she would have sworn he was incapable of feeling. He turned his blue, unruffled gaze on her. His look of accusation wasn't pleasant.

Everyone except Hunter had forgotten about them. With husbands and wives wrapped up in fighting among themselves, even Sergei was safe for the moment. Taking advantage of the small reprieve, Marina quickly collected her scattered group. Extracting a clean hanky from her reticule, she mounted the pulpit and knelt to press the cloth to Sergei's still-bleeding nose.

"There, there," she said beneath her breath, trying to conceal her frustration as she helped the *danseur* to his feet. She glanced around, looking for an alternative exit, but found none. If she'd had any other choice, she would have gone a different way, anything to avoid passing through the middle of the battle. Anything not to have to walk in front of Hunter.

"Come on, Sergei." Hoping to avoid another confrontation, she took him, busy attending to his bloody nose, by the arm. She commandeered him toward the vestibule. To her relief, the rest of the troupe followed like sheep.

Head held high, her aristocratic pride her only remaining weapon, she marched on without pausing.

Oh, please, Hunter, please, she prayed. *Back away.*

But he didn't. Just as she had feared that he would, he stepped into the aisle, blocking their escape.

"So tell me, Pretty Boy," he asked, "have you learned your lesson?"

Marina stopped and whirled to face Hunter, determined to protect sensitive Sergei from yet another physical attack. He may have done wrong, but she was the one to take the necessary disciplinary measures. It wasn't Hunter's place.

To her surprise Sergei pushed her, rather roughly, out of his way.

"This is all your fault, you son of a bitch," he accused, the very-American curse distorted by his accent. It came out sounding more like a Russian last name, Sonavich. "You will pay," he warned, swiping at the blood still oozing from his nostrils. "I will see that you pay."

Her dance partner could often be difficult and invariably temperamental, but such an outburst was unlike him. Like the curse, it was so American. Angry with Hunter for inciting Sergei to boorish behavior, she glared at him, hating him for his insensitivity. With a look, she dared him to say another word.

Hunter said no more. He didn't have to. His return glare could only be described as deadly. Why? she questioned. Sergei's threats were obviously idle.

"Come on, Sergei," she urged softly, dabbing gently at him with the blood-soaked hanky. "Let's go home where I can take a better look at your injury." She would look at his nose all right, then she would give him a piece of her mind.

"It's broken," he whined, blindly allowing her to lead him as he tilted his head back to stop the flow. "My face is ruined. Marinuska, what will I do if my face is ruined?"

"It's not ruined," she assured, patting him on the shoulder. "Everything will be all right. I promise you."

And it would be. Somehow she would see to it, even if they had to take what money they had and get as far away from Sweetwater as it would take them.

As close to tears as she had come in a long time, she gladly escaped from the church where her life, her dreams, and her expectations had crumbled before her eyes. Nothing she could do would convince Hunter of her sincerity.

She couldn't imagine how it could get any worse.

With the source of the dispute, empty threats and all, shown to the door, Hunter managed to make his way to the front of the church. In all his years he'd never seen such a brawl, not even in the days of the Songbird Saloon. He planted Rainee in the preacher's chair far from the foray so he could keep an eye on her, then he joined the frayed servant of God on his pulpit. The poor man had resorted to wringing his hands.

"Would you like me to try, Reverend Endicott?" he offered.

"Oh, please, Mr. Kincaid. Anything," the clergyman pleaded fretfully. "Oh, my. How could something so awful happen in the House of the Lord?"

Since nothing seemed sacred anymore, Hunter grabbed a candlestick from the altar. He used it as a makeshift gavel, pounding loudly and insistently until the din subsided enough so he could be heard.

"Ladies, gentlemen." Such a polite address at the moment was a far cry from what they deserved. "Stop and take a good look at yourselves," he demanded in a voice that boomed with authority.

He received minimal response. One woman charged him, an umbrella—raised like a bayonet—aimed right at his middle.

"Mrs. Davenport," he said calmly, as if he greeted her instead of sidestepped her attack. The so-called weaker sex had a bloodthirsty side that put savages to shame. The situation required stronger action. He reached for his gun, only to remember he'd left it hanging in the vestibule along with his hat. Words were his only weapon now. Words and Sweetwater's essence of community pride. Once again he banged his gavel.

"Are we going to allow a bunch of outsiders to turn us against each other?"

He found it oddly symbolic the way the contenders split up. The men gravitated one way, grumbling, the women the other, griping. As for their offspring, both male and female, they stood on the sidelines looking bewildered. At least, their parents no longer fought. For the moment, anyway.

"Just where do you stand on this, Kincaid?" The question came from Jeb Granger. "With them?" He jerked a thumb toward the group of women that included his own wife. "And their foolish notions that one of those outsiders might actually be fit to marry one of us? Hell, everybody knows you can't hitch a horse to a coyote. Are you with them or with us?"

Hunter stared at his fellow rancher. Them or us? Insiders, outsiders. Therein lay his own personal dilemma.

Without a doubt he would never stand by and allow Rainee to take up with the likes of Sergei Bozzacchi. He would send her away first, far enough away to guarantee her safety until the Russian left town. However, when it came to himself, it seemed he wanted to play by a whole different set of rules.

Marina. In spite of it all, in spite of what Della had done to him, he still wanted her to stay. It would be better if she didn't. More than anything, he wanted to believe it might be different with her, yet his hard-learned cynicism warned him such wishful thinking only spelled disaster.

Them or us? The decision had to be made, but he found the choice impossible.

"Sorry, Jeb. In this case, the only side I'm on is my own."

Ignoring the animosity directed at him from all angles, Hunter forced a protesting Rainee out of the church. Yes, he was more than prepared to do whatever he must to protect his daughter.

"Sergei, how could you have gone against my express wishes?"

They had returned to the dance academy. His nose had stopped bleeding and he had washed his face, but the *danseur* insisted on a clean handkerchief.

Marina led him to her room; she sat him on her bed. From a drawer of the rickety dresser she retrieved one of her own and pressed the delicate lace-edged square into his impatient fingers. Odd, she thought, as he snatched at the offering. She had never noticed how soft and uncalloused his hands were.

She watched as he continued to dab at his upper lip. His hand, the gesture, even the handkerchief, none of it made him any less masculine. According to Russian standards, such mannerisms were perfectly acceptable. Even her father, a battle-hardened soldier, had carried lace handkerchiefs her mother had tatted for him. Yet, she couldn't conceive of a man like Hunter Kincaid adhering to such a custom.

Had that marked cultural difference been a part of what had attracted her to Hunter in the first place? That and his unfailing honor? True, he could be unreadable and infuriatingly impossible, at times even brusque, but no one could ever question his honor.

Sergei, however, was a different matter altogether.

"You must believe me. I didn't do anything wrong, Marinuska," he insisted.

"No, I suppose you didn't, but only because Sarah's father put a stop to it before you could." In the future she would have to watch Sergei more carefully.

"You believe that *kulak*, that farmer, over me? How can you?" he asked, his voice laced with indignation.

Wordlessly, she produced the crumpled note she had retrieved from the floor of the church. She spread the paper out for him to read.

"I've never seen that before," he declared.

"I'm sure you haven't, but you know as well as I do, it was intended for you."

"So what if it were, Marina?"

"Then you betrayed my trust, Sergei. These people live a much simpler, straightforward life than we do."

"You mean more bourgeois." He sniffed arrogantly, once again pressing the bit of perfumed cloth to his nose. "One would think you actually found their quaint lifestyle to your liking." He laughed, then stood up and began to pace. "Surely you aren't willing to give up everything you've worked so hard to attain for this?" With a sweep of his hand he indicated their anything-but-elegant surroundings.

She stared at him in silence.

"You, of all people, prima ballerina of the Royal Russian Ballet, a princess of the realm. I'm surprised at you," he hissed.

"And I am disappointed in you," she countered.

"Don't be, Marinuska." His voice took on a note of pleading as he suddenly rose from the bed and knelt before her, taking her hand in his. He kissed the knuckles in a chivalrous gesture.

Startled by his unexpected change in attitude, she tried to retrieve her hand.

"We can have it all again, Marina. You and I. The world will be at our feet. All you have to do—"

"Sergei," she cut him off, trying to be gentle in her rejection, but unwilling to succumb as other women did to his sophisticated, yet empty promises. "I'm not one of your paramours."

"Of course, you're not. You mean so much more to me.

You always have. None of the women in my life have ever mattered. But you knew that, didn't you? I couldn't have you. The snow princess, untouchable. That was what you wanted me to think, wasn't it? That no one could ever have you."

"Sergei, please," she protested in a horrified whisper. She had had no idea that he harbored such feelings for her. How could she have been so blind?

"If anyone betrayed another's trust, it was you. You with that cowboy. Why else do you think I wasted my time with foolish little girls like Rainee Kincaid? I hoped to make you as jealous as you made me. I thought to prove to you that Kincaid's only concern was for his daughter. Then you started to care for her, even more than you cared about me. However, I forgive you, my darling. Surely you'll forgive me." Turning over her hand, he pressed his lips to the pulse point in her wrist in a lavish, sensuous caress.

"Sergei, don't," she objected, pulling away.

"Why not, my love?" Trapping her hand once more, he brought it to his mouth. "You know we would be good together. Otherwise, we could never dance the way that we do." His lips traveled the length of her arm.

Unmoved except for pity, her heart lay quietly in her chest. Sergei had been the very first man to ever touch her. As her dance partner, he had held her tightly, even caressed her body, before an audience of hundreds, yet she had never thought of him as a lover. Physical desire had never once played a part in their relationship.

He was Sergei. Someone she could trust; someone who understood what it meant to work hard for success. Someone who shared her love for the stage, the thrill of an approving crowd, the dedicated life of the ballet.

"Please, you must stop," she pleaded softly.

"Why?" Rising to his feet, he tried to gather her into his arms. "Is it because of that uncouth cowboy? That Hunter

Kincaid?" He sought her mouth with his. "He is the one who betrayed your trust, not I."

"No, you are wrong," she said with confidence, turning her face away from his.

"Am I? Then why don't you ask him about the deal he struck with Dmitri in Russia."

"Deal? If you mean the cattle negotiations between them, Sergei, that was for the good of the people of Russia, to feed them, give them work." She struggled to escape the clinging, unwanted grasp, the lips that were cold and unpleasant against her face.

"How very noble of you, Marina. Not every woman would be so proud to commit adultery for the sake of the Russian people."

"What do you mean?" She ceased to fight him, fearful of what he knew or thought he knew.

"The infamous Nicolaiev proposition. Bed my wife and I'll buy your cattle." His mouth curled contemptuously. "Everyone in St. Petersburg talked about your supposedly innocent part in that affair, but now I wonder. Did you revel in the fact that you were the envy of your female peers? Not every woman can claim to have a husband willing to make arrangements with her lover."

"No. That is a vicious lie, Sergei. It didn't happen that way." Yet in her heart she knew Dmitri capable of such warped judgment. She couldn't count the times her invalid husband had suggested she take a lover, even thrusting men in front of her. Would he have used Hunter in the same way? Yes, she had to admit that he would have, thinking to make her happy. He had sent them off alone to the country, and—now that she thought back to it—had even seemed to know without being told what had taken place.

But what role had Hunter played in her seduction? Turning, she ran toward the door, determined to learn the answers.

"Marinuska, where are you going?"

"I'm going to ask Hunter."

"No, Marina. Stay here with me. I'm twice the man that he is. I love you more."

"I'm sorry, Sergei, but I don't love you, not like that."

"Marina, don't forsake me or I'll do something we'll both regret."

His angry words followed her down the hallway. She didn't heed them. Already she had done so much that she regretted. What more could Sergei possibly do to make matters any worse?

"Hunter, you can't be serious." Chloe LaRocca's intelligent eyes widened with disbelief.

"Very serious. Please, Chloe, I need you to do this for me."

Hunter Kincaid didn't often ask for help. This time, however, he realized that without Chloe's assistance he could never hope to accomplish his goal. While driving home from church with Rainee, he had reluctantly come to a decision, one he had put off making for a long time, stubbornly refusing to believe it necessary. But after what had happened today, he dared not procrastinate any longer.

The time had come to pay attention to Rainee's education. He must enroll her in a reputable finishing school, and the closest one was in St. Louis. Such a drastic step was for her own protection, of course. The last thing he wanted to do was send her away, but he would if it meant holding on to her in the end.

With Rainee off at school, and under the watchful eye of someone he trusted, he wouldn't worry about her. Eventually she would come back home, he assured himself, all rebellious notions stripped from her mind.

"All right, Hunter. I can understand why you want to do this, but why ask me?" Chloe pressed.

"Because I know I can trust you to see her there safely."

"Me? A madam? A whore?" She snorted contemptuously.

"You did all right by me, Chloe." Hunter covered her aging hand with his own work-roughened one.

"For a girl it's different." Slipping her hand from beneath his, she patted his knuckles. "A little childhood taint never hurt a man. In fact it gives him an air of . . ." Lifting her gaze to the ceiling, she made a spiraling motion with her hand as she searched for just the right word. "Sophistication," she finally said.

"Aren't you always telling me that if a legitimate offer came along giving you a way out of here, you'd take it?"

"Yes, that's true, Hunter," she conceded. "Still—"

"Still, nothing, Chloe. I'm making you one damn-fine legitimate offer."

Chloe's eyes darted left, out the window, then right toward the door that led to the front parlor. He could see that his words were beginning to have a positive effect.

"In St. Louis, you could take up residence on the west side of the city." Only the wealthy and influential resided west of the downtown district. He dangled temptation like a carrot in a horse's face.

"A mansion on Grand Avenue with lots of rooms. I have to admit that would be awfully nice."

"As many rooms as you want, Chloe, and servants to keep them tidy."

"And a carriage with high-steppin' horses." She giggled, totally caught up in the prospect.

"If that's what you want." Hunter laughed, too, warming to her enthusiasm.

"And all I have to do is keep an eye on Rainee. Make sure she stays in school and out of trouble."

"That might not be an easy task," Hunter warned.

"She's only one little girl. I've had to manage dozens over my lifetime."

"There," he stated emphatically. "Now you can see why I figured you're well-qualified for the job."

"St. Louis." Chloe sat back nurturing her dreams. "Hell, I might even find myself a rich husband."

"Personally, Chloe, I think you'll do a whole lot better than that."

"No, Daddy. I don't want to go to St. Louis. I don't want to leave my friends." Rainee stood up from the table and threw down her napkin.

"Of course you do." Unruffled, Hunter continued to eat his Sunday supper. "Now sit down."

"What if I refuse?"

"Refuse? To what? Sit down or go to St. Louis?"

Her pretty face stiffened, just like her mother's used to. He didn't want this to turn into a battle of wills. Hadn't he been through enough of those with Della? All he wanted was for his daughter to be happy and safe—above all, safe.

"Look, Rainee, you've got it all wrong, honey." Abandoning his own meal, he stood and came around behind her, placing his hands on her shoulders. Resistance met his kneading fingers. "I think it would be best if you got away from here for a while. I've already wired the school in St. Louis and paid your tuition. Classes begin soon." When she refused to relax, even a little, he grew frustrated. "Damn it, Rainee, I figured this would please you."

Hunter couldn't begin to understand Rainee's negative reaction. He had truly thought his plans would thrill her.

"Very well, Daddy. It seems you've already made up your mind. So if that's what you want, then I'll start packing."

Like a brave little wooden soldier she turned, pushed her way past him, and marched toward the stairs.

"Rainee?"

Responding to his summons, she faced him from the first landing. The tight set to her jaw indicated her resentment.

"Believe me, honey," he said, trying hard to convince her. "You'll be glad I did this in the long run. I promise you, some day you'll even thank me."

She didn't thank him then. Instead, lifting her stubborn chin, she continued up the staircase.

But nothing short of a miracle or a natural disaster would make him change his mind, not when it came to the welfare of his daughter. Rainee would be on that train to St. Louis with Chloe even if he had to drag her to the station himself.

And by damn, he would have a peaceful Sunday dinner.

He started back toward the dining room, but paused at the unexpected knock at the front door.

Now what? he wondered as he watched Sierra hurry to answer the impatient pounding. After the day's disaster it could be anyone.

"Kindly inform Mr. Kincaid that the Princess Marina Nicolaiev is here. I insist on seeing him right away," Marina demanded when the Indian woman answered the door.

"Yes, ma'am," the woman said, hustling off and leaving Marina standing in the foyer.

She knew she looked a mess with her hair coming down from its pins. Spying her image in the hall-seat mirror, she brushed at it with her fingers, but it did no good.

"What are you doing here?"

"Hunter?" She whirled in surprise at his sudden appearance in the opposite doorway. Still dressed in his best clothes and handsome as always, he looked anything but pleased to see her.

She regretted her impulsiveness. Perhaps she shouldn't have come. But she was there and she had to know.

"May we talk?" She lifted her chin with stoic determination.

"If you don't think enough has all ready been said." He eyed her calmly, assessing her with an open frankness that made her doubt herself.

Had he looked at her in the same way in Russia? Had he found her wanting there, too? No wonder he had been anything but pleased at her unannounced arrival in Sweetwater.

"This way, then," he said with a sigh when she didn't relent.

She followed in silence as he led her into a spacious room. A massive fireplace covered one wall. The heads of deer and elk and many animals unfamiliar to her decorated the others. The room of a predator, a man who took what he wanted without asking or regard. Had she, too, been just another trophy? That thought brought tears so close to the surface she wasn't sure she could control them.

He indicated a seat, but she refused it.

"I want the truth, Hunter," she managed to say.

"Don't we all, darlin'?" They stared. "The truth about what?" he finally asked.

"About Russia."

At that he quirked a brow. "What about Russia?"

"I want to know what part I played in the negotiations between you and Dmitri." She searched his face for an immediate response.

His expression never changed. His eyes never wavered.

The moment of truth, yet she found herself unable to face it, or the man, so she turned away, staring blankly into the glassy gaze of some poor beast, another innocent victim.

"Daddy, what's going on?"

Marina glanced up, discovering Rainee standing in the doorway, her eyes darting with uncertainty between the two adults.

"Go on, Rainee. This has nothing to do with you," Hunter stated rather curtly.

But the girl was looking at her for reassurance.

"It's all right, Rainee. I'm here to see your father for personal reasons."

Rainee's smile conveyed relief. The moment she departed, Marina resumed her study of the wall display.

"Marina." Hunter came up behind her, cupping her shoulders with his hands. "I'm not going to deny that your husband made me a tantalizing offer no man could refuse."

She shook him off and moved away.

"My God, you were everything I ever dreamed of having." Once more he touched her shoulders, this time gripping them so tightly she had to struggle to get away.

"Oh, Hunter, how could you have agreed to something so dishonorable?"

"I didn't agree," he defended himself, forcing her to face him. "At least not in the way you're accusing me of doing."

"What do you mean?" she asked, seeking some kind of hope to cling to.

"Oh, face to face, I told Dmitri no. Hell, I had no problem doing that." Dropping his head, he buried his face in her hair. "But when I saw you alone in that carriage, even when I suspected what your husband was up to, that he was manipulating me . . ." His voice caught with emotion and he lifted his face. "I swear to God, Marina, the cattle contracts had nothing to do with it. I won't deny that I was fully aware of what he wanted from me. I just thought I had enough integrity to defy him." His mouth jerked up in one corner. "I didn't.

Even one night with you would have been worth more to me than my honor."

"And now? What am I worth to you now, Hunter?" She looked up into his face, seeking reassurance.

"What more do you want?" His expression turned suspicious.

"I only want your trust."

At that she saw him falter. Crushed, she pulled away, turning toward the door, needing desperately to escape. He caught up with her on the porch, claiming her arm, refusing to let her go any farther.

"How do you expect me to trust you when there are so many things about you I can't be sure of?"

"Such as? Ask me, and I'll gladly tell you anything," she cried. She offered no resistance when he settled them both in the swing on the far end of the porch.

Dusk was only minutes away, the fiery ball of the sun making its descent behind the barn.

"Sergei? How much does he mean to you?"

She listened to the *squeak, squeak, squeak* of the chains as he set the swing in motion. Did he really want to know?

"Enough that I cannot desert him," she finally answered. And that was the truth. Regardless of every thoughtless, even spiteful, thing Sergei had done to her of late, she couldn't callously abandon him.

"I see."

"Hunter, you must understand. He and I have been through so much. He's like a brother to me." She touched his arm. He didn't pull away. "After Dmitri's death, there were several attempts on my life. Without Sergei's help, I would have never reached America."

"Attempts on your life? Who?" He gripped her hand.

"It doesn't matter. That's all behind me, left in Russia."

"Are you sure? After what happened in front of the general store . . ."

"No, no, I'm certain there's no connection." Not that she could fully explain what had happened then or afterward, she was sure it had nothing to do with Russia. How could it? She had nothing of value or importance anyone would want, at least nothing worth following her halfway around the world for.

Holding hands, they swung in silence until the peaks of the distant mountains swallowed up the sun. She was sure he had more to ask.

"What about your dancing?" The question rang out in the dusky stillness. "How much does it mean to you?"

"Ballet is a part of who I am, Hunter," she answered honestly and without hesitation. "It's the same as breathing or eating or loving to me. Are you asking me to give it up?"

"No, I would never ask that of you."

There was another question he wanted to ask. She could read it in his eyes, but couldn't be certain what it was. She only knew what she wished it to be.

If only he would ask her, she had her answer ready. Yes, yes. She would marry him. Just ask. She leaned forward as his mouth opened.

"I would ask you to stay tonight, but . . ." His gaze reflected his hesitation.

Disappointment shot through her. It wasn't what she had hoped for.

"Oh, no, I agree. It wouldn't be right, not with Rainee here."

"I could go back with you to town." He sounded hopeful.

"No, not with Sergei there."

"Of course. I understand."

But she was sure that he didn't. It was best right now that

Sergei not see them together, not until he'd had a chance to calm down.

"I should be going now."

"I suppose you're right, but it will be dark soon. Maybe I should take you back . . ."

She shook her head.

"I don't want you going alone."

Even as they discussed it, she saw the shadowy figure of a cowboy leading a horse from the barn cross in front of the house.

"Paco. Where are you going, son?" Hunter asked in an authoritative voice. "Tomorrow is an early day, you know."

"Yes, sir. I know. Evenin', ma'am." He touched his fingers to the brim of his hat. "To town, Mr. Kincaid, but I'll be back early." The young man turned, the last of the light reflecting on his face. Marina tried to place where she had seen him before, but couldn't remember.

"See that you are. In the meantime, I would be obliged if you would escort Miss Nicolaiev back to her place."

"My pleasure, ma'am." He tied his horse to the back of her buggy, climbed up, and took up the reins.

Hunter led her to the vehicle and lifted her onto the seat.

"I'll come to see you this week." His hands lingered on her waist.

"I'd like that." Her gaze clung to his face.

Paco flicked the reins, and the horse moved ahead, pulling her from Hunter's arms. Settling on the seat, Marina glanced once more at her escort, trying to remember where she had seen him.

Of course. How could she have forgotten? He had been the boy who had once delivered a message to Sergei from Rainee.

Nineteen

The next morning Marina accepted the steaming mug from Fanny.

She sat in the middle of her bed, sipping hot coffee—a very American thing to do. In Russia, one drank tea or, if privileged, hot chocolate—and always from a glass. But it was rather nice, she had to admit, to curl both of her hands about the warm ceramic cup and stare into its steaming contents.

Dear Fanny. She could feel her friend fairly bubbling with questions, yet she said nothing, asked nothing, just sat down on the edge of the bed keeping her company, sipping her own drink.

"So tell me, Marina," she finally said. "Do we stay or do we go?"

"Oh, Fanny, I'm so unsure." In order to free her arms for a hug, she turned to deposit her mug on the small table beside the bed. "My music box?" she murmured. It was missing.

"Are you sure you didn't move it?"

"No, no. I'm certain it was here yesterday after church when Sergei . . . surely he wouldn't have?" Her heart skipped one anxious beat.

Sergei? Out of spite had he taken her music box? If so, what did he plan to do with it?

Angered by such childish antics, she threw back the covers.

"Marina, what are you going to do?"

Still dressed for bed, she hurried out the door and down the hallway to Sergei's room with Fanny right behind her. She pounded on the door, but, of course, got no response. How like him to play such games.

"Marina, do you really think Sergei took your music box?"

"Wake up, Sergei," she cried. "This has gone far enough." She hammered on the door once again. "I *know* he did," she replied. "And I'm going to get it back."

She rattled the doorknob in frustration.

"Here, let me." Taking a pin from her hair, Fanny stepped forward decisively. She bent and inserted the pin into the keyhole on the door and, with only a little effort, she released the lock.

"Fanny, I didn't know you could do that."

"A little trick I learned in New York," the young woman explained with a shrug, putting the pin back into her hair.

"Sergei?" Determined, Marina rushed into the room only to discover no one there, the bed undisturbed—the window open.

"Where do you think he has gone?"

"I don't know, but if he's taken my music box, I have to find him." She began to search, starting with drawers, hoping for a clue.

"Marina, look at this." Fanny handed her a piece of crumpled paper. Her pixie-like face worked with worry.

"Where did you find this?"

"Thrown on the floor."

Marina read the note. It was from Rainee Kincaid, asking Sergei for a rendezvous at the abandoned line camp near the river. Her hand began to tremble, her mouth to go dry. "Oh, Rainee," she whispered.

"Surely Sergei wouldn't actually run off with that child, would he?" Fanny asked.

"I'm not sure anymore what he is capable of doing. I just

know I have to find them, stop them if I can, from doing something we might all regret," she replied, remembering his threat of the day before.

Her decision made, Marina quickly dressed.

"If I'm not back by this afternoon, then you must find Hunter and show him that note," she informed Fanny as she raced down the stairs.

"Marina, maybe it would be best if you sent for him now."

"No, Fanny." At the door, she turned and squeezed the other woman's hand. "You have to understand. First, I must try to do this on my own. I owe it to Hunter, to Rainee, and even Sergei. Please."

Fanny nodded.

"Thank you," she said, rushing out of the building. She made her way to the livery.

The deserted line camp near the river. Although she had only been there once before, the day of the picnic with Hunter, she felt certain she could find her way there again. Too much was at stake for her to make a mistake now.

"Mr. Kincaid, thank goodness you're back."

The housekeeper's worry-etched face greeted Hunter at the back door.

"What's wrong, Sierra?" he asked with only mild concern, because in the Indian woman's eyes every minor disaster constituted a crisis. Dusting off his hat and jacket, he hung them on the appropriate peg.

On a cattleman's hunch, he had ridden out long before dawn to check on a small herd of selectively bred cows due to calf at any time. Just as he'd sensed, one had been in trouble, and he had spent most of the morning pulling her and her calf through the long ordeal.

"It's Miss Rainee. She's gone."

His hand on the buckle of his holster, Hunter stiffened. Rainee gone? No one had to tell him what that meant.

"When?" he demanded, reaching for his hat and coat to put them back on.

"I-I-I'm not really sure, Mr. Kincaid. I checked her once, early this morning, but she was still asleep, or so I thought. When she didn't get up on her own, I went in to wake her a little later. I discovered she'd stuffed pillows under the covers to make it look as if she were still in bed."

Before he had left this morning, he, too, had peeked into her room and seen what he had thought to be his daughter burrowed under the covers in her sleep. Perhaps he, too, had been deceived by one of the oldest tricks in the book. She might have left just before Sierra went in to wake her up or in the middle of the night. He had no way of knowing.

"Mr. Kincaid, this is all my fault." The woman wrung her hands in distress. "I should have—"

"No, no, Sierra. Don't blame yourself. I should have seen this coming." Uncradling his pistol, he checked the cylinder to make sure it was fully loaded.

"Mr. Kincaid, what are you plannin' to do?" Sierra asked, worry once again shadowing her dark eyes.

"I'm going to find my daughter and bring her home." He holstered his weapon.

"Then you know where she is?"

"Not exactly, but I have a damn good idea where to start looking."

Hiring a horse and buggy, Marina traveled the south road out of town, trying to recall the exact spot where Hunter had turned off the main route the day of the picnic. If she remembered correctly, he had driven well-beyond Chloe's place.

So she breezed past the way to her friend's home without even slowing down.

There had been no actual crossroad, only a faint wagon path through an open field, but had the trail been before or after the road that led to his ranch?

Pressured by the need to make the right choice the first time, Marina battled a rising sense of panic. She had to hurry. Time was of the essence. Instinct, however, warned her to slow down, and she reined the horse to a walk.

Leaning precariously over the edge of the buggy seat, she watched the side of the road, looking for a sign of the faint trail. At one point she stopped, thinking she had found the place. But no. She didn't remember that line of cottonwood trees in the distance. The field had been much more open and not nearly as rocky.

Frustrated, she clicked her tongue at the horse. They started forward again, moving so slowly it would take hours to cover the section of road. Hours she might not have.

She had to find the couple, convince them both not to do anything foolish. Whatever motivated Sergei, she doubted it had anything to do with love for Rainee. It was more like revenge—against Hunter, against Marina herself—for not taking his confession of love seriously. But surely they had been friends, partners, much too long to allow a misunderstanding to come between them. If only she could talk to Sergei, she felt certain she could convince him to see the error of his ways.

Just as important, she cared deeply for Rainee. If anything happened to the girl—well, she felt responsible, and not just because she was Hunter's daughter. Perhaps, in spite of that fact.

Battling the frustration, she glanced down at the side of the road and saw the beginnings of the faint trail that cut across the open field.

"Whoa," she called out, reining the horse to a halt. She stared out over the landscape. Yes. This was it. She had found it. In fact, she had almost passed it.

She tried to make the horse back up, an impossible task, of course. So, steering the confused animal off the road, she drove the buggy in a wide circle in the field, a little too quickly and sharply, for the vehicle listed to one side.

Unmindful of the danger, she urged the horse on.

As they went bumping and bobbing down the narrow path, Marina had only one concern. She must get to that deserted line camp in time.

She heard the roar of the distant falls long before she actually spied the small clearing near the river, but at least she knew she followed the right trail. Up a small rise, and there it was. The shack, built only a short distance from the sheer cliffs, was just the way she remembered it. She brought the buggy to a halt.

At first she saw no sign of life in the distance, but then she caught a glimpse of a pair of horses tied to a tree in the rear. Instantly she recognized one of them as the mount Rainee had always ridden into town for her lessons. As for the other one?

Her hope faltered. Oh, please let her have gotten there in time.

"Get up there," she cried, slapping the reins against her horse's rump. It took her a few moments to descend the rise and drive to the front of the cabin. Thinking only to stop something irreversible before it happened, she scrambled out of the seat and ran toward the building. Without bothering to knock or announce her presence, she threw open the door.

"Rainee?" she called out, looking around when she heard a small, muffled whimper to her left. The interior of the cabin was so dark, she could see nothing.

"Marinuska, how timely that you could join us." The *dan-*

seur's voice boomed loudly from her right. "How unlike you to have come alone, but I'm so glad that you did. It makes what I must do so much easier." He laughed as if delighted. "I knew you would never allow another woman to take your place."

"Sergei!" she exclaimed, angling toward him, but unable to make him out. "Where is Rainee?"

"Where is Rainee? Where is Rainee?" he mocked like a mindless parrot. "The Kincaids. Are they all you ever think about? Well, let me show you something that will undoubtedly change your mind."

With a hiss, a match flared and touched the wick of a lantern. The small halo of light illuminated only the right side of the cabin and Sergei as he snapped the glass cover back in place. He sat in the only chair at a rickety table, her mother's music box before him. Pieces of the mechanism, scattered on the flat surface, glinted in the lamplight, mocking her just as his voice had.

"How could you, Sergei?" she choked, assuming he acted purely out of spite for her earlier rejection. Angered beyond caution, she lurched toward him, thinking only to reclaim what rightfully belonged to her. What did he hope to gain by destroying her most prized possession? Surely not her love.

Meeting her halfway, he caught her by the arm and shoved her, none too gently, across the room. She landed in a dark corner, luckily on an old bedstead that groaned in protest from her sudden weight. The muffled sounds that followed were human, as were the glittering, frightened eyes that clung to her.

"Rainee?" she whispered, discovering Hunter's daughter huddled against the wall, hands tied, mouth gagged, looking scared to death. "Sergei, what have you done to her?" she cried, turning to inspect the girl for injuries.

"Done? Why nothing. I don't want her, you know that. All

I ever wanted was you." He snorted, patting his shirt pocket. "But I'm more than willing to take the money she brought thinking I would run away with her."

Rainee whimpered, her innocent eyes filling with disillusionment.

"How could you, Sergei?" Pulling the girl to her, Marina glared at him. Her throat tightened around the rest of her angry rebuke. Fear like she had never known before gripped her. Sergei, the one person she had thought incapable of physical violence, held a gun in his hand pointed straight at her disbelieving heart.

Driven by a need to get there as fast as he could, Hunter rode cross-country instead of following the road into Sweetwater. As dangerous as it was to gallop over rough terrain, he nonetheless urged the horse to go faster.

Every minute counted, and his mad dash would save him precious time. He had to find Rainee and stop her before she managed to leave town. Once she was gone, he knew from experience how impossible it would be to track her down.

Upon reaching the ridge on the outskirts of town, he allowed the tired mustang to slow its pace to a fast walk. But he stopped for nothing and no one until he reached Marina's place. There he dismounted, leaving the lathered horse standing in the middle of the street. Without bothering to knock, he burst through the front doors.

"Rainee!"

Receiving no response, not that he'd figured his willful daughter would present herself on command, he headed toward the stairs leading to the floor above. In his haste and determination he took the steps two at a time.

"Rainee, I know you're here. When I find you, I swear to God . . ."

"Mr. Kincaid? What do you think you are doing?" Fanny stood at the bottom of the steps, staring up at him as if she thought she'd conjured him out of thin air.

"Where are they, Fanny?"

"I-I-I don't know what you mean." However, her look said differently.

"Very well, if you won't tell me, then I'll find them for myself." Nothing and no one would interfere with the tracking down of his daughter.

He began a systematic search of the premises, starting with Sergei's room at the end of the hallway. He vacillated between disappointment and relief to discover it unoccupied. At least if he had found Rainee there, even if his worst fears had proven to be true, his quest would have been over. But it wasn't over, not by a long shot, he suspected.

Room after room, he left no door unopened, no hiding place unrevealed. By the time he had finished upstairs and started on the rooms below, it dawned on him. Not only had he found no sign of Rainee or Sergei, but Marina was nowhere to be seen, either.

"Marina," he demanded, turning on Fanny who had surprisingly enough followed his progress without saying a word. "Why isn't she here?"

"M-M-Marina?" Stuttering, she stepped back, cowed by his aggression. "Why—she's gone out for a while. She promised to be back soon."

It wasn't so much what she said or even the way in which she said it. Instead, something in the quick shift of Fanny's eyes as she refused to look his way made him suspect Marina's absence had a connection to Rainee's disappearance.

Did Marina know of the girl's plan to run away and perhaps even condone it? No, he refused to believe that. Though after her confessed loyalty to Sergei yesterday, he couldn't discount the possibility.

"How convenient," he said, not bothering to hide his skepticism. "When she does return, you give her a message. You tell her that if I find out she's encouraged my daughter's misbehavior in any way, I'll personally hold her accountable. You got that?"

"Y-Y-Yes, sir." Eyes wide with fearful respect, Fanny wobbled her head.

Suspecting he'd accomplished about all that he could there, Hunter headed toward the front door. Having been through the ordeal once before, he knew what his next step must be. Inform the authorities before proceeding with his search. But this time he had no intention of sitting around and waiting for them to find his missing daughter.

"Mr. Kincaid," Fanny called after him.

Harboring hope that the woman had decided to help him, he turned.

Fanny swayed in indecision. Her hand, buried deep in a pocket, clutched and unclutched a concealed object. For a moment it seemed she was about to confess.

"You're wrong about Marina," she offered without explanation instead. "You've got to believe me. She would never do anything to harm Rainee. She loves her like a daughter."

"I hope you're right, Fanny. In the meantime, if you suddenly think of anything that might help me, I'll be at the sheriff's office."

He was already in the saddle when she finally raced out into the street. Reaching up with a trembling hand, she pressed a piece of paper into his.

"Marina made me promise not to tell you where she had gone unless she didn't return. She wanted a chance to make this right herself."

He read the note, recognizing Rainee's handwriting and the recklessness of Marina's action. A sick feeling invaded the pit of his stomach, his concern now twofold. Marina could well be in as much trouble as his foolish daughter.

"Thank you, Fanny," he said, cramming the note into the pocket of his shirt.

Hunter headed back in the direction from which he had just come. If only he had taken the road instead of riding the way the crow flies, he might have intercepted Marina, preventing her from blindly rushing into a situation for which she was ill-prepared.

In his heart he knew a man like Sergei Bozzacchi would stop at nothing to get what he wanted. And what he really wanted was anyone's guess.

"Why are you doing this, Sergei? What do you want?" Marina pleaded, glancing longingly at her music box on the table behind him. She slid back on the bed, rubbing her shoulder where it had hit the iron bar of the headboard. Beside her, Rainee began to struggle against her gag, as if trying to tell her something. As much as she wanted to turn and reassure the girl, Marina dared not take her eyes off Sergei, not even for a second. Not with that wicked-looking gun in his hand.

"Don't be coy with me any longer, Marina. You know as well as I do what I'm looking for." Reclaiming his seat, he propped the gun on the table where he could easily retrieve it, his attention once more fixed on disassembling the music box.

"Please stop," she cried, edging forward on the bed. What did he think to accomplish by destroying her music box besides breaking her heart?

"Very well, Marina, I'll stop." Grabbing the gun, he settled back in the chair. "Just as soon as you give me the documents."

"The documents?" she asked. "What documents?"

"You know what documents." In emphasis he jerked out another and yet another piece of the music box, tossing them on the table with the rest.

She flinched with the desecration, as painful to her as if he ripped vital organs from her own body. Closing her eyes, she tried to make sense of his demand. There was very little she would hesitate to give him in order to save her mother's music box. Surely he must know that.

"Damn it, Marina! Where are they?"

She jumped at his sudden outburst, at the desperate look in his eyes as he rose and started toward her, at the unwavering pistol still leveled on her.

"Honestly, Sergei, I don't know. But perhaps if you tell me, I can help," she suggested in a hoarse whisper.

When he still looked unconvinced, she scooted as far away from Rainee as she could, hoping to keep the girl out of the line of fire if Sergei should decide to pull the trigger. She prayed that wouldn't happen, that he would believe she told him the truth.

"The list of names, Marina," he said through gritted teeth, his knuckles whitening as his grip tightened on the trigger. "The incriminating list your dear Dmitri ordered compiled . . ."

"Dmitri?" Her eyes widened in surprise. What did Dmitri have to do with this? Unless . . .

Could these be the same documents the officials had searched for after his death but never found? Suddenly it all began to make sense, terrible, frightening sense.

"Yes, Dmitri," Sergei confirmed. "The list that named those supposedly responsible for the failed attempts on the tsar's life. Guilty or not, they were all to be executed, you know."

"Dmitri would have never allowed that," she defended, "He was much too honorable."

The word stuck in her throat like a bitter pill when she remembered the anything-but-honorable way Dmitri had handled the negotiations with Hunter. If her husband had been willing to use her as a political pawn in one way, why not in another?

"When the list couldn't be located in Russia, it was hoped that the prince had destroyed it since some of his friends' names were on it. Later, with some . . . convincing, his manservant confessed otherwise."

"Feodor?"

"Yes. With his dying breath he swore he helped Dmitri hide the list in this music box. But I didn't learn that until we reached New York. Now I must find it and destroy it."

"Why is this list so important to you?" she asked.

"My father and brother are implicated. I have to protect them at all cost."

"At all cost, Sergei? My life included?"

"No, no. I tried to protect you, too, Marina. I swore to my father you were innocent, that if he would just let me take you away, whatever you might know would never be revealed."

"Then it was your father who murdered Dmitri and was behind the attempts on my life in Russia."

"If Dmitri had only given him the documents when he asked for them, none of that would have happened."

"And what about what happened here in Sweetwater? Surely your father wasn't behind those attempts, too."

"No, no, I swear. I only meant for you to be frightened— the way you were in Russia. I wanted you to flee as you did then. I couldn't take the chance that you might decide to send the documents back to Russia."

"Sergei, if I had known about them, why would I have betrayed you now after all this time?"

"Hunter Kincaid. With him, you didn't need me anymore.

With his connections in Russia, it would have been easy to send the papers back to the authorities. What better way to get rid of me than by destroying my family?"

"No, Sergei, you're wrong. I would never have done that."

"Wrong?" He laughed. It was neither a pleasant nor a comforting sound. "We'll see how wrong I am."

As fast and frightening as lightning, he whipped around and snatched Rainee from the bed. Holding the whimpering girl to his chest, he put the gun to her head.

"The papers, Marina," he threatened, pulling back the trigger. "I want them now."

An emotion welled in Marina so strong it gave birth to a courage she had never known she possessed. Rainee. She would do whatever she must to protect the girl.

"Just let her go, Sergei, and I promise I'll give you whatever you want." Stalling, she frantically searched her mind for a means to gain time, even a few minutes, as long as he let Rainee go. "The key," she lied. "I can't get to the papers without the key to the music box."

His hand relaxed, a barely perceptible amount, but enough to give her encouragement.

"It's in my purse, in the buggy," she explained hurriedly, praying he would believe her. "I'll go get it."

"No. I'll get it." Accepting her explanation, he thrust Rainee in her direction and started out the door. Then thinking better of his logic, he whirled and waved the gun at them.

"Stay here and don't move."

Marina nodded her head in agreement, relieved that he had willingly left them alone for the few minutes it would take for him to search the buggy. But it wouldn't take him long to realize he had been deceived, that her reticule wasn't even there. In her haste to find Rainee she had not bothered to bring it with her.

The moment Sergei disappeared through the door, she flew

into action. Quickly she untied Rainee's hands and removed the gag from her mouth.

"Hurry, Rainee, we have to get out of here before he returns."

"You're so brave, Marina," the frightened girl gasped. Thank goodness, she didn't argue and took the lead out the back door.

Marina started to follow her, then remembered her music box. She couldn't leave it behind. If she did, Sergei would surely destroy it in his anger. Torn in indecision for only a moment, she hurried back to the table and gathered the scattered pieces of the mechanism, placing them inside. She picked the box up.

She'd forgotten how heavy it could be. Still she refused to give it up. Lugging it across the room, she stumbled once under the weight. When Rainee returned looking for her, she gratefully accepted the girl's help.

Once they were outside, she realized there was no way to take the music box any farther without jeopardizing their safety and possible escape.

"Go on, Rainee," she ordered over the roar of the falls, struggling to get herself and the music box on the back of the horse. She kept an eye on the cliffs, only a short distance away, as the horse refused to cooperate, backing up in fear at the unfamiliar object in her hand.

"No, I won't leave you," the girl cried, urging Marina to climb into the saddle so she could hand her up the music box.

As they struggled to accomplish the nearly impossible task, Marina saw Sergei come around the outside corner of the building. She had never seen him look so angry. Still clutching the music box, she whirled to confront him, putting herself between her one-time friend and Rainee. He would not get his hands on the girl again, not if she could help it.

"You lied to me, Marinuska." In spite of the familiar endearment and the hurt in his eyes, he lunged for her.

Stumbling backward toward the cliffs, she pushed Rainee along with her. Nearly dropping the music box, she valiantly managed to hold onto it.

But Sergei kept coming, closer and closer, forcing them to continue backing away. Finally, Rainee, who was still behind her, refused to take another step.

"Marina?" Terror laced the girl's thin-voiced plea.

Marina looked back. The girl teetered dangerously close to the end of the cliff. Only a few more steps and she would fall to her death. Then, out of the corner of her eye, she saw Sergei raise the gun and aim. Marina continued to clutch the music box. Her only weapon.

"Rainee, get out of the way!" she cried in warning, the girl's safety uppermost in her mind. Calling up every ounce of her strength, she flung the music box with all her might.

She saw it hit Sergei, saw it glance off his chest, crash to the ground, and splinter into a hundred irreparable pieces. The sacrifice gave both Marina and Rainee the chance to escape. Hoping Sergei would follow her, she sprinted in the opposite direction from Rainee, running along the edge of the cliff.

Her plan worked. She could hear Sergei behind her, cursing her. He drew closer and closer until suddenly he had her, his arms like a vice around her middle, squeezing the life out of her. Then she was falling, falling.

Rainee's screams—or were they her own?—followed her descent.

Twenty

On the ridge above the line-camp clearing, Hunter paused only long enough to get his bearings. What he saw below, taking place dangerously close to the cliffs, caused him to put spur to horseflesh.

He had noted the buggy parked in front and the two horses tethered behind the cabin when Sergei came out the front door. Immediately afterward, two women slipped out the rear exit.

He watched until he saw sunlight glinting off the pistol in Sergei's hand.

If only he could get there faster, but the relentless mustang had already given its all. As they neared the line shack and lost sight of the activity behind it, Hunter felt the horse stumble in exhaustion.

Dismounting, he tossed down the reins and groped for his own gun cradled in its holster on his hip. He came around the building, running, pistol cocked and ready, but all he could see was Rainee, standing on the edge of the precipice, looking over.

"Marina! Marina!" Her repeated screams pierced clear to the core of his heart. His emotions, too long kept dammed up, burst forth, running as freely as blood.

"Ma-ri-na!" His own cries blended with those of his daughter's.

By the time he reached her side, Rainee's hoarse shrieks

had dissolved to bitter, remorseful sobs. Without questioning his appearance or that he would forgive her, she turned, burying her face into his chest.

"Oh, Daddy, I'm sorry. It's all my fault. How could I have been so stupid to have listened to his lies?"

"Did he hurt you, Rainee?" he demanded, shaking her fiercely when she didn't immediately respond.

"No, he didn't," she finally replied between sobs. "But if Marina hadn't come along when she did, if she hadn't been willing to put herself in danger to protect me, he would have."

Marina. Had she truly made such a sacrifice for his daughter? Fearfully, Hunter leaned over the ledge. He saw them lying on a precarious shelf on the face of the cliff several yards below. Sergei and Marina, their bodies intertwined as if caught in an eternal dance.

Until then, he had never known the true meaning of loss. What he had felt when Della had left him or even in the end when he had found her dying, none of that compared to the pain he experienced at that moment. It was as if a part of him lay battered on that ledge. The part that made him whole. Closing his eyes, he buried his face in his daughter's hair.

Marina. He felt the unfamiliar catch in his chest and didn't care if it labeled him less than a man in some people's eyes. He only knew he could not go on living without her beauty, her vibrancy, her unquestioning love of life. He would gladly risk it all for another chance to hold her, to simply tell her that he loved her, that he accepted her the way that she was. And God help him, he would trust her, no matter the consequences. No matter that she might decide to leave him with time. Even a day, a week, a month, a year together would be enough. Whatever she would be willing to give would make him happy. If only he had another opportunity.

But, being a cynic, he expected no such miracle.

"Daddy, look."

At Rainee's urging, he opened his eyes.

The movement was ever so slight, the groan so soft. He couldn't be certain of either one. But if there were a chance, even a small one . . .

"Stay here, honey. And keep away from the edge."

He released his hold on Rainee only when he was certain she was no longer in danger of falling. Then he raced toward the spot where he had left his horse, seeking his lariat, a means to lower himself onto the ledge where Marina lay. Out of the corner of his eye he saw Rainee drop to her knees beside the broken remains of what he realized had once been Marina's music box. It had been so important to her, and now it was destroyed, forever silent. He could only hope the woman had not met the same fate.

"Daddy, I think these are the documents . . ."

"Not now, Rainee. Just stay back," he ordered. Whatever she had found, it could wait. His only concern for the moment was to find a way to save the woman he loved more than life itself.

Marina awoke.

"Mama?" she murmured, aware of the weight of another human pressing down against her aching body, crushing her. Straining, she listened for the familiar sounds. Odd, how the roar of the cannonade never ceased, and yet she did not feel afraid. And the music? She listened again. When had it stopped? Did that mean Papa would find her soon?

But it wasn't Papa she wanted to rescue her.

"Hunter."

"The American won't help you now, Marinuska."

"Sergei!" She opened her eyes. Slowly, she looked around, discovering that, miraculously, she lay on a small shelf, dangerously close to the edge, the groaning *danseur* draped across her like a broken doll. She remembered toppling from the cliff, remembered hitting the ground, but Sergei had been beneath her then, softening the impact. Afterward, they must have rolled. Thankfully, they had stopped inches from the edge, for the bottom of the canyon was far below. No one could survive such a fall.

Mist from the not-so-distant waterfall, the source of the sound she had mistaken as cannonfire, sparkled in Sergei's blond hair like sequins. It reminded her of how they used to glitter their headdresses and costumes before a performance.

Those days seemed so far away now, hopelessly out of her reach, like the spot high above from which they had plummeted. Had Rainee managed to escape? Perhaps even now she rode for help.

"Marina, my legs. They hurt. Why can't I move them?" Sergei asked groggily, attempting to shift his weight. When he did, a smattering of rock rolled from the ledge, too close, much too close.

"It will be all right," she comforted. "But you must be still." Otherwise they might both slip from their perilous position.

Extracting herself from beneath him, she slid as close to the solid wall as she could, clinging to an exposed tree root. Reaching out, she grasped Sergei's arm and tried to pull him toward her, but she was not strong enough.

He began to struggle and then to scream. To her horror, his oddly bent legs refused to budge. He must have broken them when he hit the ground.

"My legs. I'm maimed!" His twisting and thrashing increased.

"No, no, Sergei. I promise you, they'll be all right." Tears streamed down her cheeks unchecked. "But you must lie very still until help comes," she insisted, reaching out to stroke

his head as if he were a wounded bird. She glanced up, looking for a sign of activity. Refusing to give up hope, she kept
telling herself it could take awhile for Rainee to ride to town
and get assistance. In the meantime, she had to hang on and
convince Sergei to do the same.

Beneath him a piece of the ledge broke away. She darted
a nervous look at the lip. The echo of the ricochet confirmed
her warning.

"Sergei, please, please be still. If you don't, we'll both
die," she repeated.

"Do you blame me, Marina? Please, don't blame me." His
irrational behavior grew steadily worse. Ignoring the danger,
he continued to struggle. More loose stones, just beneath him,
chipped away from the edge as he slowly, painfully dragged
himself toward her.

"I don't blame you, Sergei." She reached out her hand to
help him.

"This is not how it is supposed to be. I always promised
to be the one there for you." Their fingers touched. "A
woman needs a real man. Why wouldn't you allow me to be
that for you?"

"Sergei, I care about you. I never meant to make you feel
less of a man or to hurt you."

"Then you *do* love me, Marina?" His look conveyed an
intensity of longing as he clutched at her hand, pulling himself up next to her, propping his battered body against the
wall of the cliff beside her.

"Yes, I love you, Sergei, but not in that way." She couldn't
lie to him.

"Then if I can't have you, no one will."

He grabbed her so quickly around the throat, she didn't
have the breath to scream. She heard the ominous click of
the gun against her head and knew that her compassion had
been foolishly squandered. She should have searched Sergei

for the gun and taken it away from him when she'd had the chance. Her folly would cost her her life.

Strangely calm in the face of death, she clung to the root and waited for him to pull the trigger, knowing that nothing she could say would change his mind. No one could save her now. No one. She squeezed her eyes closed in resignation.

"Marina, where are you?"

That voice. More comforting than an angel's. She would recognize it anywhere.

"Hunter, I'm here," she managed to get out before Sergei smothered her mouth with his hand. She didn't question how he had found her or what he planned to do. If she got out of this alive, she swore never again to criticize him for his Western ways of dealing with crises.

"What do you want, Kincaid?" Sergei demanded.

"You know what I want, Pretty Boy."

"Well, I won't give her to you." Sergei laughed, a demented croak.

"Are you sure? Not even for the papers that were in the music box?"

"The list? How can I be certain that you have it?" Sergei demanded. Then he shot her an accusing look. "I should have known you would have given it to him."

Clawing at his restraining hand, she vehemently shook her head in denial.

"I have a gun, Kincaid. Give them to me now or I swear I'll kill her," he shouted.

A few minutes later she saw a rope snaking its way down the side of the cliff. It stopped just out of reach. Attached to the end was rolled paper. Was it truly the document Sergei wanted or only a ruse?

"Lower, Kincaid," Sergei ordered, releasing her and swiping desperately at the bait without success. Moaning, he gave up.

"Oh, no, Bozzacchi." Hunter spoke with deadly calm. "You'll do this my way or we won't do it at all. If you want those papers, first you must throw away your weapon." He jerked the line, dangling the documents like a carrot.

Hatred blazing in his eyes, Sergei swayed in indecision, then hurled the gun over the precipice in a wide arc.

"Very good, Bozzacchi. Now you'll send Marina up to me."

"And how do you expect me to do that? She doesn't have wings."

"Hunter, listen to me," Marina interjected, hauling herself to her feet. "Sergei's legs are badly injured. They're so mangled, he can't even stand up." She glanced at Sergei with renewed compassion, knowing there was nothing more he could do to harm her. "Lower the rope so I can give him the papers."

"Are you sure, darlin', that that's the right thing to do?"

"Trust me."

Would he? Could he?

The rope descended. Hoping it was truly the list Sergei wanted, she reached up and untied the rolled document, careful not to lean too far over the edge. Tentatively, she knelt and placed the papers in his outstretched hand.

He unfurled the paper, his eyes scanning the Russian characters. When he came to the second page, his eyes closed with relief.

"Did you find what you were looking for?"

"Yes. Now my family is safe." Crumpling the papers, he clutched them to his chest. "Oh, Marinuska. Why couldn't you have loved me or given these to me?" His eyes, so full of pain, focused on her face.

"Sergei, don't you see that if you had only asked me, we could have looked for them together?" She laid her hand over his clenched fist. "Together we could have destroyed them.

Then this need never have happened." She glanced down at his shattered legs, unable to disguise her pity.

"My legs are ruined, aren't they?" He followed her gaze. "Look at me. I am doomed. You know as well as I do, I'll never dance again, and who is Sergei Bozzacchi if he cannot dance? Just another cripple for you to take care of."

"No, Sergei, that's not true." But noting with horror the odd angles of his lifeless lower extremities, she saw that it was. Tears of compassion sprang into her eyes. What more could she possibly say?

Their eyes locked. As in all the times when they had danced together, each sensed the other's move in advance. As hard as she tried to hide it, there could be no denying what the thought of caring for yet another invalid meant to her. Still, for him, she would endure the constraints of such a life.

"How many years have you carried me along, Sergei? Let me take my turn."

She saw the very moment he relinquished the will to live.

He shook his head, his eyes looking beyond her to the rim of the ledge. Pitching to his side, he began to roll, the paper firmly clutched to his heart.

"No, Sergei." She lunged toward him, grabbing at his shirt as he neared the edge.

"It's better this way, Marinuska." As Sergei plunged into the canyon, he left her with a look of resignation to his chosen fate. Like a nightmare, it would be forever etched in her memory.

"Marina, let go." Hunter's cry of distress from above blended with the sound of tearing fabric.

The burden ripped from her grasp, she pulled back and stared with disbelief at the shredded remnant of cloth in her fingers, all that was left of Sergei. She buried her face in her hands, unable to look, engulfed by the terrible roar of the falls.

"Listen to me, darlin'. Grab the rope." Hunter's urgent plea barely reached her through her haze of grief.

Looking up, she realized she teetered precariously on the quickly crumbling edge, Sergei's fate soon to be her own. The rope. She could see it swinging just out of her reach. Grasping for it, she came up empty-handed. She scrambled to her feet, taking one final, desperate lunge at the lifeline, and the unstable ground gave way beneath her. She started to fall and knew there was nothing she could do to stop herself.

"Hunter," she screamed. But he couldn't help her either. She, too, would die, battered on the rocks below. No. No.

Suddenly, her arms were jerked up over her head, almost torn from their sockets. The feel of the rough hemp rubbing against her palms burned and she wanted to let it go. She looked down and saw nothing beneath her dangling feet but the jagged rocks and roaring river far below. Her chest began to hurt, her head to swim dizzily. How much easier it would be to just let go.

"Hang on, Marina. I've got you."

"I can't," she cried, feeling her hands slip as the rope began to ascend. She looked down again, wondering how long it would take her to reach the bottom. Would she feel it when she hit or would she mercifully pass out long before?

"Marina, look at me."

"I'm afraid," she said in a small voice.

"Then let me be your strength, my love, the music to get you through the storm. Look up. Have faith in me, darlin'. I won't let you go."

Yes, she must look up. Just like when she danced she knew better than to watch her feet. Invariably it caused a misstep. Slowly Marina lifted her face. High above her, Hunter's outstretched hand beckoned to her. She found his eyes, clung to them, to the hope, the confidence, and the love they showered upon her. And she did hear the music, music more beautiful than any she'd heard before. Somehow for Hunter's sake, she must hang on. She must ignore the agony in her arms and bleeding hands as he slowly pulled her up.

But it was hard, so very hard, especially when her bruised and aching body smacked against the side of the cliff again and again. Then, when her knuckles scraped painfully against the rocks, her grip loosened and the rope slid between her fingers like sand.

"Hunter," she whispered, fearing she would never reach him, never be held in his arms again, never know his love at its fullest.

At that terrible moment of uncertainty, she felt the warmth of his hand clamp over her wrist, catching her just in time. Dangling, knowing that only his strength kept her from plunging to her death, she knew what she must do. Just like when she danced, she had to trust and rely upon her partner's skill.

"Give me your other hand," Hunter instructed.

She lifted her arm, straining toward him, his fingers only inches away.

"Come on, you can do it, Marina."

She could see his knuckles clutching her other wrist. They turned white and started to tremble, the muscles in his arm bulging to their limit; but he refused to give up. Closer and closer their fingers drew, so close yet just out of reach. With a final thrusting stretch, she grasped his hand. Did he have the strength to pull her up?

"From this day forward, my life—my heart—is in your hands, Hunter," she whispered.

If one could believe in miracles or, better yet, the power of love, then it came as no surprise, least of all to her, that he somehow managed to pull her up the rest of the way. In doing so, he delivered her not only from the immediate danger of the unstable cliff but the crumbling remains of her life. Sitting on the edge of the canyon, she discovered that it was his arms holding her, his mouth kissing her, not the solid ground beneath her, that provided all the security she would ever need. The storms of life could never frighten her again.

"How did you know where to find me, Hunter?" she asked as he helped her to her feet despite her shaky legs.

"Fanny. She had enough sense not to keep her foolish promise."

"And the documents?"

"For that we can thank Rainee and her Kincaid stubbornness. Even when I tried to ignore her, she refused to give up. She found them among the ruins of your music box. Probably, it had some kind of false bottom."

"My music box," she cried, turning to look for it.

There, not far from the edge of the cliff, she saw its scattered remains. Rushing forward, she knelt among them, touching the splintered pieces of carved rosewood. She started gathering the scattered springs and gears. Then she found the all-important cylinder, the source of the music. So many of the delicate pins were broken off. She knew then, it could never be repaired.

The pain of her loss clutched at her heart and brought tears to her eyes.

"I'm sorry, Marina." Hunter knelt beside her.

She buried her face in his chest and allowed the tears to flow unchecked. She wept for so much more than the music box.

"We'll get you a new one," Hunter promised.

"No, no. It's irreplaceable," she said, sniffing and wiping at her eyes to clear away the tears.

But was it truly irreplaceable? If only she had Hunter, then she wouldn't need it anymore, she wouldn't need anything, she swore. Looking up at the man she loved with all her heart, she prayed that she hadn't lost him, too.

"Marina," Hunter began, his face unmasked by emotions, "I—"

"Daddy? Marina?" Rainee rushed forward and knelt beside them, throwing her arms around Marina's neck.

"I'm so sorry," she sobbed. "I was such a fool. Can you ever forgive me."

"You mustn't blame yourself, Rainee." She cupped the girl's tearful face. "You had a dream of becoming a ballerina and thought only to fulfill it. Tell her, Hunter." She looked at him over Rainee's shoulder. "Tell her it's not wrong to follow your dreams."

Their eyes met, challenged. His indecision seemed eternal, and she thought for a moment he wouldn't relent. Finally he smiled and welcomed Rainee into the circle of love, making it complete. It was a bond, a silent—yet solemn—pledge.

"No, honey, it's never wrong to go after what you really want. Hell, it's what I've always done. Look what it's gotten me. A wonderful daughter and a—"

"Oh, thank you, Daddy." Rainee interrupted. "You'll be proud of me. I promise. I'll go to school in St. Louis and become a fine lady. And then I'll dance around the world and meet Prince Charming." Gaining her feet, Rainee whirled away in a cloud of happiness.

"A wonderful daughter and a what?" Marina asked when finally they were alone.

"I didn't think you would catch that," he said, flashing her a grin.

"Ah, darlin'," she said, mimicking his low, Western drawl, "nothing about you ever slips past me. And don't you dare be careful about what you say. So what has it gotten you, Hunter? A wonderful daughter and a what?"

"Hopefully, a wife, if you'll have me." He kicked at the dirt like an uncertain youth. "If it doesn't interfere with your dreams and plans. Your friends and dancing and responsibilities."

"That is my dream, Hunter. You and Rainee are my friends and responsibilities. And if I wish to dance . . ." She put her arms around his neck and led him in a whirl on the grassy ledge with no music except the rhythm of their hearts beating together. "From the first time I met you, when we waltzed that night in Russia," she said as they continued dancing, "you were all I ever wanted. To dance for you, Hunter Kincaid, what more could I want?"

"Me? You wanted me? What would a confident, shimmering princess in silver want with a rustic ol' cowboy like me?"

"A cowboy, yes. But a man to put a prince to shame. I would much rather be a cattle queen than a Russian princess any day."

"Are you sure? I wouldn't want you to have regrets later."

Coming to a halt, she pressed herself against him. A gentle breeze whipped her skirts about his legs, her unbound hair around his shoulders, enveloping him, binding her.

"Hunter Kincaid, I have never been more certain of anything in my life."

Epilogue

August 1874

It promised to be the wedding not to be forgotten, at least not by the citizens of Sweetwater, Wyoming.

Marina sat in the vestry of the little church reading the batch of letters she'd received just that morning.

The first was from Rainee, away at school now for several months. She missed the girl more than she could have ever imagined, but reading of her antics in St. Louis brought a smile to her lips. Nothing at all to be concerned about. In fact, it all seemed very mild indeed for a young woman off to finishing school. Nonetheless, she would gloss over many of the details when she relayed to Hunter his daughter's news and words of love.

The next envelope also came from St. Louis. She looked at the return address for a moment, not recognizing it. Curious, she tore it open and shook out the pages. An article from a newspaper fluttered into the lap of the stylish Dolly Varden walking suit she had recently received from New York.

As she flipped to the last page, the closing signature caught her by surprise. Fanny? Why, she should be in New York by now. What was she doing in St. Louis? Almost a month ago she and Hunter had arranged passage for the entire troupe back East. Had something gone awry?

She frowned, then the corners of her mouth lifted as she

began to read Fanny's letter. Something indeed had gone awry, but not for the worse.

Upon reaching St. Louis, the troupe had had a two-day layover waiting for their connection to the East Coast. During that time, Fanny had discovered that thriving St. Louis had no resident ballet company. She and John had immediately formed one, convincing almost all the original troupe to stay with them. As for money-supporting patrons . . . Chloe brought them in by the armload.

Reaching the last paragraph of the letter, and the request she read there, she paused. Her frown returning, she picked up the article that had fallen into her lap.

"Are you ready, Mrs. Kincaid?"

Distracted from her reading, Marina glanced up and spied the Reverend Endicott standing in the doorway, smiling at her.

"Yes, of course. Whenever you are." Standing, she collected the scattered pages of the letter and set them on a small table. She couldn't quite decide what to do about Fanny's offer. What would Hunter think of it? Picking up the notes she had placed in the vestry earlier, she followed the preacher down the short hallway to the rear door of the church.

"You have a passel of anxious brides waiting for you," the reverend warned her.

"No more anxious than their prospective grooms, I hope."

"To be honest, they're on tenterhooks," the preacher admitted with a nervous laugh of his own. "They're not sure what's going to be expected of them."

"Good, that's how they should feel, at least for a little while longer. Don't worry, Reverend Endicott, the day will go smoothly." Smiling sweetly, she moved to take the lead.

Once outside, she glanced around. Rows of chairs, all sizes and shapes, had been set beneath the shade of the aspen and cottonwood trees. Thank goodness a gentle breeze stirred the hot, summer air. As had been the way of things in Sweetwater since that infamous Sunday several months ago, the women sat on one side, the men on the other. But today, if all went as planned, that would change.

Her gaze came to rest on the tall figure of the handsome cowboy sitting among the rest of the men. Hunter. She smiled at her husband, her heart welling with the love that seemed to grow stronger every day. With a proud look in his eyes, he responded with an encouraging nod.

Marina took the podium placed in the shade of the church steeple and waited for her audience to give her their full attention.

"Ladies, gentlemen, good afternoon," she greeted, placing her hand on the crown of her straw hat to keep it from fluttering off her head. Looking out at the crowd once more, she cleared her throat. "It seems all of the grievances are in. As you requested, I have organized them into separate lists, one for the men and one for the women. Each of you should receive a copy. I'll give you a few moments to look them over."

As she spoke Annie Shackelford and Sarah Granger handed out the printed fliers. She watched each recipient's reaction. As she had expected, not one woman showed surprise at what they read. The men, however, looked anything but pleased and began to grumble.

"Is there a problem, gentlemen?" she asked.

No one wished to be the first to speak. Finally, Jeb Granger stood up.

"It says here the women demand an equal right to join all organizations includin' the Cattle*men*'s Association." His extra emphasis on the word "men" got chuckles from his cohorts.

"That's right, Jeb," Marina answered. "Wives have just as

much at stake and do just as much work as their husbands. Everything you own is half Elvira's. It seems only fair to allow her a say in the decisions. If you have a problem with the name of your group, may I suggest you change it to the Stock Raisers' Association."

Her proposal received twitters from the ladies.

"Hunter Kincaid, you mean to tell me you plan on lettin' your wife have a say in your ranch?" Jeb swung around to glare at Marina's husband.

"Why not?" Hunter shrugged. "She's got some damn good ideas."

"Then what about the Ladies' Committee?" Jeb demanded, looking satisfied with himself.

"Jeb Granger." Hatty Shackelford stood up, too. "We welcome you in the Ladies' Committee. We'll even put you in charge of it, if you want."

That evoked laughter from both sides.

"And for your sake," the mayor's wife continued, "we'll even agree to changin' the name to a town council. Maybe if we'd had some men on our committee in the first place, all this discord wouldn't have happened."

Catching Hunter's eye, Marina smiled. If there had been men on that committee, she might not have ever come to Sweetwater, and that would have been a tragedy indeed.

"Sit down, Jeb," Mayor Shackelford growled, tugging on the rancher's coattail. "Just take your medicine like the rest of us."

Clamping his mouth shut, the protester did as he was told.

"Are there any further objections?" Marina asked. When no one spoke up, she turned to the waiting preacher. "All yours, Reverend Endicott. I believe these couples are ready to renew their marriage vows."

The ceremony proceeded quickly and painlessly, if one didn't count Mrs. Davenport's rendition of the wedding march. Once that was over and she'd joined her spouse, the preacher requested all the couples to unite before him as he read the revised vows written by Marina asking both sides to love, honor, respect, and listen to each other. Uncertain how much it would actually change the public image of Sweetwater, Marina suspected this renewal of vows would at least add a little spark to the private lives of its citizens. A little renewed spark went a long way toward keeping the peace.

Afterward, Hunter joined her in the churchyard.

"I'm proud of you, darlin'. You've done what no one else was capable of, reuniting this town." Reaching into his pocket, he pulled out a dried rosebud and presented it to her.

"What is this?" she asked, studying the ancient petals.

"It was in your hair our last day together in Russia."

He had saved it all this time. She didn't ask why. She didn't have to. Without saying a word, she took off her hat and weaved the flower into her hair once more.

"We got a letter today from Rainee," she informed him as they walked along, arm in arm, a couple in love.

"How are her grades?"

"Fine."

"And her social life?" he asked, his brow quirking with skepticism.

"Quiet."

"Good. I know Chloe keeps that girl straight."

At that Marina smiled secretly. "I'm sure you're right."

They walked on a few moments more in silence.

"Hunter, there's something I need to ask you," she said, finally making up her mind to tell him of Fanny's offer.

"Whatever you need, darlin', you have only to ask."

Did she?

"Excuse me, Mr. Kincaid?"

She looked over Hunter's shoulder and saw a stranger standing there.

"Yes," Hunter answered curtly, turning.

"Mr. Hunter Kincaid?"

He nodded cautiously.

"Sir, my name is James Bishop." The man stuck out his hand and Hunter clasped it in greeting. "I'm a personal emissary for President Grant. Could we talk a few moments in private? Ma'am," the official said, looking at Marina only briefly before turning his attention back to Hunter.

"I have my things to gather in the church," she offered. "Hunter, I'll meet you at the wagon in a few moments."

A few minutes turned into a half hour. At last when Hunter joined her and helped her into the wagon, she noted the tightness of his jaw and knew something had disturbed him.

"What is it, Hunter? Is something wrong?" she asked as they drove out of the churchyard.

"You might say that. But then you might think it's something good. President Grant has heard about my cattle negotiations with Russia. Bishop says it caused a stir in diplomatic circles in Washington."

"Your President? He is like the tsar in Russia, right?"

Hunter nodded.

"Is he upset with you?"

"No, he's not upset exactly, but several other countries have approached him wanting to arrange a similar deal. He's asked me to negotiate them."

"Why, Hunter, this is wonderful," she exclaimed, clapping her hands.

"Is it, Marina?" He glanced at her from across the wooden seat, taking in her smiling encouragement. "This doesn't trouble you in the least, does it, darlin'? International negotiations, diplomats, and government. You just take it all in stride, don't you?" Reaching out, he gathered her into his arm. "Hell, you'd probably be better at this than I'm gonna be."

"Never. You just have to promise me that if anyone offers you their wife, you won't take them up on it."

At first he looked at her seriously, then succumbed to the teasing twinkle in her eyes.

"Why would I when I have the woman of my dreams right beside me?" He glanced at her earnestly. "You will go with me, won't you?"

"Where will we go and how soon?"

"Immediately. First we head to Washington, then it could be anywhere after that. James Bishop mentioned Australia, South America, maybe even the Orient. I've thought about the running of the ranch, but absentee owners have successful operations all the time. I have good men I can leave in charge."

"The best," she agreed. "The ranch will be fine. Hunter, do you think we could stop in St. Louis first?"

"To see Rainee? Of course. Maybe we should consider taking her with us."

"You should ask Rainee what she would like to do. In the meantime, how would you feel about me dancing again?" she asked quietly. Although she had kept up her exercises and teaching, she had not given an actual performance in a long time.

"What did you have in mind, Marina?" His hand tightened on her shoulder.

In as few words as possible, she shared the unexpected turn of events in Fanny's life. Then she explained how well received the troupe had been when they had first come through St. Louis on the way west.

"If I honor her request and give a performance, it will help boost their ticket sales. Hunter, I wouldn't want to do anything to upset you."

"This would make you happy, wouldn't it?"

"Yes, I admit I miss dancing."

"Then I want you to do this, with my encouragement. In fact, I want you to reestablish old contacts back East. Let them know we'll be there soon. I can share you with the world, Marina, if you can share the world with me."

"Oh, Hunter." She threw her arms around his neck. "I can't tell you how much I love you."

Hunter brought the wagon to a halt in the middle of the main street of Sweetwater and pulled her into the circle of his strong arms for all of the world to see.

"You don't have to tell me. You show me every day by greeting me full of hope and anticipation when I come home tired and dusty. Just knowing you're there makes my life complete."

"Always, Hunter. I'll always be there when you come home."

Just as she knew he would always be there to shield her from whatever storms swept into her life.